She felt a whisper of soft breath on her face . . . like a gentle kiss. Then she felt the coldness in her throat. A piece of ice was lodged in her windpipe. Caroline McKelvey opened her eyes . . . wide and blue as sapphires. She tried to gasp, but the air would not come.

There was blood . . . everywhere.

PRAY GOD TO DIE

Pray God to Die

CAREY ROBERTS

AVON BOOKS ◆ NEW YORK

This is a work of fiction. Names, characters, places, and incidents either are the product of the author's imagination or are used fictitiously. Any resemblance to actual events or persons, living or dead, is entirely coincidental.

AVON BOOKS
A division of
The Hearst Corporation
1350 Avenue of the Americas
New York, New York 10019

First Avon Books Printing: November 1994

AVON TRADEMARK REG. U.S. PAT. OFF. AND IN OTHER COUNTRIES, MARCA REGISTRADA, HECHO EN U.S.A.

Printed in the U.S.A.

RA   10   9   8   7   6   5   4   3   2   1

ACKNOWLEDGMENTS

I would like to thank some generous individuals who helped me set an accurate background for this novel. My appreciation goes to the D.C. Police Department, Criminal Investigation Division, and particularly to Detective Anne Evans, then a member of the Homicide Division; to Capitol Hill players, Susan Stubbs and Thomas Sneeringer; to Anne Sprague of ABC News in Washington; and to RHD for helping me discover the Washington Cathedral. My deepest love and thanks to my wonderful family and to LRB for never-failing support and a special note of appreciation to Susanne S. Kirk, Executive Editor, Charles Scribner's Sons.

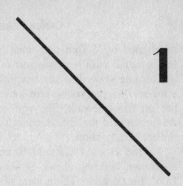

1

The young woman waiting for the light to change at the corner of Massachusetts Avenue was not thinking of danger.

It was twenty minutes past six on a Thursday evening in early October. The streets were crowded, the evening beautiful. A lamp shone from the window of the old stone apartment building across the way. But it wasn't dark yet. Not so dark that Caroline couldn't see the faces in the cars passing by and laughter in the eyes of a boy and girl standing next to her. They were linked arm in arm, caught up in some private joke.

The day had been warm but now there was a light cooling breeze. It was Indian summer in Washington and there was nothing for Caroline McKelvey to fear. Not anymore. Not since she had settled matters . . . put things right.

The light changed and Caroline stepped from the curb. A middle-aged man crossing toward her from the other side of Wisconsin Avenue looked at Caroline, looked away . . . and then looked at her again. She was used to that. Men had stared at her all her life. She wasn't in the least vain about it. She had been a beautiful baby, and the beauty had remained.

It was all in the bones. At least that's what Simone said. And in the wide-spaced blue eyes, sapphire-hued and fringed with dark lashes. And the shape of her mouth, sweet and curving with a short upper lip. It was the kind of face that men dream about, romanticize about, " . . . and aren't

1

threatened by.'' That was what Simone said, and Simone had laughed with her own sort of irony when she said it.

Caroline slowed as she reached the west side of the avenue and let the young arm-locked couple move ahead of her on the sidewalk. She walked slowly past the Italian restaurant and the café carry-out and dry cleaners and the unisex beauty shop.

As she crossed Garfield Street, she looked up at the apartment building ahead. Simone's apartment was on the front, fourth floor. There were no lights on and the sliding glass door to the balcony was closed. It was usually open when Simone was home. She liked city noises, she'd once told Caroline. She liked feeling the pulse of the city.

Her own apartment was on the sixth floor. It was on the back of the building and looked out toward Rock Creek Park. A view of treetops. It was lovely and quiet on the back. It would have been lovelier if she hadn't had to share the apartment with Nicky. But then Nicky had been living there first. She'd found the apartment and invited Caroline to share it and had introduced her to Simone.

The Alhambra's lobby door was unlocked. It wasn't supposed to be. Harold was supposed to be standing here in his green uniform, ready to open the door and take her packages and push the elevator button for her. Supposed to be, but sometimes wasn't. That was Harold.

Caroline chuckled and shifted her package to the other arm. She pushed the elevator button for the sixth floor. There were only six floors in the building. Why it took the old brass elevator so long to make the trip up or down always puzzled her. The elevator was something like Harold . . . pleasant but slow, and undependable. Once it had stopped between the third and fourth floors when she and Nicky were aboard and it had taken Harold almost an hour to get them out. Nicky, who had claustrophobia, had had to sit on the floor in the corner and breathe into a paper grocery bag they'd emptied. ''I really haven't any nerves,'' Caroline now said to herself, surprising herself by saying it out loud. "I have faith. That is what I have. Faith. That's the important thing."

The light was dim in the elevator. She was the only passenger, although she saw old Mr. Forrester coming in the front door of the building just as the elevator door closed. She reached for the button to stay the door but it was too late. She tried to give him an apologetic smile as the door closed but she wasn't sure he even saw her. Dear old fellow, she thought. He can't see or hear worth a hoot but somehow he manages. Edward Forrester had the apartment two doors down on the sixth floor.

Slowly the ponderous old elevator rose to the top floor. Caroline stepped off into the shadowy hall . . . more shadowy than usual because two ceiling lamps were out. Blast Harold! He'd said he was going to fix them.

Not that it mattered. It was light enough to see. The walls were creamy plaster with nice molding and the carpet was pale rose. She passed the widely spaced doors, just eight apartments on each floor, four on the front side and four on the back. When Nicky had first called and said, "Come see what I've found, a great old building, newly renovated, just down the avenue from the Washington Cathedral. Posh as hell, Caro," she'd been doubtful.

Not about the apartment, the "posh" building just down the avenue from from the Cathedral. But about living with Nicky Nelson again. They'd been unlikely roommates during their freshman year at college. There had been no scenes, but no real closeness either. After that first year, they had gone in different directions and hardly done more than wave across the campus.

Nicky Nelson was nervous, quick-talking and ambitious . . . a child of New York if ever there was one. The fact that she, like Caroline, came from Manhattan was the reason they were placed together. But it wasn't enough of a match. And "the media thing" . . . they had that in common also. Both their fathers were in the national spotlight and well known. Even that had not been enough. Caroline had edged off.

Since college, she had not given Nicky Nelson a thought until this past July when they'd bumped into each other shopping. She'd given Nicky her phone number and said certainly she'd like to get together sometime but she couldn't say exactly when because she was getting married at Christmas and life was hectic . . . and she was busy at work and looking for a new apartment because her present lease was almost up and . . .

Well, here she was, three months later, living with Nicky in a sixth-floor apartment on Wisconsin Avenue across from the Cathedral. She wasn't quite sure how it all happened except that Nicky had swept her into it. That was Nicky's way . . . to sweep you along. Which was one of the reasons they hadn't lasted as friends and roommates at Bryn Mawr. Caroline liked being her own person. She didn't like being swept along by anyone.

She reached her door and shifted the package again so that she could search in her bag for the key. She fished out the red leather key chain and sorted through the keys. One was to her father's apartment in Manhattan, rarely used since she went up only once or twice a year. The second key was for the office on Capitol Hill. She pursed her lips slightly as that one slid through her fingers. She wasn't going to let herself think about all that now. Caroline's fingers closed around the apartment key and she thrust it into the lock.

As she opened the door, she glanced down the hall and saw the white light come on over the elevator. It was probably Mr. Forrester. Embarrassed that she had not waited for him, she stepped quickly inside.

Through the sliding glass doors opening to the balcony, she could see gold sky darkened now to copper above the treetops. That wide patch of autumn sky threw enough light for her to make her way into the dining area. She put the grocery bag on the bar that separated the dining area from the kitchen.

As usual, Nicky had left clutter—several glasses, a coffee cup and a cereal bowl, banana peel and empty yogurt container on the bar . . . not to mention *The Washington*

Post spread about everywhere, one section on the bar, another on one of the leather-covered stools and the rest in a messy pile on the floor.

A note stood propped against the toaster oven. It read, "Caro, missed you this morning. You were gone before I got up but then I was dead—exhausted! It was a late night and very interesting." Both *late* and *interesting* were underlined in Nicky's overstated way. Had she been on a date or just working late? Caroline couldn't remember and didn't much care. The note went on, "I'll be late again tonight. There's some cold pasta in the refrig. Be my guest. See you, Nicky."

For a moment Caroline slumped against the bar. Her mood had nothing to do with Nicky's note. She was relieved that her roommate would be staying out. It wasn't the mess in the kitchen or the weariness she had been carrying around with her all day. It was the weight of the decision that lay like a stone on her heart. No, she wouldn't let herself think about that. It was over . . . done with. She was going to have to carry on alone.

Caroline straightened her shoulders. The only way not to think about the tragedy of her life—yes, the tragedy of it— was to stay busy. She kicked off her pumps and began to clear the mess away. The newspapers from the bar were folded and thrust into a bag under the sink . . . dirty dishes clattered into the dishwasher. She ran the yellow sponge over the bar and the small countertop beside the stove.

Just the act itself, the act of straightening and cleaning, made Caroline feel better. She'd always been neat . . . always liked to have things clean and right where they were supposed to be. She looked at the grocery bag on the bar. First, a cup of tea, then she'd unpack and put away.

While she was waiting for the teakettle to whistle, she leaned her head against the cabinet over the sink. Why was her head throbbing? The day had gone just as planned. She had said her piece . . . done what was right. She could feel tears right behind her eyelids . . . tears ready to fall if she'd let them. She wouldn't.

She reached into the cabinet for the tea bags. The water

was rustling to a boil. She glanced at her watch . . . six thirty-five. She would get out some Oreo cookies from the grocery bag and sit down for a few minutes to watch the national news. Perhaps Simone would have a spot. Simone was the Capitol Hill correspondent for ABC News and routinely had a few minutes of air time on the nightly show.

Caroline walked around the bar with the cup and saucer in her hand, the tea bag floating in the darkening brew. She switched on the television set standing on a bookcase in the dining ell. The bright square lighted up the dark room. She glanced toward the living room and saw the expanse of sky beyond the balcony had grown darker, the room was almost all in shadows.

There was an edge of light on the carpet. Was the front door still open? Maybe she hadn't shut it properly because she'd been carrying the groceries.

A flicker of movement and she caught the shape of shoulders in the shadows. Someone was standing just inside the front door of the apartment half in and half out of the darkness. Someone was in the living room . . . standing still between the curio cabinet and the sofa. Someone was standing there and watching her.

Another movement from the shadows. A step across the carpet toward her, then another. A pause beside the sofa. The voice was soft and flat. Ironic, and without the usual charm. "Sorry, I didn't mean to startle you."

Caroline struggled against the race of her heart, struggled to regain her composure. How could she have been so careless? She forced a smile, as though to confirm that she'd been startled . . . but she was not concerned. No, not concerned. And most certainly not frightened.

She reached for the switch to the overhead dining room light. Light equalized things, took away the advantage of surprise. The glow was steadying, encircling them both. Yes, that familiar face. This could be managed certainly. She felt her confidence returning. "Was there some misunderstanding about today?" She raised her hand as if to ward off argument. "Please understand that I'm entirely determined. I meant all that I said today. Everything is . . . entirely over.''

There was no response. Caroline caught just a slight shrug that conceded nothing. She imagined something coiled, tension held close, like the ridge in a cat's back, something suppressed and taut about the shoulders. Anger . . . Was it anger? Was that what she saw in those searching eyes?

Caroline moved backward, using words as a shield between them. "It's a question of doing what's right. You do understand?''

"I understand, Caro.'' Now there was a reassuring smile. A hand went deep into a pocket. It was a casual stance. Unexpected.

Caroline saw herself reflected in the dining room wall mirror.

How white her face was! She looked beautiful. The silk dress. The heat in her face. She always looked beautiful, she knew that . . . it didn't matter. She knew that too.

Turning to the kitchen, she balanced the teacup carefully so that it would not spill again and betray her feelings. She had misjudged her power and persuasiveness today. She'd been a fool and now she sensed she was in danger. Real danger. Her only chance was to hold on to this charade of civility.

"I'll make a cup of tea for you.'' Caroline busied herself turning the kettle on again, reaching into the cabinet for another cup and saucer. She turned toward the bar, a reassuring barrier between them. She put a tea bag in the cup she had placed there.

There was a rustle from the crumpled newspaper on the floor. One step closer. The space between them narrowed. They were facing each other across the bar. So cold, so still those eyes.

There is really no emotion there at all, Caroline thought, no pain or sorrow, no anger.

"Don't you want what's right?'' She tried a pleading smile.

"Right?" The word seemed to amuse, but only for a second. There was a sobering of expression. Then came a request. "Please close your eyes, Caro."

"Close my eyes . . . but why?"

She was conscious of the flicker of the television on the bookcase, of Simone's low-pitched, intense accents. "Now, a special report from Capitol Hill . . . "

"I just want you to." The voice was oddly hypnotic.

Dear God. Caroline closed her eyes. She felt a whisper of soft breath on her face . . . it was like a gentle kiss. Behind her the kettle began to scream.

Then she felt the coldness in her throat. A piece of ice was lodged in her windpipe. Caroline McKelvey opened her eyes . . . wide and blue as sapphires. She tried to gasp, but the air would not come.

She could see them in the mirror. Two profiles caught. The glitter of the upheld blade. There was blood rimming like a crimson necklace on the neck of her dress. There was blood . . . everywhere.

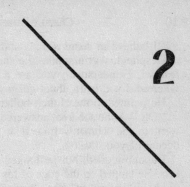

2

"I don't believe in angels," said Dakota.

The big, broad-shouldered homicide detective twisted his Super Bowl ring as he spoke. He had played tight-end for the Redskins in his "salad days," a time so recent and luminous in his memory that rubbing the gold ring with its huge ruby still gave him a pleasant buzz. "No such beings, Fitzhugh," he said now with a certain firmness. "I wouldn't trust an angel if I saw one."

He was looking at his partner's beautiful legs as she sat on the corner of her desk across the aisle from him in the squad room.

"What about devils . . . do you believe in devils?" she asked.

He shook his head to indicate negative.

She laughed . . . and crossed her legs.

Dakota leaned back in his chair and studied Anne Fitzhugh through narrowed eyes. Detective Anne Fitzhugh had great legs. She'd finally given up wearing those damn high heels. The shoes she had on this morning were much better, stacked heels with a blunt toe. They looked Italian, maybe Ferragamo . . . or something fashionable anyway. He judged those shoes would be worth a week's pay for an average detective on the force. But he liked the leather. And, the color.

"What *do* you believe in, Dakota?" She was teasing him, gray eyes silvered with laughter, black-lashed, beautiful.

9

"I believe in *gargoyles* . . . and *grotesques*."

Despite his grim tone, she laughed again. "The *grotesques*, I understand, you are a homicide detective. But where did you learn about *gargoyles*?"

He pointed to the church bulletin lying on his desk.

"Oh," Anne sobered, answered her own question. "You went to the woman's funeral at the Cathedral. That was decent of you, Dakota."

Dakota nodded, but he looked absentminded. And restless. He tapped on the edge of his desk with his thumb, the old habit that meant, Anne knew, he was thinking of something else. "Do you know what *gargoyles* are?"

He didn't wait for Anne's answer. "Waterspouts, that's all. Medieval engineering feats. They look like decorations along the edges of the roof but they're designed to project outward and send the rainwater clear of the walls."

Anne pictured the nightmarish little stone creatures that adorned the high outer walls of cathedrals and churches she'd seen. "Who told you that?"

"Anthony Jesse Clore. He's one of the canons at the Washington Cathedral. The Reverend Canon Anthony Jesse Clore. He conducted the service and showed me around afterward. He was shook up about the woman's death. Seems he knew her pretty well."

"Did he give a reason?"

"She'd been in counseling with him. That's his specialty, counseling the forlorn . . . working with people with problems."

Anne started to ask, "What kind of problems did she have?" But she'd caught something in Dakota's voice. "What's he like," she asked him instead, "the Reverend Canon Anthony Jesse Clore?"

"He's all right . . . for a man of the cloth." Dakota smiled. "Not what you'd expect, actually. A big guy, easy to talk to. Intelligent, I'd say . . . *handsome* maybe, you'd say. A dark-haired Billy Graham with a Harvard accent."

Anne Fitzhugh's laugh was a deep throaty chuckle.

She was just back from vacation, two weeks down in Tidewater Virginia country. "Just lazing about," was all she'd told Dakota. But whatever she'd done had been damned good for her, he'd decided. She looked rested and ready to get back to work. She'd shown up at the Indiana Avenue headquarters early this morning, ten minutes early for the 7 A.M. shift . . . beautiful and bright-eyed. And, Dakota noted, as usual just slightly sassy.

"Dakota, lay the case out for me," she said. "You say you haven't got a handle on the Caroline McKelvey murder. Well, tell me everything you know right from the very beginning. I mean, you might hear yourself say something you didn't *know* you knew."

He studied her face. Was she putting him on? He hadn't wanted Anne Fitzhugh to be his partner on this case. Hadn't chosen her or wanted her. It was sixteen months now that Anne Fitzhugh had been working Homicide and, for the most part, Don Dakota avoided her.

She was a good cop, he admitted. She had proven her stuff. The rest of the team had ragged her hard in those first months, called her "Foxy Fitzhugh" . . . "Magnolia cop." She had taken their testing in stride. A very classy female. Plenty smart, he'd give her that too. She hung on. She'd made her peace with the rest of the squad because she carried her own weight.

The fact was the lady in question tied him in knots. Double knots. It all went back to her first case, and what had gone on between them. The personal thing. The man-woman thing. The sizzle. Dakota still thought about it more often than he was willing to admit. His mind would play over those weeks they'd worked together on that first case of hers, that odd, spun out situation in Georgetown . . . and when the case was solved, that one long sweet night they'd spent together.

Regrettable. That was the word she'd used later. But not forgettable.

It shouldn't have happened, that was the point. Forget it, he'd told himself that, forget it, Dakota. The lady is not for you.

She'd turned him down cold in the morning. She'd blown him off in the light of day. "Regrettable"—that's what Anne Fitzhugh had said to him the next morning. "Just a mistake on my part, Dakota." She'd said it quietly. No arguments allowed.

No, he didn't trust her and he didn't trust himself with her.

Every time Captain Terry Wilson assigned them as partners, he'd managed to switch off. But not this time. No options available, said the chief. He was caught with Fitzhugh on this McKelvey case.

Dakota centered the McKelvey folder squarely on his desk blotter. The lady wanted it brisk. So, she'd get it brisk. "O.K., Fitzhugh, listen up. Three days ago, it was on Friday morning. The call comes in about 6:30 A.M. I'm in the building already with nothing to do. So I take the call . . . start my day early. I go out to this snazzy apartment building on Wisconsin Avenue. Corner of Mass." He looked up at Anne cryptically. "Uptown gloss. Second District, your old beat. The body of a young white female has been discovered, she's dead in her apartment."

"Discovered by whom?"

"Victim's roommate, name of Nicky Nelson. Turns out the roommate came home to the apartment about five in the morning and found her—the victim, this Caroline McKelvey—lying on the floor. To be more precise, she was slumped over a bar between the kitchen and the dining room. She'd been stabbed, sliced as it were . . . right across the jugular." Dakota made a slicing motion right about his tie knot.

Anne winced. "How long had she been dead?"

"Just over twelve hours by the time the crime lab got to her. The murder occurred on Thursday evening. Coroner says she died between 6 and 8 P.M."

"May I see the shots?" She put out a hand, palm up.

Dakota handed over the medical examiner's glossy prints and continued his account. "The roommate had gone plumb crazy . . . had hysterics before I got there. She had blood all over her feet and she'd knocked over a teacup sitting on the counter beside the dead girl and she'd used the phone and . . . spread her own prints over everything.

She had, in other words, made a mess of things. The manager of the building had calmed her down some and, when I got there, she was on the phone in her bedroom calling everybody she could think of . . . the dead girl's parents and fiancé . . . a guy in the Navy, stationed over in Annapolis. Woke everybody up, of course, stunned them cold. She even called the dead girl's boss at home. And Father Jesse Clore. She'd called him first thing, even before she called the police. He was there when I arrived.''

"This priest from the Cathedral . . . this Clore, he was in the apartment?''

"When I walked in, there he was in his black suit, white Roman collar, the whole bit. He was down on one knee by the corner of the living room sofa with his face buried in his hands whispering prayers to himself, and the roommate is talking ninety miles a minute on the bedroom telephone, and the victim is lying there on the kitchen counter dead . . . in a pool of blood like nothing you've ever seen.''

"Dead. Very dead," said Anne soberly.

She was studying the glossies the crime lab had taken at the scene.

"Very. It was odd as hell, you know." Dakota was stroking his mustache. "Like some kind of play scene I'd walked on to.''

Anne handed him back the pictures. They'd made her feel just slightly sick. But then violent death always did. In this case, the scene was particularly bloody. Not so much brutal—as just plain bloody.

From the crime lab's glossies, it didn't appear the girl had been beaten up or raped. She had been "sliced" as Dakota put it, straight on and had fallen forward across the counter. The head of soft blond curls was matted with blood, and the young woman's profile, outlined in the mire on the counter, was quite beautiful.

She looked, thought Anne, almost serene in death.

"Have you any . . . " She started to ask, "ideas about the killer?'' and thought better of it. Dakota admitted he had no handle on the case yet. The Cowboy was as good a detective as they get, and not a man to push. He was methodical and he was sure. If she gave him a chance, he would tell her all he knew.

"So"—Dakota slid the pictures back in the manila file—"I get this roommate whose name is Nicky Nelson—did I say that?—off the phone and lying down on the bed with a cold cloth on her forehead because she is now feeling faint and I call the crime lab. And then, while I'm waiting for the wagon to get there, I sit down with Father Jess. It is now about seven-forty in the morning."

"You surprise me, Dakota. You like this Father Jesse Clore."

"Why would you think that?" Dakota gave her a sharp look.

"The way you say his name. He's a *good* guy in your book."

"I don't divide the world into good guys and bad guys," he said. "That's *your thing*, Fitzhugh. But yeah . . . Jess is O.K. He told me some things about the victim that were helpful."

"Like what?"

"Like the fact that she was twenty-six and living in the apartment on Wisconsin Avenue only two months . . . and that for the past three years she's worked as a lobbyist for an environmental association but just recently she'd gone to work for Congressman Woodward from New Jersey . . . the one who's always up there in the news with sound bites like, 'Good Government is Clean Government.' He's the one making headlines about trying to get the mid-Atlantic coast cleaned up."

Anne interrupted. "Why was Caroline McKelvey in counseling with this priest, Dakota?"

"She had some family pain to work out. That's just how Clore put it, Fitzhugh. Caroline had 'family pain.' "

Anne raised an eyebrow.

"For what it's worth," added Dakota, "her father is Marcus McKelvey who used to be the U.S. ambassador to the UN. Now he writes books, mostly about world peace . . . that kind of thing."

Anne recalled the name and the face. A handsome man,

Marcus McKelvey, vigorous, white-haired, in his late fifties. He looked a lot like Eric Sevareid.

"Her mother divorced McKelvey or maybe he divorced her, I don't know which, when the kid was about ten. Her mother's been remarried for years to Peter Carver, the Washington builder, and Caroline got along pretty well with her stepfather and her mother. They were both at the funeral."

"What about her own father . . . Marcus McKelvey?"

"He was there. Came down in a limousine from New York. He was alone. He looked different, older, more remote than I remembered him. He and Caroline didn't see much of each other."

"Is that what the priest told you?"

"No. It was the roommate. She kept coming into the living room. Then she'd take one look around and begin hiccuping and getting herself more and more worked up. I could see she was going to fall apart if I didn't get her or the victim's body out of that apartment."

"What's she like . . . Nicky Nelson?"

"Fast-talking . . . skinny, untidy. Neurotic as hell, I suspect, but not unattractive. Lots of curly black hair, a mouth that doesn't stop. Her father is Jay Nelson, the guy with the late night talk show out of New York."

Anne's attention was caught. "These roommates were both daughters of well-known men. That's . . . very interesting."

"What is so interesting? They are worlds apart in every way, Marcus McKelvey and Jay Nelson."

"I was thinking maybe that was why Caroline was in counseling . . . being the daughter of a famous man isn't easy."

"We are getting off the subject. Way off. Do you want to hear what info I've got on this case, Fitzhugh?"

"I want very much to hear what info you've got on the case, Dakota." Anne's smile was wide-eyed.

Dakota stared down at his notes. "It seems Nicky hadn't seen Caroline for several days. Their schedules conflict. Nicky Nelson works for ABC . . ."

"Just like her dad," Anne put in demurely.

"Just like her dad except that he is impressive and powerful and works out of New York and she is unimpressive and powerless and works in Washington."

Dakota made a mental note that he had just scored a point. "Nicky Nelson is just a camera grip, a 'right hand annie' for the news digest show at 10 P.M. She tells me she works noon until 8 P.M. weekdays and then goes out for supper and comes back to do the show. Afterward, she winds down, goes out for drinks or . . . 'out to play,' as she put it. She didn't see much of Caroline except at breakfast and on weekends. She did say one thing . . . that Caroline had been distracted lately, had been talking like she might be about to break off her engagement to the Navy guy."

"Now, that's interesting."

"What is *interesting*?"

"That she would be making so many changes in her life."

"You mean the victim, Caroline?"

"Of course, I mean the victim, Dakota!" Anne stood up indignantly. "In the space of the last two minutes, you've told me that Caroline McKelvey recently moved her residence, changed jobs and now you tell me she was about to break off her engagement!"

Dakota leaned back. He narrowed his eyes. "Well, don't make a crime out of it. The girl was twenty-six years old, finding her way. Do you have some problem with people making changes?"

Anne crossed the narrow aisle and perched on the corner of Dakota's cluttered desk. "Let's just say it's a piece of the 'Who was Caroline McKelvey puzzle?' and file it for further reference."

"Yes. Why don't we just say that?" he said with elaborate calmness. "Maybe you will now let me get on to the *really interesting* facts of the case."

"What are those facts, Dakota? Please go on. I am listening intently."

"You need to understand, Fitzhugh"—he was sober now, all business—"and this *is* important—the door to the apartment was apparently unlocked and the murderer walked right in. Or, it was locked and Caroline went over and opened it . . . she willingly admitted the murderer. There was no sign of forced entry.''

"So, you are ruling out . . . ''

"I'm not ruling out anything, but the evidence suggests she knew her killer. I mean, it wasn't a robbery, for God's sake! Nicky says that nothing is missing and the victim's purse was lying on the counter with wallet intact.'' Dakota shook his head. "And it sure as hell wasn't rape. So, I'm thinking . . . ''

"You're thinking this was premeditated murder and that Caroline knew the person. Only she wasn't expecting trouble. She wasn't expecting foul play.''

"Right. So, I'm wondering who would have cause to . . . ?''

"Caroline's fiancé. He's your obvious suspect, Dakota. The guy's being jilted. He's angry.''

"Daryl Swan. Lieutenant Commander Daryl Swan. No, I don't think so. He is too much in love with Caroline. Or, was. He was torn up at the funeral, cried like a baby.''

"That could be an act. I wouldn't write him off.'' Anne slipped a piece of paper from the folder on the desk. "What does the crime lab say . . . any good fingerprints?''

"Just a few clear ones. Those of Caroline and Nicky Nelson. And Father Jess Clore . . . from when he was trying to be helpful after Nicky found the body.''

"I find it very strange,'' said Anne, "that Nicky Nelson called an Episcopal priest before she called the police or Caroline's family.''

"Jess Clore was Caroline's spiritual adviser. He was just across the street. Somehow it makes sense to me. I thought we'd swing by and see him this morning.''

"Father Anthony Jesse Clore.'' Anne said the name slowly. "I picture a head of soft white hair, a little round belly, a gentle healing manner.''

"What you'll get is a man of forty-three with a lean belly and a rugged face and . . . well, I think you'll like him. Fitzhugh, I wish you could have seen Clore kneeling by that sofa. He was in pain, his eyes were closed. I heard him say, 'Caro, oh, Caro.' Then he got up and went over to the counter where her body was and stood there stroking her head. He got blood on his shoes but he didn't seem to care.''

''He sounds . . . like a man who's not afraid to show his feelings,'' Anne said.

Dakota pursed his lips slightly. ''He was also getting in the way. I told him to leave things alone, he'd mess up the evidence.''

''What did he do then?''

''He made the sign of the cross over her body and left shortly after.''

Anne was looking intently at Dakota. ''You say he managed Caroline's funeral?''

''Managed isn't the right word.'' Dakota frowned. ''Father Clore officiated at the service. He knew who I was and why I was there. Now and then, I felt like he was looking right at me, Fitzhugh. He's like that. I suspect his eyes met those of every person in the chapel at one time or another.''

''How many people were there?''

''It was a private service, only about twenty people. Her mother and stepfather were there, as I said. He is a real mover in the city and she is 'society.' '' Dakota put quotes around the word with his fingers. ''They were in terrible shock and weren't much help when I talked with them on Friday. They'd seen Caroline on the weekend before when her fiancé was in town and the four of them had lunch at the Georgetown Club. Since then, there'd been one telephone conversation. Caroline had sounded her usual . . . listen to this, Fitzhugh, I wrote it down just like her mother said it—'My daughter was her usual sweet, happy self.' ''

''This is a girl who is breaking her engagement, had just changed her job, is in counseling with an Episcopal priest . . . very interesting.'' Anne shook her head.

''Don't keep saying that.''

''Sorry. What about her father?''

''McKelvey hadn't talked with his daughter for several weeks. She'd sent him a book and a card for his birthday last month, but there had been no communication since.''

"Hadn't he even called to thank her?''

"He didn't say. He's self-contained. Just like he looks on TV. He kind of bowls you over with his calm. Not that he would bowl *you* over, Fitzhugh. Not you.'' Dakota leaned back in his chair again. Now he was riding her, a flash of amused challenge in his blue eyes. "You'd keep your cool, I'm sure about that, Fitzhugh, no matter what.''

"Get on with the story, Dakota.''

"Well, there's not much more. You've seen the death report. Very straightforward. The little lady got her jugular vein sliced at very close range. No other trauma to the body. Let's see.'' Dakota flipped through the notes he'd scribbled in his notebook. "Late Friday morning, I talked to a couple of the neighbors and the building superintendent. No one *knew* anything. No one *saw* anything. No one *heard* anything . . . except one old fellow down the hall named Forrester, a retired gent with a cane and minimal eyesight. He thinks he saw Caroline getting into the elevator something after 6 P.M. on Thursday evening just as he was coming into the building. She was alone, he *thinks*, but he isn't sure. He just caught a glimpse of her before the elevator door closed. He *thinks* she smiled at him.

"Mmmm . . . she probably was alone. She came into the building about six-thirty on Thursday evening and got murdered shortly after.'' Anne stared at her partner thoughtfully. "Why? Why Caroline McKelvey and why that night?''

"Beats me," said Dakota.

"Let's start with the roommate.''

"I started with the roommate, Fitzhugh. I spent most of Saturday morning with the roommate. She talked ninety miles a minute and broke into tears every now and then, but she didn't seem to have a clue who killed her roommate. I don't think she actually *knew* Caroline very well.''

"What about the people at her office?''

"Congressman Woodward's office. I was there on Friday afternoon. Woodward was on the floor of the House giving a speech and the other people in the office . . . all twenty-

four of them . . . Jesus, these guys have big staffs . . .
seemed real sorry about Caroline. She was well liked.
Woodward's AA—his administrative assistant—he's the
main man in the office—introduced me around. He was
helpful, but it wasn't much. She'd only been working there
a few months.''

''A lot can happen in a few months. Maybe a love affair.''

''Possible,'' said Dakota. ''She was one good-looking
woman. But I didn't pick up on anything like that.''

''What about the office she'd worked in before?''

''Closed on Friday afternoons and weekends. Just a small
environmental affairs lobbying outfit. We'll check it out
today, Fitzhugh.'' He reached for his notebook and scribbled down the address.

Anne stood in the middle of the aisle waiting for him.
She was watching him. She liked watching Dakota, but
only when he didn't know she was watching him.

Anne shook her head and allowed herself a deep steadying breath.

Working with Dakota again would take some adjusting
to. She had not forgotten what happened before. She had
not forgotten the strong physical attraction. She was standing so close to him at this moment she could put her hand
on that head of brown-gold curls if she wished.

Don Dakota. Code name, ''The Cowboy.'' The cream of
the team. That chiseled and appealing profile should, by
rights, belong to a man of passion and tenderness. That face
totally masked the fact that this macho supercop was known
to be bad news to women: stubborn, complicated, ''oh yes,
ma'am, believe it.'' She'd heard the word around Indiana
Avenue. Don Dakota was bad news to women.

And he could make her heart beat faster than any man
she knew.

She wouldn't think about that. She couldn't afford to.

Dakota was not the kind of man to get involved with.
He was nothing but one big risk. A risk she'd never take.
He'd been married twice. He was twice divorced. Love'm
and leave'm. Not a good record in the emotions department.

He was a loner. A dedicated cop. He was scornful.

Anne smiled. It was time to put up her guard. Rein in her emotions. The vacation was over. Working again with Dakota would bring out her vulnerabilities, her fear of risks.

Yes, she'd keep her guard in place. No slips. The Cowboy didn't trust her. That was the heart of it. He'd asked her once, and quite pointedly at that, what the hell she was doing on Homicide. A fair question from a seasoned cop to a young woman lawyer whose fear of physical violence showed. She was, he'd flatly pointed out, as unlikely a candidate for the job as he'd ever seen.

And she'd offered something glib in response. A quick wit made a cover.

Anne's true feelings didn't often show and she wanted it that way. Her feelings were her own personal business. To put it simply, she had a deep and quite unreasonable rage at Death. It was a personal rage and it had brought her to where she was. This scruffy Homicide squad room. Being a homicide detective was Anne Tyler Fitzhugh's revenge.

Five years ago, her husband, Congressman Rob Fitzhugh, had been shot in the chest while campaigning on the back roads in southern Virginia. It had been a pointless and random shooting in a roadside café. An old jukebox playing, a smoky bar. Rob Fitzhugh had stopped in for a late night cup of coffee before driving back to Washington and stepped right into an argument between strangers. A trigger squeezed, a murder without malice. The killer had been a man in jeans and a plaid shirt, a man with a gun, a man no one remembered. An unknown man who got into his pickup truck and drove away into the night. Despite massive efforts by local, state and FBI investigators, the identity of that man was never discovered. . . . He was just another killer who was never brought to justice.

In the first few months after her husband's death, Anne had lived in a state of shock, her feelings blunted by her grief. Then came a growing anger that Rob's killer was not caught. Finally, depression. And, more difficult to deal with, fear. A strange sort of fear that she could not face. A fear of losing control. A fear of violence. A fear of risking anything that mattered . . . anything. She believed for a long time that she could handle those feelings on her own. She was a criminal lawyer and a good one, just like her father, respected Virginia DA John Tyler. But it was useless. She had turned inward, inward for safety, and lost her passion for the law. Finally she had given up the hard-won D.C. law partnership and gone home to the Tidewater to hide.

"Face yourself, Anne. Face those fears," her father had challenged her when a year had passed and she still did nothing but falter, brim with tears and turn away when people talked about Rob Fitzhugh . . . brilliant Rob Fitzhugh, who shouldn't have died.

No, he shouldn't have. But he had died. "Rob Fitzhugh is gone," her father reminded her. "Throw yourself into work. It's the only way you'll stop grieving so."

John Tyler was not suggesting that his daughter return to Washington and join the D.C. Police Department. That had been her own surprising choice. Two years on a beat. Two years without feeling much inside except anger. The fears had lessened. Anger was the one thing she could hang on to. She'd made it all the way to where she wanted to be, the D.C. Criminal Division. Homicide Department.

Gratefully Anne had let the work absorb her and slowly fill all the empty places. Yes, she was still haunted by fear. No, she didn't like taking risks. It was part of her vulnerability. But she was a good cop, a steady, thoughtful detective, and she threw herself into her cases. Every solved murder case helped ease her pain. Her absorption in solving difficult murder cases blotted out everything else, focused the angry feelings that still engulfed her. Even now, as she watched Don Dakota close the McKelvey folder, Anne felt her private energies begin to build for the challenge that lay ahead of them.

Caroline McKelvey. A young woman with a lovely face.

A face like an angel's, even in death.

Anne Fitzhugh reached inside herself and felt the anger, felt the familiar indignation at senseless murder flood through her. This was her own private adrenaline. Her energy was grounded in anger and commitment, and was strong enough to dispel her anxieties about working again with Dakota.

Why was Caroline McKelvey murdered?

And by whose hand?

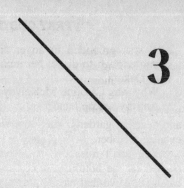

3

A Monday morning at nine-thirty, a bell was pealing in the school yard. A brisk, purposeful morning in early October. Canon Anthony Jesse Clore was not in his office in the administrative wing of the Washington Cathedral. His secretary, Alice, said he was in the herb garden.

"I'll take you there." Alice led them through the cool dark halls behind the Cathedral's nave. "Jess says gardening is a way of letting off steam."

"Your man of the cloth lets off steam at ten o'clock on Monday morning!" murmured Anne as she and Dakota followed Jess Clore's secretary down the stone steps toward the green lawn on the south side of the Cathedral. "It must be a hard life, Dakota."

He grinned, amusement in his blue eyes. "Loosen up. You're going to like the man, Fitzhugh."

She might . . . and she might not.

However, she definitely liked the Washington Cathedral. She liked it for its simplicity and cream-brown lines, its sense of serenity and strength. Ironic, Anne considered, that fourteenth-century Gothic was so entirely appropriate for the capital of the most developed nation in the world . . . and for this idyllic wooded hillside in the northwest part of the city.

The massive limestone edifice, in the shape of a cross, had been under construction for as long as she could remember. Anne had watched the twin towers of St. Peter and Paul rising skyward year by year.

Until this morning, Anne had never turned up the short winding drive and viewed the edifice up close. She sensed peace. The grounds were heavy with oaks and magnolias and deep-set gardens. The grass was deep green even now, even in October.

"You can't miss the herb cottage." Clore's secretary paused on the bottom step of the south transept and indicated the drive that ran beside the Cathedral. "Walk to the right, you'll see a small brown building on your left. That's the herb cottage. You'll find Jesse . . . Canon Clore there."

"What does she mean when she calls him canon?" Anne asked Dakota as they walked up the circling driveway under the sheltering trees.

"A canon is above a parish priest and below a dean and bishop. That's what Jess Clore is . . . a canon and, I expect, he's hungry as hell to make it all the way up."

"To bishop?"

"You got it."

"You impress me, Dakota." She gave the big rugged man walking beside her a thoughtful glance. "You really do. I didn't know you knew such weighty things."

"There's a lot about me you don't know, Fitzhugh."

She laughed then and touched his arm.

"There." Anne nudged his arm. She was looking toward a brown building caught in the sunlight. Low hedges lined the walk. "There's an herb cottage, if I ever saw one, Dakota. And, that's a canon . . . if I ever saw one."

He laughed in spite of himself. Father Anthony Jesse Clore was coming out of the greenhouse on the far side of the low building carrying a tray of small pots. The priest wore sunglasses, a black short-sleeved clerical-collared shirt, black pants and dirty white athletic shoes.

As they approached him on the gravel path, Jesse Clore paused and held out his hand to Dakota. "You're back, Lieutenant? Good to see you again."

Dakota made the introductions and looked around for a

quiet spot. "Is there a place somewhere . . . ?"

Jesse Clore motioned toward the boxwood hedge, a me-
dieval-looking gate. "In there . . . the Bishop's Garden. It's
quiet, there are some benches."

The two detectives followed Canon Jesse Clore through
the arched wooden gate. The Bishop's Garden was intimate,
shaded and tranquil. Above their heads rose the Cathedral
facade and spires.

He's a careful man, thought Anne. A big man, taut and
careful. He likes being in control. She watched him settle
himself and his seedlings on a high-backed bench.

The priest motioned to Anne and Dakota to sit down in
two wooden chairs that formed with the bench a conversation spot beneath the trees. "What's on your mind, Lieutenant? As if I don't know. . . . Caroline McKelvey." Jesse
Clore looked suddenly sober as he said her name.

"You and I have already talked at some length about
this case." Dakota was setting the tone. "I mean, you were
there on Friday morning. You said you hadn't any idea who
might have killed Caroline McKelvey. Still, there's something to be gained from going over it again. Do you mind
a few questions?"

"Shoot. Fire away. Ask me anything you like." Canon
Anthony Jesse Clore took a deep breath as if to regain his
composure.

Yes, thought Anne, a big man in every sense . . . graceful
in his movements, broad-shouldered and ready to give. It
is himself he is holding under control.

"Well"—Dakota was taking out his notepad—"first
we'll cover old ground if you don't mind. Detective Fitzhugh needs to be filled in."

Jesse Clore turned to her. He had a hawklike face, high
cheekbones and dark hair, graying just slightly at the temples. A thinker's face. Empathetic. Anne had to admit she
liked his face. Jesse Clore looked as though he had lived
hard, as though nothing came easy. Control, banked energy,
intelligence. That was what she sensed. Dakota was right.
This man of the cloth was impressive.

"You said you knew Caroline McKelvey for some five months." Dakota was checking his notes.

"About that. She came to a party last spring . . . an informal party, one of those that the Young Professionals Club at the Cathedral throws every three months or so."

"The Young Professionals?"

"Young singles of the parish . . . those between the ages of twenty-five and forty who don't get a lot of spiritual attention and . . . don't have ways of meeting up with each other. I think this one was ribs on the grill and beer and some guys I know who play mellow jazz. . . . "

"Where did this party take place?"

"At my house." Clore gestured toward the right where the grounds of the Cathedral extended into green foliage. "I rent a house with two other unmarried priests. It's shabby, but the rooms are big and it makes for a good party."

"Who gets invited to the Young Professionals' parties?"

"Anyone . . . and everyone. Word goes out. Anybody in that age group who wants to come is welcome. I haven't had anyone show up yet whom I wasn't glad to see."

"Caroline McKelvey showed up at your party in April?"

Jesse Clore smiled ruefully. "You know, I actually don't recall her being there. Can you believe that . . . a woman as beautiful as Caroline? She told me later that she came by for a short while. People come and go at these affairs . . . sometimes a hundred or more drop in during the evening."

"So, when do you actually remember meeting Caroline?"

"She heard that I run a discussion group, just a small group of serious-minded young people who want to talk about the problems of life in Washington, life in the fast lane . . . getting close to your feelings. So she came to the meeting on the next Tuesday night. Now that night I remember her. Every man in the group turned around when she came in. . . . She didn't say much, just listened. But she came every week after that."

"She didn't say *much* . . . or didn't say anything?"

"It took a while for her to loosen up."

"But she finally did?" Dakota asked.

"Not really. She was always freer when she could talk to someone 'one on one.' "

"When did you begin talking to Caroline 'one on one'?"

"Around mid-August. We can check my appointment book. Caroline had been living downtown, F Street I think. In July, she moved. She got more active in the affairs of the Cathedral. And she decided, I guess, to get down to a deeper level in her own life. It was somewhere in mid-August when she told me that she was in need of some private help . . . some counseling." Clore's mouth tightened as he spoke.

Now it gets ticklish, thought Anne. He was going to be stubborn about confiding details of Caroline McKelvey's personal life. She didn't blame him for that. She would feel the same way.

But they had to know.

As she expected, Dakota was zeroing in. "You told me that Caroline talked to you about family pain? Can you be more specific?"

Jesse Clore seemed to retreat from them. His eyes had gone darker. He responded flatly, "It isn't relevant to her death, Lieutenant. But, all right. She saw her family split at a very tender age . . . a messy divorce. One doesn't get over that. And there's a brother who's something of a mess. Her mother is quite a charming lady who remarried well and began a new life. I think Caroline felt cut off somewhere. It didn't show to the naked eye. She was attractive and self-assured. But underneath, she was in a lot of pain until . . . "

Dakota waited for Clore to go on. He said nothing.

Anne asked bluntly, "Until what?"

"Until she found God."

Anne flushed. It wasn't quite the answer she was expecting.

Dakota's head was bent over his notebook. Now, he looked up, giving her an amused smile. "You come on too strong sometimes, Fitzhugh," he had said to her more than once. "You can be so damn direct, you turn your party off. You have got to learn to work the moment."

That was what he was about to do now. She knew just how Dakota operated. He had a certain sensitivity about him, a skill at timing, a skill at interrogation, that was a treat to watch. She watched her partner close his notebook.

"This is one incredible place," Dakota said. "One of the most beautiful places in Washington, I would say."

"The Bishop's Garden," said Clore quietly. He seemed less intense now. "It's restful, I agree. Caroline liked to come and sit here. Actually, that's how she got into private counseling. I came into the garden one day and found her. She was obviously despondent over something. I knew her from the discussion group and I came over to talk to her. After that, we met once or twice a week in my office. When I think about Caroline being murdered, I get angry as bloody hell! If I knew who killed her, I'd . . . "

He made a hard fist. It was obvious Jesse Clore meant something violent and very physical.

His dark eyes suddenly met Anne's.

He relaxed his fist. It was a conscious effort. He smiled with his particular intimate charm. "I am a man too, Detective Fitzhugh. This collar doesn't mean my reactions to life aren't just like any one else's."

She nodded. "I understand. We are cops and we get angry a lot, too."

"As for Caroline, I cared about her. A few times, we even had dinner together after our group sessions. Yes, she kept active in those too. I felt as though I knew her very well."

"Who were her friends?" Anne asked.

"We didn't talk much about her friends."

"What about the young man she was going to marry?"

"Yes, she talked of him. She'd known Daryl for a long time and it was a good . . . comfortable relationship."

"Her roommate?"

A pause. "Nicky came with Caroline to a few gatherings of the Young Professionals. I don't think they were good friends. They shared an apartment—went their separate ways in general. No two young women could have been more different than Caroline and Nicky Nelson.''

"How so?'' Anne leaned forward in her chair.

"Oh, Nicky's all right. She's a tough kid. Ambitious as hell, but I couldn't say about her talent. She has the kind of manner that rubs on your nerves like sandpaper.''

"I was wondering just why she called you when she found Caroline's body?'' Anne brought out the question awkwardly. "That just seemed curious to me.''

"Caroline wasn't close to her family. She was close . . . to me. And I was right across the street. It stands to reason.''

"No. Not really.'' Anne shook her head. "Most people call the police first thing when they discover a murder. Nicky waited . . . an hour or more before she notified the police.''

"You'll have to ask Nicky Nelson about that.'' Clore looked annoyed by Anne's persistence on the point. "I can't speak for her.''

"Had you ever been to their apartment before . . . to Nicky and Caroline's?''

Jesse Clore put his hand to his forehead. "No, surely not. Nicky said 'sixth floor, the last apartment on the right.' She said Caroline was dead . . . murdered. I put on my clothes and went there as if I were sleepwalking. I don't think I believed what Nicky said until I saw Caroline lying there . . . slumped across the bar.''

There was a movement to their right. Jesse Clore's secretary was framed in the garden's entrance. Her voice was light, apologetic. "I hate to bother you, but there's a phone call. It's the bishop . . . ''

Canon Clore sighed, put his hands on his knees and rose.

Anne watched the way he reached down for the seedlings on the bench. Gentleness. Banked fires . . . control was her impression. A certain reach for integrity. She liked him. At least, she thought she did.

He looked from one to the other of the two detectives.

Again he made a tightening movement with his fist. "We can't let Caroline's death go . . . "

"Unsolved," finished Anne.

"I was going to say 'unavenged.' " The dark-eyed priest smiled sadly.

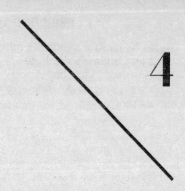

4

"Would you like to see the victim's apartment now, Fitzhugh?"

Anne nodded. "Do you have a key?"

"The super will let us in." Dakota swung the white Crown Victoria—noticeable as a police vehicle only by the swaying radio antennae on its trunk—into mid-morning traffic on the avenue headed south.

The apartment building was on the right, less than two blocks from the Cathedral.

"A good location," commented Anne, "near the bus stop and metro."

"Near Father Clore." Dakota was cryptic.

"A handsome building. Well cared for. Modern."

"Faux-modern."

He was right. The Alhambra was probably forty years old like most of the buildings along this part of upper Wisconsin Avenue. Sturdy, time-weathered apartment complexes, large and sprawling with shops and restaurants on the street level. The Alhambra was smaller than most, freestanding, with narrow balconies across the front on the upper floors.

Anne noted beds of ivy lining the walkway, the windows had been recently washed and the ornate brass door trim shone from polishing. "An expensive place to live in for two young working women," she pointed out. "The rent's probably eighteen hundred dollars a month, or more."

Dakota made a scoffing sound. "Caroline and Nicky

weren't just two ordinary working women. There's family money on both sides. Caroline had a legacy from her grandfather. I don't know how much, but plenty. I *am* sure she didn't have to work at all. As for Nicky, look who her father is. . . . " He let the sentence trail off.

An alert, young black man in a green uniform and visored hat was moving purposefully across the lobby. He opened the glass door only a crack.

Dakota showed his badge.

The door was opened with a wide flourish. "Sorry, sir. I didn't know you were the police. Mr. Harris told me to let just tenants come in and that's all . . . and we gotta get an O.K. on everybody else."

"Fine enough. You're doing your job. Where is Mr. Harris now?"

"He be back in his office. I'll get him."

"I know the way." Dakota motioned Anne toward a swinging door on one side of the lobby.

Alfred Harris was the building superintendent. He offered them straight chairs in his office. "Like I told you on Friday"—he was looking at Dakota—"I live here in the building with my wife. I've been managing The Alhambra for twelve years and haven't ever had one bit of trouble until this . . . this terrible occurrence upstairs on Thursday evening."

He looked tired, a small man with nervous habits and a head of thin shining black hair. "We had a burglary about four years ago, had the furniture taken right out of the lobby. My wife and I were in our apartment in the back having supper. We didn't have a doorman then. After that, we got people to work round the clock. It's worth it . . . for tenants' security."

Anne smiled reassurance. Through the office window she could see a narrow slice of lawn on the side of the building, the buff-colored walls of the building next door. A spray of ivy grew up that wall. It was a nice neighborhood, quiet, slightly old-fashioned, the kind of place people think of as safe.

Life is dangerous . . . fleeting, fragile. She could hear her own heart beating. And Rob was dead. Nothing is ever safe.

"As for the tenants"—Alfred Harris stroked his temples—"they've been *crazy*, just crazy since the accident. I mean, the murder. That's what they want to know . . . all the details. It was murder, wasn't it?"

"Yes, it was murder, Mr. Harris." Dakota was jingling the keys in his pocket.

"Oh, sweet Jesus, I knew it was. I mean, obviously it was murder. I was here Friday morning. I saw her lying there. But I kept thinking . . . hoping it wasn't true. And then, the Saturday paper had that story about Miss McKelvey 'found dead,' and my other tenants just went wild. I mean, they all think that someone is prowling about the building."

"Miss McKelvey let the murderer into her apartment," said Dakota dryly. "It looks like the murderer was someone she knew."

"A friend?" Harris looked confused. "You mean it was a friend who killed Miss McKelvey?"

"It *looks* that way." Anne could not resist qualifying the point. "It doesn't mean that it happened that way. It could have been a stranger who was indeed 'prowling the building' and found her door open . . . or knocked and she opened . . . "

Impatient, Dakota interrupted Anne. "You told me on Friday that the back entrance to this building is secure. It can be opened only by a buzzer from the lobby desk or from this office. And the front door is locked. Do you mean locked or covered by a doorman?"

"Well, both really. I am saying the front door is always locked. The tenants have keys *and* there is a doorman on duty. He carries groceries for the elder tenants and accepts packages and flowers that are delivered when folks aren't home. It is an amenity of the building as well as a safety thing. Like I said, the tenants have keys to the front door so . . . "

Dakota again interrupted, finishing Harris's sentence. "So, no one can enter the building through the front door unless the doorman knows them or some tenant lets them in. Or they have a key?''

Harris looked ill at ease. ''That's right, essentially.''

''What do you mean 'essentially'?''

''Yes, that is the way it works. And, like I told you, the doorman who was on duty Thursday evening . . . well, he claims he didn't let anyone strange or unlikely into the building.''

''Harold Perry's his name,'' Dakota said shortly to Anne.

Harris nodded. ''That's right. Harold Perry. He's been working for me regularly for the past two years. Harold's shift is 5 P.M. until midnight. It is a busy time around here what with people coming home from work and others going out for dinner. Harold's real friendly. He knows people by name, he does a good job.''

''The doorman didn't see Caroline enter the building on Thursday evening?'' Anne asked Dakota.

''I haven't gotten around to questioning Harold Perry yet.''

''I asked Harold myself,'' said Harris with an air of importance. ''I asked him on Friday night and he said no, he didn't personally see her come in on Thursday evening. 'Must of missed her,' he said. 'Anything out of the ordinary that evening?'' I asked him. ''No,'' he said, ''nothing out of the ordinary.' If you check by tonight, you can talk to Harold. He'll be here, working the front door.''

Dakota was ready to move on. He asked for the key to apartment 612.

''Well it *is* entirely possible, you know, Dakota,'' Anne said when they were in the elevator, ''that someone could have entered this building on a false pretense or posing as a repairman . . . ''

He sighed. ''No way, Fitzhugh. Whoever killed Caroline McKelvey met with no resistance. I am dead certain she knew her killer. They were facing each other across the bar and she didn't step back or put up her arms to defend herself. What does that tell you?''

The apartment door was sealed with wide strips of NO

ADMITTANCE tape. Dakota balled the yellow tape and put it in his jacket pocket.

"What about the roommate, Nicky Nelson?" Anne questioned.

"Staying elsewhere for a few days. She was in no mood to hang around."

The apartment had the smell of death in it. A blood-thick, cloying scent that Anne Fitzhugh had come to know well. Floor to ceiling drapes were closed across the far wall of the living room. When Dakota maneuvered them open, sunshine flooded into the room through a sliding glass door that opened onto a balcony. Dakota slid the door open and some of the scent of blood and death disappeared into the autumn morning. The view was of leafy treetops, suburban backyards.

Anne let her eyes move slowly around the living room trying to catch the mood. The room was carpeted in beige, pale in its coloring, and vaguely feminine although there was a curio cabinet on one wall holding a striking collection of beautifully carved animals.

When she moved closer, she noted a leopard coiled to spring, an elephant with tusks raised, a lion on the run. Something elegant and vicious about each one. They did not match the decor in the rest of the room. The roommates were probably not compatible. Jesse Clore had already indicated that.

"In here, Fitzhugh," said Dakota.

The dining ell contained a table and four chairs, their seats covered in pale patterned chintz. A floor to ceiling mirror hung just within the ell. On the long wall, a bookshelf held a pile of magazines carelessly stacked, a wine cooler and a matching tray with wineglasses on it. There was an African violet in a fishbowl on the bottom shelf. A television set occupied the middle shelf.

Dried blood lay in hardened pies on the parquet floor below the edges of the bar that separated the dining ell from the kitchen.

Anne looked down on a bar's surface that was a scarred and matted ocean of blood, jet black at the center, but thinning to crimson as it ran in dried-up rivers and threads to the edge of the bar. That bloody sea was marred by the profile of Caroline McKelvey . . . a clear outline of brow and nose, a mouth half-open and a small firm chin. Caught in the dried-up blood were single hairs of gold that had been pulled from her head when the body was removed.

"No smears or streaks." Dakota had moved into the kitchen.

He rested his hands wide apart on the bar, careful not to touch the blood. "The victim was standing right here, her murderer was on the other side. Caroline didn't fight. She didn't put up any struggle. Why not? For God's sake, it looks like she leaned across the bar right into the knife."

He was right. How could someone pull a knife on a young woman, bring it to her throat and not have her pull back? Perplexed, Anne shook her head. "Did the medical examiner have any thoughts on penetration point, angle, height of murderer, that kind of thing?"

Dakota nodded shortly. "A right-handed murderer. Probably of average height. There was nothing noticeable about penetration point or angle. The cut was made straight on. But here's an interesting point, Fitzhugh. The lab says the cut wasn't made by any kind of regular knife. It was some kind of duller tool. Maybe scissors sharpened. Small. Very sharp . . . razor-sharp."

"Small. Very sharp . . . razor-sharp." Anne repeated the words softly.

"The cut was made gently. Without force, says the coroner."

"A woman could have done it."

"Right." Dakota's eyes were thoughtful. Intent.

"This Nicky person?"

"No way did that broad do it, Fitzhugh."

"Sometimes the answer is too obvious to see." Anne tried to lay out a scenario. "Let's say they were here together, Nicky and Caroline." Anne stood in the dining ell across the bar from him. "Caroline is putting away groceries, getting ready to make dinner. And they got into an argument. Caroline leans forward over the bar and says something vicious. Nicky is on this side of the bar and she has these super-sharpened kitchen shears and . . . ''

"The murderer could have been a woman, I'll grant you that, Fitzhugh. But Nicky Nelson claims to have been at work that night. She has witnesses to her presence at the studio. I haven't yet talked with them. But I'll say this . . . if she did come home and kill Caroline and go back to the studio for the 10 P.M. show and then head out bar-hopping for several hours, that's one cool lady. I mean, here was her roommate bleeding to death in their kitchen. . . . ''

"Caroline died in seconds, Dakota,'' she reminded him. They were on a rhythm. Now the partnership was taking hold. Point, counterpoint.

"Damn it, you know what I mean.'' He sighed. "Nicky Nelson hasn't got that kind of cool. No, she didn't kill her roommate.''

Anne was looking at the broken slivers of a teacup on the floor by the dining room table. "Whoever it was . . . Caroline was having a cup of tea with her murderer.''

"Not quite. She was having a cup of tea by herself.''

Dakota pointed to a spot inked in red by the crime crew on the counter. "That's where her cup was found. The crew took it in to the lab, found Caroline's fingerprints and lip prints. No cream and no sugar. Those pieces of broken china you're looking at . . . apparently a second cup was standing on the bar. An empty cup. No liquid was in it and only Caroline's fingerprints were on it. When she fell, her arm knocked that cup to the floor. It broke. Pieces are here and there. Also, a tea bag which was possibly resting in it.''

"Strange that she would fix her own first, then the other . . . ''

"Did I tell you she had taken off her shoes?'' Dakota pointed to a pair of brown high heel pumps lying near the bar on the dining room side. "My theory is she is having a cup of tea all by her lonesome and someone knocks on the door. So she goes and opens it, and it's someone she knows. She invites the person in and she comes back here and starts to make her visitor a cup of tea. She has her back turned when the knife comes out . . . ''

"So, we are back to the original question, Dakota. Who could have entered this building without the doorman letting him or her in? How many people have keys to this building?"

"Every tenant. Forty-six apartments."

"What about Caroline and Nicky? Maybe they'd pass out a few keys."

"Nicky claims she hasn't given anyone a key."

"And Caroline? I wonder if she . . . "

Anne's sixth sense made her pause and turn her head at a faint sound. A key was being inserted into the lock. Someone was attempting to enter the apartment.

Dakota moved swiftly. He was around the bar and waiting at the living room arch when the front door opened. "Jesus," Dakota exclaimed. "Who the hell . . . ?"

A slim young man wearing khaki pants and a black sweater stood framed in the doorway. "I'm Paul Mc-Kelvey, Caroline's brother." He came inside and closed the door firmly behind him. "I know, you're the detectives. I heard downstairs. They told me I could come up."

"You're Caroline's brother?" Dakota's tone was doubtful. "You weren't at the funeral." Still, he took his hand down from the breast of his jacket and his shoulder holster.

The young man shook his head, his face impassive, oddly mocking. He was not as young as all that. Perhaps in his early thirties, Anne judged. Sallow-skinned and in need of a shave. Blond hair going brown, long on the collar. His eyes were dark. They had a bruised look beneath them as though he was sick or had not slept in a while.

"I didn't hear that Caroline was dead until yesterday. I live in L.A. Most of the time, L.A.," Paul McKelvey said finally. "I was visiting in Baltimore this past weekend and I . . . "

"Hell, no one called to tell you your sister was dead?" Dakota was disbelieving.

"I don't have a permanent address. I check in back East now and then." He was looking at the dried blood on the bar. A shudder of visible pain went through his body.

"What are you doing in town now?" asked Dakota.

"I called my mother's house last night and . . . "

"So what did your mother say?"

"She didn't. She wasn't taking any calls. Even from me. Apparently she's under heavy sedation. My stepfather told me that Caroline had been murdered."

Paul McKelvey's tone was steady again. Only the twitching of a nerve in his face showed his emotional state. "So, this morning I borrowed my friend's car and drove over. Here I am . . . "

"Were you close to your sister, Paul?" Anne sensed the answer would be "no."

"The reason I came here today is . . . I had to see . . . I had to know what happened." Paul McKelvey picked up a throw pillow from the sofa, then tossed it down with a hard gesture. "She was . . . "

"She was . . . what?"

"She was the only really good person I ever knew."

He did not look directly at Fitzhugh or Dakota. But he sounded, for the first time, entirely sincere. "That's the hell of it. She was the only one who ever cared a real damn about me. She hadn't any reason to . . . but she did."

"Tell us about your sister, Paul." Anne's voice was gentle.

"I can't. Not really. I haven't seen much of her in recent years."

"What about when you were small?"

Paul McKelvey went over to the curio cabinet. He bent down and picked up a tiny carved tiger, stood it on his palm and stroked the small animal with his finger. "I was four years older than Caroline. I was a real little hellraiser . . . even then. My mom walked out on my father when I was fourteen. She took my sister, the 'ever-sweet and ever-beautiful' Caroline with her."

"And left you . . . ?"

Paul turned abruptly and sat down on the sofa. He put a

hand to his temple as though his head was aching. "I was left in New York with my father, who promptly sent me away to boarding school. The divorce was a rough scene. It didn't make for closeness."

"Have you seen much of your sister over the years?"

"No," he grimaced. "Now and then I'd come to Washington for a visit which always proved disastrous. My stepfather gritting his teeth until it was over, my mother with nothing at all to say to me. Really nothing, except some kind of implied, 'Why don't you stop making me feel guilty'?"

"But Caroline always loved you?" Anne was sitting now in the armchair across from the pale young man.

"You could say that. I was shitty to her, I admit it. I guess I saw her as the favored princess ... I mean, Jesus, even my stepfather liked her! She was able to ... "

He didn't want to continue. Anne could sense that. He was a slender, tired-looking young man. There was something badly wrong. She glanced up at Dakota leaning against the arch, watching with an impassive face. He was letting her have a shot at this. She pushed Paul McKelvey to continue his story. "Caroline was able to do what, Paul?"

"She borrowed money from our stepfather. She said it was for graduate courses she wanted to take at American University. It was for me actually. I'd opened a restaurant with a friend out in L.A. and it was folding. It was going down. I was desperate. My grandfather left me some money but I'd gone through that. I mean I was in real trouble. So Caroline got the cash for me. But ... "

He shrugged, opened his palm and looked down at the carved tiger he was holding. Then he put the small animal in his pocket.

"I gather you lost the restaurant?" Anne asked.

"Yeah. Things just didn't work out."

"Are you on drugs?"

"Off and on. No big deal."

Anne glanced at Dakota again. She could not read her

partner's face. She turned back to McKelvey. "When was the last time you saw Caroline?"

"About three weeks ago. I had some business in town. I crashed for a night, here on this sofa. I'm not too welcome at my mother's, you see."

"Did your sister tell you anything that might help us in finding her killer? I mean, did she see herself in any danger?"

He paused as if considering the question. "Her roommate was here the whole time. We didn't talk about much that was personal, Caroline and me. Usually she asks me a lot of questions like she's interested in what I'm up to, you know. This time she didn't. It was like she had something on her mind. I think something was worrying her."

"What do you think it was?"

"Probably it was her precious work. She was dedicated to saving the earth, you know. The biosphere she called it. It was her own personal mission." Paul McKelvey spoke with an edge of sarcasm.

"What about her personal life? Did she mention a change in her marriage plans?"

"You mean, her plans to marry Daryl?" McKelvey looked surprised. "The last I heard they were getting married next spring. First it was Christmas, and then spring."

Dakota cut in abruptly. "How did you get this apartment key, McKelvey?"

"Caro gave it to me."

"How do you get in the front door?"

"The lobby guys know me. They always let me in."

"Why the hell did Caroline give you a key to her apartment?"

Paul McKelvey looked startled at the harshness in Dakota's tone. "In case I was in town and needed a place to . . . It is not a big deal, you know. I *am* her brother."

"Not much of one." Dakota's eyes had the color and coolness of slate. "I don't think you ever did her any favors. What's more, I think you were jealous as hell of your sister. I would even call it . . . active dislike, McKelvey."

The young man on the sofa answered without emotion. "You call it what you want to. I don't think I disliked her. She was a bleeding heart, a pushover. I take what I can . . . whenever I can. So, I took advantage of her. I'll admit that. But I sure as hell didn't murder Caroline."

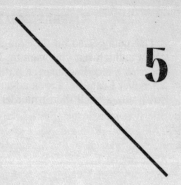

5

"**Y**ou were rough on him," Anne said to Dakota.

"Paul McKelvey is a self-serving punk."

"Granted. He's selfish, maybe a deadbeat. He is pretty honest about that. He's also a victim."

"Of what, for God's sake?"

Anne was watching the city slide by the Crown Vic's window, this affluent northwest slice of Washington. The calm, leafy streets and broad avenues of the Second District had been her beat when she was a patrol cop. She knew its glories and heartaches. She knew that the people who lived behind the front doors of these handsome houses bled when cut just like anyone else. Emotionally and otherwise. They were just passing the Vice President's sprawling, turreted mansion overlooking Dunbarton Oaks. "A victim of money and divorce," she went on. "A mother who walked out on him, a father who is remote. A disjointed family. Too much money . . . too little love."

"Spare me," said Dakota shortly. "Who has the perfect life?"

"Still. Family is . . . " Everything, she wanted to say. Anne was thinking of the gruff, warmhearted father who had raised her and given her love and direction and a strong sense of family despite the fact that her mother had died when she was three. She hadn't felt abandoned as a child. Not then. Not that she could remember. Maybe . . . maybe on some rare afternoons, in the quiet, in the empty rooms.

But John Tyler had been enough.

Rob Fitzhugh had been enough. She hadn't expected either death. She hadn't expected this abandonment. Her beloved father had died of a sudden heart attack in Richmond just over a year ago. She had never expected to be left alone by the two men in her life. If only there had been a child left for her . . . Rob's child. That would have made it bearable. Two was enough for a family.

Anne shook her head, turned from the window.

"I think Paul McKelvey is physically sick," she said to Dakota. "I'm going by his skin tone . . . and something feverish in his eyes. What do you think . . . hepatitis?"

Dakota shrugged.

"I don't think he killed Caroline, although he had a motive. He owed her money. Not to mention what Paul would gain by his sister's death . . . sweet Caroline, the favored child. With her out of the way, the bad apple may come into his own. Both with Marcus McKelvey and with his mother and stepfather."

"We'll see." Dakota sounded detached, as if he didn't want to talk about Paul McKelvey.

She glanced at her partner's profile. Dakota had lost his summer tan. He looked pale with fatigue—she hadn't noticed that this morning. She knew that he'd been working double shifts for the past few months. She'd done more than a few double shifts herself over the summer. The department was pressed, taking heat for all the unsolved cases of the past few months. It was easy to lose your perspective.

Anne started to ask where they were headed now. Dakota was chewing at the edge of his mustache, impatiently maneuvering the Ford through traffic. He was too hard on the gas pedal, quick on the horn.

"Nicky Nelson," he said, as if reading Anne's mind, "noon, at the City Café."

It was almost twelve now. The City Café was on M Street, right up the street from the ABC building. A smart, casual little café, known for its delicious food. Anne's spirits picked up.

* * *

At a small table in the back of the café's dining room, Nicky Nelson was waiting for them. She was a slim young woman in her mid-twenties, with tense shoulders and a mane of black, tangled curls.

Dakota had described Nicky as hysterical, out of control.

She did not look so to Anne. Nicky's expression seemed entirely calculating. In those black piercing eyes, Anne saw a glitter that bordered on mania. "My roommate shouldn't have died," Nicky offered flatly as the two detectives sat down at her table. "There wasn't any reason for it. Caroline didn't have a single enemy."

"Someone killed her. I call that an enemy," said Dakota.

She acknowledged Anne's presence with a hard look, then said cryptically, "I think Caroline just got in the way, that's all."

"Got in whose way?" Dakota was suddenly interested.

Nicky Nelson had said more than she intended. She fiddled with the flyer-menu lying on the table. "I believe it was a burglar . . . who got scared off finding her home."

Dakota gave her a skeptical look. "You didn't think that on Friday. Or on Saturday. Is something missing from the apartment?"

"No . . . I'm not sure yet. I haven't been there long enough to look."

Anne shook her head in wry amusement at Dakota and reached for a menu. Without being too obvious, she studied the young woman on the other side of the small table. Nicky's black silk blouse was wrinkled: the gray business suit was missing a button. She sensed Nicky's guard was up . . . way up.

"Thanks for meeting us," Anne said calmly. "I'm sure this isn't easy for you. You knew Caroline better than most. It would help a lot if you would describe her for us."

"Beautiful." A wry expression crossed Nicky's face. "We'll put that on the table first. It colored everything. Caroline McKelvey was the kind of woman men looked at . . . and liked what they saw. People turned to putty in her hands. She got what she wanted just by asking for it."

"Was she vain?"

"No." The girl turned back to Dakota and gave a brief laugh. "That's the irony. She thought of herself as lucky. I told you, she liked people and people liked her. She didn't have any enemies."

"Weren't other women jealous?"

The most jealous one of all was Nicky Nelson herself, thought Anne. It would be hard not to be. The comparison was too great. She watched Nicky struggling with Dakota's question.

"She was the only pretty woman I've ever liked. But I did like her. How could I help it? There was a kind of innocence about Caroline. Call it idealism. She had that in spades. It was why she was in the environmental stuff . . . why she was working for Congressman Woodward. 'To make the world a healthier place'. . . . That was *her* kind of thing."

The words were complimentary, but Anne heard something disparaging in Nicky's tone. It was as if Nicky considered Caroline's idealism admirable . . . but foolish.

"What's *your* kind of thing, Nicky?" asked Anne.

"Realism . . . the truth, no matter how it grates. I call life the way I see it. My greatest ambition is . . . " Her voice trailed off as if again she had said too much and regretted it. She was staring at her hands folded tensely on the table in front of her.

"Your greatest ambition is . . . ?"

"It doesn't matter a damn." The young woman's tone was abrasive. "But if you really want to know—though I doubt if you do—my ambition is to make it big in television. I'm not beautiful like Caroline but I'm tough and very smart. I'd like to produce or direct a first-class investigative reporting show. No holds barred. I'm talking sometime in the future, when a big break for me comes. I'd like to be the brains behind the show, if you know what I mean. Brains I've got."

Anne saw scorn flicker across Dakota's face as the young woman spoke. Nicky Nelson had that effect. It was too bad. She'd probably been that way all her life.

"How about we put those brains of yours to work right now," Anne said. "Let's talk about Caroline and her relationships. Her parents . . . what went on there?"

"You mean, the Carvers?" Nicky shrugged. "Pretty good vibes. She didn't tell them everything in her head but they got along well. They spoiled her with things."

"How about her father . . . Marcus McKelvey?"

"Not close. But that was his choice, not hers."

"How about her brother, Paul?"

"That loser!" Nicky ran her hand through the swirling black curls. "I just met him once. It was a few weeks ago when he was in town and looking for a bed for the night. I saw right through that guy. A loser . . . and a *user*."

Dakota leaned forward. "Of people or drugs?"

"In my opinion, both." Nicky's low regard for her dead roommate's brother was obvious. "Caroline thought he had talent . . . for what I don't know!" She motioned abruptly for the waitress. "Let's order now. I have to be at work at one."

Dakota had taken over the questioning and was carefully going over once again the events of last Thursday, the day of the murder.

Yes, Caroline had most likely taken the bus to work, Nicky related. Though she sometimes took the metro; the Tenleytown station was a two-block walk from The Alhambra. As for herself, she had breakfasted and watched a soap opera and driven into ABC about two in the afternoon. She had a five-year-old Mustang, kept it parked in back of the apartment building, space 16.

"Anyway"—Nicky was diving into her lunch—smoky grilled shiitakes with red onions—"I was at work all afternoon Thursday. We were doing a special on consumer rip-offs and there was a lot of cutting and stuff, so we had pizzas brought in."

"You never left the studio until after the 10 P.M. show?" Dakota was polite but gave her nothing. "You have witnesses who can verify your presence?"

"I do . . . for every damn minute of the afternoon and

evening! What's more, the parking lot attendant will tell you that my car stayed put in the lot till a few minutes before eleven. Then some of us went out for drinks. It was the usual, the crew from the show. I stopped by a friend's house about two, slept an hour or so and drove home about four-thirty in the morning.''

Anne broke in. "Is that your pattern?"

Nicky frowned. "I don't know what you mean by pattern. I mean, yeah . . . I'm a night person. That's when I think best, work best . . . do everything best.'' She gave Anne a sardonic look over the rim of her beer mug.

Anne slipped her notebook from her shoulder bag and laid it on the table beside her plate. "So you came home about 4:30 A.M. Friday morning and . . . then what?''

"I parked behind The Alhambra. I came around the side of the building like always. It's lighted, no sweat. I don't worry. Jack Lee was the doorman on. I said 'Hello, how goes it?' and stepped into the elevator. When I got upstairs to the apartment . . . '' Nicky paused, swallowing. Her voice was suddenly higher in pitch. '' . . . When I came down the hall, I saw our apartment door was open. About four inches open. I mean, for God's sake! That wasn't right. I came in and . . . ''

She clenched her fist and pressed it hard on the table, unable to go on with her story.

Dakota spoke softly as if to calm her. "The living room was dark. The ceiling light in the dining ell was on but you didn't see Caroline at first. You told me that on Friday. You said you noticed the television was on. The one on the bookcase. There was just the white empty square, no programing. So you started over to turn it off and then you saw Caroline lying across the bar.''

Nicky nodded. Her voice was raspy, but her emotions now appeared under control. "I thought at first she was asleep. Oh no, I knew better! I mean, all that blood everywhere! I couldn't believe it. I just stood there staring at her.''

"Then what did you do, Nicky?'' Anne asked quietly.

"I ran downstairs to Simone's apartment. I mean, I took the stairs like I was flying. I pounded on her door. But she wasn't there."

"Who is Simone?"

"Simone Gray. You know, on ABC, the . . . "

"Oh, that Simone. Why did you go to her apartment? What floor?"

"The fourth. I don't know why. I just thought of her first. She's the only person I know in the building. But she wasn't there, you see. So, I came back to the apartment and I called Father Clore."

"Why not the doorman or the police? Why did you call Father Clore?"

"For some reason, I went into Caroline's room. I sat down on her bed. I turned on the light. His number was written on the pad by the telephone. His personal number at his house on Woodley Road. Caroline talked to him sometimes late at night. And I saw the number, and it just came out and hit me. So I called him."

Anne made a note on the blank page of her notebook. It was the first note she'd made on the case. So Caroline McKelvey and Father Clore were in the habit of talking on the phone "late at night." He hadn't implied that kind of closeness. She asked Nicky, "Did your call wake him?"

"I can't say. He answered on the second ring. He sounded alert. I blurted it out. . . . I said, 'Caroline is dead, for God's sake! She's dead! Someone's broken in and killed her.' "

"How did he respond?"

"He said, 'Stay calm, Nicky. I'll be right there.' "

"Is that all? Did he ask you any other questions?"

"No."

"Not even . . . where you lived? What apartment?"

"No. Well, maybe he did ask that. I was thinking about Caroline's body and all that blood . . . that blood dripping down off the bar . . . those two big pools of blood on the floor."

"How long did it take Father Clore to get there?"

"Five . . . eight minutes. Maybe ten."

"What did you do while you waited for him?"

Nicky had picked up a hard roll. Now she put it down beside her plate. "I looked around the apartment to see if anything had been stolen."

Dakota was staring at the young woman. "You see, you did look. Nothing was stolen. That's what you said on Friday."

"I didn't think anything was stolen then. I still don't . . ."

"You were very certain on Friday morning."

"That was a first reaction." Nicky's voice was defensive. "Jesus! I mean, I didn't see anything missing. And there was Caroline's purse lying there. Still . . . "

"Still, what?"

"Well, I still haven't checked everywhere. I mean, maybe it was a burglar and he was in one of the bedrooms when she got home and then he came out and killed her and he heard noises in the hall and got scared and . . . "

Anne pushed a wing of dark hair behind her ear and leaned forward to catch Nicky's gaze. "I'm curious about something. How did Father Clore get into the building? Did your doorman just let him in . . . no questions asked?"

"Jack Lee called up. By this time I was pretty unnerved. I was crying. I was shaking. . . . I could hardly talk. I told him, 'Yes, send him up. For God's sake! Caroline is dead. She's dead!' Before I knew it, Jack was upstairs and the super too in his bathrobe and Father Clore. All three. They were standing in the living room staring at . . . "

"Who called the police?" Anne asked.

"Father Clore took charge. He told the super and Jack Lee to go back downstairs and that he would take care of everything. He was very strong actually. I guess I had gone to pieces again by this time. He put his hands on my shoulders and shook me. Real hard. He said, 'Get yourself together. We have got to do what we can to protect Caroline.' "

"But she was dead." Anne let out her breath. "How could you protect her?"

"I think he meant her . . . reputation. Funny, you know . . .

he hadn't really looked at her. I mean, he saw her lying there when he came in, but he didn't go over and look at her. I don't think he could stand to. He told me to go wash my face and get myself together. When I came out of the bathroom, he said that it was time I should call the police.''

"Why didn't he do it himself?"

"I asked him to but he said no, that wasn't for him to do. That was for me to do. Oh, he asked me one other thing. Father Clore asked me if I had told anyone else.''

Nicky looked from Anne to Dakota. "I told him about going down to Simone's apartment but that she wasn't there. He just stared at me like he couldn't take all this in. He was very white in the face. Then, he said, 'You had better call the police now.' ''

"And you did?"

"I went back to the bedroom and, when I got myself together, I called the police.''

"Whom did you call next?" Anne asked.

Nicky drained her beer mug and set it carefully on the table in front of her. "I'd already called her office,'' she answered flatly. "I mean she worked for a prominent congressman. If there was going to be any publicity, I figured they had better know.''

Anne's and Dakota's eyes met across the table. He raised his eyebrows, but did not look surprised. It isn't really that surprising an answer, his look said. She agreed. There was a certain protocol in official Washington concerning death, sex and scandal. Those in power were vulnerable . . . always. Advance information was protection.

"Congressman Woodward's office wasn't open at that early hour,'' Anne said.

"I called his AA . . . you know, his administrative aide. His name is Alex Shannon. I'd heard Caroline talk about him, so I looked his number up. His home number. He was really appreciative that I'd called. He said he'd tell Woodward right away. He said to let the office know if there was anything at all the staff could do.''

"They were at the funeral.'' Dakota murmured to Anne. "The AA and a few other people from Woodward's office.

Not the congressman himself. He had gone home to New Jersey for the weekend. There was a speech or something. But his wife was there.''

Anne nodded. She remembered Gertrude Woodward from the days when Rob had represented Virginia's Ninth District in Congress. Gertrude Woodward was a vivacious woman, sharp-eyed, always impeccably dressed, a partner in her husband's political life. Gertrude Woodward would do all that was expected of her and more.

Nicky was looking sallow and drained. "Is that all? I hope it is. I have to be at work now.''

"All for now.'' Dakota pushed back his chair.

"Just one more thing.'' Anne held Nicky with her gaze. "Caroline had just changed jobs. Can you remember what she had to say about Congressman Woodward? Did she like working in his office?''

"Of course.'' There was a low, harsh laugh. "Mr. Clean. Of course, Caroline was happy, she was right where she wanted to be. Congressman Jim Woodward was her idol. She had put him on a pedestal.''

"You sound as if you don't agree.''

"I don't believe in the Lone Ranger.'' Nicky gave Anne a bitter smile. "I don't believe in heroes. I left all that malarkey to Caroline . . . and you see where it got her.''

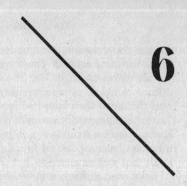

6

"Nicky was contemptuous of Caroline. No, that isn't right. She admired her roommate. She said that and I believe her, but Nicky considered Caroline naive."

"A lightweight," agreed Dakota. "Nicky tries to make out that Caroline McKelvey was just a beautiful piece of fluff. Maybe she was. But . . . "

"That's not the way you see Caroline, is it, Dakota?"

Don Dakota was sitting across the aisle from Anne in the squad room, his chair back, boots up on his desk. He had a picture of Caroline in his hands, a five-by-seven candid photograph, still in its silver frame. He had taken the picture from the apartment on Friday morning to use in the investigation.

"I got the feeling from Father Clore's eulogy that the girl he was burying had been damn bright and . . . complicated. But I already knew that."

He held out the picture to Anne as if to support his viewpoint. It was a color shot, taken in a garden. Late afternoon sun highlighted her hair as Caroline, in a white old-fashioned dress, leaned against the back of a wooden garden bench. She had turned to look at someone out of sight of the camera. Her face was thoughtful.

Anne studied the picture.

No, she was not a piece of fluff, this one.

The eyes were quick and intelligent, the mouth sensitive. Anne studied the picture, aware that the setting was vaguely

54

familiar. The distinctive greenery, the rich brown earth . . . the fine slatted arms of the wooden bench.

"This was taken in the Bishop's Garden at the Cathedral."

She handed the photo back to Dakota.

"Which doesn't mean anything," Anne continued. "We know Caroline went there all the time. Anyone could have taken this picture. Maybe it was Father Clore."

Dakota's chair creaked as he slid his feet to the floor.

He rustled through the day's mail on his desk. "Here's the medical examiner's report." For a moment, he studied the typed page.

"Well?" asked Anne. "Anything we don't know?"

Dakota's expression was bemused. "Yeah, something we didn't know. Caroline McKelvey was pregnant, Fitzhugh. Coroner says the victim was in the early stage of a pregnancy, possibly four to six weeks, sex of fetus undetermined."

He looked hard at her as though to gauge Anne's reaction.

She felt an odd stir of emotions. Surprise, envy, maybe. She said, "Caroline was a vibrant, independent young woman. She was beautiful and she was engaged to be married. Things happen."

"I don't think it's the fiancé Daryl Swan we're talking about here."

"Why not?" asked Anne. Dakota was ahead of her, on to something.

"Just my gut feeling. I met the guy. He is a real straight-arrow. I don't think he's the one responsible."

Anne could see the picture of Caroline McKelvey lying face up on Dakota's desk. "Which would complicate things, wouldn't it?"

Dakota didn't answer. He had the telephone in his hand, dialing the medical examiner's office. In a moment he was asking about the possibilities of paternity identification of a four- to five-week fetus through blood type.

"Right. The McKelvey case," he said shortly. Then, "Why the hell not?"

He looked up at Anne and shook his head.

"No luck." Dakota hung up the telephone. "The pregnancy was too early to make a paternity ID . . . even if we had a suspect."

Anne felt the edges of her notebook in her jacket pocket and pulled out the small battered book. The only note she had made thus far had been jotted at lunch—*Caroline McKelvey and Father Anthony Jesse Clore talk on the phone late at night. Why? And about what?*

"You know what I think, Dakota?" she said suddenly. "I think Jesse Clore isn't leveling with us. Your man of the cloth knows more than he lets on that he knows about the victim's life. He may not accept the fact that what he's holding back is relevant to her death but he's keeping a close hold on Caroline's secrets."

"Why the hell wouldn't Jesse Clore want to help us catch Caroline's murderer?"

"Oh, I think he does want *that.*"

Sensing that Dakota was misinterpreting, Anne spoke more softly. "I don't doubt Clore's sincerity in this. I believe he was devoted to Caroline. Maybe it's *that.* That very aspect. I suspect Father Jess is feeling bound by confidentiality between priest and penitent and doesn't know quite how much to say."

Dakota did not dispute her words. He shrugged and put the picture of Caroline McKelvey in his drawer. It was an abrupt movement that said "enough . . . for today."

"Look," Anne said, caught by Dakota's look of strain and weariness. "I'll pay a call on Congressman Woodward's office. I mean, you've been there. I need catch-up time on the McKelvey case. If anything of interest turns up there, I'll call you."

She slid her notebook into her suede jacket pocket and stood up from her desk.

She reached for her sun glasses, saw that Dakota was staring straight ahead.

"Fitzhugh." He held her with the quietness in his voice. "For what it's worth, do you really believe Jess Clore

knows? Are you thinking Caroline told him she was
knocked-up . . . in trouble, and he's keeping it to himself?''

Anne had an image of Canon Jesse Clore sitting on the
bench in the Bishop's Garden. There had been an intensity
in him that had been almost palpable. She remembered his
face, the dark triangular brows, the depth and rich timbre
of his voice.

She surprised herself with her answer. "You said I was
going to like Jess Clore, Dakota. You were right. I did.
And, without taking anything away from what I said before,
I trust him too.''

It was close to three when Anne left headquarters. The
day had turned out warm as summer and golden with autumn foliage. She put on her glasses as she went down the
steps of the Municipal Building. Her destination was only
a few blocks away. Congressman Woodward's office was
in the Rayburn Building on the south side of the Capitol.
She decided to walk.

Capitol Hill was familiar turf to Anne Fitzhugh. When
her husband had first been elected to represent Virginia's
Ninth District, Washington had seemed a marvelous, magic
place for the two of them to explore together. They'd rented
a town house on the Hill and, although they'd usually spent
weekends down home in the Tidewater or at their new farm
near Leesburg, the Hill was ''stomping ground,'' as Rob
used to say. Anne had practiced law there and Rob had
walked the cobblestone streets to his offices in the Rayburn
Building.

Anne felt the ache of nostalgia as she crossed Pennsylvania Avenue and glimpsed the imposing white marble
building on the far side of the Capitol. To her mind, Rayburn was the most impressive of the three white buildings
that housed congressional offices. She and Rob had argued
the point—a ''just for fun'' debate. The Longworth Building was smallest. ''And the darkest inside,'' Rob pointed
out. Cannon was the most impressive of the three, he'd
speculated. ''But so isolated,'' she'd reminded him, ''emo-

tionally situated, as it is, on the *other* side of New Jersey
Avenue.'' The Rayburn Building was where the action was.
They agreed entirely.

Debating with . . . laughing with Rob. Rob Fitzhugh was
always vital, always there. Loving her.

As a fledgling member of Congress, her husband had
been elated to have an office assignment in the prestigious
Rayburn Building. He'd drawn only a third-floor suite or
the back side of the building, with windows looking down
on the freeway. ''In time we'll win a view of the Capitol.
If I live right, we'll be moving . . . down,'' he'd promised
Anne.

He'd lived right. Only there hadn't been time.

''A TRAGIC LOSS FOR VIRGINIA AND FOR THE NATION,''
lamented *The Washington Post.*

As she entered the marble lobby of the Rayburn Building, she took off her sunglasses and queued to have her
handbag inspected. There were new guards posted here
now. They didn't know her anymore. She didn't bother
showing her badge. She didn't ask where Woodward's office was either. She didn't have to ask.

Congressman James Woodward was a rainmaker, one of
the most powerful members of Congress. He'd represented
his New Jersey district in Washington for over twenty years
and sat on several important committees including the
Armed Services Committee whose committee rooms were
in this building. Anne had never met Woodward, although
Rob had pointed out the senior congressman to her on the
floor of the House and at several large party functions. He
was an imposing man, physically attractive, and a confidant
of the President. He was chairman of the Select Committee
on Narcotics Abuse and Control. He had a corner office on
the first floor of this building, Capitol side.

Naturally, he had a corner office. There was protocol in
this business of politics. Woodward was at the head of the
line. Anne's heels clicked as she walked quickly down the
long white marble hall toward Woodward's office.

The New Jersey congressman's outer suite was staffed
by a fair-haired young woman in a business suit whose

name was Janet Sutton. A plaque half lost in the clutter on her desk said so. She looked up from a pile of papers, a nest of photos. Her smile was professional and welcoming and also slightly harassed.

When Anne identified herself, Janet Sutton pushed a buzzer on the desk. "I'm afraid the congressman isn't here at the moment," she explained quickly. "But Alex said to let him know whenever the police called or came by. I mean, we all care a lot about finding Caroline's killer."

Alex . . . would be Alexander Shannon, Woodward's chief AA.

Anne nodded agreeably. She would have preferred to talk with Woodward, but a top assistant would do in the congressman's absence.

"Alex doesn't seem to be answering his buzzer. Let me get you some tea or something. I'll have to find him for you." Janet Sutton stood up abruptly. A certain awkwardness. She seemed suddenly ill at ease.

"Is everything all right?" asked Anne.

A brief smile, "Well, you see . . . there's just a lot in the wind . . . "

Something indeed was in the wind, Anne agreed.

"I'm in no hurry." She sat down in a leather chair that was offered. "And I don't need any tea, thanks anyway."

Despite thick carpets and the closing of the heavy paneled door to the inner office, Anne could hear the murmur of voices and typewriters clacking away.

Rob had managed with a staff of six. A man in Woodward's position would have a large staff of assistants, secretaries and researchers. What had Dakota said? Twenty-four in this office. And probably a few keeping the home fires burning in New Jersey.

She knew the makeup for a big congressional staff. A half-dozen political pros would make up the first circle, and the rest would be young, bright and ambitious—willing to work long hours in crowded quarters until they burned out or could no longer afford to stay. The reward was the heady excitement of feeling the arteries of government pulse and thread around Washington and around the world . . . being miraculously part of the power package . . . the "in" group in the city that rules the world. "Or, thinks it does," Rob used to say.

"Detective Fitzhugh?"

Anne's reverie was broken by a voice that was calm and assured.

"I'm Alexander Shannon."

As she rose to her feet, Anne's smile hid her chagrin. She'd had an image in her mind of Alex Shannon. She'd been wrong. For a Capitol Hill player—and Congressman Woodward's AA was certainly that—this man was not cut from the usual smooth cloth. He was very casual in appearance, tanned, slightly built, not much taller than herself with sandy brown hair and a soft but engaging smile. Thirty. Maybe a few years older than that, but with a youthful, open smile. An individualist. An outdoorsman. His sandy hair was rumpled. He had on a yellow shirt, the top button undone and the tie loose.

"Sorry for the interruption in a busy day," she began. "I need to talk with you about . . . "

"About Caroline." He finished the sentence for her. "Of course. When Lieutenant Dakota was here on Friday afternoon, he said there'd be more. More questions, that is. I understand perfectly. We are in terrible shock here, you must know that."

He sounded sincere. He sounded as though he personally was emotionally affected. No doubt, he was telling the truth. The office staff would be stunned by the murder.

Janet Sutton was still standing by her desk staring fixedly at Anne.

"Let's step into Jim's private office so we can talk without any interruptions," suggested Alex Shannon. "The congressman's in a meeting over in Annex Two . . . you know, the old FBI Building. Then he's got a dinner at the White House. I'm not sure he is coming back at all this afternoon."

With the assurance of privileged position, Alex Shannon opened the paneled door. The seat of power. Jim Woodward's private office. A handsome effect, thick carpets, the lingering scent of fine cigars, soft lights burning.

All around the room, in fact, were pictures of famous men, all personally autographed. The most prominent, the one blown up and hanging over the green leather sofa, was a black and white shot of a youthful John F. Kennedy. He was laughing, in intimate conversation with an even more youthful James Woodward. Also framed in shadow boxes above the sofa were pens used to sign legislation of note. Much of the legislation had to do with the environment and drug enforcement. Over the years, James Woodward had become known as the stalwart champion of ''a healthy earth . . . the healthy life.''

''Please sit down, Anne Fitzhugh.'' Shannon indicated the sofa for Anne and lowered himself into a matching green leather chair.

''I remember your husband.'' The dark hazel eyes were studying her, gauging her depth. ''Rob Fitzhugh was one of my idols. I couldn't believe it when he was killed. I remember you too. You were visible . . . and beautiful. You still are.''

He was smooth, good at the job of politics. Still, Alex Shannon's words moved her. She took a deep breath.

''Let us go over this quickly if you don't mind. As I understand it, Caroline McKelvey had been working in this office for seven weeks. She was hired as an assistant to the congressman in the environmental field.''

''That's right,'' Alex replied. ''Caroline impressed Jim Woodward when she was lobbying him about nonbiodegradable packaging . . . aluminum, that kind of thing. He thought she was damn smart and attractive.''

Was there something contemptuous in Alex Shannon's eyes when he spoke of Caroline? Anne had the impression that something negative, or at least speculative, had crossed his face. A flicker and it was gone. Had she imagined it?

On the other hand, Jim Woodward was known to appreciate pretty women. Perhaps, Shannon was simply acknowledging the fact.

''Everyone up here liked her. She hadn't really gotten into the swing of things yet, of course. But she was working

on some environmental research for Woodward and I think she was going to prove valuable in this office. Until . . . ''
A hesitancy. Was it calculated? A certain regret in his voice.

"Until she was killed," finished Anne. "Yes, I understand. Let me ask you something, Mr. Shannon . . . ''

"Alex. Please."

"Alex, did Caroline seem perturbed or nervous lately? Did she mention anything or anyone that was causing concern?''

"No, I wouldn't say so."

"Had she made any friends in the office? I'm thinking . . . male friends?''

Alex rubbed his chin, shook his head. "She already had a boyfriend. She was engaged to a Navy lieutenant in Annapolis. I think they were getting married in the spring."

"I am interested in her relationships here on the Hill, particularly anything out of the ordinary you might have noted in this office.''

"No love interest for Caroline in this office, I can assure you of that. She generally ate lunch with the girls in the back and sometimes with me. We went to the House cafeteria, the dining room. A few times to restaurants. I don't think she singled out anybody. She was very involved in her work. Sometimes, she ate at her desk. We all do that. These are really busy times, you know."

"What about Congressman Woodward? Did she spend much time with him?''

"No, she was never alone with Jim Woodward." Shannon shook his head adamantly. "No, I am certain of that. I was always present."

He does his job, thought Anne, amused at Alex Shannon's quick response. Protecting Woodward is his first priority. It didn't mean Shannon was lying, just being careful. Despite his charm and rumpled appearance, Alex Shannon was a very cool and "in control" personality.

"Can you tell me," Anne continued, "in some detail about last Thursday? Can you tell me about Caroline McKelvey's last day in this office?''

"Detective Dakota asked about that on Friday. I was sort of vague in my answer. We've talked in the office since, of course. We've tried to reconstruct it, I mean, just where Caroline was every hour that day. There wasn't anything out of the ordinary that any of us can come up with. Except . . . ''

"Except that . . . ?'' Anne leaned forward intently.

"Well, she left early. She left about a quarter to two that afternoon. She didn't say where she was going. She told Janet that she had an appointment.'' Shannon leaned forward in his chair also. His knees and Anne's were almost touching. "The truth is, we all left early that day. It was an exceptionally beautiful afternoon and Woodward was taking the day off to play golf. That's something he rarely does. So, I guess, we all felt . . . since we work so damn hard . . . ''

His grin was easy, contagious. Anne smiled back.

"What did you do with your free afternoon?''

"I left about one. Before Caroline did. That's why I was so vague with your partner, Dakota. I really didn't know what she had done on Thursday afternoon. Anyway, I personally did what I usually do with a few hours off. I went for a jog on the C and O Canal.''

"Yes, I thought you might be a runner. You're very fit. And you have a tan.''

"I'm in training for the Marine marathon. An uncertain and not very systematic training. But I do what I can when I can. That day . . . last Thursday, I took my dog with me. Lyndon is his name. A hound, naturally.'' He smiled, his teeth very white in his tan face. "I give out before Lyndon does. Anyway, we ran about twenty miles that afternoon. I stopped for a cold drink at Glen Echo Station about four. That's a little pub on McArthur Boulevard. Do you know it?''

She nodded.

He added, "A buddy of mine works there. We shot the breeze for a while and then I ran back. My car was parked near the Great Falls.''

"What about the evening?''

"You mean, where did I spend the evening?" He frowned as if slightly affronted. "About six, I went out to Chevy Chase and had a drink with Gertrude Woodward. Jim Woodward took me out of a bad scene in a foster home when I was in my teens. He and Gertrude are the only real family I've ever known. Anyway, I left their house about ten. The rest of the evening I spent in my apartment with a pile of paperwork. You are not suggesting . . . ''

"No, I am not suggesting anything. We have to know everyone's whereabouts."

Shannon rubbed the back of his neck. "This is very uncomfortable. I mean, we're so used to being in a fishbowl. I guess I am talking about Jim and Gertrude more than myself. You understand my concern. Any hint . . . even the mildest suggestions that anyone in this office would . . . ''

"I am not making the mildest of suggestions about anything," Anne surprised herself by smiling candidly at him. "I'm just doing my job . . . as you are doing yours."

He leaned toward her. He said, "Touché, Detective Fitzhugh. I am just being super sensitive. It comes with living in a fishbowl."

Anne was looking past him at a framed photograph which stood on the end table between the sofa and chair. It was a candid shot of Gertrude and Jim Woodward taken several years back. They appeared to be mountain climbing, perhaps somewhere in the Rockies. Sunlight glittered on jagged ridges, snow-crested. They were both wearing shorts and climbing boots, and their backpacks. They were smiling up at the camera. It was a good shot of the couple, although the sunlight was directly in Gertrude's eyes. Her smile was forced, and she was squinting slightly.

"No, it isn't easy . . . living in a fishbowl," agreed Anne.

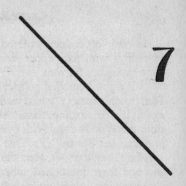

7

"How can you say you didn't like living in a fishbowl? You relished it," Congressman Alan Foley protested over dinner on Tuesday evening.

"I relished being Rob's wife," Anne said.

Alan agreed. He knew her very well, almost as well as he had known Robert Fitzhugh, his law school roommate at the University of Virginia. He had been the best man at Rob and Anne's wedding.

"You enjoyed the political life. I'd swear it, my girl."

She had enjoyed it. Not the fishbowl bit, having her picture taken all the time and the press always at their heels whenever they were in public. And having to say inane things to the media so she would appear intelligent but edgeless. An independent lady, but . . . entirely wifely. An asset to Rob and not a liability.

The challenge and excitement of political life had been marvelous, Anne conceded. Ideas under discussion. Energy flowing. Collusions and connections. Personalities to be delved into, coalitions built. That was the side of politics she'd enjoyed. Even . . . relished. Yes, that was entirely true.

She gave Alan an amused smile. Their discussions rarely had sharp edges.

The fact that Alan Foley had taken Rob's place in Congress and was her best friend in the world, and had been for years, and had stood by her through thick and thin, did not mean that he knew everything about her. Still . . .

He had, of course, ordered just right for them both. Swordfish with red pepper sauce for her, duck with mandarin pancakes for him.

"All right, I enjoyed political life. Or parts of it anyway. That doesn't mean I would want to be a congressional wife again. It's demanding, thankless and nerve-wracking. Consider the Woodwards. With every eye on Jim, Gertrude has to watch her P's and Q's. One loses one's freedom."

Alan thought about what she had just said for a moment and and then questioned soberly, "Freedom to do what? Go careening around town, poking your nose . . . your very pretty nose . . . into dirty situations, walking into crack houses where . . . "

Anne was aware that her mind was wandering. "It's not all dirty places," she pointed out now to Alan. "Murders take place in all walks of life, high and low. And for very complicated reasons."

"Caroline McKelvey was murdered for a complicated reason?" Alan looked at her soberly. "How do you know it wasn't some shabby character who came in off the street and killed the girl for money. Drug money?"

Anne shook her head. "Dakota has convinced me she knew her killer. We agree on something about the case anyway. The question is who . . . is her murderer?"

"And why? Why would someone want to kill a beautiful young woman?" asked Alan, conscious of the animation that had come over Anne's face. "It's the 'want to' question that fascinates you, Anne. That's what captures your interest. Motive."

"I did discover one odd thing." She looked up at Alan. "Odd . . . in what way?"

"Last night I went by The Alhambra to talk with the doorman who was on duty on the evening Caroline was killed. His name is Harold Perry."

She was seeing the doorman in her mind's eye as she spoke. The heavy-set young man had moved with an easy grace. He was eating chocolate Kisses from a bag behind the counter and he'd offered her some and made her laugh.

He had ready for her the names and telephone numbers

of all the tenants living in the building. He had prepared, at the super's request, a handwritten list of everyone he had personally seen entering or leaving the building during his shift at the lobby door on Thursday evening.

"Was the list of any help to you?" asked Alan.

"Yes and no. One delivery of flowers, handed in. Two deliveries of pizza but Harold himself took them up. No repairmen or salespeople or . . ."

"Or strangers with knives in their hands bent on murder," Alan quipped quietly.

"According to Harold," said Anne, "most all those who came into the building that evening were tenants or owners, people who live in The Alhambra . . . folks coming home from work, that kind of thing. He let in a few guests. About twelve if you can trust Harold's memory. At least he had their names."

"Well, that narrows it some, I should think."

She shook her head. "All the residents, and there are eighty-six living in the building, have keys to the front door. The list is only of the ones Harold remembered entering and leaving between 5 and 8 P.M. He took some people up in the elevator. He could well have missed several others who entered. And he may have forgotten some. I mean, for that matter, the killer could have been anyone who lives in the building."

"That still narrows it, doesn't it? People with keys to the building and twelve guests."

"Consider this, Alan." She pulled the handwritten list from her beaded purse and handed it over to him. "Do you notice something odd . . . surprising?"

Quickly, he scanned the list of names. "Yes. I see that Canon Anthony Jesse Clore was in the building that evening . . . and you told me he didn't tell you that."

Anne's expression was troubled. "I would have thought he'd mention it."

"How did the doorman recognize him?"

"Harold says Clore has a habit of dropping by now and then to visit parishioners. This time Father Clore had come to see a woman in her late seventies who has just lately been confined to a wheelchair—Sarah Wallace—she lives on the second floor. According to our doorman, Jesse Clore appeared about five-thirty last Thursday afternoon. He had a paper bag in his hand that looked as though it might have a bottle in it. He left again about seven-fifteen that evening, without the paper bag.''

''Well, I'm not a detective but it sounds like a man paying a call at cocktail hour and arriving properly armed with liquid refreshments of his own. And he wasn't secretive about it.''

''Not a bit. Harold called up on the house phone and Mrs. Wallace said, yes, she was expecting him. Later, when he was leaving, Jesse Clore talked with Harold for a few minutes in the lobby. He said something about the evenings getting colder, the streets darker.''

''I think you should have another talk with Father Clore.''

''I shall. First thing tomorrow. And I intend to pay a visit on Sarah Wallace as well.''

Alan was looking over the list that Anne had handed him. ''Have you checked out the rest of these names?''

''There isn't anyone there who . . . ''

''Simone Gray, the ABC Capitol Hill correspondent. Her name is on here.''

Anne nodded. ''Yes. She lives there. Harold says she came in about six, arrived in a taxi. She had someone with her. Harold had seen the same man with her several times before but doesn't know who he is. The two of them went up to her apartment and left together about 9 P.M. Again in a taxi.''

''Simone Gray.'' Alan repeated the name as he handed Anne back the list.

''Do you know her?''

''Who on the Hill doesn't know Simone Gray and tremble when she approaches with mike and cameraman in tow?''

''She's marvelous,'' said Anne with a laugh.

''She's sharp''—he grimaced—''and beautiful, but she does go for the jugular.''

Again, Anne laughed. "That's why she is marvelous."

The waiter was approaching with one lone dessert on a silver tray. The young man put it down with a flourish in front of her. A cream-filled chocolate éclair.

Anne wrinkled her nose with pleasure. "Did you order this for me?"

"I did, knowing your secret vices. You shall do it complete justice, I haven't a doubt." Alan was himself eyeing the ornate ironwork liquor shelves on the other side of the room. "Shall we have an Armagnac to finish or . . . some champagne?"

"Maybe an espresso."

"Two then," he said to the waiter.

Anne sighed, and looked around with pleasure. Mrs. Simpson's was indeed one of her favorite restaurants in northwest Washington. Suave young waiters, mirrored walls reflecting the golden light, portraits of English royalty. Glass cases held memorabilia from the late Duke and Duchess of Windsor's time in the spotlight. The setting reminded her of Wallis Simpson's fabled romance. And the young king who adored her and gave up his throne for her.

"It really was a terribly gallant gesture on his part," Anne murmured quite out of context. She was looking toward a portrait of Edward VIII when he was the Prince of Wales.

"A king giving up his throne for the woman he loved?"

Alan was reading her mind. It was one of the nice things about being with him. She never had to explain.

He continued, amused. "It was nothing, really. Any red-blooded, or should I say, blue-blooded . . . fellow would do the same."

"Would you, darling?"

"Make a sacrifice for you? Of course. Any sacrifice, no matter how kingly. Name it."

She laughed, knowing it was true. "Well, there's one small thing you could do. I'm having a hard time getting hold of the esteemed congressman Jim Woodward. Gertrude takes his calls at home and says he will call me back. He doesn't. Alex Shannon puts me off as well. It seems odd. I don't know whether Woodward is really so busy, or it's just their way of protecting him. What do you think . . . ? You and Jim are good friends.''

"You want to talk with Jim Woodward about Caroline?"

"I do, and I'm trying to keep things relatively informal. I know he probably hasn't a thing to offer. Alex assures me that is the case. Still, I want to talk with the man personally. I want to look at his face when he talks about her. I want to know what he thought of her.''

"He's not on that list that Harold gave you."

"Heavens, no!" Anne laughed.

Alan's face was dead serious. "Where was Woodward on the evening that Caroline was killed? It probably isn't necessary to ask, but has he an alibi?"

"According to his AA, Woodward took a rare afternoon off last Thursday. He played a round of golf out at the Chevy Chase Club, and then stayed at the club and dined in the Grill Room with friends. I am sure that won't be hard to check.''

"And where was darling Gertrude?"

"At home in Chevy Chase. Alex Shannon was with her at cocktail hour. He left about ten and, I gather, she spent the rest of the evening alone.''

"Naturally."

Anne laughed. "There, you see what I mean, darling! A congressional wife's lot is not an easy one. Many lonely nights.''

"Yes, poor Gertrude. I would agree in this particular case. Woodward is not an intimate man. He is not known to waste time on anything frivolous.''

"I don't call *your* interests—collecting contemporary art and fishing—frivolous," said Anne staunchly. "As for Congressman Jim Woodward, I just told you, Shannon said he was playing golf on Thursday afternoon.''

"With the right people, no doubt," Alan commented dryly. "Woodward wasn't playing for the exercise. You can trust me on that. He's an ambitious fellow, The Honorable James Mason Woodward of New Jersey.''

Anne was bemused. "I thought Woodward was the epitome of the high-minded congressman. So very, very straight.''

''He is . . . all that. He's got the cool and clever Alexander Shannon to take care of all the practical matters. Alex came to work for Woodward right out of law school. Shannon takes care of all things unpleasant for Jim and . . . does it efficiently. 'He takes no prisoners,' as the saying goes. And then, there's Gertrude. She's been her husband's office manager for years. That leaves Woodward free to move, to negotiate . . . to be *the* ecology man . . . the environmental man in Congress.''

''Where is the ambitious part?''

Alan looked rueful. ''I shouldn't have said it.''

''But you did say it.'' She pursued the point. ''What did you mean?''

''Just a gut feeling that Woodward wants to be president more than a drowning man wants air. And he has a passable shot at it. After all, he's only sixty-five and he is storing up points. There is time.''

''Any skeletons in his closet?''

''If you mean other women, I'd say no. In fact, I'd say definitely not. He admires a pretty face. Have you noticed, all the women on his staff are good-looking? But nothing more serious than that. No dalliances. He's too damn busy and too righteous. Notice I didn't say 'self-righteous.' All his environmental issues put him on the road a lot. He's hit thousands of podiums, and he honestly believes in what he preaches. I guess.''

''You are a cynic, Alan. Jim Woodward wouldn't make a bad president. Particularly with the ever-loyal, ever-sparkling Gertrude at his side.''

Alan grinned. ''Now, that's the good side of being a congressman's wife! One can never tell where it might lead. As for the ever-loyal and ever-sparkling Gertrude Woodward, I doubt if she'd mind being First Lady one little bit. She's the total political wife.''

''A provocative description, Alan. I wouldn't touch that for anything.''

As they left the restaurant, he linked her arm through his

own. "I've just thought of something. It's probably not important at all. Just an interesting coincidence."

Alan was looking up at the dark sky. "The Woodwards have been big donors to the Washington Cathedral. They are very active there. Especially Gertrude. I mean, they live close by in Chevy Chase. They probably know Father Anthony Jesse Clore well."

Anne followed Alan's gaze to the west.

The Woodwards and Father Clore. It was a connection she had not expected. Still, it wasn't that strange. Washington was a small town really, on certain levels. There were always coincidences.

Against the starlit night, the dark spires and bell tower of the Washington Cathedral rose majestically above the buildings and treetops. On the tops of the spires, small red lights flashed their warnings.

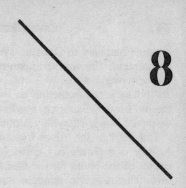

8

"We are talking about an Episcopal priest, damn it all, Fitzhugh!"

"Don't be so touchy, Dakota. I know who and what we're talking about."

They were speeding up Massachusetts Avenue on Wednesday morning in the white Crown Victoria. Dakota was behind the wheel.

Damnably handsome this morning, but still irritable, noted Anne. He had on his brown tweed jacket with the leather elbow patches. It was his favorite jacket, worn a bit and frayed on one cuff. If he were in a better mood, she would tease him about it. She decided against it.

"I think," he said testily, "you are making too much noise about this visit of Jesse Clore's to The Alhambra. He visits parishioners all the time. He probably didn't think it was worth mentioning."

"You are probably right." Still, Anthony Jesse Clore was in the building at the time of murder. That couldn't be discounted. It was important information. Anne didn't have to say it. Dakota knew that.

They found a spot by the small park across the street from The Alhambra. A call to the Cathedral offices earlier that morning had revealed that Canon Clore was out in the suburbs at a breakfast meeting for local area clergy. His secretary informed Anne that Clore would be stopping by late in the morning to see Nicky and pick up some books he'd loaned to Caroline.

Anne had said to Dakota, "We'll intercept him there."

Intercept. The word had annoyed her partner. Walk easy today, thought Anne.

"Nicky's not expecting us, you realize," Anne said as the old brass elevator chugged upward. "She's going to be surprised at our showing up this morning."

Dakota had the silver-framed picture of Caroline Mc-Kelvey in a plastic bag under his arm. The lab had made copies of the photo for the files. "We're returning this picture. That's reason enough. Anyway, she asked for this visit."

Nicky Nelson had called headquarters on Tuesday afternoon looking for either Detective Dakota or Fitzhugh. She'd told Cathy, the department secretary, that she was "nervous" about returning to the apartment.

"An ambiguous message," Anne said now.

"It sounds like she wants to go on playing out the story that a burglar broke in and was robbing the place when Caroline came in and surprised him."

"Who could she be protecting?" Anne asked.

"Well it's not herself," Dakota said. "Nelson's alibi stands up. Regrettably."

Anne grinned. The Cowboy didn't like Nicky Nelson. That was obvious. But he was right. Her alibi held. She had been with one or another of her ABC colleagues all Thursday afternoon and evening.

A knock on apartment 612's door brought no response.

Dakota knocked a second time.

The door was opened by Paul McKelvey.

"Oh, it's you, is it?" Reluctantly, Caroline's brother stepped aside and motioned the two detectives inside.

The living room was cluttered. Caroline McKelvey's clothes were spread on the sofa and chairs, shoe boxes were piled, several cardboard boxes stood open in the middle of the pale carpet. "We're packing up." Paul explained the obvious.

To Anne's eye, the young man looked better than he had on Monday but his skin was still yellow as if he were jaundiced.

"My mother doesn't ever want to see this place again. I said I'd help with the clearing out." Paul sighed slightly as if with a certain resignation.

"I thought you two had given up the case." Nicky Nelson was framed in the doorway of Caroline's bedroom. She looked harsh in a bright green cotton sweater and frayed jeans. "Oh"—she noted the package in Dakota's hand— "so you finally brought back Caroline's picture. Daryl was asking about it."

Daryl . . . Caroline's fiancé.

Anne turned and saw a young man, tall and reed slim, on the balcony. He was leaning on the railing, looking out into the treetops. She had glimpsed him when they came into the apartment but it had taken a moment to register. Now he turned and came into the living room through the sliding doors. Quick smooth movements. He also was in jeans. A dark blue crew sweater. He had dark hair cut very short, a grave sad face.

"Lieutenant," he held out his hand to Dakota. "I met you at the funeral. Is there any word? Anything at all?"

Dakota shook his head, introduced Anne. "Believe me. We're doing all we can. A murder investigation takes . . . time. Effort and time."

Swan's face was slightly swollen, the pupils of his eyes enlarged and almost black with pain. He spoke with what seemed an effort at emotional control. "I still can't believe she's dead. I can't believe that anyone would kill someone as lovely . . . as wonderful as Caroline."

He really loved her, thought Anne. His pain shows like an illness.

Daryl Swan accepted the package from Dakota and unwrapped it. For a long moment, he stared at the picture and then he said, "This was taken in the Bishop's Garden at the Cathedral. We were going to be married there next spring. Did you know that? We were planning a big wedding . . . the works."

It didn't sound as if Daryl Swan knew Caroline was pregnant.

Anne glanced toward Nicky, still standing in the doorway. It had been Nicky who claimed Caroline was going to break off her engagement to Swan. But the dark-haired girl's face revealed nothing. She stood legs apart, sullen, arms akimbo.

Swan drew a ragged breath. "We had all these plans. I can't tell you how knocked out I was when Nicky called on Friday morning and told me what happened. It's been like a bad dream these past few days. I haven't waked up from it yet. I still can't believe she's dead."

"When did you last see Caroline?" Anne asked.

The young naval lieutenant turned toward her. "I talked with Caroline on Thursday before she went to work. I talked with her that very morning. She sounded fine."

"Did she tell you anything out of the ordinary?" Anne began the litany of familiar, necessary questions.

He swallowed, cleared his throat hard. Remembering the conversation seemed to bring new pain. "We talked about the approaching weekend. She was coming over to Annapolis and we were going to take a sail out in the bay on Saturday afternoon, have dinner somewhere that night."

"Did she say anything about her week, her life in Washington . . . how she was feeling? Anything at all out of the ordinary."

Daryl Swan still had the picture of Caroline in his hands. It was as if he did not want to put it down. "She didn't say anything special. She said she had some things on her mind . . . but they would all be settled this week."

"Do you know what she meant by that? Did you pursue the subject in any way?"

"No. I rather thought she meant problems at work. It wasn't anything to do with us," Swan answered.

"Are you certain of that?"

"Of course. I've known Caroline since prep school days. We've been engaged for over a year. Lately I have been working hard and we haven't had much time together. That caused strain. But, I mean, if there was anything . . . " His voice broke.

Daryl Swan was honorable, self-contained, thought

Anne. He wouldn't be the kind who'd ask too many questions, who'd pry. He probably didn't know Caroline as well as he thought.

Anne glanced at Dakota. Their eyes caught. He was right. Daryl Swan was most likely not the father of Caroline's baby.

"I wasn't implying trouble between you," Anne said gently. "I just want to be certain there wasn't someone new in her life, someone who was coming on to Caroline. You know, giving her a hard time. Or . . . "

"Or threatening her," Dakota finished.

"No one was threatening Caroline!" put in Nicky hotly.

"Yes, I think . . . there *was* someone threatening her." It was Paul McKelvey who spoke. "I've been thinking about it. I believe Caroline knew . . . suspected she was in some kind of danger."

His words were a jolt in the room's chemistry.

Paul McKelvey continued in an exhausted rough tone. "This morning, Nicky and I've been sorting out Caroline's belongings. I found this in the drawer of her bedside table. It surprised the hell out of me." He pulled a small shiny object from his pocket and held it up. It was a mace canister.

Nicky gave a snort of exasperation. "What is it . . . a can of mace? That doesn't mean a thing. Caroline's had that thing around for ages."

"She didn't have it three weeks ago when I spent the night in this apartment. I know, Nicky. I went through Caroline's room looking for cash." Paul McKelvey rubbed the light beard on his chin with his hand, and spoke ironically. "Believe me, I'm one who knows how to go through a room carefully. There was no canister of mace in her drawer then."

Nicky moved quickly into the room, pushed aside a pile of the shoe boxes and sat down in the chair. Her tone was angry, dismissive. "I imagine she had it in her purse."

"I went through her purse. Three weeks ago when I was here, Caroline had no mace. I'd swear to it."

Dakota looked down at Nicky. "Are you really so positive that Caroline kept mace in the apartment? Are you certain this isn't a new purchase?"

Anne Fitzhugh observed Nicky fiddling with nervous fingers at the edging of her sweater. The young woman hesitated as if seeking an answer that was to her own best advantage. But why stumble with this? What was Nicky Nelson's problem?

"Caroline said that having something like that around made her feel safer," Nicky finally responded. Her tone was equivocating. She finished with, "Not that it did her any good! You see what happens! A burglar breaks in and . . ."

"You said she had the mace around 'for ages.' " Dakota took the cylinder from Paul and held it out toward Nicky. . . . "Have you ever seen this canister before?"

"Yes!" The dark-haired young woman's eyes were like black stones. "Of course I have. I think she got it last summer at some hiker-biker outfitting store near Tyson's Corner. I tell you Caroline wasn't the brave type."

There was something defiant in Nicky's face. Also, something close to controlled hysteria in the tension of her body. For the first time, Anne saw what Dakota had been talking about when he described Nicky's behavior on Friday morning.

Daryl Swan offered his thoughts softly. "It's true. Caroline was a gentle soul, not particularly brave. She didn't like being alone. That's why she wanted a roommate. I think it stands to reason she might have had a can of mace in her bedroom drawer. I don't know that it means anything in particular."

"I think it sure as hell does!"

Again it was Paul McKelvey who spoke out in his exhausted, compelling way, "Nobody knew Caroline like I did. Yeah, sure . . . she was gentle. Also trusting. But she knew this building was safe. The sixth floor, for God's sake! A safety lock on the apartment door. I don't think she was afraid of a burglar. Not one damn bit."

"What are you implying?" asked Anne.

"Something happened since I saw Caroline last. A bad situation got worse. Yes, I know"—he held up his hand—"you asked me on Monday if Caroline had said anything to me about being in danger. I said that when I was here three weeks ago, she was quieter than usual, that's all. Well, I have thought about it."

Was he grandstanding for his own private ends? Anne waited, her gray eyes calm and questioning.

"What she said to me that night three weeks ago was only a brief thing. She asked me if I knew what it was like . . . to wrestle with my soul."

Paul grimaced and then continued, "I am not so philosophical. I am a pragmatist at best. I parried the question. Caroline went on . . . she said something about the devil wearing the face of a saint."

For a moment, the compelling face of Father Anthony Jesse Clore floated before Anne's eyes. "What do you think she meant, Paul?"

Surprising color stained Paul McKelvey's high cheekbones. "I believe she'd been let down . . . by someone she admired. She was an idealist, I tell you. It would take a lot for my sister to see the evil in a person. But I think she would confront that evil. I know Caroline. I think she was pushing someone."

"Do you have any idea who that someone might be?"

"I haven't a clue. I just know Caroline." Paul turned to Nicky. "You're right, Caroline wasn't the brave type. She'd have trusted her charms, her persuasive power. If they failed her, she'd have been in trouble. I don't know what she'd have done then . . . except buy a can of mace to protect herself."

Daryl Swan gasped. "She didn't tell me anything. Wouldn't she have told me if she thought she was in danger?"

Not necessarily, thought Anne. Her thoughts were racing. She looked at Dakota, saw that he was studying Paul McKelvey. Her partner's face was unreadable.

Paul believed it was someone Caroline admired.

Or, maybe someone his sister misjudged, had been taken in by . . . maybe fallen in love with.

"This is the biggest bunch of garbage I've ever heard." Nicky Nelson had indignation written all over her face. "If Caroline was in some kind of trouble she'd have talked about it with me. I live here. I'm her roommate, for God's sake."

Anne felt an odd wave of exhilaration. She was beginning to get a grip on the personality of Caroline McKelvey. No piece of fluff. Fair-haired, complex Caroline.

Nicky Nelson was probably the last person Caroline McKelvey would have talked to about her fears. And it wasn't Daryl Swan. Regrettably. And it hadn't been her brother, Paul. The most likely person Caroline would have talked with was her spiritual adviser, Canon Jesse Clore.

And had he betrayed her?

There was a knock . . . speak of the devil!

Anne flushed at her own thoughts as Paul opened the door.

Jesse Clore wore a light gray sport jacket above his clerical black. He filled the door frame, taking in the scene. He gave the appearance of both strength and of lightness, of vigor. . . . yes, sexual vigor, and intelligence. If Caroline had fallen in love with him, and that had to be seen as a distinct possibility, it was understandable.

"Why do I feel like I am walking in on something?" Jesse Clore offered his engaging, if slightly apologetic, grin as he entered the living room.

"It's all right," said Dakota. "We were discussing some issues about the victim . . . about Caroline."

Daryl Swan turned his head away. It seemed an effort to gain control of himself.

Paul went into the kitchen to get himself a glass of water.

"I think," responded Jesse Clore after a long moment's pause, "this is a very hard time for all of us. I can't get Caroline out of my mind either. And it's O.K. It's just the way things have to be."

His eyes met Anne's.

It was as though he could see into her very soul.

Jesse Clore moved across the room and put his hand on Daryl's shoulder. "It is O.K. to grieve. Grieve like hell, old man. We don't want to forget her. We won't forget her."

Anne could feel Clore's presence. He had changed the tension of the room. He had taken command. He was enveloping them . . . and comforting them all.

"Actually we've been talking about this." Dakota held up the canister of mace. He was looking directly at Jesse Clore. "There is a difference of opinion about when Caroline acquired it."

Clore stared at the cylinder in Dakota's hand. "Mace, is it? Does it really matter when she acquired it?"

"It might. What we are trying to ascertain is whether or not Caroline knew her life was in danger. Was she frightened of someone?"

Dakota did not take his eyes from Jesse Clore's face.

It seemed to Anne that there was a slight involuntary tightening of the skin around Clore's eyes. "Frightened? Oh, I don't think so. Caroline was a damn sight more intrepid than you might imagine."

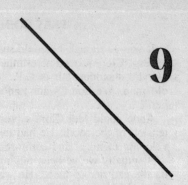

9

"I believe you knew Caroline McKelvey very well. Far better than you let on," Anne said to Jesse Clore. It sounded like a challenge.

They were on their way down to the second floor of The Alhambra to see Sarah Wallace. The priest had readily agreed to visiting his parishioner. He expressed surprise that there was any question about his own activities on the evening of the murder. But when Anne raised the issue and suggested verifying his alibi with Sarah Wallace, he did not seem in the least annoyed.

"I understand. It's wise to check everyone out . . . even someone as wonderful and holy as me." He broke into his ironic grin and made the moment all right. "As for the question of Caroline . . . "

They were using the interior stairs of The Alhambra. Jesse Clore reached the turn ahead of Anne and stood, hands in his pockets, waiting for her. "As for the question of Caroline . . . I don't think I've been misleading you and Dakota. I knew her well, I admit to that. I was her friend, her pastoral counselor."

Anne was thinking of Caroline's pregnancy. A bombshell . . . a vital complication. The young woman must have known or suspected her condition. She must have revealed this to her spiritual adviser. Certainly he knew about this complication in Caroline's life.

"I think there's something of importance that you know,

82

Jesse, a personal problem that Caroline perhaps shared with you and that you're not letting on to . . . something that would help us with this case.''

''There might be. Only I can't . . . won't risk betraying her confidences. I'll have to think about the question ethically. Of course, I'd tell you in a minute, if I thought I had any clues as to who killed Caroline. It is just a matter of . . . subtleties.''

''One of those subtleties may hold the answer.''

He pursed his lips and turned down the steps.

Sarah Wallace was delighted with their visit. A visiting nurse was fixing her an early lunch. The smell of tomato soup and cheese toast filled the second-floor apartment.

The old woman was handsome, white-haired, with intelligent blue eyes. A paisley shawl was thrown about her shoulders. It brought out the color in her eyes.

''Oh, if I could only help you!'' Sarah Wallace responded to Jesse Clore's introduction of Detective Anne Fitzhugh with a quick clasp of hands. ''That lovely girl! You know, I used to see her sometimes in the elevator when I was still on my feet. I used to think she was a vision. Not just beautiful in her features, but a beautiful spirit as well. The kind of beauty that shows in the face.''

Jesse sat down on the sofa across from Sarah Wallace's wheelchair and took the veined hands in his own large muscular hands. ''Caroline was that,'' he said soberly, ''a truly fine spirit. One of the rare ones.''

''And to think that she was . . . murdered.'' The old woman's voice faltered. She stared into his eyes as if for reassurance.

''Do you realize that Caroline was murdered while I was here having cocktails with you on Thursday night, Sarah? How painfully ironic . . . that we two should be chatting away while that atrocity was taking place upstairs.''

Sarah Wallace's eyes filled with distress. ''And we had no idea, did we? Here we sat in this living room with our bourbons and soda talking about Cathedral life.'' She turned apologetically to Anne. ''You see, I was president of the Altar Guild of the Cathedral for years and active in the diocese for many more. I am still interested in what goes on across the street.''

She arched her eyebrow in the direction of Jesse Clore. ''Of course, I keep my eye on this one!''

Anne laughed. ''He needs watching, does he?''

''I should say! He is a terrible rascal.''

Sarah Wallace had spots of bright color in her cheeks. Her affection for the Episcopalian canon so much younger than herself was apparent.

The blue eyes cleared, began to twinkle. ''I've known Jess since he was a boy. You see, my late husband was for years the dean of a boys' prep in Connecticut. When we were first married, we lived for a while on the campus and Jess was a 'new boy,' and then an 'old boy' while we were there.''

''I might have been the reason they left!'' Jesse grinned at Anne. ''I was rather incorrigible then. No one would ever have picked the Church as my future calling.''

''Oh, I don't know.'' Sarah's voice grew softer. ''There was something very . . . feeling about you. A rare sensitivity. It showed beneath the pranks and foolishness.''

''Is that what you were talking about on Thursday evening,'' asked Anne, ''old times? School days in Connecticut?''

''Yes. Old times . . . and present times. I always enjoy it so when Jesse visits. It makes a lonely woman's evening most delightful. He is going to be the Cathedral's dean one of these days . . . and I'm going to be here cheering for him.''

''How long did you stay on Thursday, Jess?''

His dark eyes met Anne's and held them in a steady gaze. ''An hour or two. Yes, almost two hours. I came at five-thirty and left at something after seven.''

''Two hours. Was it that long?'' asked Sarah Wallace. ''It seemed like minutes to me, not hours.''

''We finished half a bottle of bourbon between us,'' Jesse said. He reached out and patted the paisley-covered shoulder. His gesture was affectionate, comforting.

Five-thirty until seven-fifteen. It was exactly the time frame that Harold Perry had given Anne for Jesse Clore's presence in The Alhambra.

When they left Sarah Wallace's apartment, Jesse Clore shook his head nostalgically. "She is a marvelous old gal. She was always interested in the boys at school. I'd had a difficult home life, you see, and I needed some attention . . . little brat that I was."

He might have been. But he had grown into a smooth and attractive man. She decided to be candid with him. "I find it surprising, even disturbing, that you didn't tell Dakota or me that you were in this building at the time Caroline was killed."

"No one asked me for my whereabouts on Thursday evening." He was not defensive, just matter-of-fact. "You didn't think . . . you certainly didn't suspect . . . ?"

"No, I don't. I haven't any thoughts on the subject yet. But I need to have all the relevant facts."

"Yes," he agreed, chastened.

"Did you speak with anyone else here that evening?"

Was there a pause before he answered the question? Anne watched his face. It was so readable, that face. It seemed to her that he was struggling with something.

"I talked with the young man at the front door as I was leaving. Harold is his name. Just something about the weather."

Harold Perry. That was true, of course.

"Actually," Jesse offered suddenly, his voice grown husky, "I think it's unforgivable that I would be here when Caroline was killed. It has shaken me. I am a man who prides himself on offering comfort . . . protection against evil. A champion for good. What mockery! There I was, glass in hand, feeling self-satisfied and full of myself . . ."

Again it struck Anne that Anthony Jesse Clore hesitated, drew in his breath. It was as if he wanted to say something more. But he did not and the moment passed.

* * *

Dakota was having an argument with Nicky Nelson.

Anne could hear their voices as she and Jesse Clore approached apartment 612.

Nicky's tone was strident. "I know what I'm saying, damn it all! Someone went rifling through my things and Caroline's too."

"That's just fine. *Now* tell me this . . . what the hell is missing? What got taken?" Dakota was cool, sarcastic in return.

"I don't know. Nothing of mine. I can't speak for Caroline. Maybe something of hers is missing. I just don't know!"

They were in the middle of the living room facing each other. There was no one else in the room.

"Where are Paul and Daryl?" Anne asked.

"Gone to Spring Valley with a carload of Caroline's belongings." Dakota did not turn his head. He continued to glare at the dark-haired girl opposite him. He said flatly, "There weren't any intruder fingerprints. There would have been if . . . "

"The burglar wore gloves," she said.

"You mean, the *murderer* wore gloves."

"Same thing!"

Dakota said carefully as if talking to a child, "A burglar steals. Whoever came into this apartment on Thursday evening had murder on his mind. A carefully sharpened tool . . . scissors maybe. Razor-sharp. Whoever it was came into this apartment with an intent. An intent to murder Caroline McKelvey."

There was a pause. A stillness filled the small bright apartment.

"You can't know that." Nicky's eyes were huge and dark.

"I'd bet my badge on it. As for you, sweetie, I think this talk of yours about burglars is nothing but a smoke screen."

You are riding her too hard, Dakota, thought Anne.

She saw panic fighting with fear in Nicky's face.

"I just want it on record that someone went through her

things on Thursday night." Nicky's voice was flat, stony. "I just want that on record."

The girl turned and went across the dining ell and into the kitchen. She jerked on the tap hard and poured herself a glass of water. She didn't drink from the glass, only stood there with her back to them. It was obvious that she was trembling.

Anne followed, stood in the dining ell with her hands resting on the smooth surface of the bar. This was exactly where the murderer had been standing when Caroline was killed.

Nicky turned and made a gesture with one hand, indicated the bar, the neat kitchen. "All gone . . . no more blood. Daryl cleaned it up for me this morning. It took him over an hour. One would think your people would have cleaned up the place."

"The police don't . . . " Anne shrugged. There was no point. She changed her tactics. "You're on the offense, Nicky."

"I'm not on the offensive. I'm just mad as hell . . . wouldn't you be if someone broke into your apartment and killed your roommate and went looking through your drawers?"

"No, it's more than that."

It was, but she couldn't put her finger on what it was. She stared Nicky down. "I think you are afraid that whoever killed Caroline will come back to kill you too."

The girl's head went back. "Why do you say that?"

It had been a shot in the dark. "You act afraid. But if that's true, Nicky, why don't you help us find your roommate's killer? You offer nothing."

"I am not afraid, not in the slightest. I know how to take care of myself." Nicky's voice held its edging of hysteria.

Dakota was standing at Anne's elbow. "We can't protect you unless you are straight with us, Nicky. What would someone have been looking for in this apartment? In Caroline McKelvey's room? Why would someone have wanted to kill her?"

"I don't know. Simone said . . . " Nicky's voice broke off.

"You mean, Simone Gray?"

Nicky nodded. She looked confused and miserable. "Simone said something about Caroline being too trusting and not watching out for herself. She said that Caroline wasn't smart where the bad guys are concerned."

Dakota frowned. "What did she mean by that?"

"I don't know what Simone meant."

"Of course you do."

"I said I don't know!" repeated Nicky in a low voice. "Maybe just that Caroline wasn't careful. I told you Caroline never met a stranger. She'd have opened the door to anybody. Hell, I don't know what Simone meant!"

It was possible Nicky Nelson was telling the truth. She looked ragged. Anne turned to Dakota. She shook her head to warn him to lay off. He didn't look at her.

"But *you* are different, aren't you, Nicky?" Dakota was again sarcastic, cutting. "You're a tough little nut. You'd keep the door locked, the strangers out. We don't have to worry about you, do we?"

"Get off my back! I'm not afraid of anything or anyone. Even you, tough cop."

Anne nudged Dakota hard.

"Jesus," he muttered under his breath.

"I think we've all had enough," offered Anne. "We'll talk again when you are cooler, Nicky."

"There's nothing to talk about. Don't ask me any more questions. I don't have any answers. None at all." She sounded determined. Also vaguely forlorn.

Anne shook her head. This abrasive young woman was her own worst enemy.

"As for your being in any danger," Dakota called after Nicky as she went toward her bedroom, "I don't think you have to worry about that, kid. This building is tight. Keep your wits about you. You're going to be all right."

"Thanks for the reassurance. But don't worry about me. My wits are . . . always about me." Nicky disappeared into her room, slamming the door behind her.

"I can't get it right with that girl." Dakota flushed.

They rejoined Jesse Clore in the living room. "Sorry." Dakota still looked annoyed.

The priest was standing beside the curio cabinet. There were two books lying on top of the cabinet. He tightened his shoulders, reached for the books. "These are mine," he said. "Caroline borrowed them." He looked pale as if the morning had upset him.

"Did that make any sense to you?" Anne asked. "That reference to Caroline not being too smart where the bad guys are concerned."

"It might have just been metaphorical," Jesse Clore replied uneasily. "Maybe Simone Gray was just saying Caroline wasn't the kind to go looking for trouble."

"Trouble found Caroline!" said Dakota. "She didn't go looking for it."

"Not trouble . . . someone. *Someone* came looking for her." Anne agreed quietly. "One of the good guys . . . who turned out to be one of the bad guys."

"I have to go," said Jesse abruptly. "I have a lunch appointment."

He turned and stood for a moment in the open door.

He looked from one to the other of them, then spoke with a certain nervous resolve. "Caroline did have a personal problem on her mind. It involved a choice to be made, a decision between right and wrong. We talked about that in the past few weeks. I guess you could call it . . . the meaning of integrity. She was wrestling with her conscience."

"A decision about what?" asked Anne bluntly. "We have to know."

"No. I can't tell you." Jesse Clore held up the two books. They were both by Albert Schweitzer . . . on ethics. He went out and closed the door quietly behind him.

Dakota loosened his tie . . . obviously exhausted.

Anne felt the weariness and frustration in her own temples. She looked down at the carved animals in the curio cabinet. A leopard about to spring. An elephant with raised tusks. There was an empty spot where the tiger had been.

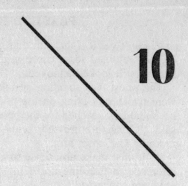

10

At Indiana Avenue a message was waiting on Anne's desk. Congressman Alan Foley had called her twice this morning. The Homicide Department secretary's scrawl read, "Call him. Important."

She dialed Alan's number.

His strong voice, with its intimate Tidewater accents, came over the line. "Just wanted you to know why you're having so much trouble getting in to see Woodward. Rumors are flying on the Hill . . . big news. It sounds like a presidential appointment is in store for Jim Woodward. I don't know whether it's true or not."

"A presidential appointment? As what?"

"How about this . . . a new cabinet position. Secretary for Hemisphere Protection."

Anne cradled the phone. "Alan, you're putting me on!"

"I'm not, darling. I'm serious. The President is creating a powerful new position, one with clout. He's taking money out of all kinds of budgets to fund it. Rumors are the new Secretary's job will be to protect our hemispheric environment. The man who gets the spot will be our watchdog, national dragon . . . our environmental big gun! We are talking everything that involves clean living in this hemisphere. Pollution, ice caps melting to the north, and drug traffic from the south."

"Wow!" said Anne.

"Wow . . . is right! The White House hasn't said anything yet. But informally, the story is confirmed. The official announcement should come today. Very soon. And Woodward is *the* man."

Anne glanced at her watch. An announcement, if there was to be one today, would come in the next hour. Just in time to break on the noon news. This administration knew how to play the media game. "I'm stunned," she whispered, "I think it is very innovative of the President."

"Spoken like a good party supporter," Alan said. "As for Jim Woodward," he paused, "his staff has already called a press conference for three this afternoon. This is a big victory. I mean, he will have to be confirmed by the Senate and all of that. And there's a lot of jealousy out there . . . but Jim has a good record."

Anne could almost hear Alan's thinking through the political process. She said, "You feel Woodward will sail through confirmation?"

"If anyone can. He is integrity plus. Anyway, that's the reason you haven't been able to get to him these past few days. He's been meeting with the President, hush, hush . . . and other cabinet members."

Anne could picture Jim Woodward with his lion's mane of white hair and deep impressive voice. Yes, he'll be a star in the nation's political sky, conceded Anne when she put the receiver down. Right up there in the limelight's glow will go Alexander Shannon and all those other dedicated staffers she had met in Woodward's office on Monday afternoon.

Too bad about Caroline McKelvey. No doubt, she'd have loved all this.

Dakota was at the far end of the squad room talking with Boccucci. She went to tell him.

The announcement of Congressman James Woodward's appointment as the new Secretary for Hemisphere Protection came over the noon news.

Anne turned up the car's radio so they could hear it. She and Dakota were on their way up Sixteenth Street to pay a visit on the lobbyist's office where Caroline had been employed before she joined Woodward's staff. Dakota was eating a hamburger as he drove, holding his soft drink with the same hand that held the wheel. He listened to the news announcement with his own kind of intentness.

Removing the shiny red paper from her own burger, Anne squeezed out an extra catsup and said, "I think we should go to his press conference this afternoon."

"You think Woodward is going to have time to talk to us?"

"Of course not. I just want to be there. I don't know why. Maybe, just for Caroline."

"Suits me. I wouldn't mind seeing what it's like. I mean, this is big time, isn't it?"

Anne turned the volume on the radio down. "Big time, for sure."

She was feeling vaguely sad, weighted and philosophic. She couldn't quite say why, but she needed to tell him how she was feeling. "It is funny about life, Dakota. A girl in Woodward's office is dead. The new girl. She hasn't been there long enough to make much of an impact. Anyway, that's last week's news. And everybody is sorry, but life goes on and Woodward gets a big political appointment and this is big time . . . more important. And it is. It really is. I guess. I mean, what do you think, Dakota? Do you think we'll ever know who killed Caroline McKelvey? And does it matter?"

"You are damn right, it matters! Hell, we are most definitely going to find out who killed Caroline! I'll bet my badge on it."

"That's the second time today you've bet your badge." She took a bite out of her burger. It was juicy and sweet with catsup. Also, she liked Dakota's vehemence. She felt better already.

Dakota turned toward her and for just one unexpected moment their eyes met and held. "That is because, Fitzhugh, we are a good team. I am one mean bastard who doesn't like to lose. And you are one exasperating, smooth as silk, cheeky broad who doesn't give up either. Hell, we'll crack this case . . . I know what I'm talking about." He gave her one of those rare sweet smiles that, in spite of herself, made Anne's heart turn over.

The small environmental office where Caroline Mc-Kelvey had worked before she joined Congressman James Woodward's staff held only two desks, two chairs, a filing cabinet and a small sofa. "We run a lean show," said Margaret Dell, chief lobbyist for a clean water organization headquartered in New York. She was a woman in her late forties, full of zest and sparkle. "But that doesn't mean it isn't an effective show. We've made some good friends on the Hill. We're making progress."

"Thanks for seeing us." Dakota showed his badge. "You know why we're here. Like I told you on the phone, the more we know about the victim . . . the faster we can do our job."

Margaret Dell paused, sat on the edge of her desk. "I can't tell you what an asset Caroline was to me. Basically, she did research and staffed this office while I was out making my calls. She was efficient and dependable . . . not to mention a darling soul to have around."

Anne was looking at the plaques on the wall, a large framed ad that spoke of the *harmful bacteria, dangerous cysts, microscopic worms, radioactive solids, asbestos and volatile organic chemicals* in our drinking water and a poster of a forest waterfall. There were glossy pictures framed above the desks of Margaret Dell chatting with various members of Congress.

"We are trying to get a handle on McKelvey's personal life," Dakota continued. "Like, who did she get phone calls from? And who did she go to lunch with?"

"Well, her fiancé, Daryl Swan. He called often."

"No one else?"

"Now and then, a girlfriend. Her brother, once or twice." Margaret Dell put her hand to her forehead. "She was very businesslike. She wasn't the kind to gab a lot on the phone. And mostly she brought her lunch and ate at her desk. Caroline was a wonderful person and maybe . . . not underneath like she seemed on the surface.''

"Can you explain that, ma'am,'' Dakota asked quietly.

"A beautiful girl, bubbly, you know that. You'd think she'd tell everything she knew. She didn't. Caroline kept her personal life to herself. She talked about other things mostly . . . our environmental projects, maybe a recent movie. If she had gone sailing on the weekend, she'd mention that. Otherwise, no . . . ''

"When did you last have contact with Caroline?''

Margaret Dell fingered her gold earring. "Let's see. She left me for Jim Woodward's office in mid-July. I can't tell you how I hated that . . . losing Caroline, but it was definitely an advancement for her. I encouraged her to take the job. We talked a few times after. She sounded . . . ''

Anne caught the pause in Margaret Dell's voice.

Dakota responded quickly. "She sounded . . . how, ma'am?''

"Well, I guess it was the last time I talked with her. I had stopped by Congressman Woodward's office. It was in early September. He's a hard man to get in to see and since he is already in favor of our bills, I don't bother him too often. But this day, I did stop by and I talked with Caroline. I had the feeling that . . . ''

"Yes, ma'am?''

"This sounds ridiculous.'' Margaret Dell put her hand to her mouth, her eyes twinkling. "I had the feeling that she was in love . . . yes, that she'd fallen in love. And it wasn't with Daryl.''

"Why do you say . . . ridiculous?'' Dakota asked.

"Because she didn't say a thing to that effect. Not one thing. But she had a look about her, sort of starry-eyed and happy. I know when I see someone in love. I think Caroline was 'involved,' if you know what I mean.''

Dakota nodded, seemed to understand. "Did she mention any names to you? I mean, even a casual remark.''

"No, she didn't. She talked about Woodward. She thought the world of him. And from what I hear, he is great to work for.''

"Was there anything else that might be helpful?''

"She told me that she'd moved out near the Cathedral and liked it out there. But I tell you, something had happened since Caroline left my office. She had worked for me for three years. I knew her well. She was different. She was in love."

"And you say . . . not with Daryl?" Anne could not resist asking. "I'm surprised. They seemed so right for each other."

"Oh, they were." Margaret Dell nodded. "Entirely right for each other, and he adored her. But love plays tricks. You know that." She smiled at Anne. "I think Caroline had lost her heart. Yes, I do. You asked. I told you."

"What do you think?" Anne asked Dakota as they headed toward the Hill. "Do you think it's possible that . . ."

"Yes, I think anything . . . anything is possible." He stretched behind the wheel, rubbed his face with his hands. His jacket was getting too tight for him. It was his favorite and he wore it anyway. "Love plays tricks, or hadn't you heard?"

"You aren't getting enough sleep, Dakota."

"Tell me about it."

"Stop working overtime. It will kill you."

He sighed. They were moving around the Botanic Gardens at the foot of Capitol Hill, heading up Independence Avenue. "Look, Fitzhugh, there's work to be done on the streets. And I need the money. You wouldn't understand that. So cut the advice." He sounded curt.

Her partner lived on a houseboat docked at the marina in the Washington Channel. A simple life, he'd once said. An unanchored life, for sure. He had a son growing up in California with an ex-wife. Anne had seen his picture on Dakota's desk. The boy was throwing a football.

She said, "Forget I said anything. It's your life, Dakota."

They were coming up Independence Avenue. The U.S. Capitol was on their left. She said, "We can park in the lot at the corner of First Street. The patrolman on the corner is a friend. He'll work it out for us.''

A spot for the Crown Victoria was managed in the crowded lot on the corner.

"Professional courtesy." The Irish cop flashed a grin.

"Where is this damn press conference anyway?" mumbled Dakota as they moved with the crowd into the Longworth Building.

"The Committee Room for Ways and Means. I guess the chairman loaned it to Woodward for the occasion. For a press conference of this importance . . . a good stage is necessary."

The Committee Room for Ways and Means would be just that. A good stage. The curtain on a new scene in the nation's political play was about to go up, and the mood in the Congressional Office Building was one of suppressed excitement. Word of the press conference had swept the Longworth. The corridor outside the main-floor committee room was chin to shoulder with young staffers from every office in the building. Everyone who could manage it was making a point of being there. To see . . . and be seen.

Lobbyists had been drawn by the lights and the coils of black cable and the sound men setting up operations outside the committee room. Scattered here and there in the crowd was a Hill personality, senator or congressman. Easily recognizable . . . as were the more colorful members of the press.

Always and forever the important press, thought Anne. The first reviewers to be played to. She noted the TV cameras banked on the other side of the high-ceilinged room as she and Dakota entered. The front rows were reserved for the press and the seats were filled.

"A nervous bunch," said Dakota. "Jesus."

"Actually, it is just the usual high-spirited political crowd," said Anne.

"Bloodhounds . . . on point," her father would probably say.

Radio and television reporters were clustered beneath the great heavy chandelier in the center of the room vying for the prepared statements which members of Woodward's staff were passing out.

Dakota said under his breath, "This looks like a circus."

"A carefully orchestrated circus," she murmured back. She'd been here before. She'd seen it as glorious and rather hokey, but it had been wonderful then because of Rob. Now she felt cynical and emotionally detached as she watched staffers deciding who would and who would not get an advance copy of the statement. "I've only got a hundred copies," she heard someone say testily.

"Feeding the sharks," it was called.

She looked toward the podium at the end of the room. On either side of the dais rose two curved tiers of seats meant for the members of the Ways and Means Committee when it was in session. The backdrop was gold velvet and from a private entrance in that handsome curtain, Woodward would soon appear. She glanced at the clock set in a high arch on the other side of the room.

"He's late." Dakota was reading her mind.

"As expected. Fifteen minutes late. He's on 'Hill Time.' "

The curtain parted, several men in dark suits with paisley or red-striped ties emerged through its folds. Janet Sutton was the only woman among them. She also wore a dark business suit. The crowd quieted. Heads turned expectantly.

"Woodward," said Anne to Dakota. It wasn't necessary. The room was flooded with hot, rich light. The focus was on Woodward. His power was set off by the deference of staff members who fell to the sides as he moved to the podium.

Only Alex Shannon accompanied his chief to the mike. The AA looked keen-eyed and "on-alert" as he handed Woodward the prepared statement to read, a certain deference and something proprietary in the gesture. Anne thought of what Rob used to say about . . . about a senior congressman being a "magnet for loyalties."

Jim Woodward patted his tie, cleared his throat. Then, the crowd having hushed entirely, he began to offer his statement in a deep unhurried voice.

"I don't know why we're here," Dakota muttered under

his breath. "We've got better things to do."

"Just keep your eyes open, Dakota. This was Caroline's world. I mean, maybe there is someone, something . . ." Her voice trailed off. She caught sight of Gertrude Woodward in the background, half hidden by a TV camera. The congressman's wife had on a red wool suit that set off her gray hair. She was listening intently to her husband.

"I see," said Dakota, "about one hundred young men in this room that Caroline might have fallen for."

"What about . . . the man himself?"

"No way it was Woodward. He's too old . . . too important for Caroline."

"She was a hero-worshiper, Dakota."

There was a flurry of applause as Woodward finished his statement. As expected, he had thanked the President for the nomination and pledged his commitment. "A challenge of great importance . . . a chance to save America's future," were the words used.

The press began to bombard Woodward with questions.

"Let's get out of here," said Dakota. He touched her arm.

"A few more minutes," said Anne. Her attention had been caught by the arresting figure of Simone Gray. The beautiful television reporter was standing back from the other questioners, her arms at her side. She was staring at Woodward intently.

The pose struck Anne as unlikely. The Capitol Hill reporter was never so passive. It was always Simone Gray on the front row, Simone Gray with her "to the heart of the matter" questions. Not today. Today was different.

Anne stood up to see better. She had Simone Gray clearly in sight and then she lost her again. The room was surging with people who had begun to move about and to talk among themselves.

"You're right," Anne said to Dakota. "We might as well get out of here. See those lights flashing over the clock. That means a vote's been called on the floor of the House. Woodward's going to be leaving anyway."

But the press would not let him go. Anne saw Alex Shannon try to clear a path for Woodward back up to the door in the gold velvet curtain. The way was blocked with questioners and well-wishers.

Bells sounded. "Ten minutes to vote, Congressman," one of the aides called out. Woodward stepped back up on the podium and held out his arms. "I really have to go. God bless."

With Alex Shannon and two of the other aides leading the way, Woodward began to move across the crowded room toward the hall door. He passed close by Anne, a big man, glossy and distinguished, in a well-cut blue suit. She had thought he might be wearing makeup. No, the tan was real. Jim Woodward was indeed the outdoorsman he claimed to be.

Again his way was blocked. Woodward paused.

Anne saw his face clearly, saw his smile fade abruptly. She realized that Simone Gray had come up to Woodward. She was standing directly in his way, blocking his progress. Simone had her notebook open as though she was about to ask him a question.

Behind the professional smile, Anne saw something angry in Simone Gray's dark eyes. She watched the correspondent step even closer to Woodward and heard her speak.

It was only a whisper made under her breath, but Anne heard it and so did the man to whom it was addressed.

"You are a bastard, Jim," said Simone Gray. "I'm going to get you . . . I am going to pull you down."

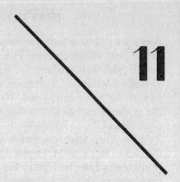

11

"Are you sure she said ... 'I am going to pull you down.' "

Anne nodded, "With 'you bastard' thrown in for effect."

Don Dakota's laugh was amused and cynical. "Simone Gray is known for being as outspoken as hell. Maybe she knows something we don't know ... or maybe she's got some personal vendetta against Woodward. I saw her block his way and say something but I couldn't hear what it was."

"I heard her clearly," insisted Anne, "and so did Jim Woodward. He jumped when she spoke. Alex Shannon heard her. He said something back to Simone, low, under his breath. Whatever it was ... was angry."

"Hell, that's politics. That's Simone Gray. She 'gets' everybody, doesn't she?" Dakota fished the car keys out of his pocket and gave an appreciative wave to the parking lot attendant. "I've had enough of this political scene. Let's hit the road, kid."

But Anne lingered beside the car. She saw the ABC News team loading its van at the far end of the lot, the crew stowing away the cameras and lights.

Simone Gray was entering the lot.

Anne felt a rush of adrenaline. The encounter she had just witnessed between Simone Gray and Jim Woodward was vivid in her mind.

True, this was politics. Big fish were open game for the media. And this was Simone Gray's style ... always on the attack. Usually the newscaster's political gestures were elegantly done, the rapier thrust . . . the perfect dagger question. And always without emotion. Simone was known for her control and lack of personal involvement in the stories she covered.

What Anne had witnessed at the close of the press conference in the Longworth Building was different. She had seen an encounter between a man and a woman, each powerful in his or her own way. It had been swift . . . over in the blink of an eye. Only a few people realized what was happening. Certainly Simone's whisper hadn't been meant for the camera. Or for anyone else to hear. Only for Woodward. Simone Gray's words had been emotional and personal. A threat.

"Wait," Anne said to Dakota through the car window, "I'll be right back."

She walked quickly between the parked cars.

A few feet from the ABC van, she caught up with Simone Gray. The Capitol Hill correspondent was carrying a leather briefcase and looked moody and preoccupied. She turned when Anne called her name and slowed her pace.

"Anne Fitzhugh, D.C. Homicide." Anne showed her badge.

Simone Gray came to a full stop. "I know who you are. You're Congressman Fitzhugh's wife . . . his widow. Of course. You're the lawyer who's now on Homicide." She stared at Anne, smiled slightly. "How can I help you?" She was taller than Anne, but more slender.

Fine-boned and beautiful. More beautiful in real life than on the television screen. It's in the eyes, thought Anne, those dark, shining eyes. And the cheekbones. I know this face, she thought. I know those dark winged eyebrows, the expression in those eyes. The feeling of familiarity struck her forcibly.

Such is the power of television, thought Anne.

She also noted signs of exhaustion in Simone Gray's face, maybe even signs of dissipation in the small lines that her makeup skillfully masked.

Anne began awkwardly but candidly. "I have to say that

I am a fan of yours. I watch you whenever I can."

Simone smiled slightly. She was obviously used to being complimented. Still, it was evident from the intent way she was looking at Anne that she realized she'd not been stopped for that reason alone. She asked in her distinctive husky voice, "What can I do for you, Anne Fitzhugh, D.C. Homicide?"

The outburst at the close of the press conference was interesting, but not relevant. What was relevant . . . was Simone Gray's relationship with the girl who had been stabbed on Thursday evening at The Alhambra.

"This concerns the death of Caroline McKelvey. My partner and I are investigating the case." She nodded toward the Crown Victoria with its prominent radio antennae. "We understand that you live in The Alhambra and were friends with the victim. Is that correct?"

There was a pause. A shadow of a frown crossed Simone's face, a look of anger, annoyance . . . maybe fear. It was brief, hard to read. She said levelly, "I knew Caroline McKelvey."

"Knew her?" The lack of emotion was surprising. Anne responded quickly, "I had the impression it was more than that. I thought you were her friend."

Simone Gray was looking toward the white squad car, staring at Dakota, who had gotten out of the car and was leaning on the hood. Her eyes darkened. She squared her shoulders slightly and stepped back from Anne. "I don't understand why you are here. Are you following me?"

Anne flushed. Simone Gray was coming across as a prima donna of the first order. "No. You're just one of several 'friends of the victim' on our list. We plan to see them all. You weren't on our schedule for today. My partner and I were . . . well, let's call it 'happenchance' that we ran into you. When I saw the van in the lot, I thought it was a chance to catch up with you."

"Do you know yet who killed Caroline?" Simone Gray asked.

"No we don't."

"Do you have a suspect?" Simone's gaze was dark and steady. She was used to asking the questions. She waited for the answer.

"No," Anne replied honestly. "We don't. That's why we need to talk with everyone close to her. You live in The Alhambra. You knew Caroline." She had started to repeat, "you were friends," but realized that Simone had backed off from that.

Curious. But then, reasoned Anne, maybe "friends" was too strong a description for the relationship between the two women. The ABC correspondent was ten years older than Caroline McKelvey . . . savvier, and far more worldly than the younger woman. More likely, it had been a case of Caroline looking up with admiration at Simone Gray.

"I would have come forward immediately if I had anything to say." Simone Gray turned away from Anne.

"You are perceptive. I believe your insight would be valuable."

Again Simone hesitated. "I can't be of any help. Really."

"Perhaps," persisted Anne, "we could set up an appointment to talk with you, say tomorrow morning?"

Simone sighed, glanced at her watch. She seemed suddenly resolved. "All right, let's get this over with. I haven't had lunch. . . . Why don't you and your partner meet me at Bullfeathers in ten minutes. I'll be happy to tell you what I can about Caro."

Beneath the striped awning in front of Bullfeathers, two girls were eating ice cream in the October sunshine. The mood was casual, sleepy. An older man in his shirt sleeves, jacket folded on the chair beside him, sat at one of the tables with *The Washington Times* spread out in front of him.

Inside the pub, the mood was livelier and sharper. The long bar was not so crowded as it had been at lunch hour or as it would be at Happy Hour. But even now, in the 3 P.M. lull, more than half the bar stools and a few of the tables were occupied. Most of the clientele were men. Some looked up, caught by Anne's vividness. Talk was politics. Talk was power.

The earnest men of Capitol Hill, thought Anne, seeing how deeply absorbed they were in their conversations. All in uniform . . . dark shoes, dark suits, power ties.

She waited for Dakota. He had paused by the bar and was admiring the picture of Theodore Roosevelt hanging above it. As he studied the picture, the big, easy-moving detective straightened his tie. He looked rumpled, bigger than life, more physical than the other men in the bar. A loner . . . with a certain integrity. And somehow vulnerable.

Damn you, Dakota, you are just a Rough Rider yourself.

She caught his eye and smiled in spite of herself. His eyes smiled back. The tension eased.

There was an empty table in the second room.

"What do you say, Fitzhugh?" Dakota ordered a beer, took off his jacket, hung it on the back of his chair. "I'm curious to see how you're going to handle this. You believe it's worth asking Simone Gray about her exchange with Woodward?"

Simone Gray had just entered the pub. She paused for a moment in the door to the dining room . . . serene, slim shoulders back. A panther on the prowl. Her dark eyes swept the tables. She came toward them.

Dakota rose. Anne made the introductions.

"I'm starved," said Simone Gray. She sat down and rested her briefcase and leather handbag on the extra chair. "You don't mind if I eat while we talk?"

"Of course not," Anne started to say.

But Simone was already addressing the waiter. "I'll have a chicken sandwich, onions . . . steak fries, with catsup, please." She eyed Dakota's frosted mug. "And I'll have a martini."

She looked from one to the other of the detectives. "I never eat. Rather, I eat just once a day. Sometimes, every other day. I mean, really dine . . . at a table, with a napkin. Otherwise I am on the go, too busy for food."

Simone's slender elegant figure showed her disinterest in

food. Her hands were slender also. She wore one large squarecut diamond, mounted in a cluster of emeralds, on her right hand.

"What did you think of the press conference?" asked Anne.

"Well managed, but that's Shannon for you."

"What do you think of Woodward and this new presidential appointment he's got?"

"He hasn't got it yet," Simone said cryptically. "What I *think* about Jim Woodward is unimportant. We aren't here to discuss politics, are we? At this moment, I am exhausted. And famished . . . and thirsty!"

Anne felt again that unexpected sense of familiarity. Even the candid, assertive manner seemed familiar. It was uncanny. It was as if they had met and talked before.

Dakota leaned forward. "Well, aren't we lucky? We can watch you having one of your rare meals . . . at a table yet, with a napkin. And we can get our interview in with you at the same time."

He's annoyed, ragging her, thought Anne with surprise but with a certain amusement. He is going to give her a hard time. Even if she is a famous television personality.

"Whatever." Simone looked hard at Dakota, sizing him up.

Anne could read her thoughts. . . . Don Dakota. Wasn't he a tight-end for the Redskins? Early eighties. Went out with a bad knee. Looks intelligent. Shoulders that don't stop, arresting blue eyes, sexy mouth, well-cut features. . . . Also, macho. Very macho. Simone responded as if challenged, "You wanted me here, I'm here."

"Talk to us about Caroline McKelvey," ordered Dakota.

"What does that mean? Can't you ask specific questions?"

"Do it my way, if you don't mind. You won't bore us."

Anne saw Simone hesitate a half second before answering calmly, "Caroline was intelligent, a young woman with curiosity and charm . . . zest for life."

"That part we *know*," said Dakota.

"I am sure you *know* it all. Why bother with this? Caro

was born to the good life . . . and she was born beautiful. She didn't let either of those good fortunes go to her head. Except that maybe . . . ''

"Maybe, what?" Dakota caught the hesitation.

"Maybe the combination made her . . . overly confident."

"That isn't what you were going to say."

"I was going to say . . . stubborn and foolish."

"There's a difference," pointed out Dakota.

"A moot point." Simone looked suddenly tired. She shrugged her shoulders and took a long sip from the glass that had been placed in front of her. She closed her eyes when she did so.

"What do you mean by 'stubborn'?" asked Anne.

"Hardheaded. Caroline was hardheaded. We had a run-in, a disagreement once or twice. I couldn't convince her of anything."

That surprised Anne. She couldn't think what Simone and Caroline would have a disagreement over.

"As for 'foolish,' " Simone continued, "what I mean is, I can't see Caroline ever being suspicious or even . . . cautious enough. It was probably her undoing."

Anne thought of the mace canister found this morning in Caroline McKelvey's bedside drawer. That indicated caution on Caroline's part. Simone Gray was wrong in that regard.

"Did Caroline have reason to be suspicious of anyone?"

Simone looked quickly at Anne. "What do you mean?"

"You said 'it was probably her undoing.' "

"She's dead," Simone answered shortly. "We don't know why, do we? I would think she probably handled something badly . . . foolishly. Nicky filled me in. It sounds as though Caroline let someone into the apartment that she shouldn't have."

Dakota's voice was husky. "You believe Caroline is dead because . . . "

"I have no idea why she's dead." Simone Gray was regal, in complete control. "You asked me what I know of her. I've just told you. I am a reporter. I judge people.

Bright, stubborn . . . idealistic. That was my impression of Caroline.''

Dakota stroked his mustache.

"How well did you really know her?'' Anne asked.

"I guess not so well.'' Simone turned to her. "You see, I'm not the person to ask about Caroline McKelvey, am I?''

"Exactly how and when did you meet Caroline?'' Anne asked.

"I met her this past summer. Her roommate, Nicky, is a camera girl on a local news show on our station. A disorganized girl . . . neurotic, but she's Jay Nelson's daughter.'' Simone raised a dark winged eyebrow, then continued. "Jay and I are old friends. We hung around a lot together in New York before I came to Washington. Well, anyway, the girl hasn't got it in her . . . in my opinion, to make it big in TV. But she will have to learn that the hard way.''

"You met Caroline through her roommate?''

Simone nodded. "I hadn't much time for Nicky but I tried to be decent . . . once or twice we shared a late supper. Then, one September afternoon, she showed up with Caroline, her new roommate.''

There was something in Simone's voice that caught Anne's attention. Some flavoring of affection for Caroline that belied her earlier hard words.

"You liked her. Caroline made you think of yourself when you were her age.''

Simone's laugh was amused, ironical. "She did remind me of myself at twenty-six. That certain confidence. That awareness that some young women have that if they set the rules, they can have their own way. It comes with good looks. It gives an edge.'' She looked at Anne. "But you know that, don't you?''

"Caroline had that . . . advantage?'' Anne smiled.

"Of course. Only with her, it was smothered in naivety. She was so damn idealistic. If Nicky Nelson hasn't enough of her clever, smart-ass father in her act, Caroline was hers . . . in spades. I interviewed Marcus McKelvey when he was our UN ambassador. One world, compassion, trust, benevolence—all that kind of rot.''

''You sound like a cynic,'' Dakota said gruffly.

''McKelvey is a prophet. He's ahead of his time.'' Simone Gray spoke with feeling. ''It would be ducky if we could all love each other and feed the poor and build habitats and throw away the bombs. But in my opinion . . . and my opinion is worth something . . . it doesn't work that way and won't for a long time. You have to be tough to get at the truth. You have to look behind the obvious . . . in this town. And this town is better than most.''

Yes, her opinion meant something. Simone Gray had been a top correspondent for ten years. She'd seen and heard a lot. Anne was thinking of the press conference. She remembered Simone Gray's passion when she was confronting Jim Woodward.

''What did you think about Caroline going to work for Congressman Woodward?'' questioned Anne.

Simone was diverted. Her lunch had arrived. She sat back, studied the plate, nodded her approval and picked up her fork with relish.

Anne waited.

Finally Simone responded, her voice cool and studied. ''I said she was naive. I think Caroline was in over her head in Woodward's high-powered office. But forget it. She's dead. It doesn't matter now.''

Dakota had moved the silk flowers from the center of the table and was studying Simone Gray with a certain watchful fascination. He did not seem to have made up his mind about her.

''Do you have any idea who the killer might be?'' Anne continued. ''Anyone at all? Perhaps . . . a new lover of Caroline's?''

Simone did not look up from her plate. She was eating quickly. Her hand was steady. She said, ''I wouldn't know about any new lover. She was engaged to a young naval officer. I met him several times, a neat guy. I *know* he didn't kill her.''

''Who else was in her life . . . romantically speaking?''

"We didn't talk about men. There are other things to talk about. Better things."

Anne sighed. "When was the last time you saw Caroline?"

"Ten days ago. She dropped by to see me at work."

"And you hadn't seen her . . . talked with her since?"

"I keep strange hours. I am rarely home and when I am home, I'm a private person. I don't see a lot of . . . anyone."

"Why did she come to see you at the studio?"

"I asked her to. There was a favor I wanted."

"What was the favor?"

Simone pursed her lips. "It was entirely personal. I'd rather not get into it." Anne sensed this was hard for Simone Gray. Her tone was flinty, edgy. She wondered if Simone was telling the truth. "Did Caroline do as you asked? The favor, I mean?"

"No. I don't know. I didn't see her again . . . alive."

Dakota was stirring. He sat back in his chair, obviously dissatisfied with the interview. He shook his head. Then, he interrupted with a certain abruptness. "Do you mind telling us where you were when Caroline was killed?"

Simone's eyes locked with his. "I don't mind, only I don't know at what hour she was killed."

Dakota was unruffled. "Just give a rundown of your activities between six and midnight last Thursday."

"I thought you might ask me that. I wondered what I would say."

Despite the perfection, the air of self-confidence, there was, thought Anne, something appealingly perverse about the woman sitting across the table. One sensed something about Simone Gray in real life that did not show on the television screen. A candidness that covered itself in grittiness. A sadness that wore a wry, sophisticated cover.

"I was on the Hill most of the afternoon," Simone began slowly. "At two, I taped an interview with the House majority leader which ran that night on the national news. I just got home in time to catch it. I guess it was about six when I got home. A friend was with me. We had a drink and watched the show. Later we went out for dinner. I guess that was about nine. We went to the River Club and then to his place for the night.''

"We'd like your friend's name," said Dakota.

"I'd rather not give it."

"Any reason?"

"It's no one's business but mine. That is my personal life." Simone's dark eyes were brilliant. "I don't divulge my personal life to anyone."

"Look," Dakota was again annoyed, "you've just told us you were at The Alhambra on Thursday evening. With this mysterious friend. Jesus, maybe he killed . . . ''

"No, he didn't," Simone interrupted. "He didn't kill anyone." She put down her fork and leaned back in her chair. "He was in my apartment the entire time we were there."

"How did you hear about Caroline's murder?"

"On Friday morning, I was in the ABC booth in the House chamber. Nicky Nelson called. She said she thought I ought to know. I was terribly upset. Of course, I felt rotten about it.''

"I didn't see you at the funeral," said Dakota.

"No," Simone responded levelly, "I went out of town for the weekend. A professional commitment. Otherwise, I would have been there."

Dakota nodded, still with a certain coldness. "It didn't matter. A small funeral. Just the family, a few friends . . . the real mourners. You weren't missed."

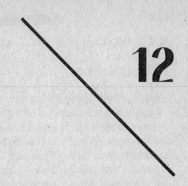

12

Anne found a pile of pink telephone slips waiting on her desk at headquarters. Most were routine. Alan Foley had called. Nicky Nelson, also.

Anne sat at her desk, rested her chin in her palms. The morning visit to The Alhambra to "intercept" Anthony Jesse Clore seemed a long way back. She'd been certain that she was on to something important. She'd been suspicious of the appealing priest.

Was she still? Her conversation with Father Jesse had been vague and seemed loose-edged now in retrospect. In fact, the whole day seemed a washout.

Anne picked up a pencil, toyed with it. Had she and Dakota come up with any new information that might help them find Caroline McKelvey's murderer? Her notebook lay on her desk. She flipped through her notes. Paul McKelvey thought his sister was afraid of someone. Thus, the canister of mace. Nicky said no. She still insisted the murderer was a would-be burglar who had searched not only Caroline's room but her own as well.

If that were true, then Paul McKelvey was a likely suspect for rifling the drawers. In fact he admitted to having done that in the past. A sad character, Paul—not quite likable but pathetic.

Margaret Dell, Caroline's former employer, said she suspected Caroline had "fallen in love" in the past few months. Maybe someone on the Hill. A conjecture, at best.

And it didn't really fit with Caroline being afraid of some-one. Or, did it?

The "good guys" . . . the "bad." Where had that come from?

Nicky had quoted Simone Gray as saying Caroline "wasn't smart where the bad guys were concerned."

Anne drew a circle around the quote on her notepad. She should have thought to ask Simone about that during the lunchtime interview. What had she meant? Probably noth-ing more than the bit about Caroline's idealism and think-ing she could get her own way by just being beautiful and assertive and knowing she was right. That certain "edge," Simone had said.

None of the men she and Dakota had thus far identified as important figures in the victim's life could be classified as "bad" guys.

Not Daryl Swan, that was for certain. He seemed to be a love of a guy, sincere and dedicated to Caroline. What's more, his alibi was unassailable. He'd been having dinner with fellow officers at the Academy in Annapolis on Thursday evening. He had given a lecture after dinner. No way . . . no way he could have killed Caroline.

Not Father Anthony Jesse Clore. Even if he was in the building the night Caroline was murdered. That appeared to be coincidence. Usually, Anne didn't like coincidence. Her father always said, "Look twice at coincidences. Con-sider the odds." Still, it didn't add up in this case. She couldn't see it.

Congressman Jim Woodward hardly knew Caroline. He gave no evidence of being a "bad guy." Nor did Alexander Shannon.

Paul McKelvey was the only obvious loser in the group. But under that exhausted angry façade was a brother's grief. In Anne's opinion, Paul McKelvey was not the murderer they were looking for.

She glanced at the notes she had made during the inter-view with Simone Gray. Nothing was helpful. Nothing. A wasted day.

Anne glanced at her watch. Five o'clock. The afternoon

shift was out on the streets and had been for two hours. She and Dakota were officially off-duty. He wasn't at his desk across the aisle. She stood up and looked over the cubicles. Dakota wasn't in the squad room, which was, at this hour, almost entirely empty.

Anne went down to Andy Boccucci's desk. She noted a weary raincoat hanging on a wire hanger, a plant wilting on the far edge of his desk. His cubicle, like the rest of the squad room, struck her tonight as shabby and untended and disorganized.

"How's it going . . . your upper-crust murder in northwest?" Boccucci glanced up, went back to his typing. "Give me a minute," he said. "I have to finish this."

I guess one could call the McKelvey case an upper-crust murder, reasoned Anne. Exhaustion and exasperation brought a sting to her throat. "Have you seen Dakota?" she asked Boccucci.

He typed another line on his report before looking up at her. "Gone home, I guess. The Cowboy, he's working eleven to seven tonight. Probably went home to get a little shut-eye."

Dakota hadn't bothered to tell her he was going. He'd been moody all day. Difficult all week. It was making her crazy. "Dakota's working too much." She sounded annoyed, and knew it. "It's making him mean . . . hard to work with."

"The Cowboy, he's always mean." Boccucci laughed. "That's why he's good. He don't take no shit." He went back to his typing. Two fingers, fast. Finally he pulled the report from the typewriter and added it to the pile on his desk. "There is another mother-fucker done." He pushed the typewriter table away. "I am only now 'bout three weeks behind with my paperwork, rather than four weeks."

Anne took off her earrings, square gold and silver criss-crossed. She stood them, one on top of the other, on the edge of Boccucci's cubicle divider. "Why do you think Dakota works double shifts all the time?"

"For money . . . honey. But you wouldn't know about that. Beautiful lady lawyer, slumming on homicide. When it gets rough downtown, you can always go back to that law practice of yours uptown.'' The small cop folded his arms behind his head, leaned back and waited for her reaction.

"That's not fair, Boccucci.'' Anne's gray eyes darkened. "I work hard. I am a good detective. Don't give me any grief. I get enough from Dakota. I don't need it from you.''

He was contrite. He stood up, a sweet-faced man with a head of glossy black curls. He was barely as tall as she was. He put an arm around her shoulders. "I was joshin' you, girl. I know you're a good cop. Dakota does too. We just can't resist giving you a hard time . . . 'cause you are so damn good-looking. So damn sassy!''

So good-looking . . . so sassy. That might be all there was to it for Boccucci. It was more complicated where Dakota was concerned. Working together was bringing it all out again between them. There were emotions to be fought. On both sides.

"You too tough on him, lady. Dakota's a good man. Listen.'' The little detective squeezed her shoulder. "You're off . . . I'm off. Come home with me. The wife is making pasta. I mean, when Angela makes pasta, she makes pasta. We'll drink wine . . . eat shrimp, some pasta . . . talk.''

She gave him a hug back but shook her head. "Thanks for the invitation but I'm too beat tonight to be any fun.''

She went back to her cubicle.

Her telephone light was flashing.

She answered, "Homicide . . . Detective Fitzhugh.'' She slipped on one earring, put the other on the desk in front of her. She thought it probably was Alan.

"Anne? Is that you? Alexander Shannon here.''

She could hear voices, exuberant laughter in the background. "I was at the press conference today,'' she said.

"I know. You and the lieutenant were both there. I saw you.''

"Your man did well. We were impressed. Impressed with the appointment and with the way Woodward handled himself.''

"Thanks." The noise in the background grew more muted. A door slammed. "It's been wild around here, you can imagine." He gave a tired-sounding laugh. "Now, the place is finally settling down. I know you and your partner are anxious to talk with Jim. That's why you were at the press conference, I gather. Look, if you would like to come by, we could manage it."

"Now . . . right now? Has he got the time?"

"There's never time." Alex laughed again. "The truth is Jim and Gertrude are having a few friends into the office for drinks. Gertrude remembers you from the Congressional Wives Club. She said she'd like to see you again and it would give you a chance to have a few minutes with Jim. I mean, you can just step into the staff room and have a little talk. There isn't much he can tell you but I know you want to see him about this . . . this Caroline McKelvey thing."

"This Caroline McKelvey thing." Anne stiffened. Again, the discounting.

Alex Shannon had said the words softly but it struck Anne as harsh and cold. "Your upper-crust murder" is how Boccucci put it. The young woman's death on Wisconsin Avenue didn't seem high priority to anyone except perhaps to Caroline's family and friends . . . and the other tenants of The Alhambra.

Love-lost Caroline. Anne moved the gold and silver earring gently around on her desk with a finger. "Yes, I'd like to spend a few minutes with Jim Woodward. Shall I come over now?"

"Right," said Alex Shannon. "What about your partner? Is the lieutenant coming also?"

"No. He is . . . otherwise engaged. I'll come by myself."

It had long been Anne's opinion that evenings on Capitol Hill owned a special mysterious charm. The Capitol, when night-lighted, appeared majestic in the dark and the white office buildings only a tunnel ride or a short walk away ringed the imposing building like sentinels.

Underground. Behind closed doors. Hideaways. The bustle of the business day was over and everything turned finer and more intimate. Even if the House or Senate were in late session, the staffs thinned down to the important and the faithful. The lobbyists and the tourists were all gone. No one was around who wasn't wanted. No one was *allowed* around, Rob used to say, who wasn't prime for secrets, strategy sessions or celebrations. It was, she used to agree, the best time on the Hill.

Anne found a parking spot for her red Porsche on the street. The sun was just setting behind the Washington Monument, streaks of purple and gold layered the sky to the west. All else was dusk and indistinct. It was getting colder and she was glad for the suede jacket. She shivered as she went up the marble steps to the Rayburn Building.

A bar was set up in the outer office of the New Jersey congressional office. "Scotch, vodka. Wine, beer . . . soft drinks. Whatever you'd like," said the bartender. He looked stoic. He had probably been at this for several hours, saying the same thing.

"A Perrier for me," said Anne, "twist of lime."

Several people were milling about. They were the press conference's remnants . . . staff from other offices, small-time reporters, no one Anne recognized. The door to Woodward's office opened. Alex Shannon came out with Janet Sutton. They looked elated.

"You must be exhausted as well," said Anne.

Janet pushed wispy fair hair out of her eyes and held up a plastic glass of white wine. "I am. When I finish this, I am going home and falling into bed."

"Thanks for coming on short notice." Alex took Anne's hand and squeezed it. His eyes were shining. An outdoor type, like his boss, thought Anne. His skin was tan, his movements graceful, taut.

Intelligent. And appealing. Alexander Shannon was also a hustler. A political shark. The Hill bred them, honed them and weeded them out. The survivors played for high stakes. It was acceptable.

"Before I take you into the party, I want to show you something," he said. "I think it might be important." He

led her through the doorway on the right into the staff room
and closed the door behind them.

The ceiling light was on. Filing cabinets, desks, telephones, a sea of untidy bookcases filled in all the spaces.
One desk close to the window was cleared and neat.

"Caroline's," said Alex. "We finally addressed that task
this morning. Janet did, rather." He pointed to a cardboard
box on the chair. "There are her belongings. I'm going to
have them sent out to her parents' house in Spring Valley
tomorrow. I thought maybe you'd like to look through
them."

The cardboard box held a gold pen and pencil set, a box
of tissues, a framed picture of Daryl Swan in his naval
officer's uniform, a bottle of Chloë hand lotion, a sweater
and Caroline's desk calendar.

"May I look through this?" She picked up the calendar.

"Of course," he responded. "To be honest, I already
have."

It was the standard issue government calendar that
flipped and showed a page at a time. The pages were empty
until July 16, the day Caroline had started working in
Woodward's office. Thereafter, there were sparse, regular
notations. "Staff meeting" came at regular intervals. There
was an occasional notation for a meeting with Alex or with
another member of the team. Only two or three times did
Anne see notations for meetings with the boss himself,
Congressman Jim Woodward.

"You see," said Alex, "she didn't get to meet with the
chief very often. She was the new member of the team, still
getting her feet wet."

Anne turned to the last page with a notation on it. The
date was last Thursday, the day of Caroline's murder. A
meeting with the press secretary was scheduled for 10 A.M.
Then came the words, "Afternoon off. See E."

"Who is E?" asked Anne.

"Yes, I thought you'd be interested." He folded his arms
across his chest. "I haven't any idea."

"You've thought about it?"

"I have. There's no one in our office whose name begins

with E—not a first nor last name. Janet said there is a girl who works down the hall named Emily. We asked her . . . she didn't know Caroline.''

"Maybe E is a friend . . . a personal friend of hers.''

"I didn't know Caroline socially at all. So I wouldn't know who her friends might be.''

"Interesting.'' Anne flipped back through the calendar. "Here it is again. 'E. 6 P.M.' on September 12. And once more. 'E. 5 P.M.' on September 22.''

"You said a friend?'' Alex raised an eyebrow. "You're probably right—6 P.M. sounds like a drink with a friend. I mean, none of those appointments were during work hours. They were on her own time.''

Anne wrote down the three dates and hours in her notebook.

She was aware that Shannon was watching. She asked, "What was Caroline working on in this office? Can you tell me about her assignments?''

He smiled at the question. "Of course! I gave them to her. She was smart, caught on fast. She started with some pretty routine stuff. Press releases on environmental issues, answering letters from constituents. About three weeks ago, I put her on a special project that has to do with disposable diapers littering the earth. I would make a bet that you didn't know about the environmental importance of disposable diapers, now did you?''

Anne shook her head. Alex Shannon was a charmer and pleasant to talk with. He was also smart as hell. She could sense that.

"Disposable diapers make up about a third of the non-biodegradable litter in this country.'' He was speaking seriously. "Something obviously has got to be done about it. Jim wanted a position paper. Caroline was doing the scut work, she was almost done with a draft. I'll show it to you if you like.''

"I take your word on it, really. You were pleased with her work? Personally pleased?''

He hesitated, then nodded. She sensed with a certain

irony that he'd wanted her to ask that very question, had
led her to this point.

"Entirely pleased. I just wish we had a dozen Caroline
McKelveys around here. She was a really fine staffer, a
dedicated person."

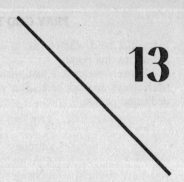

13

James Woodward of New Jersey smoothed his tie as he greeted Anne Fitzhugh. He radiated strength and vitality. The clasp of his hand was strong, the look in his blue eyes confident.

"We've not met before. I certainly would have remembered you!" He had stepped from a knot of guests in his office to welcome her. "I knew your husband, of course. Rob Fitzhugh was a good man . . . he's sorely missed."

"But I remember you." Gertrude Woodward joined her husband. She was almost as tall as he, but thinner. A chic thinness, noted Anne, that made her seem almost fragile.

"It's good to see you again, Anne, even under these unpleasant circumstances."

So, there was the reference to Caroline. Finally.

Anne was conscious of Shannon. She sensed the extraordinary alertness behind Alex's easy smile. She watched Shannon whisper something in the new secretary-designate's ear, saw Jim Woodward start slightly. In the excitement of the new appointment, he had probably forgotten the reason she was here.

Woodward looked at Anne apologetically. "I must say hello to some good friends. Don't go away. We have things to talk about, I haven't forgotten."

No, she wouldn't go away. She watched Gertrude and Alex close ranks on either side of Woodward to greet a high-ranking senator who was just entering the room accompanied by his two top aides.

"Hello, Anne Fitzhugh." The sound of her own name caught her off-guard.

Anthony Jesse Clore held a glass in his hand. It looked to be bourbon, ice sparkled. He seemed glad to see her.

"Hello, yourself." She felt a certain rush of pleasure. "Twice in one day . . . we find ourselves in the same setting."

"My good fortune entirely." His dark eyes sparkled. He lifted the glass to her. "Actually I've been thinking about you. This morning with Nicky was unsettling. I kept seeing you in my mind's eye, standing at that counter where Caroline was killed. The way you calmed Nicky down. I thought she was going to go over the deep end again. You handled it well."

"It's just part of the job."

"Not an easy job you've got. I hope you don't mind, I was also wondering about you. Wondering why you are into this messy business. Why policework? Why homicide?"

As always she hesitated, knowing there was not any kind of easy explanation.

"You're not, by chance, on the job now?" The curiosity showed in his eyes.

She smiled but did not answer. She felt emotionally exhausted. And, at the same time, oddly exhilarated, wired. She was off duty, as it happened, but always on the job on a case like this. Caroline's murder absorbed her, filled the loneliness inside. Nothing else mattered. How could she explain that?

Alex Shannon touched her arm. "You left your drink in the staff room. Perrier, I believe. Can I get you another?"

"I'll have a bourbon this time," she said, grateful for the interruption.

There were several men and women drinking bourbon. She smelled it, the deep rich scent of bourbon. Kentucky bourbon had been Rob's drink. She'd grown to like it. Jim Woodward wasn't drinking anything, she'd noted that.

Gertrude had a glass in her hand that was the color of vodka. She was deep in conversation with one of the guests.

Her eyes met Anne's across the room. She put her hand to her forehead, pressed it as if distracted, a flash of diamonds at her wrist.

Jesse was still waiting for her answer. "Sorry," he pushed her, "I just don't understand why you are here."

"I don't understand why you're here either, Father Clore," she came back with a certain spirit. "I thought this was a celebration party, a few close friends of Jim and Gertrude's."

"It is. And I am. A close friend." He grinned with his usual compelling intimacy. "And *you* are not. So, what are you doing here?"

Gertrude Woodward was crossing the room and now stepped between them. She spoke softly, just so Anne and Jesse Clore could hear. "I just want to be certain that you both understand . . . well, it isn't that Jim's not upset about the young woman who was killed. My goodness, he is. Caroline worked in his office and we know the Carvers socially. And Marcus McKelvey also. Such a tragedy for everyone."

Was she apologizing for the celebration? Did she mean to explain the air of vigor and animation with which Jim Woodward was at the moment greeting a newly arrived and quite beautiful young woman?

Anne said to Gertrude, "I understand. Life goes on."

The older woman looked relieved. "Of course, you would understand. Especially, in politics, there isn't much time for reflection, grieving. One does what the day demands."

"Which doesn't mean," Jesse Clore whispered as Gertrude moved on, "that Jim and Gertrude are heartless. They're not."

"Actually, I do understand." Anne noted that behind her mask of vivacity, Gertrude appeared tired . . . bone-tired. One does what the day demands.

Alex Shannon handed Anne her drink. "Wish I could hang around with you but the man needs me." He nodded over his shoulder at Woodward, who was patting his breast pocket and loudly exclaiming, "My passion . . . my only vice is a good Jamaican cigar."

Alex moved quickly to pass around the cigar box on the desk. "Macanudo . . . very sweet."

The bourbon was sweet to her mouth. She hoped it would balance her exhaustion and nervous energy. She looked down into the ice in her glass and said to Clore, "This appointment of Woodward's is rather extraordinary. I understand that. He has to prove he's capable and win Senate confirmation."

"He's capable. A boy from the Midwest, a truck farmer's son with a passel of scholarships for his education. He's got a Ph.D., you know. Before he made it to Congress, he was a college professor. Did some fine work in agriculture research. Grains . . . the feeding of the world's people. Jim Woodward has come a long way."

And somehow gotten wealthy along the way also.

Hadn't Alan told her that the Woodwards were major contributors to the Cathedral? Anne wondered where and how Woodward had made his personal fortune. She considered how best to ask that question.

Jesse was saying in his husky intimate voice, "Ambition is strange and rather marvelous. I hear many confessions, Anne, many confidences. There are a lot of people who would kill for this appointment. I think this new position excites Jim because it offers a chance to get some important things done in the environmental field."

"You make him sound artless . . . dedicated."

"I don't know about artless. He is actually rather canny."

"Who the hell are you calling . . . canny?" Woodward put his arm around Jesse Clore's shoulders, a rough squeeze. "You're not filling this lovely woman's ears with terrible untruths about me, are you?"

"I am calling a spade, a spade," Jesse laughed.

The congressman took the cigar out of his mouth and looked somberly down at Anne. "I haven't forgotten why you are here this afternoon, Detective Fitzhugh. I appreciate your coming. Let's go back in the coffee room. Just a hide-away in the back of the office but we can have our talk there.''

It was just that. A hideaway passage at the back of the suite connecting Woodward's office with the staff room. The passage held only shelves for supplies and the coffee-maker on a table. Paper cups, cream and sugar containers. Also a hot plate and teakettle. There were two straight chairs. Woodward sat down and motioned for Anne to take the other chair. ''About Caroline. . . . '' Woodward put the cigar in an ashtray and rested his hands on his knees. ''I'd grown fond of that girl. She was a lot like her father, you know. Did you ever meet Marcus McKelvey?''

Anne shook her head.

''Marcus is brilliant . . . remote in personality but a mar-velous man. Insightful. He is a legend in his own time. As for his daughter . . . ''

''As for Caroline?''

Woodward leaned back in his chair. ''What can I tell you? She was my newest staff member. I hardly knew the girl. Of course, I've no idea who killed her.''

''I didn't think that you did. It just occurred to me that perhaps the reason you hired her was that she was Marcus McKelvey's daughter. Could that be so?''

Woodward flushed just slightly and rather charmingly. ''I took note of that fact, yes indeed. But Caroline had done good work for the Clean Water Association. She was ded-icated, farsighted. She was qualified in her own right.''

''Her work pleased you?''

He looked vague. ''She hadn't been here long enough to judge.''

''Long enough for you to 'grow fond of her.' Certainly that is long enough to know whether or not Caroline was going to be valuable to you as an administrative aide.''

''As I say, I saw little of her,'' he answered stiffly. ''Alex Shannon would be a better judge of her work.''

''I gather Shannon had some trouble with Caroline.'' It was a hunch on Anne's part. Congressman Jim Woodward was hedging. She sensed that he was covering something and she wanted to know the truth about Caroline McKelvey and this office.

"Oh, I wouldn't call it trouble. Alex calls the shots around here. He's a hard taskmaster. I think once or twice he wasn't happy with Caroline's attitude or something. It wasn't really important. They worked it out. I stay out of those staff things, you understand."

"Alex is tough. He runs a good show for you?"

"I couldn't get along without him. Listen . . . " Woodward leaned forward and laughed as if he had made this statement before many times. "Shannon runs this office and my committees. He manages all my appointments, gets me home to New Jersey when I need to be there. And Gertrude runs everything else! I am just a man with one passion, one obsession—turning this earth, this hemisphere . . . into a safer, healthier place for tomorrow's children."

The man had a certain eloquence. Anne found herself believing in his sincerity. Quickly she went over the events of last Thursday evening with him. Yes, Woodward agreed with her accounting. He'd been playing golf that afternoon at the club. He'd decided to stay for drinks and dinner. He ran off the names of the men he'd dined with in the club's grill. "I got home about ten-thirty that night. Gertrude was already in bed, but we talked a bit about my game . . . my day."

She believed he was telling the truth.

"Well, dear lady"—Woodward patted his breast pocket as if looking for a fresh cigar—"this has been a long day. I'm sure you are weary also. Is there anything else?"

Anne understood. He wished the conversation to be over. She stood up, Woodward towered above her. She asked impulsively, "Just one more thing. Did you find Caroline physically attractive?"

A generous roar of laughter answered her question. "I'm not dead yet, my dear Anne Fitzhugh! Of course, I did. Any man in his right mind would have found her both beautiful and charming."

"And Alex. Did he find Caroline attractive?"

"Alex keeps his thoughts on women to himself. He's a

loner, you know. Really, I admire him for his self-control. So many lovely girls on the Hill. He says you can't mix 'politics and pleasure,' whatever that means!'' Woodward was flushed, joking. He opened the door and led her back out into the party.

She did not think that Jim Woodward had been romantically involved with Caroline McKelvey. Anne's instincts told her that *if* Caroline had been in love, it was not Woodward. Nor was it Alex Shannon.

At least, Anne did not think so. Still there was something odd going on. Alex was managing the scene, managing her investigation. She sensed that effort at control on his part.

She stood aside from the rest of the party in Woodward's office. There were thirty people or more in the handsome room now. Most were congressmen and senators, some no doubt were indeed good friends of the Woodwards and others only vital to the upcoming confirmation. She watched Woodward work the room with Shannon close at his side. The AA was making sure that no one was ignored, that no glass was empty and, more importantly, that his boss—the new secretary-designate—was the center of attention.

Alex Shannon was not without physical appeal. He has a certain banked-fire sexuality, thought Anne. He was astute, well educated. He'd spoken of a political science degree from Princeton and a law degree from Georgetown. The Woodwards had been generous, Alex had acknowledged that fact to her cryptically and without much emotion. Everything seemed taut, muted, under cover and under control where Alex Shannon was concerned. The rumpled casual look was just his cover. She would talk with him again.

She would call or maybe even drop by this office tomorrow. On the surface it appeared that Alex Shannon wanted to be helpful. The business about the mysterious E. on Caroline's calendar. Shannon had not been entirely candid with her concerning his own relationship with Caroline nor his evaluation of her as a member of his staff. He had, in fact, been fake as hell. It's called ''protect your rear,'' thought Anne. Such are the ways of the political animal.

She moved through the gregarious crowd speaking to a few senators and congressmen she knew, but she did not linger. She didn't make a show of leaving nor did she seek out Alex Shannon or Jim Woodward to say good-bye.

Gertrude Woodward was waiting in the outer office. ''I hope Jim was of some help. He hardly knew Caroline. Have you any idea at all who murdered the girl?''

''Not really.''

''Maybe it was just some street person, looking for drugs,'' Gertrude said almost hopefully. ''Or some kind of crazed killer. You know, like that Bundy fellow. Is it really true she was stabbed? Caroline, I mean?''

''No, not stabbed. Her throat was cut. The murderer used some kind of sharpened tool.''

''Like a knife . . . like scissors?'' Gertrude asked intently.

''Perhaps scissors. A blade of some sort that had been sharpened. We're working on it.'' Anne edged into the hallway. An apologetic smile. ''Anyway, thanks for including me in your party tonight. It was helpful. And again, congratulations on the nomination.''

A certain animation lighted Gertrude's face. ''It's a marvelous and busy time for us. Still, if there's anything more that Jim and I can do, please let me know. I have written Marcus a note. I've talked with the Carvers. They went away for a few days, you know. When they are back, I intend to pay a call. Darling people . . . they didn't deserve this.''

''Darling people, rot . . . nobody deserves homicide,'' murmured Anne to herself as she went down the marble hall. Gertrude's words irritated her. If she only knew how violence violates one's soul, how it tears at the sense of the rightness, the fairness of life. Dakota had told her once that being on Homicide was like trying to keep a chess board level in a storm at sea.

As she came into the lobby, Anne caught a glimpse of black and gray tweed, dark hair. If there was anyone in this cast of characters who'd understand that, it was Anthony Jesse Clore.

She caught up with him just outside in the cool darkness. "Hello."

He turned at the sound of her voice. "I was just thinking about you."

"Still wondering about my choice of occupation . . . why is a nice girl like you . . . " She smiled in spite of herself. "Are you still trying to figure me out?"

"I am. I was wishing I had my car and I could offer you a lift somewhere. Alas, I am traveling this evening on the metro."

"How about I give you a ride home? I know where you live. Woodley Road."

She saw his face light up, heard the warmth in his voice. "Terrific! Nothing sounds better right now."

"Actually, there's still a lot for us to talk about."

"You mean . . . Caroline?"

Anne nodded, voicing her thoughts more for herself than for his benefit. "Four days ago I was ending up my vacation. At about this very hour on Sunday, I was driving up from Tappahannock wondering what was waiting for me on Indiana Avenue. Who would I be partnered with . . . what kind of case?"

"It turned out to be this particular damnable case of murder." Jesse Clore's voice was ragged. "At least I think so. Damnable!"

Of course, it was. A damnable case! Anne felt a flood of emotion so strong and harsh she could say nothing. It was anger, frustration, more than anything else.

"I think," she said when he had settled himself beside her in the Porsche, "someone is playing games with Dakota and me. I haven't figured out who it is yet."

He turned toward her. "What do you mean?"

"There's someone out there who can help us, someone who knows more than he or she is telling. For whatever reason."

"Why do I get the feeling you think that someone is me?"

She did not deny the accusation. "I don't think you would purposely mislead us. Still, you might be more revealing. You don't offer much unless you are asked."

"I don't mean to be secretive. What do you want to know?"

She eased the car out into traffic. "Let's start with the Woodwards. Your close friends, the Woodwards."

"If you are saying that with any sarcasm, don't. I am not a political friend of Jim Woodward. Jim and Gertrude are active at the Cathedral. He has served on a couple of committees with me. They have been generous with their gifts."

"Don't be defensive. I didn't mean anything more than I said." Anne gave him a soft, easing smile. "You will have to admit the Woodwards are ambitious?"

"I do, indeed. It is no sin."

"Do you think Jim's word can be trusted?"

"Actually, I do. He is, as I said earlier, canny. Canny and ambitious. I also think he is a very straightforward fellow, basically kind. He rescued Alex when the boy was fourteen or fifteen, found him in a bad foster-care scene and brought him home. Woodward's treated him like a son. I can relate to that."

"Gertrude?"

For a moment he hesitated, then said, "She's more complicated. I think it's been a long hard road for her. In some ways, I think the 'hungry years' were easier for Gertrude than now. Jim has become a cock of the barnyard and she has to keep up. You know, it isn't easy."

"Was she jealous of Caroline?"

"Jealous? Not at all. Gertrude keeps a firm hand on her husband. She knows where he is every hour, every minute of the day."

"How does she know?" Anne glanced over at Clore. "How could she know?"

"She and Shannon are close. They make good allies, you might say. Their business is . . . Jim Woodward. They might be unlikely bedfellows, Gertrude and Alex . . . but bedfellows they are all the same."

"How do you know that?"

He laughed slightly. "You know I can't exactly say how I know it, but I do."

"What about Shannon? Did Caroline speak of him to you?"

"Yes, she spoke of him. She liked him enormously in the beginning. But . . ."

Anne gave Jesse a quick glance. "But what?"

"But they fell out somewhere along the line. I don't believe she'd seen him for several weeks before she died."

"What do you mean . . . seen him? They worked together every single day."

"Listen, Anne, this is a confidence I'm reluctantly betraying. Caroline told me she felt guilty about seeing Shannon while she was engaged to Daryl. She was confused about her feelings for Alex Shannon."

"Are you sure they went out together? I mean, socially?"

"They had dinner a few times. I am quite certain of that. At his house."

A piece of the puzzle fitting in, thought Anne. Which explained Alex Shannon's lack of candor about Caroline. A love affair . . . even Woodward did not suspect that.

"The real trouble was," Jesse offered slowly, "Caroline misread Shannon. At least, this is my own opinion. Because Alex voices all the right sentiments about the environment and saving the world from pollution, she thought she'd found a knight in shining armor. I gather he is more pragmatic than she suspected."

"I'm not following you."

"Caroline didn't talk much about the affair. Maybe it was only a one-night stand that shouldn't have happened. Sex but no passion, no feelings." Jesse Clore's voice trailed off. He went on, after a thoughtful moment. "Sex without any feelings attached is just aerobic exercise. Meaningless and pretty hurtful for someone as complicated as Caroline."

They were stopped for a light below Sheridan Circle.

Anne turned to study Jesse Clore. "You like complicated people, don't you?"

He nodded. "Caroline wanted a good world. She was willing to work for that. She was also a passionate young woman . . . looking to be swept away."

"You are talking now about . . . real passion in sex."

"Daryl had her on a pedestal. She didn't want to be there. She wanted to be desired. She wanted to be lusted after. She wanted to be swept away. She wanted sex with lasting passion, real emotion and . . . connection in it."

"Why do you think that? Did she tell you?"

The light changed. A car honked behind them.

"She didn't have to tell me. I knew Caro very well. I knew what was deviling her. I knew what she wanted."

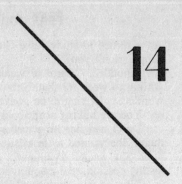

14

Was this going to be a confession?

It struck Anne that Caroline might very well have been in love with Father Anthony Jesse Clore. There was empathy in Jesse Clore's eyes, a sense that he did not judge harshly, that his heart was open. He was that rare thing—a man easy to talk to, easy to bond with and, no doubt, easy to love.

"I expect you did understand just what Caroline wanted," Anne said.

There was a silence. The car sped through the quiet darkness. The window was down on Clore's side, the smell of cold firs and falling leaves in the night air. "I'm not sure that you do understand," he said flatly. "Perhaps you're thinking that we were lovers, Caroline and I?"

She felt his eyes on her. She answered with equal candor, "Yes, I'm entertaining that possibility. I know that you and Caroline talked often, in person and on the telephone. Sometimes late at night. I know that she tended to hero-worship. I know, or at least suspect, that she'd changed over the past few months . . . maybe fallen in love with someone other than Daryl. It could easily have been with you."

Anne paused for a moment, decided to hold back her knowledge of Caroline's pregnancy. She finished with, "Yes, I've suspected that you were lovers."

"I can see how you would think that."

"That's not exactly a denial, Jess."

"Anne, how far can I go? How honest can I be with you without besmirching a lovely beautiful girl? I feel as if I am caught in a moral and emotional trap."

"You have to be true to yourself and your profession, Jesse Clore. I need all the help I can get in finding Caroline's killer. Just tell me what you can."

They were coming up Massachusetts Avenue toward the Cathedral. The twin spires of St. Peter and St. Paul loomed dark and beautiful above the trees. The red aircraft warning lights twinkled at the top of the center bell tower.

"Let's stop by my office." Jesse was suddenly resolute. "We need to talk this out. Also, there's something I'd like to show you. It has to do . . . with Caroline."

He directed her off Wisconsin Avenue, around the north side of the Cathedral toward the administration wing. All was dark or in deep shadow along the north drive except for two small buildings set close to the road. They were wooden temporary buildings. Lights blazed through picture windows, figures could be seen moving about.

"The stone carvers are hard at work tonight," Jesse commented as they passed by.

"I rather thought stone carving was a lost art."

"It is. Only a few skilled craftsmen are left in this modern world who can do work of high quality. They are artists, of course, close to God." Jesse Clore turned his head to look back at the lighted workshops as they passed.

Anne braked the Porsche in front of the administration building. "Do you really believe that artists are close to God?"

She could see his smile in the darkness.

"They create. God creates and a few of his servants here on earth have been sprinkled with that holy dust of magic and they too can make visions and little worlds appear. The rest of us poor mortals only cope."

"You *are* funny," she said, getting out of the car. "I think you are in your own way a philosopher, Jess Clore."

He opened the door of the building with his key,

switched on a light illuminating a small lobby. The hallway led past glass-doored offices marked for clergy and administration and several classrooms.

"How about coffee?" His office was a small comfortable room brimming with bookshelves. It held a cluttered desk, and a worn sofa that was layered with books and papers. He turned on the small desk lamp. "It will just take a moment to make a pot. Or, maybe some tea?"

Anne shook her head. The room smelled of leather cream and books. It made her think of her father's study at home. The window behind the desk was curtainless but the blinds were drawn. On the wall was a wonderful painting of a Byzantine-like head of Christ, all grays and browns. It was strong and young and sorrowful. There was forgiveness and compassion in the face.

Jesse Clore saw her looking up at the painting.

"The original is an altar sculpture made of shell and shrapnel. It hangs in one of the chapels in the Cathedral . . . a gift, I think, from Great Britain after World War II. It's one of my favorite heads of Christ. There's something beautiful and ironic about the use of the metal. Bomb metal, actually."

He cleared a place for her on the sofa, pulled up a rocking chair for himself. For a long moment, however, he stood in the center of the room. Finally, he sat down, pulled the chair close to her. "I am uneasy, Anne, you realize that. I have people in this office all the time, talking about all sorts of candid and personal things. But, for some reason, I feel awkward with you here tonight . . . talking about Caroline."

Anne settled back into the sofa, pulled her legs up under her. There was still a palpable intimacy between them.

"I met you three days ago. Monday morning in the herb garden. I haven't had you out of my mind since. You are beautiful, and rare and exotic, and . . . not meant to be a detective on D.C. Homicide. You are too fine-nerved for the work you do, too intelligent. And you are scared, physically scared, not brave enough for the work. And that puzzles me and interests me."

Anne laughed. She rested her head on the high back of the sofa.

He went on in an almost rueful voice, "This morning when, so unexpectedly, I saw you again, my heart jumped. Did you know that? Could you see it? I mean, that is crazy, isn't it?"

She shook her head, charmed . . . but wary. "Three days isn't a long time," she offered softly. "Maybe, if we have the chance to get to know each other better in the future, I'll tell you about myself. Maybe, I'll tell you what brought me to Homicide."

Would she? Anne looked down at her hands clasped in her lap, the gold band on her left hand.

"I know who you are, of course," Jesse Clore was saying. He was looking at her with a sudden softness. "I know what happened to your husband. A real tragedy, a loss. And more . . . I gather it was a good marriage, that you loved each other."

She nodded, unable to speak, felt tears rising.

"Don't be sad. I'd like to have had . . . at least, that. You know, I've never married." His head was bent, his face slightly flushed, the dark triangular brows hiding his eyes. "I've come close a few times, backed off. I admit that I went into the priesthood for selfish reasons. I was trying to understand myself better. I'd had a pretty bad home scene and it left scars. I ran from the pain. I spent some time on a construction crew after college. I did a stint in the Peace Corps, got my master's degree in psychology. Finally, I looked to God."

Anne believed him, touched that he was talking so honestly and openly with her. He'd turned the attention upon himself and that calmed her.

"I guess, I was a late bloomer." He smiled. "Three years ago last June, I turned forty and finished at the seminary the same month. I'm still not sure I am any good at this clergy business. . . . I am a questioner and a challenger, but I'm giving it all I've got. I believe in God, Anne."

"Despite everything?" She heard the catch in her own voice. "Despite modern science. Myth-disproving science.

And despite 'existence pain'—that's what Rob used to call it. All the heartaches and unanswered questions?''

"In some ways, I find it easier to believe when I realize how complicated and intricate it all is. I'd have had a harder time believing in God in past ages when we thought man was the center of the universe. I'd have been damned cocky. Now, I'm more humble." He leaned forward and rested his elbows on his knees as he had on Monday morning in the herb garden. It was a disarming gesture.

Anne smiled. "What do you believe?"

"I guess I have come to believe in simple things . . . like beauty and the magic of love, the innocence of children. The willingness to risk being hurt . . . the power of forgiveness."

How husky his voice had become. Anne sensed that this was not a philosophical discussion. Jesse Clore was speaking from his heart. "I am, in my own way," he said, "talking about Caroline."

She kept her eyes on his face. "Tell me."

"I want to show you, instead," he said quietly.

He got up from the rocking chair and went to his desk, opened it to the file drawer, riffled through it. In a moment, he came back with an envelope in his hand. He handed it to her.

Anne saw that the letter was postmarked September 24, only a few weeks past, and addressed to Father Anthony Jesse Clore at the Washington Cathedral. The handwriting was strong, feminine, assertive. The envelope had been opened, but the letter was still inside.

"May I read this?" She looked up at him.

"I want you to." His voice held great sadness.

Anne took out the single sheet and unfolded it. The note read, *"Father Jesse, I've been thinking about what you said to me last night. I was feeling so lonely and sad—so incomplete, if you know what I mean—and your words helped. You comforted me. I know in my heart that I am not truly alone, that none of us are. I am glad that you are there. I think you are wise because you have felt pain. You*

*have a forgiving heart, Jess. I am going to try to be strong
and honest and true to myself. Thanks for showing me the
way. Always, Caroline."*

He hesitated, then said, "You think we were lovers. No,
we weren't. It was deeper than that. We understood each
other. I told you I had known a painful childhood. So, in
her own way, had Caroline."

He sat down again in the rocking chair. "Do you know
about her family life?"

Anne folded the letter and put it back in the envelope.
She held it out to him. "Only the obvious."

Clore rubbed his face with his hands. His voice sounded
weary. "What I am trying to tell you is that Caroline was
looking for love. She was looking to connect with a man.
In particular, someone she could idealize."

Anne leaned back into the curve of the worn sofa and
studied the strong, well-cut features of the man sitting in
the chair close beside her. "She could certainly idealize a
man like you. She loved you, Jesse."

"You'd be surprised," he responded. A smile touched
his face. "My vanity would like to have you believe that
Caroline fell in love with me. But that wasn't the case. In
fact, in the beginning she rather avoided me. She came to
my discussion group but it wasn't until I saw her one day
in the Bishop's Garden that . . . "

"Yes, you told us all that. You said 'family problems.'
You said that in your counseling with Caroline, you dis-
cussed 'family problems.' But you grew closer, didn't you?
I mean, you loaned her books. You talked on the telephone
late at night."

"You are challenging me, Anne. I am trying to be honest
with you."

She was subdued. She pushed the dark hair from her
eyes. "Go on, please."

"It didn't take long to see that Caroline's relationship
with her father was enormously painful to her. It was a
major thing, unresolved, in her life. And it affected the way
she felt about men. I mean, she was beautiful. She could

have any man she wanted, any kind of lover. And this is where the problem begins. Two Carolines begin to emerge here."

"Two Carolines . . . two sides to her personality?"

Jesse hit the chair's armrest with the palm of his hand. "One was the Carvers' perfect daughter, McKelvey's perfect daughter. She is engaged to a conservative, high-minded young naval officer. They do not sleep together. They are waiting for marriage before they take that important step. She works for clean water . . . and then for the admirable congressman Jim Woodward. She spends her free time volunteering here at the Cathedral, which is her mother's church. She smiles with her own special Caroline serenity, and works with children and tutors in English."

"But, you are saying, there was another Caroline?"

He nodded. "One who was in pain with her life. It was that Caroline who came into counseling with me. It was that Caroline who revealed herself in our talks and won my heart and my compassion."

"I think maybe *that* Caroline is the one who was murdered." Anne spoke with a certain irony in her voice.

"I don't want you judging her. That is important to me. You have to understand the complexity in all this."

"There isn't much I haven't seen, Jess. I don't judge."

"We are talking about a passionate young woman, emotionally banked . . . stalled, needy to give and get love. Daryl is respectful . . . too controlled. He cannot meet her needs. And so, there were several affairs. I am not talking about a lot of men. Just a few, but all of them strange, unsuitable. She didn't seem to know the difference between the good guys and the bad."

Anne started . . . that phrase again. Nicky Nelson had also used it talking about Caroline, had quoted Simone Gray. She nodded. "Did Caroline tell you all this herself?"

"It came out as we talked. She picked the damnedest guys. One was a young stockbroker, brilliant, yes. But he had a cocaine habit. He almost got them both killed picking up the stuff down on Fourteenth Street. Another was a guy in the CIA, top security. He gave her a black eye. She was afraid to go to the police. She just broke off with him despite some threatening telephone calls.''

"Maybe, he is . . . ''

"He was killed a year ago in a car accident. He's not your killer."

"That would have been too neat." Anne shook her head.

"There is one other you should know about." Jesse Clore stood up, thrust his hands in his pockets, looked down at her. "This one is as unlikely as the others. It's one of the stone carvers at the Cathedral. A young Italian artisan here on a work permit."

Anne felt a rising excitement. Finally something tangible. She repeated, "Caroline was romantically involved with someone who works here at the Cathedral at the time she was murdered?''

"No. It was over and had been for several weeks. I am not sure it was a 'romance.' " Jess put the word in quotes with his fingers. "It was something intense, but I'm not sure they went all the way with it. There were complications."

"Did she tell you that this relationship was over?"

He gave a slight shrug, then a nod. "All of Caroline's choices were dead-end. Dangerous choices. She saw something in all these men that made it worth it. At least, she thought she did. And then, for one reason or another, they were . . . over.''

"She set herself up to be hurt.''

"That's right.'' His voice was sad, toneless. "It was as if she set herself up to be hurt. It was as if she was repeating . . . .''

Anne could not help interrupting again. "Tell me about the stone carver, Jess.''

Jesse Clore was staring at the head of Christ on the wall.

"You see, I understood Caroline. My mother was a manic-depressive. She also had a drinking problem. Sometimes she would be the world's most devoted mom, someone you could look up to and lean on. That's mostly what the outside world saw, the people in our town.

"And then, she would change without warning. She'd

be depressed as hell for days, cowering in the backseat of the car in the dark of our garage. It was horrible. You never knew what to expect. My heart used to be hammering in my chest when I walked into the house every day just wondering if. . . . My mother committed suicide when I was fourteen. One of my sisters killed herself shortly afterward and the other is . . . well, complicated. You don't come unscathed out of families like that.''

Anne heard the tremor of pain in his voice. She rose and stood beside him.

"You see why I understood Caroline." Jesse Clore's voice was now steady and controlled. "I understood her better than she understood herself. I believed in her. And she was getting stronger, changing every day. She'd found God. She was living her faith. She was coming to understand herself.''

Anne touched his arm with gentle fingers. "Tell me about the Italian stone carver. Is he still here at the Cathedral?''

"Yes. He's still here. He might be working tonight. But I can't believe he is your man. He's a gentle fellow. What's more, he hadn't been with Caroline for several weeks before her death. They had agreed to part . . . not to see each other again. She was committed to that. She had good reasons for breaking off with him.''

"What reasons?''

"He has a young wife back in Italy and a little son. He'll be going home soon when the work is finished here at the Cathedral. There was nothing that could last between them. Caroline realized that. She stopped the relationship before 'things went too far.' It was the first time she'd been strong enough to do that.''

"She told you that?''

"Yes. It was right after Labor Day. And then, she never spoke of him again.''

"You don't realize how important this is, Jess. May I use your phone? I want to call Dakota and see if he's out with a car. Maybe he can meet me here.'' Anne moved toward the desk, already reaching for the telephone.

"Tonight?"

"Absolutely, tonight." She was dialing headquarters.

The lights were blazing in the workshops on the long drive bordering the north side of the Cathedral. The murmur of men's voices and the steady buzz of a drill came faintly through the night as Anne and Jess Clore approached on foot.

"Dakota will be here in ten minutes. Let's wait outside."

There was no response. Clore had turned his collar up against the night's chill. Even in the darkness, he seemed somber and ill at ease.

They were approaching broad picture windows, designed, Anne realized, so that visitors to the Cathedral could watch the stone carvers at work. The windows would serve a good purpose tonight. "Can you point out the man we are looking for?"

"I said he might be working tonight . . . *might*."

Anne was already standing in the shadows beside the picture windows. Makeshift but complete workshops, these temporary buildings. Brilliant fluorescent lights shone below great squares of dark skylighting on the north side. The raw plywood walls were hung with files and hammers and drills. Stone dust lay everywhere. And everywhere, men . . . men intent upon their work, mostly young men in jeans and flannel shirts, their boots and legs brushed with powdery white dust and stone chippings.

Some talked and laughed. Most were lost to their work and their own thoughts as they moved among the blocks and columns of limestone. They moved hard and quickly, with sleeves rolled up, muscles rippling and dark eyes intent upon their tasks.

Beneath their hands, great shapes and figures smoothed and arched and rose from the stone. An exquisitely carved limestone lamb nestled at the feet of an angel with a half-cut face. A lengthy serpent lay, as if carved in secret, along a slender branch.

"I don't see him," Jesse Clore whispered. "Really, I don't. Unless maybe he's one of those." He touched

Anne's shoulder to indicate several young men who were clustered at one side of the larger room. They wore yellow hard hats and surgeon's masks over their noses and mouths. They were working with drills and hammers and picks and and chisels on a towering statue of a saint with arms outspread.

In front of Anne, somewhat blocking her view, was a sheet of plastic that covered a large half-carved stone. She moved to one side and glimpsed a young man working alone. He was down on one knee beside the stone. He was fixing chains to it, chains that hung from a pulley in the ceiling.

Jess Clore was following her gaze.

"Where the rib vaulting meets at the peak of each ceiling arch in the Cathedral, goes a 'boss stone.' Pressure from both sides, stone upon stone, holds the boss stone secure and cements the arch . . . without cement."

"What a miracle," said Anne. She was watching the young man placing the chains around the stone. How competent he was and how beautifully he moved . . . how beautiful he was. Rough dark curls and golden olive skin, how smooth was the arch of his back.

Jesse's hand tightened on her arm. "That's the one, Anne. You've found him. That is Emile."

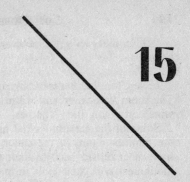

15

Dakota reached the Cathedral in less than ten minutes. He was alone in the squad car, driving too fast. He came toward them, moving easily in the arc of the street lamp. He shook hands with Jesse Clore but his eyes sought out Anne. "What's this all about, Fitzhugh? You said 'come,' I came."

She had an odd sensation, seeing Dakota there in the gold dark glow of the street lamp. It was just after eleven. He looked exhausted and as edgy as usual, fiddling with his tie, stroking his mustache. His presence reassured her.

Quickly, she filled Dakota in on what she had learned from Jesse Clore.

Anne looked from Dakota to Clore. "I saw Caroline's calendar at Woodward's office earlier tonight. There were several references on it to a mysterious E. The office staff could give no help. Two dates on that calendar *since* Labor Day referred to 'E,' and a specific hour was given. A third was the afternoon that Caroline was killed. No particular hour was marked, just the notation, 'see E.' "

For a long moment, neither man spoke.

"What's this Italian stone carver's name?" asked Dakota.

"Emile Farrare." It was Jesse Clore who answered.

"Is he in there?" Dakota was looking toward the lighted workshops.

"Yes," responded Anne. She was shivering in the crisp night air. "A young man, dark hair. He's hard at work."

"O.K., then, let's go." Dakota turned toward the work-shops.

Jesse Clore led the way, swung open the unlocked door. The room was dusty and warm and smelled of chalk and wine and young men's bodies.

Some of the carvers looked up from their work. Seeing the familiar figure of the canon with two visitors behind him, most turned back to their tasks but others remained motionless with their tools in their hands.

The young man kneeling with the chains at the boss stone was absorbed in what he was doing. He did not look up until Clore put a hand on his shoulder.

Then he rose quickly, wiped his hands on his jeans.

He is so beautiful, thought Anne, so beautiful in the face, like in a Botticelli painting. He was a man in his mid-twenties, or so she judged, with the quick shy ways of a boy. He glanced quickly at her and at Dakota and then looked at Jesse Clore with dark questioning eyes.

"Do you speak English?" Clore kept his hand on the young man's shoulder.

"A little." Emile Farrare gave a deprecating shrug.

"Caroline was tutoring Emile in English," Jesse Clore explained in a low voice. "I believe that's how they met . . . got to know each other."

At Clore's words, the young Italian stone carver straightened his shoulders. "I do not know, sir, what this is about." He began to tremble just slightly.

"Let's step outside," said Dakota. He turned on his heel.

"Tell him to bring his jacket," said Anne. "It's cold."

"And his toolbox," Dakota called over his shoulder. "Tell him to bring all his tools with him."

There was a brief conversation between Jesse Clore and the young man, and then a longer exchange, complete with shrugs and gestures, with the foreman of the Italian work unit.

Through the picture window, Anne and Dakota watched Emile Farrare cover his stone carefully with plastic and gather up his jacket and black lunch pail from a table at the end of the room. His tool belt was strapped around his waist. His expression was self-contained, vaguely sullen. He did not speak to any of his workmates as he left the building with Jesse Clore.

"We're taking him downtown," Dakota said to Anne. "He can ride with me."

"I have my car. I'll follow. Shall I bring Jesse along?"

"If he wants to come. We don't need him." Dakota gave her a quick studying look. "What are you doing here with Clore anyway? You're off-duty, Fitzhugh. You ought to be home."

It was said as a reproof.

I don't ought to be anywhere, Anne thought to herself. "I do what I want on my own time, Dakota. Just be glad my efforts paid off."

In the glow of the street lamp, Jesse Clore looked pale, agitated. She decided not to ask him to go downtown with her. They watched the stone carver get into the car with Dakota. The squad car moved away in the darkness. Crickets were singing in the hedges.

Jess Clore put his hand under Anne's elbow as they walked down the drive toward her car. His hand was warm, and made her realize how chilled and miserable she felt. "It didn't enter my mind that Emile might be Caroline's murderer. My gut tells me that he's O.K., an honorable sort of fellow. It's so unlikely."

"We'll check it out." She was bone-weary and cold. She didn't want to talk about it anymore.

They rode in silence the few blocks to Woodley Road.

"I'm exhausted," said Jesse Clore.

"Me too," said Anne.

Jesse reached over and touched her cheek with gentle fingers. "You are so vulnerable. You listen . . . your eyes listen. You have a good heart."

She wanted to say "thank you," she wanted to say, "I am vulnerable." She only shook her head as he got out of the car. "I'll call you tomorrow, Jess, and tell you what happened with Emile."

*   *   *

At night, the Municipal Building on Indiana Avenue did not reflect the fact that during daylight hours it was the hub of the D.C. Police Department, seat of the Criminal Investigation division, the heart of the First Precinct. In the hours after midnight, the imposing white marble building looked like any other D.C. government office building, hushed after a busy day.

It was just after midnight when Anne parked in front of the building. The lights on the third floor were on. She took the elevator up. Like the Capitol, this building had its own after-hours ambiance. Footsteps sounded loudly on the marble floors, doors opened and were banged closed along the hallways. There were no casual visitors at night. Only the invited. There were silences, the creak of the cleaning wagons, the squawk of police radios from the command centers, only occasional voices ... occasional laughter.

Detective Andy Boccucci, off-duty tonight, but revived by his wife's shrimp and pasta, had come in response to Dakota's radio call to help with the interrogation of Emile Farrare. He was waiting in the squad room with a cup of coffee in his hand. He raised an eyebrow as Anne came in. "This kid is an innocent, if you know what I mean. He is probably also guilty."

She put her handbag in the drawer of her desk, saw a pile of pink telephone slips beside her phone. She looked up at Boccucci. "Where did Dakota take him?"

"Down the hall to room C. Dakota went out for fries, maybe some Big Macs. He'll be back in a sec."

"Dakota eats too many Big Macs."

"The kid was hungry. I should've brought him in some pasta." Boccucci grinned. "Should've brought you some too."

She hadn't eaten since lunch, an "express burger" in the car with Dakota. Maybe that was why she felt so tired. She went down the hall to room C. In the bare cubicle of the interrogation room, Emile Farrare sat in a straight chair with his hands folded on the metal table in front of him.

His jacket lay on the table, his tool belt beside it.

"Hello," she said. "I'm Detective Fitzhugh."

If he recognized her, he did not show it. He stood up, gave a slight imperceptible bow. He had an Old World sort of charm, but there was great tension in him. He was like a bow pulled tight. She could see it in his shoulders, the pulsing of a vein in his forehead.

"We brought you in to headquarters for a talk, Emile. You're not under arrest. You haven't been charged with any crime." Not yet, thought Anne, not yet. "Do you understand what I am saying?"

He nodded solemnly. He waited until she sat down at the table, then he did also. He folded his hands again in front of him. The fingers were long and strong, white with limestone dust. He said, "Lieutenant Dakota . . . he say maybe I should get a lawyer."

"If you want, Emile. That's certainly your right. We can get you a lawyer from Legal Services, if you want."

"I don't want." He shook his head. "I don't do nothing."

She wanted to start in with questions. She wanted to ask him about Caroline. But Dakota would be angry as hell if she started the interrogation without him. There was no point in riling her partner any more tonight. She decided to wait.

"Where do you come from in Italy?"

"I come from Assisi," he said, "from near Assisi."

"I've been there . . . it's beautiful. The old basilica on the hill and the narrow streets, and the swallows flying at dusk over the valley. I lost my heart to Assisi."

"I live there in the valley below. My home is . . . there."

For the first time she saw a smile curve on his lips. His voice softened. "My father carves the stone and his father before him. My brothers, too. It is our life." How marvelous he was. Simple. Ageless. Young man, half-angel.

The aroma of food filled the room. Dakota was suddenly there, the scuff of his boots, and under his arm, a white paper bag bulging with foil-wrapped burgers, Cokes, cones of french fries. He spread the food like a feast in the center of the table.

Boccucci was behind him. "I mean, I just ate. But if you insist . . . "

The young man said nothing but reached hungrily for a cone of french fries, a cold drink.

Dakota and Boccucci pulled up chairs to the table.

"Jesus," said Dakota, opening a burger, "I forgot the damn catsup."

"Frank keeps catsup in his desk. Also mustard, pickles and bicarb." Andy Boccucci pushed back his chair. "I'll get the catsup. He'll never know."

They were making it easy. It was all part of the game. Dakota was a master at this. Anne had learned to marvel at the Cowboy's way of charming suspects as well as witnesses.

"Nice boots," he said to the young Italian. "I like boots. I like your boots. High heels . . . hand-tooled leather. You get those here in America?"

Already the young stone carver seemed more relaxed. He was unwrapping a burger. He nodded. "*Grazie*," he murmured.

When they had finished and the wrappers had been stuffed back in the white paper bag, Dakota leaned back in his chair. He had a straw in his hand and he began to fold it slowly into inch-long segments from one end. He kept his eyes on the straw as he asked, "Emile, how long have you been in the U.S.?"

"How long?" The young man frowned. "You mean, when do I come here? I come in June to Washington."

"You like it here?"

Emile shrugged. "I like it O.K. Sometime I like it."

"Are you homesick for Italy?"

Boccucci translated the question.

"I am missing my family. *Sì*, I am missing Italy some."

"Have folks been nice to you? Friendly people here in America?" Dakota was folding and refolding the paper straw.

"He says some people have been friendly." Boccucci translated the young man's response. "He says he doesn't know many Americans, says he hangs around with the other Italians on the project.''

Dakota looked up then, his eyes very blue and ice cold. ''Ask if he knew a young woman named Caroline Mc-Kelvey?''

''I know her.'' Emile Farrare did not need to have the question translated. ''Surely I know Caroline. But now she is dead. She is killed . . . murdered.''

''How do you know that she was murdered, Emile?''

''Everyone know. The newspapers say so. People at the Cathedral are talking . . . everyone say that she is dead. I know because I go to see her . . . and she is gone. Killed . . . dead.''

''When did you go to see her?''

''I go to her flat. The man at the door, he tell me this. At the Cathedral there is a mass . . . no, a service for her funeral and I go there. I wait outside and I see her mother and father and you. . . . '' He looked clear-eyed and hard at Dakota. ''I see you there too. I think you are mourning for Caroline.''

Dakota threw the straw on the table in front of him. ''I am investigating her murder, Emile. I didn't know the girl. You knew her . . . I didn't.''

Something like a sob came from the young man's throat. His dark hair was a tumble of curls, his eyes like dark burning stones. ''Caroline is beautiful woman. She is an angel . . . like I carve for the Cathedral. I carve it now, for Caroline.''

''How well did you know her?'' Dakota's tone was brusque.

Boccucci translated, listened intently as Emile poured out a rush of Italian. The young man spoke for several minutes and then put his hands to his face, looked down at the table.

''He says he met her a few weeks after he arrived. She was assigned to help him with his English. It was one of the visitor services offered to the stone carvers. They were friends, he says. Caroline was his friend. He says she was *adorabile*, easy to love.''

"Ask him did they sleep together?" No quarter given.

When Boccucci repeated Dakota's question, the young man flushed. He gave back a torrent of words.

Andy Boccucci grinned, looked from Dakota to Anne. "In his own way, he says it ain't any of your business! But since Caroline is dead and you're trying to find her killer, he will tell you the truth. No. He says . . . there was no sleeping together. Just love between a man and a woman that is pure."

"Tell him that I think he's lying."

Dakota picked up the straw and began to refold it.

"You want me to tell him you think he is lying about . . . ?"

"No. I've changed my mind. Ask him instead when was the last time he saw Caroline. Ask him when did he see her last . . . alive?"

Again there was a rush of Italian between the two men. Anne sat very still, listening. Dakota was doing just fine. He was homing in. It was better for her to stay out of it at the moment.

"He says Caroline was supposed to see him on Thursday afternoon, the day she was killed. He had asked her to meet him. They hadn't seen each other for a while and he was missing her a lot. She said that she would come, that she would meet him at a certain place on the grounds of the Cathedral. He waited, but she didn't show up."

Boccucci was speaking quickly and intently as though he did not want to forget one thing that Emile had told him. "So he went to find her. He went to her apartment building that evening and he waited outside. It was about six-thirty, he says. There is a little park right across the street from the building and he waited there. He thought he might see her come in or out. But she didn't."

"So, what did he do then?"

"He went home. He took the bus. He's staying with some of the other stone carvers nearby in Adams Morgan. The work foreman got the place for them."

"I don't believe him," Dakota said again. "If Caroline stood him up and he wanted to see her . . . if he wanted it

badly enough, why didn't he go across the street and see
if she was home?''

"He says he'd never been to her apartment, that he had
walked home with her after a tutoring session once so he
knew where she lived. He says he was afraid that she didn't
want to see him.''

"Why not?''

Boccucci turned to Emile Farrare. *"Perchè Carolina non
vuole vedermi te*?''

Emile hesitated and then responded with a certain harshness in English. "It is because we have a quarrel over this,
we are lovers and we are not lovers. It is hard to be so.''

"Ask him if anyone saw him sitting in the park. Did he
have a conversation with anyone?''

Boccucci asked, then said, "No. He talked to no one.''

Dakota was looking at Emile's tool belt lying on the
table. "Ask him to tell us about his tools,'' he said to Boccucci.

The young man took the belt in his hand and pulled
out each tool. He laid them on the table. Two hammers,
a wire cutter, drill bits, a file, several chisels. "They are
mine.'' he said. "All belong to me. I bring them from
home.''

"May I?'' Dakota picked the sharpest-tipped chisel. It
resembled an ice pick. He ran his fingers down its length.
"You keep your tools very clean, very neat.''

"*Sì*. I keep my tools very good.''

"This one . . . makes a good murder weapon.'' Dakota
held the chisel flat on the palm of his hand. Its tip appeared
sharpened, it looked freshly serrated. "Did you sharpen this
tool, Emile?''

"It is to carve stone with.'' Emile took the chisel from
Dakota. He held it with his fingers. "See, you put like this
and hit like this . . . so easy with the hammer. It is for the
delicate . . . the very fine work in stone.''

"I understand,'' said Dakota. "I understand what it is
intended for.'' He took the chisel back from Emile. "I'm
going to hold on to this, if you don't mind. I'll see you get
it back.''

Emile Farrare's face showed his confusion. "I need this tool. I need the chisel for my work."

"You'll get it back after the crime lab has a look at it."

The young man leaned forward with his fist clenched. He said something earnestly to Boccucci.

"What's he saying?" asked Dakota.

"He says he is sorry that Caroline is dead . . . that if he could, he would kill her murderer with his chisel. He says he would do that and feel no regret about it, that it would be his pleasure and his honor."

"Jesus," said Dakota. The chair scraped as he stood up. He looked at Anne. "Let's go out in the hall and talk about this, Fitzhugh."

The door closed behind them. The dark empty hall offered a kind of intimacy. Dakota folded his arms across his chest, leaned against the wall and stared down at her. "How come you were so quiet in there? That's not like you, Fitzhugh. I expected to hear a few 'my instincts tell me' . . . but no. You sit there, quiet, just watching the show."

"You didn't need any help from me. You were doing fine."

He leaned his head back against the wall and said, with something mournful and aching in his face, "You want to tell me why you were at the Cathedral with Clore tonight, Fitzhugh? Or is it none of my business?"

"It's none of your business. I was off-duty, remember."

He was silent for a moment, staring at her. "So," he said, finally. "About this Italian kid, Farrare, you think we've got enough to hold him, Fitzhugh? I mean, overnight, 'on suspicion of'?"

"What's the point?" She could be abrupt as well. "He isn't going anywhere. Send the chisel to the lab in the morning and see what they have to say."

"You think Farrare did it?"

She was too tired to think. So was he.

She could see the lines of fatigue etched in his face, a stubble of beard. This difficult man—how he touched her heart at times. "I don't trust my instincts tonight, Dakota." she said wearily, "not about anything."

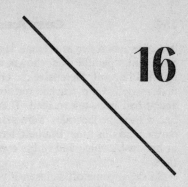

16

Thursday morning came too soon. She was struggling out of a dream. She and Dakota were in a rowboat caught somewhere above a waterfall. Where were the oars? Lost . . . forgotten. Had they fallen overboard? Anne let the telephone ring three times before she reached to answer it.

"Sorry if I'm waking you." Alan's warm, intimate voice was like a reassuring hand touching her. It brought her out of the dream. She raised her head from the pillow and looked at the clock on the bedside table. Almost seven.

"We talked about dinner tonight, but something's come up in the home district that I need to attend to," Alan explained. "If I stay the night, I can also attend the peanut farmers' dinner. Which, by all rights, I probably should."

"You want me to talk you out of it." She smiled, in spite of herself. "The truth is, Alan, I was working last night until late, too late. I probably need to relax by myself anyway. Stay down home like the good congressional representative that you are, and I'll unwind. We can spend some time together this weekend."

She buried her head back in the pillow. Alan Foley was always there for her, her friend. Maybe, in time . . . her husband. It was what he wanted. Did she? She'd probably not regret it if she married him. Anyway—and she had to accept it—no one was going to be really right after Rob. She was out of the love country, out for good.

Or . . . was she?

She stared hard at the ceiling, thinking of how Dakota

153

had questioned her in the hall last night about Jesse Core. Something painful had shown in Dakota's eyes. She'd brushed him off. Defensive . . . oh yes, Anne, you were as fake as hell. He'd reached out to her on a personal level, and it had been unexpected. That's what had thrown her. She'd thought the rules were set, a cool and professional partnership this time. But he'd let his feelings for her show in his husky voice and in his eyes. He'd lowered the barriers.

So she'd come off as insensitive. Maybe that was just as well. Stick with safe, Anne buoyed herself. No matter that he thinks you are a sassy rich girl, spoiled rotten and playing detective just to keep yourself occupied between lovers. Stay cool and professional, and Dakota can't hurt you. Keep your mind on the work, Anne . . . the all-healing work.

"I don't see how you can look so damned bright in the morning when I'm feeling like hell," Dakota mumbled when Anne arrived with a paper tray of doughnuts and coffee.

"I wasn't the one up all night." She took coffee and a doughnut to her side of the aisle. It was going to be all right between them. She took a deep breath.

The phone rang on Dakota's desk.

"Right," he said into the receiver.

He hung up with a glum look. "Well that's that, kid. The lab spent five minutes with Farrare's chisel this morning and knew it wasn't the murder weapon. Caroline was killed with a shorter, finer-edged blade. You drove him home last night." Dakota leaned back in his chair. "What do you think, Fitzhugh?"

"I think he's a scared young Italian stone carver with the face and physique of a Botticelli angel. A passionate angel . . . a young, far-from-home angel. It's possible he killed her."

"Loved her and killed her. Just another crime of passion. How did he get into the apartment building, you think?"

Anne was twisting a lock of dark hair around her finger.

"The doorman didn't see Caroline enter the building last Thursday night. One of the tenants, a half-blind old man at that, *thought* he saw her getting on the elevator and *thought* she was alone. Maybe she wasn't. Maybe Emile Farrare came into the apartment building with her."

"So you think Farrare wasn't stood up last Thursday afternoon after all. You think maybe they met in the garden as planned and Caroline took him home with her?"

"It's possible, Dakota. Caroline clearly had 'see E' written on her calendar. Emile claims she never appeared. That's what he says . . . it doesn't mean it's the truth."

"You can't make love on a garden bench. Having sex was on Emile Ferrare's mind . . . right square on his mind whether he could articulate it in English or not."

"Emile said they weren't sleeping together, Dakota."

"I know what he said. I heard him."

Anne's mind went back to her conversation with Jesse Clore in his study. There had been an implied confidentiality in what he had told her about Caroline—the girl searching for love in all the wrong places.

"She was sexually active," Anne said. "I mean, Caroline was pregnant."

"An unpleasant complication that could spoil a love affair for a romantic type like Caroline," said Dakota.

"It doesn't have to be Emile Ferrare."

He laughed. "You're thinking some other guy knocked her up and then walked away?"

"Dakota, you can be gross sometimes."

"I can be gross most of the time. I am thinking lewd thoughts *all* the time." He grinned, but it was guarded. He wiped jelly off his fingers.

Anne had spread her telephone messages from the day before on the desk in front of her. "Nicky Nelson's been trying to get us. She called three times yesterday asking for you or me. What do you think?"

"Give her a call. See what she wants."

Anne dialed Nicky's number. After four rings, the answering machine came on. It was Nicky's slightly surly voice with a slightly surly request for the caller to leave a message. Anne responded that she was returning Nicky's calls from yesterday. She would try to touch base later. She had barely replaced the receiver when the phone rang on her desk.

"I hope you slept better than I did," said Jesse Clore. "I'm something of an insomniac anyway."

She looked across the aisle at Dakota. He avoided her eyes. He was tapping his thumb on the edge of the desk. How the devil did he know who this was?

"I was going to call you. About Emile Ferrare," she said into the receiver.

"He's on my mind also. How did your talk with him go?"

"I think he's a troubled young man, lonely and far from home, vulnerable to Caroline's charms. She was beautiful and kind to him. He probably fell for her and was tremendously hurt when she pulled back."

"Have you got him . . . under arrest, Anne?"

"No. There's no evidence to say he killed her, Jess. We haven't gotten that far."

He sounded relieved. "I'm glad. Is it all right if I talk with him? He could probably use someone in his corner right now."

"Yes, talk with him by all means. You should find him at work this morning as usual."

"It will have to be this afternoon. Actually, that's why I called you so early. Virginia Carver and her husband have returned home and she called about putting flowers on the altar this Sunday in memory of Caroline."

"How is she taking her daughter's death?"

"With a certain philosophic calmness, one might say. She spoke of 'God's will.' " There was a certain tension in Jesse Clore's voice as he spoke. "I don't know why, but that phrase irritates me. I seem always to be in a kind of struggle with God and his will. I don't understand people who accept tragedy so well."

There was a pause.

"We have more in common than I realized," Anne said.

"Yes," he said. "I rather thought we did."

She glanced across the aisle. Dakota was gone. She saw him at the far end of the squad room, just disappearing through the door.

"Listen," Jesse continued, "I'm going out to the Carvers' house this morning. I mentioned you . . . and the fact that you were working with Lieutenant Dakota on the case and they said it would be fine if you two came along. They want to be as helpful as possible. Virginia said she was up to facing it all now, that she would, in fact, be happy to talk with the two of you."

"Dakota and I haven't matched our plans for the day yet. I'll talk with him. One, or maybe both of us, will be there . . . around ten."

"I hope it is you," Jesse Clore said. "You are prettier."

The Caroline McKelvey file still lay on Dakota's desk. The picture of Caroline that the photo lab had copied for Dakota was near the top of the file. Anne studied it for a long moment, studied the curve of cheek, the full lower lip. There was something wonderfully innocent and at the same time very sexy about this girl's face. Someone should have loved her. But someone had killed her.

Anne turned to the coroner's report. That "someone" had murdered Caroline McKelvey in a most unusual way. Directly, face-on. Caroline would have trusted Emile. In the beginning, at least. Especially if they'd been lovers . . . in denying that, she might have lied to Jesse Clore, embarrassed to admit the truth . . . and the fact she was pregnant. *If* she and Emile Farrare were lovers, then unquestioningly there'd been a lovers' quarrel.

Emile had said, "We are lovers and we are not lovers. It is hard to be so." Caroline would have seen the futility in the situation and, in telling Jesse Clore, her father confessor, that she was pulling back from Emile, she would have been telling the truth. Had Emile Farrare threatened her then, even in a subtle way? Thus, the mace and her reluctance to see him again. And yet, in the end, she had agreed to.

Possibly she had brought him back to her apartment to

talk things out . . . to soothe him. She was making tea when their conversation turned into an argument. Anne re-created the scene in her mind—Caroline turning from the stove unexpectedly. There Emile stood on the other side of the bar with some sharpened tool in his hand. Anne searched through the manila file for the photos taken at the scene by the crime lab. The broken teacup lay on the floor.

Perhaps, Caroline had been frozen with fear at his approach. Anne pictured Emile's impassioned face, those dark eyes ablaze. Quickly he'd raised the weapon and sliced the girl's throat before she could react.

Anne studied the picture. Caroline had fallen over the bar, her face caught in profile against the backdrop of blood. On the counter beside her outstretched hand was a grocery bag.

A grocery bag! Anne frowned. Where did that fit in?

Caroline and Emile might have stopped for groceries, planning to have dinner in Caroline's apartment. A reconciliation that hadn't worked out. Where had that bag of groceries come from? Was Emile Farrare with Caroline when she bought them?

Anne dug out her notebook from her purse. She wrote down "Is there a grocery store between Cathedral and apartment?" Also, "Ask Nicky where Caroline usually shopped for groceries?" She put the file back on Dakota's desk. He was just coming back into the squad room. He looked distracted, preoccupied. His blue eyes were dark and thoughtful.

"Listen," she said, "I was just thinking . . . "

"You listen." His shoulder brushed hers. "I'm not up to theories this morning. I've got things on my mind."

"Dakota, which case are you working on anyway?"

"Don't give me any grief, Fitzhugh. I don't answer to you."

His curt tone stung Anne. "You are such a bastard sometimes, Dakota! I don't think we should work together again. Ever."

There was something both angry and remote in his face.

"That suits me fine, lady. You don't know what policework is all about anyway. You are playing at it, thrill-seeking, aren't you? A little high-class dalliance on your part? You don't really get your feet wet, Fitzhugh."

He turned abruptly and walked out.

There was only one other detective in the squad room. Lee Williams, a tall slim black man. He walked slowly past Anne. His eyes said he agreed with Dakota. Still, he whispered over his shoulder, "You are right, honey, Dakota is some kind of bastard."

Anne took the McKelvey file to her own desk. Dakota was off doing his own thing. This was fine with her. She would work on the case by herself—in her own way, with pleasure.

She scooped up the telephone messages, three from Nicky Nelson, all yesterday's calls. One from Alex Shannon. It read "Sorry I didn't see you leave last night. Hope you got all the information you wanted. No need to call back." There was one from Alfred Harris, the building super at The Alhambra. It was for Detectives Dakota and Fitzhugh. "Can you stop by sometime? A matter of some interest."

There was a message from Simone Gray. No telephone number given. The message said, "Will call you tomorrow." The department secretary had written at the bottom of the pink slip, "Is this *the* Simone Gray?"

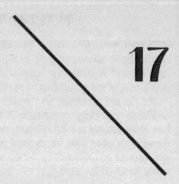

17

Virginia and Peter Carver's home lay in the northwest section of Washington, a handsome part of town called Spring Valley.

Anne Fitzhugh knew it well. It was part of her other world—that influential and restless Washington political-society world in which she and Rob had lived. Without Rob beside her, that world seemed to her spun out on money and "who was in and who was out"—like fine sugar . . . like angel food cake, without substance.

An unfair judgment, admitted Anne, slamming the car door behind her. The educated and elegant of Washington were just that. Educated, elegant, powerful . . . and diverse. Perhaps she only wanted to suffer. "Eat bitter bread if you must," Alan had said to her soberly, "you will come back where you belong in time."

The Carvers' house was English Tudor in its design, the stone walkway was lined with boxwood. Mums of palest bronze filled massive planters which stood like sentinels on either side of the front double doors. The house sprawled on a wide lot, three floors and a turret above the dark slate roof, a glassed-in sun room on the far right, garages in back. There were black wrought-iron burglar bars on all the lower windows. It was the setting of wealth and containment. One imagined order within.

Anne heard the doorbell chime. She waited, then pressed the bell again.

Virginia Carver opened the door. "Sorry . . . so sorry to

keep you waiting.'' She held out her hand to Anne, a cool but gracious squeeze of fingers. ''Detective Fitzhugh, isn't it? Please come in. We were expecting you.''

The carpet was deep and springy; the house smelled of lemon polish and the lushness of flowers. Roses, lilies, flowering plants were artfully arranged everywhere.

Virginia Carver said, ''Our friends have been wonderful, so supportive. We found the house absolutely brimming with flowers and food when we returned last night. It helps, you know. Every little bit of love and support helps.''

She ushered Anne into a high-ceilinged morning room in the back of the house. A silver coffee dispenser, cups, dainty napkins, waited on the coffee table before the bright-patterned chintz sofa.

What had Dakota said once about walking into a play scene? Something unreal and very real at the same time. She sensed it here as well.

''I am very sorry about the loss of your daughter,'' Anne said. She could see herself in the tall mirror above the desk in one corner of the room. There was color in the cheeks but her gray eyes were deep and calm, like winter on the pond. ''And I'm grateful that you will see me today. This can't be easy for you.''

Caroline's mother was small and erect in her bearing. She wore a black knit dress, simple and expensive. There were pearls in her ears and at her throat. She gestured for Anne to sit down and said just a shade wearily, ''I thought we had told all we knew about this terrible thing . . . this tragedy of ours . . . to Lieutenant Dakota over the weekend. It is so hard to talk about, so painful to go over yet once again.''

''I know you want to put it behind you,'' Anne said. Yes, that was it. Virginia Carver wanted to put it behind her. No resolution necessary, no questions asked . . . no answers necessary. It was not the reaction she had expected from Caroline's mother, but she understood.

Now that she had met Virginia Carver, even in these few minutes, she understood. Ugly business was not for this small regal lady. An investigation meant prying into things, holding the family up to scrutiny. The press could be terribly intrusive, especially in Washington. She could read Virginia Carver's thoughts. And it could be cruel. Nothing was ever portrayed correctly in the papers. Caroline, Virginia Carver would say, did not deserve that.

"She is dead," Virginia said with a quiet sort of dignity. She sat with her shoulders back, her hands quiet in her lap. "My beautiful daughter is dead and nothing can bring her back."

As if that was somehow settled, she reached to pour Anne a cup of coffee. Her hands were careful and steady, freshly manicured. An emerald ring encircled with pearls sparkled.

Virginia Carver went on rather briskly, "We've talked with Nicky Nelson, Caroline's roommate. She says it was a burglar, some kind of street-smart fellow who managed to get into the building despite the security. I mean those things happen every day. Whoever it was probably just knocked on the apartment door and Caroline opened it. She was like that, so trusting. She would have opened the door to anyone."

"No," Anne said, "no cream or sugar." She took the delicate Lenox coffee cup.

"Where is the other detective, the one who is handling the case, Lieutenant Dakota?" Virginia Carver sounded querulous.

"We're both handling this case, actually. This morning my partner is occupied . . . elsewhere."

"I went over everything with him, of course. We spent several hours together on Saturday morning. He came here, I showed him Caroline's school yearbooks, her cotillion pictures, her scrapbook, everything. He was marvelous. He came to her funeral, did you know that?"

I know that, Anne wanted to say. She wanted to say I was out of town myself. I was not yet assigned to the case. Don't try to put me down, Mrs. Peter Carver. Don't compare me with Dakota. I want to find Caroline's killer just as badly as he does. Just give me some help, that is what I need from you. She said nothing. She sipped her coffee.

"Well, hello." Jesse Clore stood in the doorway. His smile encompassed them both.

He came into the morning room followed by Peter Carver. Equally tall, but with elegant sparse bones, the older man wore a white silk shirt, a dark scarf at his thin neck. He seemed but a long shadow of the broad-shouldered young canon.

Carver acknowledged his wife's introduction of Anne with a nod and a vague smile . . . a smile that did not hide the fact that his eyes were shrewd and had taken her in carefully.

Jesse Clore sat down beside Anne on the sofa. He smelled just slightly of spice and leather. She remembered the scent from the night before.

"This has been the most horrendous few days," Virginia Carver was saying. "You can imagine. Some friends lent us their house down on the North Carolina coast . . . at Duck, you probably know it. Peter and I left right after the funeral. We had to get away, and we thought we'd stay a week or maybe more . . . "

Her husband interrupted. "It had been a real nightmare over the weekend. Reporters calling, friends, the police. A bloody nightmare! However, it didn't seem to help whether we were here or there, we were so terribly depressed. So, after a few days, we decided to come back home and try to . . . go on with life. It is all one can do, really."

Peter Carver took a cup from the tray and smiled for the first time. "Again, thanks for coming out this morning, Jesse. I am particularly glad we got our business all set-tled."

Clore turned to Anne. He said in a low voice, "We were in Peter's study when you arrived. The Carvers want to underwrite some new stone work at the Cathedral to com-memorate Caroline's life. They thought maybe a bench in the garden, in the Close . . . or a statue in the Cathedral itself. Perhaps an angel."

The irony was in Jesse Clore's eyes, not in his voice.

"My daughter loved the Cathedral so much," Virginia Carver said. "She saw it as a place of beauty and serenity."

"And solace," said Jesse.

Virginia frowned. "I can't imagine that Caroline needed solace. But, let's say, that a memorial to her is appropriate there."

"You'll be pleased to know that others share your thoughts. In my mail this morning I found a letter from Gertrude Woodward." Clore drew an envelope from his breast pocket. "The Woodwards would like to make a donation to the Cathedral in Caroline's name. They used the same word . . . 'appropriate.' "

"Oh, I am pleased." There was a graceful clasp of hands. " . . . so kind of Gertrude and Jim. You did not know my daughter." Virginia Carver was looking directly at Anne. "She was quite lovely, spiritual in nature."

"I've heard a great deal about her in the past few days. She was special, remarkable. I would entirely agree with that."

It seemed the time to get on with the substance of the interview. Anne began with some passion, "Mrs. Carver, I can't discount entirely Nicky Nelson's theory . . . that a stranger, a potential burglar, if you will, killed your daughter. But it doesn't hold up, you know. The evidence suggests otherwise. My partner and I are convinced that Caroline was killed by someone she knew. I'd like to talk about that."

Virginia Carver put her cup down carefully on the silver tray. "I think that suggestion is ludicrous! It suggests that someone she knew would have *wanted* to kill Caroline! She worked for a distinguished congressman. She was engaged to be married in the spring to a fine upstanding young man whose family I have known for years. There was no one . . . no one in her life who had the slightest reason to murder my daughter. I find the idea insulting."

"Did she talk to you about any other men, Mrs. Carver?" Anne knew the question had to be asked. "I am talking about lovers . . . complications, maybe a heartbreak, even a threat?"

"Absolutely not! Never! Lovers, what an idea! She had beaux in college, lots of them, darling boys . . . nothing serious, however. Then, she got engaged to Daryl, and there's been no one since.''

Anne nodded her acceptance of Virginia's version of Caroline's romantic life, conscious of Jesse Clore, who was still and silent beside her. Virginia Carver obviously did not know or want to know about the real Caroline.

''Did you ever hear Caroline mention the name Emile Farrare?''

Virginia Carver's face was blank. She shook her head.

''Is that a name we should know?'' Peter Carver asked.

''If you don't know it, then you don't.'' Anne sighed. ''I rather thought you wouldn't. Emile is, however, someone Caroline knew well. What about the people in Woodward's office . . . did she ever talk to you about any particular person that she worked with on the Hill?''

It seemed to Anne that Virginia Carver brightened somewhat. ''My goodness, she talked about her work a lot! And about a lot of people. . . . Congressmen, senators! You know how she was about environmental issues. She adored Jim Woodward, thought he hung the moon! I keep thinking now how pleased she would be about his appointment yesterday. She would have been right there with him too in all the limelight. If only . . . ''

For just a moment, it looked as though Virginia's eyes glazed with tears. The moment was passed, the emotion controlled.

''Did she speak of Alex Shannon, Mrs. Carver?''

''Of course. Actually, for a time there, I rather thought . . .'' Virginia waved her hand as if to brush something away.

Anne straightened on the sofa. ''What did you think, for a time, anyway?''

''You know the men were always smitten with Caroline. I believe Alex was quite taken with her for a while, but she was always true-blue to Daryl! That was how Caroline was!''

''What led you to think Shannon was smitten with Caroline?'' Anne pressed the point.

''Well, this may sound strange. But he came by to see

me one day to talk about her. She had been working there for about six weeks and one Saturday afternoon, here was Alex standing at my door. He hadn't called or anything. He said he was going jogging on the canal and he thought he'd stop by. He did have his dog in the car actually, so I guess that was true."

"You knew Alex . . . personally, socially?"

Virginia wrinkled her nose. "I don't think we've ever been with the Woodwards when he wasn't along. He's doted on by them both. Alex was something of an incorrigible boy before the Woodwards got him, that's the story anyway, but he's quite brilliant. An opportunist I've always thought, but quite brilliant. Jim says he'll have his own seat in Congress one day. Or a prestigious law office or a lobbyist firm. Jim and Gertrude depend on him for everything. You know how Jim is, rather scattery!"

"Really, darling." Peter Carver was amused. "Scattery! You are talking about a man just appointed to a cabinet post!"

"No matter! Jim Woodward has his head in the clouds. He's scattery . . . visionary, ever so charismatic! Gertrude has the business sense . . . and Alex knows how to use the political scalpel." Virginia's words were quick and knowing.

"And Alex Shannon wanted to talk with you that day about Caroline?" Anne said.

"Yes, he said he just wanted to tell me what a marvelous job Caroline was doing in the office. But it was more than that." Virginia plucked an invisible thread from her black skirt. "He asked me a million questions about her. Just like a man who is smitten with a girl. He wanted to know about her friends and her interests. He wanted to know about Daryl."

"Did you talk about this with Caroline?"

"I don't know that I did." Virginia looked vague.

"Oh yes, you did, my darling," Peter Carver interrupted. "You told that same story at dinner a few weeks later and Caroline said rather hotly, 'Mother, they are not even in the same league. Daryl has integrity and Alex would do

service for the devil if it would serve his own ends.' I
remember that clearly because only a few weeks earlier,
she had spoken well of Shannon.''

"What had she said of him?" asked Anne.

"Oh, I don't know." Carver rubbed his chin as he
thought. "Perhaps only that Shannon was intelligent, persuasive. Caroline had quick enthusiasms and high expec-
tations of people. No doubt she observed Shannon playing
a political game or so, and it disillusioned her." He chuckled rather softly. "She was like that, you know. Quite
starry-eyed. I say, do you know the ABC correspondent,
Simone Gray?"

Anne felt Jesse Clore jostle her arm with surprise.

"Of course," she said. "Why do you ask?"

"Well, I was just thinking of something quite amusing."
Peter Carver sat down in a vivid green wing chair, stretched
his long legs crossed at the ankles in front of him. It was
obvious that he was going to relate a favorite anecdote.

"Don't go on, Peter. You are going to make Caroline
sound foolish," said Virginia.

"No, it's an amusing story and so typical of the girl."

Was there something malicious in this? Anne sensed that
there might be. Peter Carver was enjoying himself too
much.

"Well, you see," Carver began, "Simone Gray happens
to live in the same apartment building. Caroline got to
know Simone quite well. Or, at least, she thought she did.
She was always going on about 'Simone this' and 'Simone
that.' I would almost call it a schoolgirl crush, and rather
typical of Caroline, if I do say so."

"Really, Peter," murmured Virginia crossly, "this isn't
necessary. You are just gossiping."

"Gossiping is a cultivated art form in Washington,"
said Carver. "Politicians and the media are always fair
game . . . you have to agree with that, darling!"

"Go on then, if you must."

Pleased with himself, Carver leaned forward in his chair.
"Actually, it was Nicky who told us this story, but Caroline
didn't . . . couldn't deny it. It seems that Simone frequents

a well-known bar on occasion . . . and she has been known to get more than a little smashed and do things she is sorry about later. That surprises you, I am sure, the cool and lovely Simone Gray.''

''What has this got to do with Caroline?'' Clore stirred uneasily, clenching his hands together.

''Hang on. It seems that Simone brought someone back home for a night cap recently, some high-flyer businessman she met at this bar. The guy was a sadist. He had Simone's clothes off and was pounding her around. She managed a call upstairs and whispered to Caroline that she was in trouble. Of course, Caroline and Nicky go rushing down. It's three in the morning and Caroline is in her PJ's. The guy gets totally bluffed by Caroline with the butcher knife in her hand and slinks out of there. Picture it, wide-eyed Caroline helping out the famous Simone Gray. Nicky tells it better than I do. She said Caroline was shaken right down to her toes by that one.''

''I think that was a pretty rotten story,'' Anne said to Jesse. His car, a battered Volkswagen, was parked behind hers. They had left the Carvers together. ''Just what the point was, I'm not sure.''

Jesse Clore looked distracted, close to anger.

The meeting with the Carvers was in its own way helpful. She said, ''I think I understand Caroline McKelvey better now.''

''Yes. I thought you would.''

He squeezed Anne's arm hard. ''The bastard, telling an ugly story like that! I almost hate to take his money for the memorial to Caroline. I'd like to have thrown it back in his face.''

He was trembling. The pain in Jesse Clore's face stayed with Anne as she drove away.

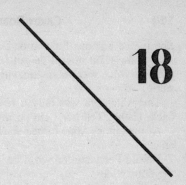

18

Peter Carver had told a rotten story. Pointless, actually.

What was interesting was what it said about Peter Carver, a sort of meanness of spirit covered with only a thin veneer of intelligence and charm.

Jesse Clore's reaction to the story about Simone Gray had been surprising. He was a worldly man and had no doubt heard stories worse than that. Especially in Washington. Yet, he had reacted strongly, with more than disdain . . . with a visceral sort of anger.

She liked that. There was a lot she liked about Father Anthony Jesse Clore.

In the splintered sunshine, Anne rode up Nebraska toward Ward Circle. It was only eleven. She was uncertain how to spend the rest of the morning. Somewhere in the back of her mind, there was Don Dakota. Where did he think he was anyway . . . still playing tight-end for the Redskins? Why couldn't he just get his act together and focus on one case at a time?

The trouble was, Dakota was a man driven. Maybe he had been on Homicide too long. One of the older detectives, she thought it was Quantrille, had said once, "The Catch-22 of the whole thing is . . . if you're sharp enough to be in Homicide, then you are sharp enough to understand that it is so messed up you don't want to be there."

The walkie-talkie was squawking on the seat beside her. Anne flipped it on, "What is it, Cathy?"

"Nicky Nelson called again. The one from yesterday.

She is real anxious for you or Dakota to get in touch. She is at home right now. I've got her number here." Cathy's familiar voice was pragmatic, vaguely sweet and filled with static.

The Alhambra was only a few blocks away. "Call her back, Cathy. Tell her I am on my way."

At the circle, Anne turned south onto Massachusetts Avenue.

Harold Perry smiled when he saw her approaching, held the door wide.

"What are you doing on duty in the daytime?" she asked him.

"Just fillin' in," he said amicably. "A little extra money in my pocket." He patted the side of his uniform trousers.

She stepped into the cool of the lobby. "While you have a moment, Harold, let me just go over a few points with you again. The night Caroline McKelvey was killed, you were on duty but you didn't see her come in. That's what you told me."

"Naw. I must have been carrying some groceries upstairs for one of the old folks, or something. I didn't see her. She must have used her key."

"Are you sure this front door was locked? You are certain of that?" She'd asked him before. Now she asked again.

"Absolutely, for certain the door was locked!" Harold spoke in a tone of complete righteousness. "I know my job. I wouldn't go off and leave the street door unlocked so anybody could come in off the street. Mr. Harris is strong about that."

If it had indeed been Emile Farrare who'd killed Caroline, then he'd entered the building with her. That covered "access."

"Harold, you gave me a list of all those who came into the building last Thursday evening while you were on duty. Did anybody go *out* of the building later that you had missed coming in? I am thinking in particular of a young man, probably in work clothes, maybe high-heeled cowboy boots . . . fancy boots with pointed toes, dark curly hair?"

He shook his head. "I didn't see anyone like that. But leaving is a different matter than coming in. You see, you just push the door and it opens. The same is true of the delivery door in back. You can't get in without a key, but you can get out easy enough."

Anne rode up to the sixth floor in the brass-walled elevator. An older woman with a wire pushcart full of groceries in brown paper bags rode up with her. "May I ask you," Anne said, "is there a grocery or deli close by?"

"Up the street a bit." The woman nodded. "The apartment building on the corner, where the Italian restaurant is, has a nice little shop. Fresh veggies. I recommend it, I really do."

"You mean the building across from the Cathedral?"

"Down from there some, the next block. It is across from St. Albans school. Don't go at three in the afternoon. Those boys are all in there buying candy and stuff."

Close enough, between here and the Cathedral.

The elevator doors opened on the sixth floor. Anne said goodbye to the little lady in the hat. There had been a ceiling light out on this floor when she was here yesterday. Today it was fixed.

Nicky opened the door before Anne knocked. She looked just out of the shower. She had on a ratty green bathrobe. Her head was wrapped in a towel. "Harold called and said you were on the way up. They're being extra careful around here now. All I can say is thank God for that."

It seemed to Anne that Nicky Nelson was talking in a more staccato voice than usual. Jumpy, she motioned Anne in with a quick look down the hall, slammed the door shut behind them and bolted it. It was a dead-bolt, newly installed.

"Is something wrong, Nicky?" The apartment was a mess. The charm that had been Caroline McKelvey's was gone.

The girl threw herself down heavily on the sofa. "Yes, something is wrong! Something is very wrong. I believe someone is after me, someone is actually trying to kill me."

For a long moment, Anne stared down at her.

It would not have surprised her for Nicky to be staging some kind of dramatic scene and yet there was authenticity in Nicky Nelson's pallor, her look of fear.

Anne pulled a footstool close to the sofa and sat down. "What makes you think someone is trying to kill you, Nicky?"

"Things . . . keep happening. Someone has been calling here and then hanging up when I answer. I mean, I didn't mention it to you yesterday when you were here but I am certain someone is watching, keeping tabs on me."

"Your name has been in the paper. There are crazies that get their kicks from reading about murders in the paper and . . . getting involved. The phone calls will probably stop in a couple of days."

"Then, my keys disappeared from my purse. I can't say just where or when but yesterday when I went to get them out of my purse at work, they were gone. Thank goodness, I keep a spare set. And the third thing, I guess it was about three o'clock this morning, I was coming home and I parked in back as usual. I got out of my car and I was starting to walk around the building and I heard someone behind me. Someone was there, waiting for me, I sensed it."

"Did you see anyone?"

"Yes, I saw someone, for God's sake! At least, a shadow. As it happened, another car pulled up on Garfield Street. Some kids were in the car and they must have frightened away whoever was following me. In a minute, headlights came on at the back of our parking lot and a car slid out and pulled away fast. I think it was a dark sedan, medium-size, like a Volvo or a Honda."

"Is that all?" Anne felt vaguely let down.

"Isn't it enough? I mean whoever got Caroline is trying to get me. I know it, I really do. I want some protection." There was something both scared and bitter in the girl's face.

"Let's talk about this rationally, Nicky. On Monday and again on Wednesday, you did your best to convince Dakota and me that Caroline's killer was a burglar who just *hap-*

pened to be in this apartment when she got home and just *happened* to kill her. An unfortunate *happen*stance. And now it is Thursday and you are saying 'whoever killed Caroline is out to get me also.' You can't have it both ways.''

''I called my father this morning.'' It was as if the girl did not hear Anne but was listening only to herself ''I told him I was coming up to New York for a few days. I told him I would be up on Saturday.''

Nicky looked at Anne in a determined way. ''I want protection from the police until then.''

Anne's head was beginning to throb.

''Let's go about this from a different direction. Let's say that you are right, and someone is after you. Then, why are they after you? Surely, you know or suspect the reason.''

There was no answer. Nicky's mouth was a stubborn line.

''What do you have, Nicky . . . that someone wants?''

''Information, probably.'' Nicky brought the words out slowly. ''Maybe I have a suspicion who Caroline's killer is. I am not saying I do, but maybe I do.''

''Well, for God's sake, share it with me! It's called 'withholding evidence.' Here I am beating my brains out trying to find my way through the sticky molasses and you are saying 'maybe I know who Caroline's killer is and maybe I don't.' ''

''No, I am not prepared to do that at this point.''

''Nicky, you are impossible!''

''I might be . . . but I am also scared and I need your help.'' Nicky gave a thin smile.

''All right, I'll trade you, protection for some questions answered. Honestly answered.''

''I am not promising you anything.''

''Did Caroline talk with you about her private life?''

''Not really.'' Nicky took the towel from her hair and began to dry the springy curls with her fingers. ''Caro kept a lot to herself.''

''You told Dakota that she was going to break her engagement to Daryl Swan. I want to know why you said that.''

"I said I *thought* she was. It was just a gut feeling on my part. She'd been talking lately about the future and what she wanted to do with her life and I didn't hear much about Daryl in it. Most people who are getting married in a few months are full of wedding plans. Caroline's mother was. But Caroline wasn't."

"What did your roommate want to do with her life?"

"Make a difference somewhere. Her work was important to her. That's all I can say."

"No, I think you can say more," Anne said. "You could tell me about the other men in Caroline's life."

"Like, who do you mean?"

"What can you tell me about Emile Farrare?"

"Oh," Nicky sighed. "I think I see where you are headed with this? O.K., so Caroline and Emile had this thing going for a while. She used to go over to the Cathedral . . . there is a sitting room downstairs beyond the Bethlehem Chapel. She was tutoring him in English after work some evenings and then afterward, they'd walk down the block for ice cream or coffee. They'd sit outside under some street umbrella. He was really hooked on her and it was very romantic for a while . . . just Caroline's thing. She saw him as a young Jesus, a depressed young Jesus . . . right out of the Italian hills. I swear she did!"

"How do you know this?"

"I met him once, and she talked about him. Trouble was Emile is Catholic and he's married to a girl back in Italy and has a little boy. A penniless stone carver here on a six months' green work card. When I heard that, I said, 'Caroline, break it off now. This guy is hopeless. He'll drag you down.' She agreed. She liked him but she wasn't really in love with him, just carried away with his troubles, his angst, his passion for her. She said she was going to let him down easy. And she did, she broke it off a few days later."

"Before she broke it off, did Caroline ever bring him here to the apartment? Do you think they were lovers, Caroline and Emile?"

"I really don't think so." Nicky spoke carefully as

though she was not entirely sure of her answer. "I can't say for sure. But I don't think so."

"Is it possible Caroline got pregnant with Emile's child? Do you think that is a possibility?"

Nicky stood up, suddenly restless. "Don't ask me all these questions! Caroline never talked to me about anything like that. She never said anything about anything like that! If she talked with anyone about personal things it was with Father Jesse. He was her best friend. Not me. But I will tell you one thing." She whirled in the green bathrobe. "Emile was very jealous of Caroline. When she broke off with him, he used to sit in the little park across the street and watch for her. He wanted to see if she was going out with anyone. He told Caroline he would kill anyone else that she fell in love with."

"How do you know that?"

"Caroline told me. She thought it was funny, actually."

"What did you think, Nicky?"

"I didn't have any use for Emile. I don't like pretty boys in high-heel boots."

There was a sudden firm knock at the door.

Nicky and Anne both looked toward the door. Nicky said, "I just had a new lock put on the door this morning, a dead-bolt. I am not having anything happen to me like happened to Caroline."

"It's me, Alfred Harris." The voice of the building superintendent was muffled but clear through the door. "I'd like to talk with Detective Fitzhugh. Is she there, Miss Nelson?"

Nicky sprung the lock and opened the door.

Alfred Harris had a large plastic bag in one hand. He stepped inside the apartment. There was a nervous look about his face, also a sense of excitement. "Harold told me that you were up here," he said to Anne. "I have something important to show you." He nodded to Nicky. "I guess . . . to both of you. At least, Harold and I think it is important. He should have mentioned it to you, Detective Fitzhugh. He should have told you that I wanted to see you." Alfred Harris's tone was reproving.

"My fault actually," said Anne. "I had a note that you called yesterday. I just hadn't gotten around to responding." Her eyes were fastened on the plastic trash bag.

"Well, this is just so strange. I mean, it has to be important to the case." Alfred Harris sat the bag down gingerly in front of him. It appeared to be lightweight.

Anne bent down, and opened the bag. It was filled with newspapers stained red with blood. She emptied them out upon the floor. "What is this, Mr. Harris?"

"Well, you see it is like this . . . these newspapers showed up in our trash bin. I mean, isn't this amazing? We try to keep newspapers separate from the rest of the trash but sometimes people just drop their papers right down the chute . . . there is a trash chute on every floor . . . and that is what happened here. Someone dropped these newspapers down that chute and Harold found them."

Alfred Harris bent over and touched one of the papers gingerly. "You can see how dried the blood is. It just happens that yesterday was Wednesday, the day for us to put our newspaper stacks out for D.C. pickup, and Harold was downstairs and he noticed these particular papers in with the trash. They could have slipped by so easily, these papers, with all the other trash. Anyway, Harold noticed. He pulled them out."

"Oh my God, look at this!" cried Nicky. She was down on the floor on her knees beside the papers. "Look at the date on this newspaper. It's last Thursday, the day that Caroline was killed."

"It's hard to say just when these papers went downstairs," Harris said. "The trash gets thrown in a big dumpster and that's where Harold found 'em."

Anne masked her fingers with tissues from her pocket and began to stuff the papers back into the plastic bag. What the crime lab would make of them, she wasn't sure. But they were a valuable find, that was for certain.

"Do you think this blood is Caroline's?" Nicky asked. She had moved away from the pile of papers.

Anne nodded. "The date on the newspapers is not just coincidence, Nicky, and this amount of blood is from big-time bleeding. The crime lab will tell us but I'm certain it's Caroline's blood.''

"The papers were probably on the floor," said Nicky. She stood up and moved toward the bar. "Some papers on the bar and some lying on the floor. That's why there wasn't any blood right there below the bar stool.''

She was right. Anne recalled clearly the crime lab's pictures. Two pools of blood on either side. There was no blood on the parquet floor directly at the foot of the bar. Why hadn't she and Dakota noticed that?

"Why would anyone go to the trouble to clean up and throw the papers away? That is what I wonder.'' Mr. Harris was looking around the apartment with a curious eye. His gaze followed Nicky, lingered on the bar area. As usual, the kitchen was littered. A newspaper was spread in some disarray on the surface of the bar.

"I mean,'' he continued, "how very curious that the murderer stopped to throw away some bloody newspapers.''

There were several things that Anne wanted to say. She didn't. She was looking down at the last section of the newspaper she was stuffing in the bag. There was the outline of a shoe's toe caught in the bloody pulpy papers in her hand. It looked like the toe of a boot. The pointed toe of a cowboy boot. The sight of it made her heart race.

"Tell Harold for me,'' she said calmly, "that he has a sharp eye. That was good detective work on his part.''

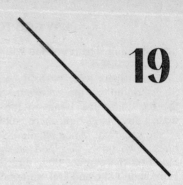

19

Anne placed the trash bag of newspapers in the trunk of the car. She hadn't a doubt that the blood on them would prove to be Caroline McKelvey's. Would the print, which appeared to be the outline of a pointed toe, be confirmed as just that—the toe print of a man's cowboy boot?

She slammed shut the trunk and decided to walk up the street in the direction of the Cathedral. Nicky had identified the store where Caroline bought most of their groceries as Dolkin's, a deli-grocery store located in the apartment building on the corner of Cathedral and Wisconsin.

As for the grocery bag found on the bar after Caroline was murdered, Nicky had listed its contents competently and quickly for Anne. "I emptied it out on Saturday," she said. "Threw away a package of boned chicken breasts. It had been sitting there since Thursday night and, anyway, I couldn't quite see myself eating Caroline's dinner." She'd made a wry face.

Did it seem to be dinner for one? Or dinner for two?

Nicky said there was a small loaf of French bread, a couple of potatoes for baking, the makings for salad, lettuce and a tomato, some radishes, garlic, a bottle of Paul Newman dressing, also a carton of strawberry yogurt and chocolate cookies. The cookie bag was already open . . . and there was a bottle of wine.

Anne had the wine with her now, the unopened bottle stuck in her shoulder bag. It was, ironically enough, an inexpensive Italian wine. She would ask the proprietors of

Dolkin's if they could recall the young woman who had purchased it last Thursday afternoon. Had she been alone or had there been someone with her?

"Ma'am . . . just a minute, ma'am!" Harold Perry called after her as Anne started up the street. He came out to the sidewalk.

"I wanted you to know that I've been racking my brains to be of some help. Miss McKelvey was one of the nicest folks I ever knew. I'd like to be all the help I can."

"Finding those newspapers was really special, Harold."

"That was just luck, but I thought of somethin' else that might be helpful. Somebody . . . it sounded like maybe a young guy or a woman, different-sounding, soft, you know . . . called The Alhambra 'round about quarter to six last Thursday afternoon. Wanted to know if Caroline McKelvey was home yet. I rang upstairs. There wasn't no one home."

"Different sounding . . . like an accent, maybe?"

"I don't know, ma'am. I mean, I could hardly hear. It was a muffled sort of voice. Like I said, it could'a been a woman. In all the 'citement since, I just forgot about that."

"Would you recognize the voice if you heard it again?"

He shrugged. "I don't know for sure."

It was a vague sort of clue, it wasn't much help.

Nor could the oriental woman who ran Dolkin's offer any assistance. She shook her head regretfully. "So many people come for their suppers. Come right in evening time. Last Thursday is now so far past. Memory all gone for then."

Anne came out of the cool cave of the store with a gritty sort of determination to make the woman remember. She would return later with Caroline's picture and one of Emile Farrare as well.

Better yet, if the blood on the newspapers was Caroline's and what looked like the toe of a boot was indeed a fancy cowboy boot print, she would come uptown tomorrow with a warrant for Emile's arrest. They'd stop by the deli-grocery, confront its proprietor and hope for an identification. This wasn't the kind of information you ignore.

* * *

Something out of the ordinary was happening on the third floor, Municipal Building on Indiana Avenue. As soon as she came into Homicide's outer office, Anne sensed something stirring in the air.

She gave the plastic bag to Cathy to send to the crime lab, and went back to the squad room looking for Dakota. She hoped to find The Cowboy in a better frame of mind than he'd been in in the morning. She had a lot to tell him. The squad room was buzzing. Anne saw Dakota, with his coat off and his shirt sleeves rolled up, at the far end of the room.

He was standing by the conference table with several other investigators and detectives gathered around him. Chief Wilson was with them and a couple of the DEA boys. They were studying a city map.

Boccucci motioned for Anne to join them. His dark eyes gleamed. "We've got a strike set for this afternoon. You want in?"

Anne looked to her partner; the big broad-shouldered detective was leaning over a map on the table. Dakota's head went up and he acknowledged her with a glance that lingered for a brief moment, but said nothing. He gave her a slight nod.

Chief Wilson said, "We can use you, Anne."

She moved in closer and listened. Dakota began to lay it out for the detectives, his usual low-pitched voice coming off taut. "This is the way it reads. I've got this little guy, see? A little 'big guy,' name is Donnie O. He saw his buddy murdered a few weeks back and he says he's going to play ball with us and testify. He's got a record, but not bad enough to make him unreliable. He'll pass."

Boccucci poked Anne in the ribs. "We're promising Donnie O a few favors . . . not to mention saving his hide. To prove good faith, he's going to pinpoint some big-shot drug dealers, one of whom killed his good buddy. It's going to happen this afternoon. We're gonna be there."

"Where?" asked Anne. "Where are we setting up?"

"Drake Place. Otherwise known as Death Valley or the . . . morgue."

"Logical place," whispered Anne, "and it's about time." She knew Drake Place well, its squalor and seamy reputation.

"Quiet down, Boccucci. Are you listening, Fitzhugh?" Dakota was staring pointedly at them.

"Listening, Lieutenant."

Dakota had the strike well organized. There'd be three unmarked cars going in to Drake Place, several more in the vicinity with uniformed cops waiting for word by radio to close in. Roadblocks were going up. Dakota would be in the advance car, the witness with him. Donnie O knew what was happening and when. He was going to take them right to it.

"This is a group down from New York, the Caribbean Mafia . . . right out of Jamaica, Haiti. They got rocks of crack with them. My guy says they'll be on the ridge above Drake Place about three this afternoon . . . yeah, that's right, this afternoon, not three in the morning. They're setting up business with their local warlords, one of which is the guy that stilled our man's buddy."

"What are we after . . . specifically?" asked Anne.

Dakota turned to her. "We're after justice, in general. We're after a few fellows in particular."

"We're expecting trouble," Buccucci murmured to Anne. "You could get out of this if you want. There's enough other stuff going on to keep you busy."

Anne was mesmerized by Dakota. She was caught by his fire. He was high on his own adrenaline, high on the prospect of action that had a bite in it. "I'm going along," she said. "I know Drake Place. We cruise down there enough. I know what we're supposed to do."

Anne went back to her desk. She opened her shoulder bag and took out her pistol. Usually she didn't wear a shoulder holster. Today she would. No encumbering purse, hands free. She took the holster out of the drawer and slid it under her jacket, stood up to buckle it.

"You're riding with me," said Dakota. He was in the aisle beside her desk.

"Is that a question or a statement?"

"It's going to be rough, Fitzhugh. Bullets are going to fly. Count on it."

She *was* counting on it. She laid the pistol on her desk. It was new, a new issue—a Glock 17 automatic. Its nose was shorter than her old six-shot Smith & Wesson .38. This 9 mm had a seventeen-round box magazine. It fired every time the trigger was squeezed, ten additional bullets before reloading.

She stared at the pistol. She wasn't entirely comfortable with it yet, although she had spent more than forty hours target practicing with the Glock.

"You know how to use that thing, Fitzhugh?"

Anne flushed. He didn't trust her nerve. That was part of the tension between them. She wondered if she trusted herself. Her fingers were cold and trembling slightly. She stood up, slid the revolver into her holster. "I'm riding with you, Dakota, you'll see for yourself."

Drake Place was in the southeast part of the city in the D.C. Metropolitan Police Department's Sixth District. It was an area of sloping gray pockmarked streets. A decaying complex of two-story apartments called East Gate Gardens lined one side of Drake Place and a large vacant lot and a string of bungalows ribboned the other.

Drug sales were the main and only business on Drake Place. At night, the area closed down except for those who wanted to live dangerously. Some of that overt drug action had slowed over the summer because of the constant patrolling by unmarked squad cars. Still, sales went on. There'd been eighteen deaths on Drake Place alone in the past six weeks; thirteen of them were unsolved.

At ten of three, the strike team left Indiana Avenue. Dakota drove the advance car, a four-door gray Crown Victoria, last year's model. Anne was on the passenger side. Donnie O sat huddled in back. The second car followed close behind with Boccucci at the wheel. They rode in silence. The walkie-talkie kept everyone linked. Chief Wilson was staying close. He remained in the command center on Indiana Avenue.

"You think these guys are sporting automatics?" Dakota

said over his shoulder to Donnie O as they turned down East Capitol Avenue.

"Naw." The young black man's voice was thick and nervous. "Mostly they got .45's and .32's. They be jumpy, quick to shoot."

Clear your head, Anne told herself. Concentration, keen eyes, steady hands. She focused on school buses, kids coming home from school, even on Drake Place. It was just after three.

They were at D Street now, the corner of D and Fiftieth. She caught glimpses of idle men standing amid the clotheslines in the vacant lots, a few women lazing away the afternoon with babies on their hips. Two boys who were almost young men, but too well dressed for their years, were greeting each other ahead of them on a debris-strewn sidewalk; they slapped palms. Gold bracelets gleamed in the sunlight.

Face your fears. Anne thought of her dad's steely command, remembered his face, the warmth of his hands on her shoulders.

Two cars were pulled up on the ridge. One was a champagne-colored Buick Riviera. Both front doors were open, a dozen men stood around it, some with their arms crossed over their chests as if they were the secret service, private guards for someone important and powerful.

"That's them," said Donnie O. He was leaning forward, his hand gripping the back of Anne's seat. "The guy in the backseat of the Buick is Paris Paul Jackson. He down from New York. You want him and you want the one standing close by the door. He from here. He called Taubert Derron. He the one that killed my friend down in the projects . . . over nothing."

Dakota turned with a squeal of brakes and headed for the ridge.

Anne relayed the information to the other cars.

The honor guard saw them coming. Someone slid into the front seat of the Buick, turned on the motor. Car doors slammed, men moved agilely down the ridge. The other car pulled away.

"I'm going to block the Buick. Tell Boccucci to pull up behind. When I stop, fan out," ordered Dakota. He had slipped his revolver from his shoulder holster. He had it in his right hand as he drove.

The Buick lurched toward them, rocketing down the ridge. Someone in the front passenger seat leaned from the window and fired a pistol. The car was out of control, the shot went wild. The pale gold car came down the ridge and rammed into a parked car on Drake Place. The impact sent men out of all four doors, three men . . . one man was still in the backseat, huddled down.

Anne was out of the car as soon as Dakota slammed on the brakes. She went down on one knee beside the hood on the left side. Dakota was out on the right.

"The big guy from the Buick," she called to him, "he ran into the building on the left."

"Cover the one still in the backseat," he ordered. "Don't let him get away from us."

Boccucci was already there, his pistol braced with both hands. A tall, thin black man was climbing out the backseat with a dazed look on his face. His head was bleeding. Shots were coming from the apartment building that Anne had indicated to Dakota. They sounded like firecrackers. Where was Dakota?

He'd made it inside. A metal door banged shut behind him.

Two homicide detectives from the third car were headed down the alley.

"Stay put," Anne ordered Donnie O, who was still in the backseat. "There'll be squad cars on the scene in a second. Tell them to make a hit . . . *that* building." She pointed to the apartment building in the center of the court, the building that Dakota had entered looking for Paris Paul Jackson.

Taubert Derron had been standing on the sidewalk. He was looking back up the ridge at the police cars. As Anne watched, he disappeared inside the same building, slithered inside the broken side door like a quick black snake.

Anne came down the slope of the ridge. It was only a few yards of tattered grass and mud. She crossed the street, both hands free. Four cement steps to the broken door. She stepped into the cool rank-smelling darkness of a hallway. There were footsteps racing above her on the stairs, voices upstairs loud and angry. A shot rang out, somewhere a woman screamed.

All the anger and the old pain were twisted into a strong rope that pulled Anne tight inside and held her to the moment. There was no fear or weariness in her. Only a vital sort of wariness. She had not felt so alive in a long time.

"Where'd they go?" Boccucci and a black detective whose name was Jeffrey Hill had entered the building behind her. They shouldered against her, breathing hard. Both had guns drawn.

She caught a glimpse of a shadow, a flick of movement in the shadowy first-floor hall. It was Derron. She knew the set of his head and shoulders now, the gold-colored shirt, dark trousers. He disappeared inside an apartment on the first floor. A door slammed behind him.

"Where the hell is Dakota?" Jeffrey Hill muttered. He was close behind Anne as they moved slowly down the dim hallway. There was a bucket blocking the way. Anne circled around it. She had drawn the automatic from her shoulder holster. She couldn't remember just when. It felt good in her hand.

Dakota was suddenly beside her. He came out of the darkness. He kicked the metal bucket, it ricocheted off the wall. "Damn," he said. "Slow down, will you? Are you after Derron? Where'd he go . . . which apartment?"

The apartment doors all looked alike, a line of battered and dirty doors, a filthy brown color. She thought it was the second door from the end. She whispered a question. "Where's the other one, Jackson? Did you lose him?"

"Yeah, I lost him." Dakota swore under his breath.

"I think it's the second door from the end." Anne's hand tightened on the Glock.

"Let's try it." Dakota looked over his shoulder at Hill. "We're going in," he said. "This one's not getting away."

The coterie of detectives in the hall had grown to six. Two more from the second car had come inside the building. Their eyes were on The Cowboy. There was no question that Dakota was running this strike.

He hammered with his fist on the second door from the end, then dodged to the right, hugged the wall. Anne also pressed her face into the dank cement, waited for shots from inside. There were none. Only silence.

"You certain it's this apartment?" Dakota was already moving back to the door.

"No," Anne whispered, "not at all certain. But I think it was this one."

"Open up," Dakota called. He banged again with his fist. "Police . . . open up! Show your face or we're coming in."

There was no response.

Dakota stepped back and kicked in the door.

The door swung open. The room inside was cluttered and half in darkness. A television was playing, its volume turned low. There was a walk-in kitchen on the left. It was empty, no back exit. On the right was a closed door, most likely a bedroom.

"Take it," Dakota ordered Jeffrey Hill. He motioned for the other detectives to move back, to get set. If there was no direct gunfire, they would rush the room.

Hill moved down the side wall close to the battered sofa. He reached gingerly and turned the knob, gave the door a shove open and stepped back. The room was in utter darkness.

"Police," shouted Dakota. "Come out or we're coming in."

The black hole yawned empty before them.

Was this the wrong apartment? Anne felt the crush of disappointment. She was on Dakota's left as they entered the room. Shadows took on shapes in the darkness of drawn curtains. An unmade bed, a crib, a battered dresser came into view.

The smell was nicotine, sweat, urine . . . and fear.

A flash of gunfire from beyond the bed was like lightning striking in the room. "Hold it!" shouted Dakota. The bullet passed between Don Dakota and Anne Fitzhugh and struck Detective Jeffrey Hill. He grabbed his neck, groaned and fell to the floor.

Anne went down on one knee, her gun outstretched. She thought she could make out a figure on the floor on the far side of the bed. She trained her gun on the darkness there.

Or had the shot come from the corner beside the crib?

Out of the corner of her eye, Anne saw Dakota moving toward the foot of the unmade bed. "Get up," he ordered. "Get the hell up and out of there. I want your hands above your head."

A second burst of fire was the response.

Dakota dodged to the right and fired into the darkness beside the bed. There was a scream of pain. Another scream, then a curse came from the corner by the crib. From the doorway, the back-up investigators were rushing the corner.

Anne swirled, firing into the darkness there.

The tall hulking figure of Taubert Derron climbed from under the crib, got to his feet. He loomed in the small murky room, moaning. He fell at Anne's feet.

She stepped back and felt for the light switch beside the door, found it. The room swam into view, feebly illuminated by the low-hanging ceiling fixture. Derron lay on his back, knees up, blood staining the front of his shirt. He was still moaning softly.

Anne went down beside Jeffrey Hill and felt for his pulse. He was still alive but his pulse was thready. She looked up at Dakota. He was at the foot of the unmade bed, staring beyond it. He drew in his breath as if he did not believe what he saw.

Lying tight against the wall, as if huddled for safety, could be seen a still figure. It was a young woman, wearing a bathrobe. She was hunched over a baby of maybe a year in age. Cradled beneath her mother's protective arm, the baby girl looked up with wondering dark eyes, but did not cry.

The young woman lay in a growing pool of blood.

It was obvious that she was dead. She'd been shot in the back.

20

Stretchers carried out the bodies. There were two dead.

One man had been killed upstairs, a local drug lord who was protecting Paris Paul Jackson. The man had fired at the police from an upstairs window and taken a bullet in his head from the ridge.

The other was a young unmarried woman who had been living with her baby and her boyfriend in this apartment. Dakota had shot her in the back.

"These things happen," someone said. "Tough luck, buddy." One of the other detectives patted Dakota on the shoulder. "Look, you were making a strike . . . what can I say?"

Boccucci only threw up his hands in frustration. Some detectives avoided meeting Dakota's eyes as the strike force and the backup team from District Six walked back to their cars.

"We don't know who the woman is. Or why." Anne said as they got in the Crown Victoria. "I mean why did Derron pick that apartment?"

Dakota said nothing. Donnie O was gone from the back-seat, taken back to headquarters in one of the other squad cars.

"It was probably just bad luck on her part," Anne said. "Derron found an unlocked door." She could see Dakota's set face. He looked white and exhausted. She felt the same. She went on talking, her voice as steady as though nothing had happened. "They found Paris Paul Jackson and a couple of his boys in an apartment upstairs with a stash of automatics and small arms . . . rocks of crack like you've never seen. At least we got him."

The team left Drake Place, moving slow. Ambulances had already pulled out with sirens wailing. Taubert Derron was in one of them. Paramedics were working feverishly over Jeffrey Hill in the back of the other. A crowd had gathered, and the narrow street was thronged with teenagers. One boy ran by with a piece of the yellow and black police tie-off cording around his head like a bandanna. A young woman was wailing hysterically.

"Shit," said Dakota. "I hate these people. I hate them all."

It was his pain talking. At the moment, however, Anne felt the same way.

On Indiana Avenue, Chief Ambrose Riley, head of the Criminal Division, was all smiles. He was talking with Homicide chief Terry Wilson and a cluster of reporters and investigators out in the hall when the strike team reached the third floor.

"Very successful. You done good, boys." He smiled his benediction at Anne, including her too. He always said "boys" when he was giving out compliments. "You got three with long-standing warrants on them. It'll be good for the numbers."

From her desk, Anne called D.C. General Hospital and inquired about Taubert Derron. The doctor in the ER said, "A shoulder wound, he'll be O.K."

O.K. to be booked, to go to jail if Donnie O would testify.

She called down to the administrative officer and asked about Jeffrey Hill. A car was on its way to notify his wife that he was in critical condition. Anne looked down at her hand. She was making a fist. There was a bruise on her thumb.

"What about the woman who was killed in the strike?" she asked.

Her boyfriend had been called. He worked at the Eastern market. A neighbor would look after the baby until he could get home.

Dakota's head was bent over his desk. He was writing his report. He knew the official procedure and so did she. He'd shot a civilian, an innocent bystander. He would go on administrative leave pending an investigation. He had to put it all down on paper, just the way it had happened.

She was his partner. She wanted to say something. But what?

He hadn't spoken the whole way back to Indiana Avenue. For a while, she'd tried . . . tried to say she was sorry it happened, that it would be O.K. He didn't want to hear any of it. They'd made the trip back to headquarters in silence. Only the walkie-talkie had blared its obscene, squawky news of crack and arrests and deaths. It had been a successful strike.

After a while, Dakota pushed back his chair. He didn't look at her or at anyone. He shouldered through the men and went down the hall to Chief Wilson's office.

As he left the squad room, the noise level lowered in sympathy. Shooting a bystander was rough . . . it could happen to anybody. Thank God, it had happened to someone else. Voices rose again. Someone in the back of the room had a bottle of Jack Daniel's. It was against regulations to have liquor in the squad room, totally against regulations. The bottle passed from hand to hand. Someone found a jug of wine.

When Anne left the Municipal Building, night was falling.

She drove out Massachusetts Avenue toward the section of town called Adams Morgan and the condo on California Street that she'd moved into shortly after Rob died. A funky area, Adams Morgan, full of change. Changing upward for the most part, full of Spanish restaurants and renovated brownstones and ethnic enclaves and good spirits. It was a place for separating yourself from who you really were. Anne's friends had been shocked when she moved there.

A few good friends had tried to understand. Even about the policework. They were there for her when she needed them . . . when *she* called, but for the most part, they stayed away. They were giving her time to get over Rob, to find her way back.

Her condo was on the second floor at the front of the building. She turned on the lights in the living room and opened some windows. The trees were heavy and full of night insects, languid leaves brushing against the screen. Still, the night air was crisp and smelled of autumn. Some people were laughing outside on the sidewalk, she wasn't sure what language they were speaking but they sounded happy.

In the kitchen, she made herself an omelet, browned both halves of an English muffin and lathered them with cream cheese and apple jelly. She needed the sugar, she told herself She couldn't think right now about anything that had happened. She was exhausted down to her bones.

She took her supper over to the living room sofa and switched on the television. The evening news was half over . . . another oil spill off the Alaskan coast. Peter Jennings was assured and charming and, as usual, the master of his coverage.

She only half-listened, unable to shake her tension.

Her hands were dirty. She could only stare at the dirt. She left the sofa and poured herself a glass of wine from the half-gallon jug of Chablis she kept in the refrigerator. She sipped some of the wine while still in the kitchen.

When she returned to the living room, Jennings was saying, "Now, for a direct comment on the oil spill from our new cabinet secretary-designate for Hemisphere Protection, Congressman James Woodward, we take you to Capitol Hill and ABC correspondent Simone Gray."

The correspondent stood on the grass outside the Capitol. Behind her in the distance was the Longworth Building at night, lights on. Simone wore a red jacket and a scarf against the night's chill. Her hair and makeup were perfect.

"Peter, I have Congressman Woodward who has just attended a meeting of key members of Congress called tonight to discuss this new potential disaster to America's northwest coast. Congressman Woodward, will you join us please.''

He was there beside Simone silhouetted against the Capitol steps. Their shoulders were almost touching. ''Well, Simone . . . '' Woodward spoke as politicos usually do on camera to members of the press . . . with that blend of ''we are old friends . . . we are in this together'' professionalism that is part of the show.

Anne thought of the press conference yesterday and the encounter she'd witnessed. She had witnessed it, hadn't she? For a moment, she wasn't sure she hadn't dreamed those few seconds of angry confrontation between Simone Gray and the new secretary-designate.

She turned off the television set and switched on the FM radio instead, her favorite station, turning it up when she went into the bedroom to take off her clothes. All of them. They were dirty, filthy. She thrust them into the laundry hamper and put on a terry robe. The ring of the telephone cut through the music. For a moment, she stood in the middle of the bedroom, not sure she wanted to answer. If it was Alan, and it probably was, she didn't want to talk about the day. He'd get it out of her somehow and then he'd be disapproving and concerned and make her feel foolish. Still, he'd be comforting. She could use that.

She answered the bedside telephone. It was Jesse Clore.

''I hope you don't mind my calling you at home.'' His voice was low-pitched and oddly anxious. ''I've had you on my mind ever since we were at the Carvers this morning.''

''It's all right, Jesse, I'm glad you called. I just came in, just had some dinner. I'm planning to turn in early.''

''Oh, really? I was hoping . . . '' He sounded disappointed. ''Well, another night, then. I just wanted to get your reaction to this morning.''

How sad she felt, how heavy in her heart. Anne leaned against the windowsill, looked out into the night. ''You mean, the Carvers? I liked her . . . all right anyway. I didn't care for him.''

"Virginia isn't a bad sort. She has her priorities screwed up. Image, comfort. She's not so different from a lot of people. Still it is a damn tragedy for her. And for Marcus McKelvey. Especially when you think of Paul dying, too."

Anne grew still. She wasn't really surprised. Perhaps she had already guessed the truth. "He has AIDS, I take it."

"I know that and you know that. The Carvers have written Paul off. They don't want to hear about his problems. He's let them down and they don't want to know the details of his 'sordid life,' as they put it. He will die among friends—not with family."

Anne felt tears rising unexpectedly behind her eyelids. "I don't want to talk anymore about any of this, Jess. I can't really tell you why . . . but I'm tired and it's not a good night for me. Could I give you a call tomorrow?"

"Of course . . . maybe I could see you. I have a service in the Cathedral at four tomorrow afternoon. Nothing planned for afterward. Are you interested in dinner?"

She was . . . she wasn't. "Let's see how the day goes." She was thinking of tomorrow, all the unanswered questions.

"Oh." Jess Clore's voice was gentle. "I did spend some time with Emile Farrare today. You've got him scared, very nervous. He says he wants to go home to Italy now."

"I don't doubt that," she said. She was wondering if the young Italian would try to bolt. It was a chance she'd just have to take until the lab came up with something conclusive on the bloody newspapers. She said, "I'll talk with you tomorrow, Jess." There was one call she had to make tonight. While she had the telephone in her hand, Anne dialed information and asked for the number of ABC News.

Nicky Nelson was going to keep her informed about her whereabouts. If she needed a police escort, Anne had promised to provide one. Getting to the studio in broad daylight wasn't a problem, Nicky said. They'd agreed to talk again in the evening. Anne was late in calling, but she was calling.

"I wondered if you had forgotten . . . or just lost interest." Nicky sounded less hysterical than she had in the afternoon. But adversarial in tone, as usual.

"It was a rough afternoon," Anne said. "Sorry."

"You weren't part of that crack strike down on Drake Place, were you? Our crew just got back from police headquarters. People down there are going around patting themselves on the back like they just cleaned up crime in D.C." Nicky's snort was condescending. "I mean, it was just one little strike."

"True," said Anne. She was staring out the window into the trees. " 'One swallow does not a summer make.' But it was a victory for our side, Nicky, however small."

"Some detective killed an innocent woman." Her voice was scornful. "Shot her in the back. I mean, you'd think . . . really!"

"Yeah, you'd think, wouldn't you? I suppose you news types could do a better job if you had the clout and the guns, right?"

"You're being defensive." Nicky laughed with a bitter sound. "They wouldn't give the detective's name down on Indiana Avenue. He's been put on administrative leave. It's going to leak, you know. Maybe you can tell me who it is. I'd like a scoop."

"Let's talk about you, Nicky. Any threats today?"

"No . . . no telephone calls to the apartment, nothing unusual. Which doesn't mean that I'm not in danger. I am. I can sense it."

"What do you want me to do?"

"Just stay in contact for now. I have this friend, this guy, who is going to take me home tonight and maybe sleep over. I'm O.K. for now."

"We'll stay in touch," Anne said.

A long hot shower helped. Soap and hot water and a long time just standing there. When she had toweled off, she blew dry her hair and put on a nightgown. She wasn't even going to read tonight. She left the radio on, turned low . . . for company.

Sleep did not come. She lay wide-eyed. Her chest hurt. It was as if there were a well of tears deep inside that had her filled up. A deep ache in her throat. She hadn't cried when Rob was killed. Not real tears. Nor when her father died. The real tears were there, but they stayed inside. She lay very still, looking up at the play of light on the ceiling from the streetlights outside.

Was all this misery because Rob was dead? Was it all because they hadn't found his murderer and nothing made sense to her without some kind of resolution to that major tragedy in her life and dreams?

The old litany of reasons wouldn't come.

Anne sat up in the dark and hugged her knees. She knew why her heart was hurting tonight . . . she didn't want to face it, didn't want to risk it.

She had to face . . . what? Loving and losing that love.

You loved somebody and he disappeared. You loved somebody and he didn't love you back. You loved some-body and he walked away from you. You might cry . . . die. That was the risk you had to take.

She dressed hurriedly in the dark.

She didn't bother with makeup. She grabbed up her keys and the leather shoulder bag.

In the kitchen, she reached for the bottle of Bailey's Irish Cream she kept on the shelf above the refrigerator. It was one of Rob's tested remedies for a bad night.

This was, without question, a bad night.

She took Fourteenth Street to Maine Avenue. The city glowed and pulsed with its own kind of night music, deep-ening to a sort of water-washed quiet as she neared the Washington Marina. This was lowland Washington. A hun-dred years ago, there'd been only swamp and marsh here. Even now, the night air held the salty scent of the bay and the pungent smell of fish close along the docks.

He'd said he kept his boat at the southwest waterfront. He'd mentioned the Channel Inn. She came to a long flat pier like a boardwalk. Lights flickered on the dark water and she could see the ribbings and masts of yachts and sailboats. She left her car near the inn and walked slowly up the long dock. It was probably hopeless. So many boats . . . just a bad idea.

A long pier extended out into the channel. She decided to give it a try. Near the end, she saw his houseboat.

She had forgotten that he called it *The Reliable Source*

until she saw the name on the bow. A houseboat . . . a sail-
boat. She wasn't quite sure what it was, only that it had a
certain girth and sat low in the water and was swaying
gently in the night. She heard the creak of ropes as it pulled
at its mooring.

There were portholes set close to the water. A light was
on inside. She walked down the plank and stepped over the
railing onto the deck. "You are a damn fool." That was
what he was going to say when he saw her. "You are a
fool, Fitzhugh, to come out here in the night, uninvited . . .
and unwanted. Who asked you, anyway?"

She rapped on the door that led below. Her knuckles
seemed fragile. There was no answer. She opened the door
and went down the narrow steps. A lamp hung low in the
galley, illuminating with a yellow glow the larger space
which was a sort of cluttered sitting room. She stood for a
moment looking at the pictures on the pine walls. There
was a bookcase with a few books on its shelves, a picture
of his son in a bathing suit holding up a fish in triumph.
There were some trophies . . . a plaque.

She moved around the table. She saw Dakota's tweed
jacket lying on a chair; draped over it was his shoulder
holster. It was empty.

There was a closed door at the far end of the room. She
opened it. For a moment, her eyes met only darkness. Then
she saw him and saw that he was asleep.

He had only a sheet over him. He lay on his back with
one arm thrown out across the expanse of bunk. His chest
was bare, his face turned away to the curving wall.

She turned to leave, and he stirred. Dakota came instantly
awake. He went up on his elbows and instinctively reached
under the pillow for his gun.

"It's me," Anne said quickly. "I just came to see how
you were."

He looked up at her as if he did not quite believe she
was standing there. Then, he swung his legs over the side
of the bed and sat up with a groan.

"Don't say I'm a fool, Dakota," she cautioned him

quickly. "Don't. Because I am a fool and I know it. I feel like a fool . . . but I wanted to come."

"Why are you here?" Flushed with sleep, he was watching her. "Are you feeling sorry for me?"

"Maybe . . . yes. I feel bad for you. I feel bad for me too."

"You didn't kill anybody, Fitzhugh. Lighten up. It was my mistake."

"It wasn't your mistake, damn it, Dakota!"

She heard the anger in her own voice. "You returned fire. We all did. I might have shot the wrong person, or Boccucci! How could you know that Derron had a woman in there? She didn't cry out. She didn't let us know she was there."

He was sitting very still on the side of the bed. He put his hand over his face and swayed for a moment. He said, "Sometimes nothing makes any sense, Fitzhugh. Nothing in this whole damn life makes any sense."

Anne sat down beside him on the rumpled bunk and slid her arm around his waist. She didn't anticipate it, didn't mean to. She put her head against his shoulder. There were tears rolling down her cheeks.

"Look, I don't need sympathy," he said gruffly. "Especially not from you."

But his arm went around her hard. He pulled her close against him. She could hear his heart beating.

"It's more complicated than that, Dakota," she whispered. "The tears aren't just for you, damn it. I don't know why, but I'd like to sleep here tonight. I'm exhausted, and so are you. I just don't want to sleep alone, that's all."

He leaned back and looked at her. He touched her face in the dark with his fingers, felt the wetness on her cheeks.

"Do you want me to hold you?" he asked. It was the Dakota she'd known, would like to know, caught glimpses of. The one whose eyes were warm and blue and whose touch was gentle.

She lay back with him in the bunk, settled her body against him. The warmth of his arm was beneath her, the steady heartbeat, fine soft hairs on his chest against her cheek.

"I didn't plan to come. I don't know why, I just had to come . . . some instinct told me . . . "

"I know," he said.

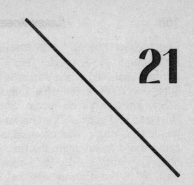

21

The Washington Channel waters were ruffled and smelling of fog when Anne pulled away from the river on Friday morning. It had rained most of the night. There was mist in the air and no one was stirring about except for a few early rising fishermen.

She reached the squad room after seven and missed roll call. The jubilant mood of Thursday afternoon was gone from the third floor. Jeffrey Hill had died during the night. Someone from the eleven to seven shift had straightened his desk and placed a glass vase with a rose in it next to the picture of Jeffrey and his wife.

Boccucci leaned on the divider above Anne's desk. He looked exhausted, wiped out. "Want some coffee?" he asked. He had a steaming mug in his hand.

She shook her head. "Already had some." She'd gone home to California Street before coming into work. She had ground fresh beans and let the coffeemaker drip while she was showering.

"Too damn bad," he said, "about Jeff Hill."

"Too damn bad," she echoed. "He was a good detective, a good man."

Boccucci looked down in his cup. "Too damn bad about The Cowboy too. It was . . . just one of those things that happen."

"Right," Anne said.

"He'll get cleared, he'll be back . . . causing us grief, before we know it. Trouble is . . . " Boccucci frowned. "You

see, I know Dakota . . . he's going to take this hard. He
looks tough. He *is* tough. That's his problem. He has got
a tough shell and when a man is like that, it's because he
hurts easy. You know what I mean?''

She knew what he meant. She sat for a while, when
Boccucci had gone back to his own desk, staring out of the
window. Nothing was changed, she told herself, just because she'd found again the fine, gentle side of The Cowboy. The hurting side. He'd seen the lost child in her as
well. What did it mean? She and Dakota were as they had
always been. The night was only a dream that happened.

He'd held her in his arms. He had not made love to her.
When finally they slept, it had been deeply. They had
stayed in each other's arms all night.

The crime lab's report was waiting on her desk.

Anne tore open the envelope. The report was affirmative.
The blood on the newspapers belonged to Caroline Mc-
Kelvey. It was her blood and hers alone. There were fingerprints on the papers as well. Several clear prints. And a
boot print.

That's what it said. ''The toe print of a boot, right foot.''

There were steps to be taken. She wasn't sure in what
order. She'd like to talk about it with Dakota. But she could
handle it alone.

She called the Court Liaison Division. She had a buddy
there named Gill. ''Do I,'' she asked him, ''have enough
to ask for a bench warrant for my suspect?'' She told him
about Emile Farrare.

She could fill out a PD 163, a prosecution report.

But, he cautioned, she needed to match the boot print
before she could make the arrest. ''You don't want to do
this wrong. You don't want to screw up,'' Gill said. ''Ask
this guy if he is willing to come in for another talk. Go
pick him up, make sure he is wearing his boots. Once you
get him downtown, you can get those boots off him. If they
match up, then you make an arrest.''

Before she left the office, she called Alfred Harris at The

Alhambra. "You'll need to come down to headquarters. I expect your fingerprints are on the newspapers and we need to take them to be able to eliminate those prints."

It would be his pleasure, Harris said. "What about Harold?"

"By all means," said Anne. "We need Harold's prints as well."

Had Nicky touched the papers yesterday when they were dumped out on the rug? Anne dialed the now familiar number.

After only two rings, the familiar voice answered.

"I thought you'd be calling to check on me," Nicky said. "I thought you'd have called earlier. But, it's O.K. So far, so good. But I'm very antsy, you know?"

"Is your friend still with you?"

"He's still here. We are going out to get something to eat."

"Nicky, here's a question. Did you touch the newspapers that Alfred Harris brought to the apartment yesterday? Can you recall whether or not your fingers came in contact with those bloody newspapers?"

There was silence. Then, "No way. I didn't touch those damn papers. What are you trying to pull?"

Keep your calm here, Anne told herself. She said, "We have prints, Nicky, from the newspapers. I am trying to eliminate those that are not suspect. I rather thought yours might be in that category."

"Well, I didn't touch the papers! I wouldn't have been caught dead touching those awful bloody papers!"

"I rather thought you didn't. I was just making sure," Anne said. "Look, I am leaving the office. If anything comes up, if you have anything specific to report, call here and they'll reach me by radio. Otherwise, I'll check with you at work around five this afternoon."

"The newspapers . . . whose fingerprints do you think they are?"

"I assume they belong to Caroline's murderer," said Anne.

* * *

She borrowed the old black umbrella that Dakota kept stashed in his desk drawer and called down for a car. As she passed Boccucci's desk, she asked, "Are you going to be around this morning? I'm bringing Emile Farrare in. I may need some help with him."

"Something new come up?"

"Right, some evidence that might make a difference."

"You need help bringing him in?"

She looked at his cluttered desk, the pile of telephone messages. "I can handle it, thanks. I don't expect him to give me any trouble. He doesn't know what's up."

"I'll be around here all morning." Boccucci turned back to his typewriter, then called to her as she neared the door, "Fitzhugh, the funeral is on Monday. Hill's funeral is at St. Elizabeth's in Rockville, two o'clock on Monday. Full dress. I'm calling Dakota . . . he'll want to be there."

Again, the rain had let up. It was going to be one of those days. Off again, then on again in downpours. That's what she had heard driving in to work this morning. The sky would be gray and overcast all day.

The mood in the city was subdued. The sidewalks were empty, headlights crisscrossing the streets. The federal and municipal buildings were deepened by the rain from white to gray, from cream to the color of mud.

She was at the Washington Cathedral before nine o'clock. She'd considered going first to the apartment building where Emile was staying but she thought he might already be on the job. He was there . . . bending over his boss stone in the stonecarvers' workshop.

When he saw her, Emile Farrare straightened. He was down on one knee on the dusty workshop floor. He rested his chisel on his knee and watched her approach.

"I'd like to talk with you," Anne said. She had the Glock in her bag. She doubted she'd have to use it. Still, her heart was beating loudly in her own ears. She hoped that her forced composure was convincing.

He rose. He was not so tall, only a few inches taller than

she. He stood close and looked at her with that angry innocence that was all his. "What I do now?" he asked.

Anne saw that he was wearing the fancy cowboy boots. That made it easier. She said, "Emile, I need you down at headquarters again. Sorry. It's necessary."

"Do you know, señora, who is the killer of Caroline?"

"We grow close to the truth, Emile."

They stared into each other's eyes. His were dark and stormy and fathomless. He said, "O.K. then, I come with you."

The foreman of his work unit shrugged in exasperation and threw up his hands. Emile, stoic as usual, got his jacket and went out to the car with her. There is a job that has to be done sometimes. You don't think about it, you just do it, Anne told herself. She didn't look over at the young man. She found him appealing and vulnerable. If he had killed, then he had done it out of some misguided passion. She could accept that kind of killing more easily than she could the scum who killed for greed, for excitement, for power.

They came out of North Drive onto Wisconsin Avenue. Anne swung over into the right lane and slowed in front of Dolkin's grocery. She pointed to the store's awning. "Do you know this place?"

He stared at the arched window. "*Sí*, I know this store. It is where Caroline buys apples."

"When did Caroline buy apples here, Emile?"

"One time, I walk home with her from the Cathedral. And Caroline buys apples."

"Just one time you went into this store with her?"

"*Sí*. One time, I go in this store. It is in maybe August. We sit in the park across from her building and we eat the apples. Then, she leaves me and goes across the avenue. I go home."

"Another time, maybe? On the afternoon that Caroline was murdered, she may have shopped in this store, Emile. She bought some groceries. She bought wine. I think you were with her then, too. Do you remember that?"

"I remember only the truth," he said. His mouth had a stubborn pouty look. He did not look at Anne. "I remember I wait for Caroline at the Cathedral. She does not come. I walk to her building and sit there on the bench. That is all that there is."

A car behind them honked impatiently.

She stepped on the gas.

They drove in silence. As they neared downtown, she glanced at him. His sleeve was turned back. There was a swollen raw, red scar on his wrist. It was oddly round like a circle. And it looked new.

"What's that . . . did you burn yourself?"

"*Sì.* I burn myself." He spoke flatly.

"How did you do that? Was there an accident in your work at the Cathedral?"

"I do it for penance. I do it for Caroline, for her memory. I burn myself with a cigarette to remember always."

She could think of nothing to say.

Anne tightened her hands on the wheel. For penance . . . for her memory. She wanted to ask him more but she felt it was not the right time. She wasn't badgering Emile. She was talking to him, only it might not look that way in court. She needed to read him his rights before he told her anything that was incriminating.

"My Caro," he murmured softly. "She want to be good. She want to do good in her work . . . in her life. Is a mission for her, yes?"

"Perhaps," Anne conceded grimly. But what is good?

She could not resist one more question. Her eyes still ahead on the traffic, she asked, "Was Caroline killed because she wanted to be . . . good, Emile?"

"I don't know, about getting killed."

The problem was to get the boots from him. On the third floor, the young Italian craftsman went docilely into the interrogation room. Anne told him to sit down and wait, she'd get coffee. She got Boccucci as well.

"Explain to him that we need to have his boots for a while," she said as they went down the hall. "I mean, he's going to throw a fit over this. He's no dummy. If he's the killer, he saw the toe print. That's why he threw away the newspapers."

Boccucci nodded. "When we want to examine his boots, he's gonna know the newspapers didn't burn in the incinerator. Game's up, kid!"

She waited in the hall. She kept thinking of the burn on his arm. A strange, stormy killer angel, this one. She hoped he wouldn't give Boccucci a hard time.

Andy Boccucci came out of the room with the boots in his hand. "No sweat." He was grinning from ear to ear. "I told Emile I wanted to see his boots. I told him I wanted to get a pair just like them. I said, 'I want to show your boots to some guys down the hall. You give me those boots for twenty minutes and I'll buy you a real Italian pizza for lunch.' "

She took the boots down to the crime lab herself.

"Hand-tooled leather . . . great-looking boots!" exclaimed one of the guys in the lab. His name was Michael Whitaker. "I wouldn't mind a pair like this." He took them from her and disappeared into the back.

Boccucci was waiting upstairs with Emile. Anne sat down on the weathered sofa and considered what needed to be done next. It was hard to get a conviction without a confession. A match of the boots to the toe print would be enough to book him. Then, they would get him a lawyer in from Legal Services and start talking.

She'd need Boccucci to work on this with her. Emile was a strange sort. He had his own truth, his own visions. She would have to work with him until he felt he could share those visions with her.

Michael Whitaker was back in less than ten minutes. He had Emile's boots in a plastic bag. He held the bag out to her. "Strike out on this."

She took the bag from him. "What do you mean?"

"Not a match. You are talking absolutely a no-way fit."

"But I was sure . . . " Anne was in shock.

"Look, you want to see?" He took her back in the lab. He had made a quick print of the toe of Emile's right boot. It was overlaid on a copy of the bloody newspaper.

"See what I mean? This guy's boots are about three sizes too large for the bloody print. I mean, your murderer is small. This print looks big seen by itself but the truth is . . . the toe that made the print on the newspaper is dainty, you know what I mean? This guy is not your killer."

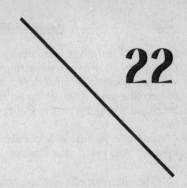

22

Anne was standing by the brass rail in the Members' Section of the House of Representatives' Viewing Gallery looking down at the floor of the House chamber.

Once this had been her personal privilege—to be in this gallery as the wife of Congressman Rob Fitzhugh. Now she was here as the friend of a House member. "Mrs. Fitzhugh," one of the security guards murmured to another as she had walked by. "Congressman Foley's fiancée," responded the other. She knew that rumor was going around. In a way the description amused her.

She did not see Alan. Some of the members were sitting quietly at their desks on the floor waiting for the vote to be called, a few read or did paperwork. Others moved restlessly about in the aisles, pausing to talk, hands in their pockets. Just casual talk.

Directly below the Speaker's chair, a half-dozen representatives were tightly circled as if in a football huddle. The majority leader was talking hard and low, issuing directives. It was apparent even from the gallery that there was strong support for the bill on one side of the aisle, strong opposition on the other. Directly across from where Anne was standing was the press gallery. That glassed-in section of the gallery was packed with reporters. She could not make out the smooth fair head of Simone Gray.

"There ought to be a perfume called 'The Political Arena,'" someone remarked behind Anne.

She turned to see Gertrude Woodward in a chic navy suit

that set off her silver hair, sitting alone in the front row of the gallery. It was no surprise to find her here. Gertrude was a professional wife, devoted to her husband and his career. She gave Anne an ironic smile. "Or maybe it could be called, 'Waiting in the Gallery for Something to Happen.'"

Anne slid in beside Woodward's wife on the polished bench. "Ah, yes . . . the strange exotic excitement of politics."

"The circus smells like elephants and hay and peanuts." Gertrude narrowed her eyes as she watched the floor. "This arena smells of private tears and public blood."

She was right, of course. One had to want power terribly to risk so much. Anne saw Jim Woodward just entering the chamber. He had Alex Shannon with him. Handsome men, those two . . . the older one with his mane of white hair, his craggy, tan face. Woodward was already flashing a majestic smile toward the TV cameras in the press gallery.

Gertrude nudged her. "Alan's trying to get your attention."

The Virginian had just entered the chamber below. His glasses caught the reflection of the overhead lights as he looked up at Anne. He gave his umbrella a shake as he furled it. Rain, he was saying . . . what a drive up from the Tidewater! She could read his mind. She always could.

Someone in his office must have told Alan that she'd called and said she was coming here this morning. She'd say hello later. But first she wanted to find Simone Gray in the press gallery.

"You aren't leaving yet?" said Gertrude Woodward. "Actually, I've been thinking about you, wondering how the investigation of the murder is coming along."

"It's difficult. I wish I could say I'm close to the truth."

"The truth," offered Gertrude, "is often a strange and nebulous thing . . . hard to catch hold of."

A gavel rapped. The Speaker of the House was now on his feet. The chamber quieted.

Anne felt a wave of nostalgia. It was nostalgia for Rob, for all this magic. The moment of the gavel's rap was like the opening seconds of the play or a symphony. The lights go down, the conductor raps for attention, a hush falls and then, it begins. A rather raucous play, this one. She'd seen it before, a hundred times with one vote or another.

Anne pressed Gertrude's hand and left the gallery.

She made her way around the chamber and up the narrow winding stairs to the ABC desk above the House press gallery where she was told by a news director in jeans that Simone was outside, preparing to do a news break as soon as the vote was in.

"Where is she setting up?"

"She's under the elm on the lawn. She's got a remote to the floor. As soon as the vote's in, she is going to . . . "

"I know . . . a news break. Thanks."

Down on the floor, the motion was being read.

On the lawn under the spreading elm, its leaves still dripping, Anne found the ABC crew set up for the live spot. Simone Gray was fiddling with her earpiece as she waited. Anne stood quietly behind the camera, out of the way. Simone would be the first on the air with this story on the trade bill vote. She was always the first television reporter to break any story involving Congress. She was a lady in control.

In control . . . and maybe in trouble.

Things were coming together in Anne's head, a new design for the puzzle. She studied Simone's well-cut gray suit, the colorful shoulder scarf. The correspondent was wearing a pair of gray suede boots. Well-fitting, expensive high-heel boots. They were also her trademark. Somewhere, Anne had read that Simone Gray had boots in all colors to match her different outfits.

Simone looked up with a frown. Their eyes met. Simone raised an eyebrow. "I was wondering when you were going to get back to me."

Anne suddenly remembered that Simone had called headquarters on Thursday looking for her or for Dakota. Why?

"I'll wait until you are done," Anne said.

She did not smile, neither did Simone.

The spot was less than a minute. The bill had passed by a narrow vote, but it had passed. Simone explained its implications in a few brief sentences. She flashed her embracing smile to the TV audience.

Simone took off her earphone and tossed it along with the microphone to a member of the crew and motioned to Anne to join her.

"A clean, neat slice of news," said Anne. "You never seem to get nervous. Do things ever go wrong? Do you ever lose it, Simone?"

"Come on. You know the answer to that, Anne Fitzhugh. You know what being a professional is all about. One isn't paid to lose it . . . is one?"

A point scored. Anne gave a wry smile. "Look, is there a place where we can talk privately for a few minutes?"

Simone moved away from the crew toward the gravel path. "I gather you're here on business. What gives?"

"I apologize for not returning your call. It was a rough day. Sorry. Do you want to tell me what that call was about?"

"Is that why you're here? You bothered to come over here in answer to my call? I doubt that. And, I am curious . . . where's your handsome stud partner . . . he of the hard line?"

"Don Dakota would be flattered at your assessment," Anne said back just as coolly. "And no, I am not here in response to your telephone call. Still I would like to know what was on your mind when you made it?"

"A whim . . . forget it," said Simone.

"Something about Caroline?"

"Probably. It really wasn't important."

"Everything about Caroline McKelvey is important to me."

Simone stared at her. Something softened in her face. "Yes, I rather thought so. You never even knew Caroline but you care about her. Odd, I can tell that. You like her."

"You liked her too, Simone. You were a hell of a lot closer to Caroline than you intimated to us on Wednesday." Anne was fishing. "You shared your personal life with her. Some of your *very* personal life."

"Did Nicky tell you that?" Her eyes darkened.

A point for my side, thought Anne.

"Yes, I trusted Caroline with some personal business of my own." Simone's voice was surprisingly ragged. "I asked her to use that information wisely and carefully. I asked her for some help. I'm afraid she let me down. But if you are going to ask me what kind of personal business it was . . . I am not going to tell you."

Anne saw the set look to Simone's mouth. "I want to know why you lied about not seeing Caroline on the day she died." It was a shot in the dark.

Something flashed in the brilliant dark eyes. "I didn't see her. She called me about two that afternoon. We had a few items to talk about."

"You argued."

"You could call it an argument. We disagreed strongly on something rather important. I said that we'd catch up with each other later in the evening. She had some notes of mine and I wanted them back."

"Will you tell me what those notes concerned?"

"I won't tell you . . . sorry."

"I think it's important for you to know that you are a suspect in this case," Anne said quietly. It was a challenge.

The look that came into Simone Gray's face was more resignation than fear. "I had a feeling it was going to come to this. I didn't kill her, you know . . . I really didn't."

"I want you to come in to headquarters this afternoon. You can bring your lawyer. This has to be talked out."

Simone Gray shook her head. "The timing is wrong. Today's Friday. I'd like to put this interrogation off until Monday. I'll be freer to talk then."

Control seemed an issue. There was a certain insouciance.

"Sorry," Anne responded. She thought about the disdain her dad used to have for a "witness who muddies the waters."

"I want you down at headquarters today at 2 P.M. unless

you can give me a better reason. We're talking about a murder.''

"For God's sake, I know that. No one knows better than I that Caroline was murdered. No one is more guilt-ridden than I!'' She colored slightly at that, but went on stubbornly. "Still I insist the timing is wrong to open this up. There are some things I am willing to talk about today, and some I am not.''

"Two o'clock, today, Simone. The D.C. Municipal Building, third floor.'' Anne looked at her watch. "You have an hour and forty-five minutes. If you aren't there, I'll come get you . . . with a warrant.''

"You won't believe this,'' Anne told Dakota over the telephone. She was calling from one of the green phone booths in the lobby of the Rayburn Building. She filled him in quickly on the developments in the case.

"So Simone Gray's your suspect now. I didn't like that bitch when I met her.''

"I don't know about that. You called her a slippery, sexy blonde. I sensed lust on your part.''

"As I recall, my exact words were a sexy . . . cold as ice blonde. There is a difference. Respect maybe, no lust.'' For the first time, there was some laughter behind his voice.

"Dakota, I'm convinced that Simone Gray is involved in this murder right up to the top of her gray suede boots. First of all, she was there . . . in the building on the night that Caroline was killed. Accessibility is obvious. And Caroline would have opened her apartment door to Simone.''

"Have you established a motive?''

"I sense motive. Something complex and personal between Simone and Caroline. I haven't figured it all out yet.''

"What about the bloody newspapers . . . you're going for a boot match? Maybe fingerprints, as well.''

"Of course. We'll start with the fingerprints at two. And then I'll get a search warrant for Simone's apartment.'' Anne cupped the receiver. The House vote was over. The hallway behind her was filling up. The House had adjourned for lunch. "Listen, I have to go. I just wanted you to know where the case stands."

There was a pause. "You are coming over tonight?"

She heard a question in the tentative quality of his voice. There was an openness, a wanting that was unexpected.

"I hadn't planned on it." She kept her voice steady.

"Other plans. O.K., I understand. You have a full life, Fitzhugh."

"I'm not prepared to fall in love with you, Dakota. It's . . . well, not in my best interests."

"I would agree with that," he said evenly. "I am not the pick of the catch."

"That's not what I meant at all. You know that."

There was a pause. Then, "You have to handle this, Fitzhugh. You know how I feel. So, I guess it's in your hands now."

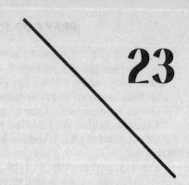

23

"You're certain there's nothing more I could do for you?" asked Janet Sutton.

It had been a whim on Anne's part, this stopover in Woodward's office. She sipped the steaming coffee that Janet had provided. "No, thanks anyway. I just wanted a word with Alex. I'll wait a few minutes and see if he shows up."

For a moment there was a silence, an awkwardness between them.

"I gather this office will be moving over to the executive side of town now that Woodward is entering the President's cabinet," said Anne.

Janet nodded. "As soon as Jim's confirmation is behind us, we'll relax and start focusing on the future."

"You don't anticipate problems with the Senate?"

"My heavens, no!" The young woman shook her head vehemently. "I mean with Jim's marvelous record in Congress, he'll sail right through. Of course there're always a few assassins lurking out there looking for trouble."

"By chance do you mean the well-meaning ladies and gentlemen of the press?"

A contemptuous nod from Janet. "If they can find a smear of dirt anywhere, they will! They'll turn over any stone, look in any black hole, just hoping to find something negative to run with. Any dumb kind of scandal! Since the cabinet appointment two days ago, we've had reporters in

214

here from all the major newspapers, the big three TV networks, not to mention all the small fry."

"It's been rough, has it?"

"Rough isn't the word. Deadly is what it is!"

"What about Simone Gray?"

"No, she hasn't been around. Except at the press conference on Wednesday. Some other people from ABC News have been in, but not Simone. I don't think she and Alex get along."

"Why is that?"

Janet Sutton straightened her shoulders. She put down the paperweight, ran her fingers up and down the lapel of her jacket. "Oh, I don't really know why. I'm sure Alex has his reasons."

There was commotion in the hall. Framed in the door was Jim Woodward with his wife beside him. Alex Shannon and two young men with earnest, eager expressions were close behind them.

"A resolution to a difficult problem." Jim grasped Anne's hand. "The trade bill was a reasonable compromise, of course. Isn't that what life turns out to be most of the time . . . but I would say, a breakthrough, a new avenue . . . a fresh wind to the back of our economy."

Anne could not help laughing. Just exactly what he'd said, she wasn't quite sure. But she got the gist of it. Jim Woodward was all exuberance this afternoon, pleased that the trade bill had passed the House.

Shannon also seemed pleased. But as ever, there was something watchful in Alex's face. He looked at Anne speculatively. "I hear you want to see me?"

"If you've got a few minutes."

"Let me get Jim settled down. Then I'll be right with you."

Janet opened a door into a partitioned space off the large staff room. "Here's Alex's private chamber. Make yourself at home. He'll be with you shortly."

The space was small, but had its effect. A few meaningful pictures of Alex Shannon shaking hands with political greats, a handsome desk, his degrees above it, a battery of telephones.

Anne sat down across from the desk. She wasn't sure just why she was here except that it seemed a place to start . . . in figuring out Simone Gray.

When he came into the room, she said, "Alex, I thought you'd like to know that we discovered the identity of the mysterious E on Caroline's calendar. His name is Emile . . . Emile Farrare."

"Oh, really." He glanced at his stack of telephone messages on his desk. "Has he . . . this Emile anything to do with the case?"

"I'm afraid not. I'm moving in another direction now. Actually, I hope you can help me."

He gave her his full attention. "You know I will if I can."

"I'd like to talk to you about Simone Gray."

There was not the flicker of change in Alex Shannon's face. "You're talking about one tough lady. We've had our moments, Simone and I."

"You mean moments of confrontation?"

"All-out war is more the way it is. Simone and I crossed spears a few years ago. She has a thing about congressional members making money. It's her idea that a man is supposed to come here poor and go home poor."

"One used to call it . . . being a public servant."

He grinned at her and loosened his tie. "The fact that Jim Woodward has prospered—legally through solid investments and some successful real estate deals—annoys Simone no end. How, says she, can a man be strong for a healthy environment and 'save the whales' and be a capitalist as well? A successful capitalist, at that?"

"Perhaps you can answer that for me," said Anne. "I am also surprised that in his many years in Congress, Jim Woodward had the time or interest to amass a fortune. He is so . . . committed to what he believes in. That total dedication to his work is what makes him Jim Woodward."

"Precisely, Anne. The man is solid and clean as a bar of soap. Biodegradable soap, for sure!"

He laughed, and she laughed with him.

"How did he pull if off?"

Alex leaned back in his chair. "Gertrude is the power behind this man, Anne. The practical power, the Lady Bird to his Lyndon, Nancy to his Ron. You get the idea?"

"Absolutely. But I'm not sure I buy what you are selling. Simone Gray wouldn't waste her time unless she had reason to be suspicious. You had better tell me if there's real smoke here, Alex, because if you don't, I think Simone will."

He studied her for a moment. "Why are you interested in Simone Gray?"

"I'm not at liberty to explain that, except I think Simone is going to be ... important in the Caroline McKelvey case."

"And what has that got to do with me ... with Jim Woodward?"

"I am not saying that it does. However, I witnessed the exchange between Simone and Congressman Woodward on Wednesday at the press conference. It's been bothering me. I thought you might explain."

"Fair enough." Alex was still staring at Anne intently. "I'd just as soon you know what kind of crazy lady you are dealing with."

"I'd like to know anything you can tell me about her."

"Well, let's start at the beginning." Alex picked up a pearl and gold encased cigar cutter from his desk and began to finger it. It was a curious gesture. Deliberate. He put his finger through the circular cutter at the end and then just as carefully laid the cigar cutter back on his desk. "I met Simone twelve years ago when I first came to Washington," he began. "She was working on the local news desk for ABC out of Boston; every now and then she'd be down in Washington covering a story that involved Massachusetts. Her name wasn't Gray then. It was Simone Simmons."

"When did she change it?"

"Simmons was her first husband's name. She was married then. The guy was an alcoholic, she divorced him, and married one just as bad. I don't remember his name. I believe he crashed the car into a cement partition on the freeway. He'd been drinking, big time. A few months later, she quit her job and came to Washington. It was then her career picked up.''

"How do you know all this, Alex? I'm getting the impression you know Simone very well."

"Not so well. I was involved with a good friend of hers in those days. I'd see Simone now and then. She was good-looking, she was cheap, she was out on the town." Again there was something cold, even contemptuous in his eyes. "To be honest, I wouldn't have thought that she would pull herself together and come so far."

"But she has." Anne made the point. "What caused the transformation?"

"Apparently she managed to get a job on a local ABC affiliate out of Baltimore. A major story came along. It went national, and she covered it. The big guys in New York were impressed with this classy cool blonde in Baltimore and the next thing you know she was back in Washington. This time big time. This time she was on her way up, and now she was called Simone Gray. Don't ask me why."

"All this is very interesting, but I don't see the crossed spears. Where do you come into the story?"

"Somewhere along the line, Detective Fitzhugh, our girl becomes a man-hater. I'm serious. She got screwed up somewhere in this story and she started going for the jugular. Give Simone Gray a man with clout, power... particularly one who acts like a decent sort, and it's like she's found an enemy. I hadn't been with Woodward a few months before I found that the one person on the national media scene that I couldn't handle was Simone Gray."

"I don't follow what you mean."

"You tell her something is black, she looks to see if it is really white. You tell her a candidate is committed to a cause, she starts checking his PAC money to see if he's been bought off."

"I call that being a tough reporter," said Anne.

"She's brought down a couple of influential men over nothing. That's where she gets her jollies, tearing a man's balls off. I've seen her in action. A few years ago, she started nosing around Woodward. Why, God knows.''

"You still insist she had nothing to go on?"

"I am saying she thought she did. She was always out on the town with this lobbyist or that and somewhere she got the idea that Woodward was raking in too much PAC money from environmentalist groups. There was nothing to it. A PAC can contribute five thousand dollars in a primary and five thousand in a general election. There are a hell of a lot of environmental associations. That means a lot of support.''

Anne nodded with a certain gravity. . . . She was not a novice at politics. Or the funding of politics. She understood PAC money and its implications. There were those candidates who'd accepted more than a million dollars in the last presidential election. It brought up the ugly issue of—who owes who if elected? Graft . . . complicity came to mind.

"Woodward accepts PAC monies up to the legal limit?"

"Absolutely. We aren't hiding anything. I showed Simone our books when she asked, but she wasn't satisfied. She gets these obsessions about men in power. Ask around on the Hill, you will find out it's true. Now, she has got Jim Woodward in her sights and she is looking for a trigger to pull.''

It all rather fit with what Anne had heard about Simone.

Alex went on in a flat, passionless voice. "You know, I went to her apartment one night and tried to talk to her. This was about a year ago. I said, 'Look, I have known you a long time, Simone. You've got problems, big-time problems. But Jim Woodward is not your problem. Lay off, will you? Find some real bastard and go after him.' ''

"What did she say to that?"

"This is not a story to my credit. You have to understand, the evening had started off well. We were about to share a bottle of vintage wine that I'd brought along. I thought straight talk would go down with her, but I guess I was wrong. . . . We were in the kitchen and she was fixing cheese and crackers to go along with the wine. She had just unwrapped the cheese. She had the knife . . . you know, the little cheese knife . . . in her hand and she turned to me and said very slowly, 'I know a real bastard when I smell one. And you, Alexander Shannon, stink to God.' I mean, I looked at that knife and I thought maybe she'd flipped her lid. I got out and got out fast. Since then, Simone Gray is persona non grata in this office and in my life.''

"You think she is unstable?"

"Yes, maybe paranoid as well. I don't know that I would trust anything that she tells you.''

"You've been helpful, Alex.'' Anne rose. "I'll be in touch.''

Upstairs, she found Alan Foley in his office.

"Where the devil did you disappear to after the vote?'' He was in his shirt sleeves working at his desk.

"I'm working a case, remember? D.C. Homicide. I am a detective, wretched at it as I am. I wasn't in the gallery just to watch history in the making . . . although I will say I thought you were the handsomest man on the floor.''

"All right . . . all right, flattery will get you everywhere.'' He reached for his coat. "How about a quick lunch? The House dining room. Soft-shelled crabs. Toast points.''

"You're on.'' I'm starving for lunch, she thought. How did he know?

Minutes later, they were sitting at a table for two in the dining room reserved for House members on the lower level of the Capitol.

She asked him, "Alan, do you take PAC money?''

"I do. Not a great deal, but I do. It is hard to turn down.''

"No strings attached? Just donations from Public Action Committees?''

"I'm not for sale, you know that.'' He looked vaguely indignant. "The people who contribute . . . who support me financially, know that. It's nice, however, to keep one's war chest well stocked with silver and gold. Just in case . . . ''

"Just in case some challenger with big campaign money

to spend comes along and wants your seat?''

"Precisely. The way it is now . . . because of PAC's, there are not many upsets, not many new faces on the Hill unless somebody holding a seat in Congress dies, gets in hot water with the press or chooses to leave."

Anne ate her Caesar salad in silence. He was right. There weren't many upsets in congressional elections. The incumbents always had the edge. Alan had inherited his congressional seat from Rob, had won it for himself in reelection, and would probably hold onto it as long as he wished . . . as long as he stayed out of trouble.

That was the media's job . . . looking for trouble.

"Alan, what is Simone Gray's reputation on the Hill?"

"You are full of questions today. What's up?"

"I know we covered this the other night. As I recall, you said Simone was sharp . . . and beautiful."

"She is." He leaned forward. "Not as beautiful as you are, but beautiful."

"You know the inside scoop, Alan. Level with me. Is Simone thought to be unstable? Is she known to be a man-hater?"

"Are you suggesting those two are synonymous? If so, I would say 'yes.' But if you are really serious, we can break it down into two questions. Is Simone unstable? There is indeed a rumor that she is sometimes unreasonable, sometimes slightly delusional. But always, sharp."

"And, the man-hater part . . . ?"

He spooned seafood sauce on his crab. "Needs flavor, just a tad."

"The man-hater part? Please tell me, I need to know."

"She is aloof, often alone. There is some talk she runs around with unsavory characters. I don't know, Anne. I've no personal encounters with her to report. This is all hearsay."

"Alan, I have a feeling that she's involved in the Caroline McKelvey case." She waited for his response. "You don't act surprised."

"I'm not. You told me Simone lived in the same building as your victim and that she was home, or rather she was seen entering the building that evening shortly before Caroline was killed. You also told me the building was secure, that no one could enter unless the doorman let them in or they had a key. Therefore, Simone Gray was and is . . . one of your suspects." He was looking at her intently. "Do you want to tell me more?"

Briefly she explained about the newspapers found in The Alhambra's incinerator. "It's Caroline's blood. And there is a footprint . . . just the toe, actually, a boot's toe. A woman's boot. 'Dainty' is how the crime lab described it."

"Not Nicky Nelson's?"

"Not hardly."

"Yes, I see." He nodded. "It could well be that Simone killed the girl. She might have held on to the incriminating newspapers, kept them in her apartment until she thought they would pass through the trash unobserved."

A waiter was standing at Alan's shoulder. He handed over a white envelope. "Mr. Woodward of New Jersey sends you this with his compliments, sir." Across the room, Jim Woodward was sitting at a round table with his wife, his two guests and Alex Shannon. Woodward nodded to them.

Alan tore open the envelope. "He's inviting us to a reception tonight at the Willard Hotel. It's in honor of his appointment to the cabinet . . . hosted by the salmon industry on the northwest coast. The President will be there."

"Woodward is courting your support," said Anne.

"Don't be a cynic." Alan's blue eyes teased. "We belong to the same party and he is senior to me. My support won't do him any good. Maybe he just thinks we are a charming couple, you and I."

He walked her out to her car after lunch. "I am stunned by your suggestion that Simone Gray could be a murderer. I mean, I see where you're coming from with this. Anything is possible, the human heart being what it is."

"I've instructed her to appear at police headquarters this afternoon. She's due there in about twenty minutes. I told her to have a lawyer with her."

Alan took her keys, opened the door of the Porsche.

"I have been mulling over what you asked at lunch . . . the man-hater bit, in particular. I rather think you're right. There is something off-putting and scornful about Simone. Still, I have seen her in the company of powerful men. She seemed to be having a good time for herself."

"Such as?" Anne slid behind the wheel.

"She used to go out occasionally with Senator Koubec, but he's retired now and gone home. I believe I've seen her with Judge Principato." He bent and kissed her through the open window.

"Thanks for lunch, darling," she said.

"Oh, and another time," Alan finished, "I recall quite clearly . . . it was, in fact, this summer, maybe in June or July. I had some constituents in town. We were dining at the Jockey Club and someone in my party said with great awe, 'There is Simone Gray' . . . members of the TV press being famous personalities in their own right. Sure enough, there was Simone Gray in a far corner of the room tête à tête with Father Jesse Clore from the Cathedral."

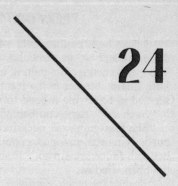

24

At two in the afternoon, Anne was waiting at police headquarters on Indiana Avenue. She had alerted Cathy and requested an interrogation room. At two-forty, she was still waiting for Simone Gray to show up.

"I don't know, Fitzhugh." Dakota was skeptical when she called to tell him that she was on her way to The Alhambra to arrest Simone. "The lady is bad news, but I think you might be jumping the gun here. You're going on circumstantial evidence and gut feelings. I was there Friday morning. I saw Caroline. Something tells me a man killed her."

"Simone wasn't alone that night. Harold Perry said a man came home with her and Simone admits that. It's possible that two people are involved in this murder, but *she* was there, Dakota. Simone was there and I am going to prove it."

At three, Anne called the U.S. Attorney's office and asked for a warrant to search the apartment of Simone Gray. In less than fifteen minutes, she was on her way out Massachusetts Avenue in a light falling rain.

Consider the human heart, Alan had said. He'd made it an apologue, a vindication and excuse. And more—a justification, an acquittal, a reprieve into grace.

The human heart is a wayward thing, thought Anne. And fragile. So easily hurt, so quick to break . . . so easily inflamed.

Rob Fitzhugh had been her first passion. The law had

been her second passion. Both were lessened now by the passing of time, by all the little deaths. Where was her own heart now?

She passed the graceful white Greek church, St. Sophia. On the right was St. Albans school and the spires of the Cathedral. The intersection with Wisconsin Avenue lay at the top of the incline. She parked on Massachusetts Avenue across from Bryce Park. The Alhambra was just across the wide avenue.

"Well now, it's Detective Fitzhugh here again." The doorman was the young man who'd been on duty this past Monday morning when she first came to The Alhambra with Dakota.

"You have a good memory. How do you know my name?" Anne shook out her umbrella.

"Harold told me. Fitzhugh is the lady detective, he said, and Lieutenant Dakota is the one with the mustache." He grinned shyly. "You sure ain't the one with the mustache."

"What is your name?"

"I'm Jack Lee. I work 12 to 7 A.M., and sometimes day shifts."

Anne rested her heavy leather shoulder bag, which contained both the Glock and walkie-talkie, on the lobby table. She said, "You were on duty here last Friday morning when Miss Nelson called down and told you that Caroline McKelvey was dead."

"Not exactly, ma'am. It was the preacher from across the street that told me. She call him and he came here, came knocking on the door. I was sitting in that chair right there, sort of resting, and he came knocking hard on the door."

Of course, that was the way it had been. "You are talking about Father Jesse Clore from the Cathedral?"

"That's right, ma'am. He claim Miss Nelson called him and it was an emergency and he had to go up right up to the sixth floor. He says 'Miss Caroline McKelvey is dead.' And I called up and she says, 'That's right, she dead . . . Miss McKelvey's been murdered.' So I let him go right up."

"And then you woke up the building superintendent?"

"That's what I did and we went up too. It was right terrible. Miss Nelson was crying and shaking, and there was blood everywhere."

"Jack, did you see any of the other tenants moving about that early in the morning? I was thinking maybe . . . Simone Gray. You didn't see her by chance?"

"No'm. She went out before I came on duty. I know that's the way it was 'cause the preacher, Mr. Clore, he asked me if I'd seen her and I said no."

Anne paused, taking in that bit of information. "Say that again, Jack. It was five o'clock on the morning that Caroline McKelvey was killed and Father Clore asked if you had seen Simone Gray around?"

"Yes, ma'am. He asked me that right 'fore he got on the elevator to go up to six. I told him Harold said Miss Gray went out about ten that evening. She gonna be out of town for a few days."

"Does Harold always tell you about all the tenants . . . their comings and goings?"

"Well see, I feed Miss Gray's cats when she goes away. She told Harold she'd be gone all weekend. The preacher say . . . " Jack Lee hesitated.

"What did the preacher say?"

"The preacher, he say, 'She didn't tell me she was going away, Jack. You know where she's gone to?' I said no, I don't. The preacher, he got on the elevator and went up to six."

"Do you know why he was asking about Miss Gray?"

"No'm, I don't. He comes over to see her sometimes."

Anthony Jesse Clore and Simone Gray. It gave Anne an odd thud in her chest to consider the possibilities. Friends, lovers . . . what? It was not a combination of personalities that made any sense to Anne. She remembered the unease that Jesse had shown when Peter Carver told his shoddy story about Simone. It struck her now that his reaction was more personal than he had been willing to admit.

As for Simone, where was she?

"What about right now? Is Miss Gray in her apartment this afternoon?"

"No, ma'am. She's not there now."

Anne pulled out the official envelope containing the warrant. "You see this? This warrant gives me permission to enter Simone Gray's apartment. I want you to take me up and unlock the door."

He looked uncertain. "Mr. Harris, he'll be out right now."

"It's O.K., Jack. Let's go." Anne was moving toward the elevator.

Simone Gray's apartment was on the front of the building, facing the Cathedral and the park across the street. It was handsome, well furnished in a sparse, expensive sort of way. The color scheme throughout was black and gray and white. The carpeting was white. There were in the living room a few accents of red. A pile of unopened mail lay on the coffee table.

It looked to Anne like a place that was not used often. She switched on a lamp, pulled open the drapes. "That will be all, Jack. If Mr. Harris comes in, tell him I'm up here. If Miss Gray appears, ring up and alert me, will you?"

He did not want to leave. "You don't think Miss Gray is the killer, do you?"

Anne heard the unease in his voice. She responded with her own questions. "Jack, what do you know about Miss Gray? Can you tell me anything about her?"

"She's nice, you know what I mean. She's got two cats and she loves 'em a lot. She tells me about 'em. She says, 'Jack, a cat, she is a smart animal . . . she walks by herself and she don't let nobody get to her.' Both her cats are females. One named Amy'thist and one named Pearl. Here they are . . . "

He swung open the bedroom door. "Hello, ladies."

The Persians were curled on the gray satin comforter. They looked up languidly, one stretched a paw. A dark tail flicked.

"They're two lazy ladies," sighed Jack Lee with obvious affection. "I feed 'em for Miss Gray when she's away. They don't go anywhere."

"Miss Gray travel a lot?"

"Yes'm. Most every weekend, she goes somewhere."

When he left the apartment, Anne went straight to the closet in Simone's bedroom. She counted five pairs of boots. All were suede and in the same style with the same pointed toe. They were in shades of navy, brown and gray. There were two pair of black boots as well. They were lined up neatly in the back of the closet and had boot-stretchers in them.

Except for one pair.

Anne found the last pair of boots in the bathroom at the end of the hall. They were of a light camel color and had just been cleaned. The suede cleaner stood beside the freshly brushed boots on Simone's wicker linen chest.

When she picked up the right boot, it was obvious to Anne that its sole had been recently scrubbed, scrubbed hard. It was very clean and the suede around the edging of the boot right at the toe was still slightly damp and discolored. Simone Gray had not been able to get the bloodstains entirely out of the stitching.

Anne found an empty Lord and Taylor shopping bag on the closet shelf and packed the camel-colored boots to take them back to the lab. She put the bag beside the front door and decided to make a cursory search of the apartment.

Just what she was looking for, she wasn't sure.

Anything . . . to link the elusive Simone Gray more closely to Caroline McKelvey.

The apartment was spacious. It was well kept and neat, the bedroom closets were orderly . . . both held Simone's clothes, one for winter and one for summer.

Anne looked for evidence that Simone ever shared the apartment with anyone . . . in particular, a man. There was no second toothbrush, no aftershave lotion, no man's bathrobe in either of the two bathrooms.

The second bedroom was both guest room and den. It contained an upholstered sofa bed, end tables and a chest in black lacquer. A Chinese inlaid desk held Simone's electric typewriter, a file cabinet stood behind it. Above it was a wall of plaques and candid pictures, some in black and white and some color shots, of Simone Gray at work on the Hill. In them all, she looked beautiful, wary and self-contained.

Like a cat that walks by herself, thought Anne.

She opened the desk drawers. Nothing unusual caught her eye. She tried the drawers of the filing cabinet but they were locked.

The living room had the same neat, impersonal character. Also the dining room with its handsome Japanese screen over the buffet. The kitchen was all white and extremely neat. It appeared that Simone Gray rarely ate at home. There was nothing in the refrigerator but champagne chilling and a plastic-capped can of cat food.

Simone's bedroom was far more expressive. It captured the dual nature of the woman. The color scheme was in the same cool shades, but the textures were sumptuous and inviting. The gray and white tufted carpeting was thick, the drapes and spread of silk. There was a red velvet chair at the dressing table, the scent in the room was Shalimar.

As Anne moved around the room, the cats watched.

On one side of the bed, the black telephone stood beside a small Roledex. Quickly, Anne flipped through it. Of course, Caroline and Nicky's number was there. And Anthony Jesse Clore's. It was under the C's, but said simply *Jesse* in pencil. There were two numbers, office and home.

She looked under the W's for Jim Woodward, found nothing. Nor was Alexander Shannon's number listed for Simone's bedside telephone reference.

There was no clutter anywhere in the room, no trash in the tall enamel bucket beside the chest, no book half-read on the bedside table. No letters or jottings or reminders anywhere. Was there nothing more personal in this room?

On the dressing table Anne glimpsed a cluster of small silver-framed pictures. She moved closer.

They seemed to be family pictures. One was of children on the beach. They were laughing, running into the surf. Probably taken in the early sixties or even the late fifties. Three children in bathing suits. One of the two curly-haired little girls was almost certainly Simone herself.

The second picture also appeared to have been taken years ago. It was a photographer's shot of a handsome man and woman. No doubt, these were her parents. They were holding hands. There was something of Simone in the woman's dark eyes and well-molded cheekbones. Also, something pained about the mouth.

She picked up the third silver frame and gasped. The face that looked back at her belonged to Jesse Clore. It was a sober and serious image of him, unquestionably recent. He wore his clerical collar. His hair was graying at the temples. There was tenderness in his eyes. Across the bottom of the picture was scrawled *To Simone, with shared memories and my steadfast love—for always, Jesse.*

Anne could not say why her heart was beating so hard. It was as though she was invading some private world where she was not supposed to be. But she was not at fault. If anything, *they* were at fault for not being honest with her. Jesse and Simone.

And yet he had seemed to come on to her. Provocative. There was a chemistry. She hadn't imagined that intent. Jess Clore had come on to her, and she had responded with warmth from somewhere deep inside of her. Only a possibility between a man and a woman. That was all, but still Anne felt oddly betrayed. Why had Jess Clore not told her?

The frame was still in her hand when she heard the front door open. Anne turned her head, but stood quite still.

The door had opened. She was quite certain of it.

And now, as she listened, the door was shut by a firm hand.

She replaced the silver frame on the dresser and moved across the room toward the door to the hall. Where was her purse with the walkie-talkie and her pistol?

At the bedroom door, Anne listened. If the intruder was the doorman, she felt certain that he would have called out to her. There was a footstep. Another. Someone was moving about in the living room.

The purse? Suddenly, she remembered.

She had put it down on the floor in the bathroom when she was examining the camel boots. Thank God, the hall was carpeted. Anne moved like a quiet shadow into the bathroom. The purse was just where she had left it.

Kneeling, she took out the pistol and slipped it from its holster. Her hands were cold and trembling.

Perhaps Simone had gotten past Jack Lee and come up to her apartment unseen. She might be armed. Anne rose and stood behind the half-open door. Through the crack, she could see the hallway. A shadow fell as someone approached.

The intruder was Nicky Nelson.

Anne glimpsed the dark-haired girl as she entered Simone's bedroom. She looked pale and intense. It was obvious that Nicky was caught up in her own thoughts and did not suspect that anyone was in the apartment.

There came the scrape of drawers opening and, as quickly, closing. The closet door banged against the wall. Anne winced. Nicky was clumsily searching in the apartment for something.

Whatever it was did not seem to be in Simone's bedroom.

Anne heard Nicky enter the second bedroom. She heard the sound of drawers being pulled open, one by one, and then, after a measured time, slammed shut. She heard murmured swearing when the file cabinet proved to be locked.

The telephone rang suddenly.

Anne could almost hear Nicky's sharp intake of breath. The girl was now close, out in the hall.

The pistol in her hand, Anne stepped from the bathroom. "My God . . . my God!" Nicky Nelson fainted dead away.

It took only a slap on the face to revive her.

Nicky stumbled into the living room and threw herself on the couch. "I can't believe this. What the devil are you doing in here?"

"I have a search warrant. You don't. I'd like to know what you are doing here."

"I guess I'm looking for the same thing you are!"

Anne studied the untidy figure lying on Simone's couch.

"Sit up, Nicky. Damn it, this is serious! I have to know what you're doing in this apartment. Otherwise I am going to arrest you for breaking and entering."

Nicky struggled to a sitting position. "I am looking for Caroline's portfolio," she said angrily. "I have reason to believe that Simone has it, and I want it."

"How did you get in this apartment?"

"Caroline had a key. Simone gave it to her. I'd been looking for it and I just found it this morning. She had put it in an empty yogurt container in the refrigerator. Can you believe that!"

"Why Caroline . . . not you, Nicky?"

"They were friends. I was the outsider." There was something both angry and poignant in Nicky's voice. "Some nights, Caroline would come down to this apartment and they would talk for hours. I was working, of course. Even if I'd been home, they wouldn't have wanted me."

"How do you know they were such good friends?"

"Caroline told me. She had no artifice. She didn't even see how that would hurt me. Simone Gray was my ideal. I mean, *I* was the one who knew Simone . . . *I* was the one who had talked Caroline into moving in here!"

Anne found a seat in the gray chair across from Nicky. She said with some urgency, "Tell me about Caroline's portfolio. I want to know what it is . . . and why you want it. No stalling, no game-playing now, Nicky. Or I'll book you for breaking and entering, for impeding an investigation. I'll book you as an accessory to a murder."

Nicky ran her hands through her tangled hair. "Well, I can't find it anyway, so what's the use!"

"Spit it out, Nicky, I'm waiting."

The girl looked at Anne with dark troubled eyes. "I might as well tell you what I think. I think Caroline was murdered because of what she was on to."

"On to?"

"Simone Gray had convinced Caroline that something was amiss in Woodward's office. I'm not sure just what the big deal was . . . graft, scandal, something like that. It was Simone who talked Caroline into applying for a position on Woodward's staff, and, sure enough, before long apparently something turned up. Caroline had this leather portfolio . . . you know, like a small notebook except it had pockets in it and she was keeping all her evidence in it."

"Did Caroline tell you? Did you see this evidence, Nicky?"

"No, she didn't tell me but I listened . . . I snooped. About ten days ago, I came into the apartment and overheard Caroline talking with Simone on the telephone in the kitchen. They were arguing, I mean really going at it, about how to 'handle' the materials that Caroline had found. Caroline didn't hear me come in. I went into her bedroom and there lying on her bed was the portfolio. So I looked through it."

"That was a pretty aggressive move on your part."

Nicky laughed, a short, hard sound. "I am naturally nosy. Damn it all, I felt I was being left out! Anyway, what I saw were some letters and some Xeroxed papers. They had to do with contributions made over a period of years to Woodward by some big environmental group called Safe Guard America. Maybe some more things too. But I saw that much."

"Are you telling me that the portfolio is missing now?"

"Exactly." Nicky clasped her hands together nervously. "Last Friday morning when I found Caroline dead, I went all to pieces. It never crossed my mind that her death was in anyway connected to this thing with Simone."

"You changed your mind. Now, you think it was?"

"Now I know that's why Caroline was murdered. You see, when I was looking to see if anything had been stolen from our apartment, it struck me pretty quickly that the portfolio wasn't there. I remembered, as clear as anything, how Caroline sounded when she was arguing with Simone on the telephone. She said, 'Nothing you can say or do is going to make me change my mind. I don't owe you anything, Simone.' Nicky paused for effect. "Three days later, Caroline is dead and the portfolio is missing."

Anne stared at her. "Dakota questioned you on Friday.

We were both here on Monday morning. All you could talk about were burglars and . . . Caroline's trusting nature.''

Nicky's face was contorted. ''Well, that was part of it. The portfolio was gone and, damn it all, Caroline *had* let the murderer into the apartment.''

''I want all of it now. What was your game plan, Nicky?''

''Well, I got to thinking. It had to be Simone. I think she is planning some big exposé of Woodward . . . right now, before his confirmation hearing on the new cabinet post. I said to myself, why is Simone Gray pulling this off? Why not . . . me? If I had Caroline's notes, I could put together a news special that would knock the socks off ABC.''

''So that's why you are here in Simone's apartment. You're looking for the portfolio?''

''Only I am scared to death. I swear to you, Simone knows that I know the truth.'' Nicky's eyes grew black with fear. ''She's following me, watching me . . . or someone is. Someone is going to kill me unless you help me, Anne Fitzhugh.''

25

A knock at the door . . . a discreet knock. A soft voice saying Anne's name interrupted the moment. It was Alfred Harris.

Anne opened the door.

The building manager spoke nervously. "Detective Fitzhugh, I was told you were here. I called up to the apartment a few minutes ago, but there was no answer. I thought I'd better check." He saw Nicky on the couch. "Oh, Miss Nelson! Is everything all right? I mean it's highly irregular . . . "

"Everything's under control, Mr. Harris." Anne picked up the shopping bag containing Simone's boots. "Come on, Nicky. Isn't it time you were at work? I'll walk you to your car."

"It's O.K.," the young woman said. "I'm fine driving downtown by myself. And I'm not worried while I am on the job. I'll just stay out of Simone's way if she shows up on De Sales Street."

"She won't," said Anne. "She knows I am looking for her."

It galled Anne to accept the fact that the person who could best help her find the suspect was right across the street. That man was Simone's covert lover, Father Anthony Jesse Clore.

"He is in the Cathedral right now." Jess Clore's secretary explained when Anne appeared in the doorway. "There is a special four o'clock service this afternoon. It's

235

for the school. The dean asked Jess to assist him. You can wait here or . . . ''

"Thanks, Alice. I think I'll go over to the Cathedral." Anne followed the covered passage past the small stone Chapel of the Good Shepherd that was open day and night into the huge sanctuary. The lower level of the cathedral smelled warm, waxy and English. She wandered along stone-floored corridors past a chapel with walls made from glittering bits of glass. She found the stairs and climbed them, hearing music as she climbed, and found herself in the nave of the great church.

The service was in progress. She heard Jesse Clore's rich encircling voice somewhere to her left leading the congregation in prayers, voices rising and falling in response to his readings.

The main sanctuary was large, with so many bays and arches and chapels that she felt anonymous and invisible, able to wander at will while the service went on. Above her head were the pointed arches.

The rib vaulting of each arch seemed light and frothy, the lines and curves like creamy lace. The arch was in fact stone upon stone. She looked up and saw a boss stone directly above. It made her think of Emile Farrare.

The small chapel in front of her was marked Holy Spirit and was designated for meditation. A dozen candles burned before the altar which had hanging above it the picture of a light-haired, robust, virile Christ. Death . . . pain . . . rebirth. She turned and walked down the nave toward the great rose window above the west façade.

She would wait for Jesse Clore in the narthex. She would stand where she could see him. If he looked beyond the congregation, he would see her as well.

The organ sounded. The music, led by boys' voices, was resounding into the last hymn. A few minutes later, Jesse Clore came down the aisle to Anne standing in the narthex beside the west doors.

"I saw you waiting here." He was still wearing his vestments, lace over his dark trousers, pale satin at his neck. He looked serious, troubled. "I saw you clearly standing here watching the service. Why didn't you come closer?''

"I didn't come to pray. I came to talk to you about Simone."

She saw the way his face went white, the skin around his eyes tightened.

"It's important that we talk now . . . about Simone Gray." A flat statement.

"Well then"—he sounded resigned—"let's find a quiet place."

Anne waited for him to change from his vestments, the cowl and gown. When he returned from the dressing room in his black shirt, familiar white collar and sports coat she noted his face was still very pale.

"Shall we go to your office?" She was all business.

"No. I know a spot here in the Cathedral where no one will bother us." He led her down the stairs and through a series of brown wainscoted passages to a narrow door which he opened with a key from his key ring. It was a sitting room.

Rather, thought Anne, with a certain irony, it is a confessional. She noted the room's sparse intimacy, the cross on the wall. She watched while he threw open a window. The smell of rain-scented earth came in.

"All right." He turned to her with a certain hardness. "We'll talk about Simone if that's what you want."

"I trusted you, Jesse. I feel that you betrayed me." She was surprised at the heat in her tone. She faced him, saw that he was staring past her, avoiding her eyes.

"I didn't think you needed to know everything," he said simply, "only what was relevant to Caroline's death."

"*You* made the decisions. You didn't think Simone's effect on Caroline was relevant . . . the fact that Simone had talked Caroline into spying on Jim Woodward! You knew that, and you didn't tell me."

"*Mea culpa*," he replied softly. "I knew. I didn't tell you. Simone has a nose like a bloodhound for moral indignities . . . but sometimes she's wrong. I've long admired Woodward so I hoped this was one of those times that Simone was wrong."

"Did you know about a portfolio of incriminating documents that Caroline purloined from Woodward's files?"

"I've just learned of it," he said.

"You've seen Simone today then?"

He rubbed his face with his hands. "Yes, I've had a long and sobering talk with her. There was a lot I didn't know that I know now. All I can say, Anne, is that I am sorry. I misled you, I'm afraid."

"You misled me about Emile Farrare. You wanted me to think he was Caroline's murderer."

"It came out that way. I was trying to make you understand Caroline. It sounded as if I was leading you to suspect Emile of her murder. I never thought he did it. I told you that."

What did it matter? Anne shook her head wearily.

He reached out and put a hand on her shoulder. It seemed to her a caress as a gesture of support. She pulled back stiffly and said, "I've just come from Simone's apartment, Jess. I found some incriminating evidence. I have a pair of boots with Caroline's blood on them. No doubt, Simone was wearing them last Thursday night. I've reason to believe they will also match a piece of bloody newspaper with the toe of a boot outlined on it . . . a boot print made in Caroline's blood."

"Yes," he said quietly. "I rather think you are right."

"Then Simone admitted as much?"

He groaned as if explaining all this to her was difficult for him. "Yes, Anne, she was there. Simone has admitted that to me. She found the body shortly after Caroline was killed. She said she went up to the girls' apartment shortly after she returned to The Alhambra last Thursday evening. She saw the door was ajar and she went in. Caroline was lying on the counter in a pool of blood. She was quite definitely dead."

"Did she also tell you that she and Caroline had quarreled over a portfolio of letters and clippings from Woodward's office that Caroline had taken? Did she tell you that the portfolio is now missing?"

He blanched. "You are suggesting that Simone killed

Caroline because of some damn papers? You're wrong. She didn't. She wouldn't. Killing is not in her!''

For a moment they stared at each other.

"I don't believe you have the judgment to make that call, Jess. You are, after all, her lover.''

His dark eyes dilated. "Wrong. I'm not her lover . . . I'm her brother.''

She was not sure that she'd heard him correctly. Stunned, Anne repeated slowly, "You are Simone Gray's brother.''

He loomed over her in the small room. His voice had a hard edge. "Look, this is private stuff, Anne. I don't like talking about it. But if it will help you . . . if it will help Simone, I will.''

"I think you'd better. Nothing is making sense.''

"Simone is the younger of my two sisters. We were born in a family in Connecticut that, I guess, started off happy enough.'' Jess began to pace the room as he talked. "I was the firstborn, then came my sisters. We lived in a house with a front porch and a garden out back. My father was quite a gardener. Roses, that was his specialty. I get sick when I smell the scent of certain roses.''

"What happened to your family, Jesse?''

"On the surface nothing . . . for a long time. Underneath, it was rotting like a stinking fish. I told you my mother was ill. When she was feeling up, we had a picture-book life. The house was always sparkling clean and filled with home-baked pies, homemade dresses for my sisters. My mother could do anything when she was manic and she charmed and delighted us with her love and her kisses . . . and songs at the piano at night. We'd just be getting used to that and she'd have a depressive period. It was like a yo-yo. We never knew what to expect.''

Anne nodded sympathetically. She had read enough to know the syndrome that sends a bipolar personality reeling from high self-confidence and marvelous accomplishments to the very depths of despair.

"When she was down, it meant weeks of a gray sort of death in our family,'' Jess continued. "My mother would stay in bed with the shades drawn, or worse. She'd be cowering somewhere in the house, like behind the sofa . . . she'd be still in her nightgown when we got home from school.''

"Couldn't doctors help? There is medication for . . . ''

"We didn't believe in admitting our failures. Not in our family,'' he said bitterly. "My father was a small-town, God-fearing, self-made man. He was the president of our local bank. He was a deacon in the church, and he grew roses. When my mother was having her down times, he would say to friends and neighbors, 'Peggy is sick with her asthma again. Just resting . . . and staying in the house is all she can do. No excitement, no guests. We are managing fine, thank you.'

"Only we weren't.'' She heard the break in his voice.

"My father was a tyrant at home. When my mother was down, we had to make it all work just like normal. I mean, it was a fantasy of his. The older of my sisters ran the house, cooked the meals. And it all had to be perfect . . . just perfect, or off would come his belt. Yeah, he was handy with his belt. And he knew just how to whip you so the stripes didn't show.''

"Oh God, Jesse. This is a terrible story.''

"It gets worse. My sister Jill ran the house like she was born to it, baking pies and scrubbing clothes. I took care of my mother. Strange isn't it, but I was the only one who could manage her when she was having a down time. I fed her every meal she ate, coaxed each bite into her mouth. I sat with her in the night when she couldn't sleep. She was fearful. Someone had to be with her or she'd begin seeing things . . . hearing things. That was my job.''

"Where was your father through all of this horror?''

"He was playing 'normal.' He was sitting down to a big breakfast that Jill cooked, he was off to the bank. He was tending his roses or . . . he was in bed . . . with Sally. My little sister, Sally . . . who is now Simone Gray.''

Anne drew in a breath. She had known it was coming to this. The explanation seemed an obvious final horror.

"How long did this go on?''

"Four or five years. My mother went out one day when

I was in school and drowned herself in a pond behind our house. Jill found her. A few months later, Jill cut her wrists in the upstairs bathroom. She was a lot like my mother and she knew it. That left Sally and me. If I had only known, you see . . . ''

"You weren't aware then that your father was sexually abusing your sister?"

"I didn't know, or didn't want to know, I can't say which. I got a scholarship to prep school and gladly took it. A few months after I left, Sally ran away from home. She was fourteen. She was found and sent home but . . . God was kind.''

He smiled with a certain cynicism and continued, "My father was killed by a speeding car as he crossed Main Street a few weeks later. You should have seen my father's funeral. Everyone turned out . . . what eulogies! He was a righteous man, much admired, much respected in our community.''

"What happened to Sally?"

"His life insurance was her good fortune. She had guts and beauty. She boarded with some neighbors until she finished high school, the insurance paid for college. She was fine . . . she seemed fine for a few years. She wasn't fine at all. She still isn't.''

"I think," said Anne, "that I am beginning to understand.''

Jesse Clore sat down across from her and buried his face in his hands. "We didn't see much of each other for a long time. I was a coward about facing up to the truth about my father and my sister. Finally one night when I'd been in Washington about six months, she rang my doorbell. She was drunk, Anne, and she was crying. I've never seen anyone in so much pain.''

He was struggling with the memory. There was sweat on his forehead. He went on. "Simone Gray is a marvel. She's bright and tender and loving. She is also hard and cynical and she doesn't trust men, especially men who sound off on themselves. The only men she can love are . . . losers. Which brings us to Caroline.''

Anne pushed a wing of dark hair behind her ear. "I'm making the connection already."

"Yes, I thought you would."

He reached out and took both of Anne's hands. "Caroline's story wasn't nearly so terrible but there were similarities. The father's public image, the child's private pain and isolation. Like my sister, Caroline couldn't get her relationship to men right. I tried to help. I let her lean on me."

"Was Simone jealous of your relationship with Caroline?"

He looked stung by the suggestion. "No. They became friends. Simone doesn't love easily, but she loved Caroline."

"They argued, Jess. Nicky heard them arguing."

"As a man of God, Anne, I swear to you that Simone did not kill Caroline."

"How do you know that?"

"Because she told me the whole story." He did not let go of Anne's hands. "Come with me. I'll take you to her now . . . let Simone tell you for herself."

Simone Gray was sleeping, curled like a child on the green leather sofa in Jesse Clore's office. She had an afghan over her. She pushed it away and sat up as they entered the room. "How did you find me?" she said to Anne. There were spots of color in her cheeks, her eyes were glazed.

"It's all right." Jesse sat down on the edge of the sofa. "You have got to come clean with all this, Simone. You have to tell the police the truth."

"Damn it all, Jess! I didn't give you permission to . . . "

Anne interrupted. "Simone, I've been to your apartment. I found your boots. They're all I need to book you on suspicion of murder . . . you might as well talk with me."

The slender blonde woman sat quietly for a moment. All the fire and tension seemed out of her now. The glamour, as well. She seemed older than her years and very tired. She said to Anne, "Actually, I guess . . . I need your help. I need your help very badly."

"Shall I call a doctor for you, a lawyer? It is your right."

"Just listen to me." It was said abruptly, the old Simone.

Anne pulled the rocking chair close to the sofa. "You and Caroline had a falling out. That's how it began. You were angry."

"I was angry at Caroline, annoyed as hell at her. Idealistic little fool." Simone took a long shuddering breath. "You know how I feel about hypocrisy." She was looking more at Jesse than at Anne.

He nodded, strengthening his sister with his compassionate eyes.

She went on with the story. "For a long time, I've been suspicious of the good Congressman James Woodward of New Jersey. The man reads honest, talks integrity and lives . . . so very, very big. I couldn't seem to put it all together. But I had other things on my mind, other targets. I just let it be.

"Then, about a year ago, I spent a weekend with a man . . . a dalliance actually, nothing more. We were holed up in a plush apartment in Atlantic City, snowed in . . . boozed in, whatever. He told me more than he should have. He told me about a fake environmental organization that was, in fact, the cover for some serious offshore dumping of waste hazards for the chemical industry."

"You're talking about Safe Guard America," suggested Anne.

"You're damn right I am." Simone was sitting up ramrod straight now, her old vigor was coming back. "I did some checking around. It looked legit. I couldn't find a single connection to the chemical industry. The only thing that struck me was the amount of money that this organization poured into Jim Woodward's campaign chests."

"More than the legal limits?" Anne asked. "I thought that was pretty well monitored."

"You are talking direct contributions. You probably don't know about something called 'independent expenditures.' A 1976 Supreme Court ruling opened the door to unlimited funding for candidates by PAC's as long as the payments are made on *behalf* of the candidate *without* his or her knowledge. We are talking 'unlimited.' We are talking big money and we are talking about Jim Woodward.''

"Have you got proof of this, Simone?"

"That's where Caroline comes in." Simone tightened her lips. "She didn't want to believe me, of course. I made her look for the evidence. I made her snoop and spy. Shannon, that bastard, caught her in the private files. There was a scene. Pretty scary. She talked her way out of it. She had the charm, you know. She thought she was invincible."

"What happened?" Anne could sense where this was going.

"Caroline found the evidence she was looking for. She told me that but she wasn't prepared to give it to me. She wasn't prepared to bring Jim Woodward down. 'He was,' she claimed, 'making a valuable contribution to the nation, the world.' She was 'in a moral dilemma,' as she put it."

"She tried to tell me," Jess Clore broke in. "She didn't make it clear. When we talked, Caroline would present situations as hypothetical. I couldn't tell which were real and which weren't. I only knew that she was struggling with something."

Simone was staring hard at Anne. "We were supposed to meet last Wednesday night. Caroline stood me up. Again, on Thursday afternoon. I had an interview scheduled and couldn't make it. 'That evening,' we finally agreed, 'after dinner, maybe about nine.' "

Simone took a ragged breath and then continued. "When I got home, I wasn't alone. A man was with me, a nobody, a lightweight . . . he isn't involved. We talked for a while. Then I fixed him a drink and told him to make himself comfortable, I'd be right back. I thought, 'ten, fifteen minutes, and Caroline and I will settle this.' It was a little after seven. I went to her apartment. She was dead . . . murdered. I stood there and looked at her. She was beautiful, even lying there in her own blood, she was beautiful."

"You got blood on your boot," Anne said, "Caroline's blood."

"My footprint was on the newspaper as well. I panicked. I got a plastic bag from the kitchen and I put the bloody papers in it. I took them back to my apartment and put the bag under the sink. It was there for days. I didn't know what to do with it. I thought about burning the papers. But how . . . in the sink? Finally, I decided it was safe to throw them away. I didn't think . . . ''

"Simone, damn it! You discovered a brutal murder. Why didn't you call the police? Why the hell didn't you?" There was anguish in Jesse Clore's voice.

The dark eyes, so very like his own, shone with a hard brilliance. "Because I know who killed Caroline. I needed the portfolio to prove it. I wanted revenge and justice. I still do. And I'll get both . . . my own damn way!"

26

There was a long moment of silence in the room, broken only by the sound of rain beating against the window. Anne studied Simone's intent face and said, "Nicky Nelson says she is being followed. Are you harassing her? Are you following her?"

"I wouldn't waste the time of day following Nicky Nelson."

"Nicky is quite convinced she is in danger. Why would she think that?"

"Because of the portfolio." Simone clasped her hands together. "The portfolio of incriminating papers. Nicky keeps fooling around with this burglary theory because the portfolio is missing. Nicky is trying, in her own not so subtle way, to tell me that she hasn't got it. I accept that. Earlier this week I took Nicky's keys from her purse at the studio and I searched her apartment. I had to be sure. No, the portfolio is not there. Someone else . . . ''

Jesse broke in again, a look of astonishment on his face. "Damn if I can think of Jim Woodward as capable of murder."

Simone's words were cold and bitter. "Woodward isn't gutsy or . . . rash enough to kill. The actual murderer was someone with as much to lose as Woodward. I can't prove it yet but I believe Caroline's killer is Alexander Shannon. I'm now convinced that he killed her and took that damning portfolio. With Woodward's tacit approval, of course."

Anne suspected Simone would say just that. "Is that why

you confronted Woodward after the press conference on Wednesday?''

''I shouldn't have shown my hand,'' Simone admitted. ''But I was seething inside about Caroline. I had to let them know that I was on to the truth.''

''I'm beginning to understand, Sally,'' said Jess Clore soberly. ''The way you see it, Shannon realized that Caroline was about to turn those papers over to you . . . and you were going to blast Woodward out of the political waters. Blast him away as only Simone Gray can do it! You were going to show him up as a fraud.''

''Jim Woodward *is* a sham . . . a damn greedy hypocrite!''

''Shannon had his back to the wall, fearful that this would be the end of Woodward's political career . . . '' Jess was stroking his chin.

''His own career as well! Alex is fiercely ambitious for himself. He's a boy from hell who has worked hard to get where he is. He has everything riding on Woodward's coattails, particularly his credibility. He had to save Jim Woodward. If it meant getting rid of Caroline to preserve the show, Shannon was up to that.''

''Alex has an alibi for Thursday evening,'' Anne pointed out. ''What's more, he didn't have access to The Alhambra.''

Simone sighed wearily. ''That's the part I can't figure out.''

''Perhaps the alibi is a cover. Gertrude just might cover for Alex. Maybe Caroline took Shannon home with her that evening,'' Jesse suggested. ''But would she have?''

''I doubt it.'' Anne shook her head. ''From what you've told me, she admired him extravagantly at one time . . . maybe even saw him as her white knight, but they'd argued. She knew enough to be wary of Alex.''

''I'll admit that I don't have all the answers yet,'' offered Simone stonily. ''All I know is . . . it has to be Shannon. He's protecting Woodward, that self-righteous bastard. Shannon and Woodward . . . they're both guilty.''

Simone was enormously convincing. But that was part

of Simone Gray . . . part of her showmanship, parcel of her charm. One had to take that into account. Anne was trying to see it as Simone did. "Alex Shannon came to The Alhambra last Thursday evening without any particular idea how he was going to get in . . . but he did. And he killed Caroline to silence her, and he took the papers back. Everything tidy, back in its place. In other words, Woodward and Shannon got away with it. Case closed."

"That's what I believe." Simone closed her eyes wearily. Again there was a long silence.

"It just doesn't work," said Anne finally. "Shannon is far too organized, too careful. He'd never have risked it."

"Oh, Alex would take any sort of risk, and do it quite coolly for what he wanted. In this case, he did risk it. And he won. He now has the incriminating papers back and Caroline McKelvey is dead."

"*Does* he have the incriminating papers back?" Anne asked quickly. "That's the odd part. If Alex Shannon is the killer and he's got the papers back, then who is now after Nicky Nelson, and why?"

Simone's face was alert, all exhaustion submerged into the possibility of challenge . . . a thrust. "Do you think Caroline might have hidden the portfolio somewhere and Alex never got the evidence back . . . you believe maybe, we still have a chance?"

"Yes, maybe we still have a chance." Anne's gray eyes were like silver. "We need to establish that Shannon could have gotten into the apartment building on Thursday evening. Who could have . . . would have given him a key?"

"Perhaps he didn't need one," offered Jesse slowly. "I've been to call on parishioners at The Alhambra. Once, I remember the front door wasn't locked. I just walked in. If it happened once . . . "

"My God," exclaimed Simone, "we're not trusting Harold Perry's word, are we? If he told you the front door was locked, that doesn't mean it was. Harold is inclined to say whatever will make it go right for him."

Anne took out her notebook. It was getting dog-eared. She'd have to get a new one when this case was finished . . .

if this case was ever finished. She flipped back through her notes. Dakota said: "No one saw anything except old fellow down the hall named Forrester. *Thinks* he saw Caroline getting into the elevator about 6:30 P.M. just as he was coming into the building . . . caught a glimpse of her before the elevator door closed. *Thinks* she smiled at him. She was alone, he *thinks*." Anne turned to Simone. "Do you know an old gentleman on the sixth floor who uses a cane?"

"Of course. His name is Ed Forrester. He's talkative, lonely. He likes to tell me whenever he has seen me on the news."

"Come on." Anne stood up quickly. "Let's see if he is home."

An hour later, Anne said to Dakota on the telephone, "My dad used to tell me that you build a stone wall, one stone at a time. 'And that's how you build a case, Anne.' is what he used to say. Well, we had a false stone here, Dakota. It was an assumption that the door was locked. Actually, Harold has a history of leaving the front door unlocked. He's likable, say the tenants, but undependable. And unreliable about details."

Dakota swore softly. "Jesus . . . "

Anne continued, "It was the super, Alfred Harris, who insisted the front door was always locked, because that was the way he wanted it to be, believed it to be."

"You think Harris was protecting his ass when he said it was locked that night. I don't know, Fitzhugh, the other guy, the one who was working the door on Friday morning . . . Jack Lee, he said the door was always locked. Always."

"Maybe it was locked when Jack Lee was on duty. But it turns out Harold Perry's not so tight about the rules. I've just been talking to him. Now that he is pressed, he admits he can't remember rightly whether the front door was locked or not last Thursday night around six-thirty. But . . . and here's the important *but*, Dakota"—Anne's voice held suppressed excitement—"the old man named Forrester, you know? He says he recalls the door being unlocked when he followed Caroline inside on Thursday evening."

"Hell, why didn't he tell me that when I questioned him?" Dakota asked. "The old man didn't say anything about the front door being unlocked."

"Maybe he was rattled on Friday, Dakota. He couldn't think."

There was a silence on the other end of the line. "Are you saying I am not much of a cop, Fitzhugh?"

"You're putting words in my mouth, Dakota. All I am doing is talking over this case with you."

"Why bother talking it over with me anyway? It's your case, babe. I'm on administrative leave." His voice was gritty now and impersonal. "You believe that the murderer is Alexander Shannon. It sounds right in my book considering what you're telling me. Well, go after him, Fitzhugh. I don't have to give you permission."

"Thanks for nothing, Dakota."

Anne hung up sharply. Why did Dakota cause her this pain deep in her chest? Damn the man! She was making the call from the guest room in Simone's apartment at The Alhambra. Grays and blacks and touches of red. Somehow, the colors hurt her eyes.

She went out into the living room just as the clock struck 6 P.M. Jesse and Simone were making drinks. She heard them talking in the kitchen, heard the murmur of their voices. Their voices sounded alike, they looked alike . . . the same dark winged eyebrows. Why hadn't she noticed that before?

"You only see what you look for. . . . " Her father used to say that also.

Jesse came into the living room and held out a glass to her. Two fingers of golden liquid, an ice cube. "You drink bourbon, I remember." His eyes held hers. "Thanks, Anne. Thanks for being open and letting Simone have her say."

"Why didn't you tell me she was your sister?"

"I had a feeling . . . a fear that she was going to be involved. I knew that she and Caroline had quarreled. It had me worried. I saw her in the building that night with this lousy guy . . . they'd been drinking. I thought discretion was the better part of valor."

"I want to know something, Jess Clore," Anne questioned. "For a while there, did you have your doubts? Did it cross your mind that Simone might be the murderer?"

She saw the skin tighten around his eyes. "My sister has been through a sort of hell in her life. But I have never doubted her integrity. Caroline had it too. They're the kind of people you count on in the long run. I just wasn't sure how the world would see it."

Anne drained her bourbon. She was conscious of the press of the hour, of twilight darkening to night outside. The pain in her chest had turned into an ache that felt like homesickness. She couldn't shake it off or even understand it.

Jesse Clore put his hand on her shoulder, turned her gently around to face him. "Just one hug? Just one hug between friends. It's due, Anne."

She was suddenly in his arms, held tight and warm against Jesse's heart. Had she hurled herself there? She pressed her cheek against the rough tweed jacket and then raised her face to his. His black lashes brushed her cheek and eyebrows. More than a hug? Yes, she wanted more. She let him find her mouth with his.

"Jess . . . "

"Mm . . . no talking." His arms tightened around her.

It was hard to pull away. It took all the energy she had.

"I've got to go, Jess. Ironically enough, I am going to be with Alex Shannon tonight. And the Woodwards. I'm going to a dinner in Jim Woodward's honor."

Simone was just coming into the living room. "Oh yes, the dinner at the Willard Inter-Continental." She nodded with a certain cynicism. "Tonight's affair has been carefully staged for right before the confirmation hearings. Alex's skillful hand at work. He's on a roll now. Nothing can stop him."

"I don't know," said Anne. "I can stop him."

* * *

The ABC News division on De Sales Street was close to the Mayflower Hotel. Anne left her Porsche with the doorman at the Mayflower, flashed her police credentials. Time was an issue. The receptionist in the ABC building was reading a magazine when Anne came into the lobby. "Nicky Nelson? I'll call up."

In a few minutes, Nicky stepped off the elevator. She had on jeans, and a frayed sweater.

"Where can we talk privately?" Anne was imperative.

Nicky shrugged. "We can use an editing room."

Only a cubicle, TV monitors. The trash can was overflowing. Nicky pulled a chair up and straddled it. "What's all this about? How come you are all dressed up? Where are you going anyway?"

"Listen, Nicky, do you want to break the Woodward story?"

"You know I do. I just don't know how."

"You saw the correspondence that Caroline took from Woodward's files. Then your roommate is killed and the portfolio disappears. If you only had that portfolio, you could break this story wide open. Isn't that right, Nicky?"

"But I haven't got the portfolio! Although someone sure as hell thinks I do. I thought it was Simone. Now, I don't know. I don't know what I think anymore. I'm scared as hell. But yeah ... I'd like to break the story wide open."

"How would you do that, Nicky? How would you break the story?"

The girl's face took on a surprising animation. "I would put together a show around the portfolio. I'd write it myself with strong visual shots ... like a '60 Minutes' take off. I'd take it to our station manager and I'd ask him to get Koppel to schedule a 'Night Line' interview with Woodward to follow. We'd spring my segment on the ten o'clock news. Koppel would follow with his quiz show ... I mean it would be dynamite!"

"We might work that out, Nicky," Anne offered coolly.

The young woman was skeptical. "I haven't got the portfolio. I can't set this up without it."

"I know you haven't got it. But the murderer thinks you do or fears you have copies of the incriminating papers . . . something is loose, not battened down, and I sense it. We have to use you as our bait."

"Use me? How? What do you mean by that . . . use me as bait?"

"I'm going to lure Caroline's murderer into the open. You have to help me. You and Simone Gray . . . working together."

"Simone hates me. She'd never work with me."

"She's going to work with you tonight," Anne said.

"Are you talking . . . dangerous?"

"Dangerous, yes. And it's going to take some bluffing and some real assertive action on your part." Which, thought Anne, will be right up your alley, kid. "It's your big chance, Nicky. Take it." Would she? She stared Nicky Nelson down.

"I'm scared as shit, but I'm on. What do I have to do?"

"Listen carefully," said Anne. "I've got a plan for tonight."

Ten minutes later, Anne was using the telephone in the ABC lobby. "Yes, this is my case, Dakota. Most definitely, this is my case and I'm calling the shots. But I could use some help . . . informal help. I figure you haven't anything much to do tonight and you could stand a little excitement in your life."

"What do you have in mind, Fitzhugh?"

He sounded wary, but just vaguely interested.

"I want you to tail Nicky Nelson. She's going to set a trap for me and she might find herself in trouble."

"Oh Jesus." She heard him groan. Then, "What do I have to do?"

"Nine-thirty tonight. I want you at the National Press Club. Show your badge, take a seat at the bar, order a drink . . . put it on Simone Gray's tab." Anne couldn't resist a chuckle, then sobered. "You'll see Nicky come into the bar and sit down at a table by the window. Someone's going to join her. I'm not sure who that will be. But someone is going to get lured out . . . Dakota, don't let me down, please.''

"Fitzhugh, where the hell are you going to be while I am tailing this damn obnoxious . . . Nicky person?''

Anne could see herself reflected in the glass door of the phone booth. A gold lamé dress, rubies set in gold sparkling at her neck and ears, the sheen of dark hair. "Dining on lamb and hearts of palm. And sipping some fine California wine, Dakota. Just where did you think I would be?''

27

When the President of the United States attends a private party in Washington, there is always an air of subdued excitement. An impressive line of black and gray cars are parked outside the building and men and women with Secret Service pins in their lapels and serious, intelligent faces stand around at windows and in doorways.

Anne arrived ten minutes late for the dinner at the Willard Hotel and was waved through the security check. She had no weapon with her. She'd left the Glock in the glove compartment of her car.

Alan was waiting beside a potted palm on Peacock Alley, the Willard Hotel's handsome mezzanine of shops and dining rooms. He gave her a long admiring look and whispered as they entered the glittering Crystal Room, "A fancy affair tonight, Annie, and a certain amount of tension in the air. I can't say just why. I'm afraid something's in the wind about Woodward's nomination."

She hadn't planned on that. Still, it might work to their advantage.

Handsomely dressed people moved in couples and in clusters around them; cultivated voices rose in greetings, confident voices full of amusement. Anne sensed the energy in the room. It was reflected and magnified in the great crystal chandeliers and in the shining mirrors. It was an energy she understood. Money and power and position . . . tentative and elusive as political power and position always are . . . wafted like invisible smoke.

"Where is our guest of honor and his wife?" she asked Alan. "I don't see the Woodwards." Nor did she see Alexander Shannon.

"That's what I mean," Alan murmured back. "The guests of honor aren't here yet. That's why there's tension in the air."

The salmon was delicious, not to mention beautiful to look upon . . . miles of moist pink delight bedded on silver trays in nests of pale green lettuce, set off with sour cream and mounds of capers.

"I love what they've done to this marvelous old hotel," someone from the West Coast was saying to the senator from California. "Hasn't the Willard been a landmark in this city for simply ages?"

He nodded, charmer that he was. "Ages before your time and mine. Shades of Mark Twain, Jenny Lind . . . their ghosts haunt the lobby. Not to mention President Ulysses Grant, who used to walk over from the White House for an afternoon brandy and cigar in the Willard's lobby. They say businessmen and such, wanting a word with the President, would wait in the lobby for a chance to talk with him, thus the term . . . 'lobbyist.' "

The pretty West Coaster, herself a lobbyist, laughed.

Anne saw a cluster of powerful senators and congressmen near the caviar. They were talking quietly, their faces unduly serious. "Yes," she said to Alan, "something's in the wind."

The moment dispelled. The Woodwards had arrived. They came in with the President and the First Lady. "Just having a few private moments upstairs together," someone beside Anne said with assurance. "Everything is all right, really."

Alex Shannon was in the party that had just entered.

He and the Secretary of State lingered to one side, still intent upon their private conversation. Alex wore his tuxedo well. He looked slim, fit and sun-burnished. He stood with his hands clasped behind his back, listening thoughtfully.

Obsequious? No, never that. Alex had, however, a way of standing very still and giving his full attention. Responsive, brilliant . . . sometimes brutal. These were the words those in the political know were wont to use about Woodward's chief aide. It would not be surprising, thought Anne, if the impressionable Caroline had fallen for him. It was no wonder he was expected to go far.

It was only a *wonder* that she could think that he could be a murderer.

She wasn't going to rush judgment. There was something coldly disconcerting about Alex Shannon, a certain lack of emotion . . . or, was it just steely control? Anne was bothered by his lack of affect. Maybe it was just a personal reaction on her part. She wasn't going to judge him too quickly, no matter what the volatile Simone Gray said.

The doors were opening from the private reception room into the larger room that was set up for the dinner. Anne glimpsed round tables flickering with candles, bright with flowers, soft-skirted, and set with the Willard's best table settings. Nothing had been left to chance for this dinner in honor of the secretary-designate for Hemisphere Protection.

All through the toasts, the gracious witty words that lauded the achievements, the vigor and the vision of the congressman from New Jersey, Anne Fitzhugh watched Alexander Shannon.

If he was nervous tonight, he did not show it. His hand, holding the wineglass, was steady, his movements assured. His eye had not yet caught hers. He was the backbone, the "handler," the strength behind Woodward. He and Gertrude Woodward were the private Woodward team.

Anne noted that Shannon was sitting beside the guest of honor's wife. Their relationship had an odd "bonded" quality to it, a certain intimacy. Had Gertrude become a real mother to this boy adopted in his mid-teens? The relationship seemed tense, more brittle than affectionate. One could hardly suspect anything of a romantic nature. Anne smiled wryly to herself at the thought.

Gertrude Woodward, in a dress of black velvet that did become her well, was totally focused upon her husband. She fingered a pearl and diamond bracelet on her arm and watched him with cool appreciation. So did Alex Shannon.

The congressman was their bird of plumage, he was their lodestar. In some odd way, thought Anne, he was also their unwitting captive.

James Woodward responded to each toast ... in particular the gracious words of the President, with his usual quick candor. He did not stay long on his feet. He acknowledged the kindness and best wishes. He indicated his willingness to serve. His smile and confident look around the crowded room were enough. Dinner was served.

"You're rather quiet," Alan whispered to Anne over the lobster bisque. "Are you ready to tell me what's on your mind tonight?"

"Not yet." Anne put down her spoon. Entering the room, late but with his usual dignified flair, was Marcus McKelvey. "Alan, there is Caroline's father."

"He's a big fan of Woodward's. They have the same goals and ideological stance. He is backing this nomination to the hilt. But you know that."

She knew that ... or would have if she'd thought about it. She could also see how it would have complicated things for Caroline if she suspected Woodward of being a fraud. A sham ... "a hypocrite" is how Simone Gray put it.

Simone had talked Caroline into searching for the truth. The ugly truth that Jim Woodward was taking private money and lots of it from chemical companies that were polluting America. The younger woman had probably not wanted to accept that truth. Then, she found the evidence for herself in Woodward's files.

"You aren't eating," said Alan. "That's not like you. You love lobster bisque."

Anne touched Alan's arm. "Watch. Watch Alex Shannon's face."

Janet Sutton had come into the room through a side door. She was standing by one of the green marble columns. Now she approached Shannon's table. Things were going according to plan.

The slim woman with the wispy fair hair bent and whispered something to Shannon. For a moment, Alex sat quite still. Then, he folded his napkin and put it beside his plate.

He leaned over and said something to Gertrude. There were smiles, brief apologies. Together they rose from their table and, with Janet Sutton, they left the dining room.

No one was paying much attention. Even Jim Woodward gave only passing regard to the departure of his wife and his chief aide.

"What the devil is all that about?" Alan asked Anne.

"That's the curtain going up on Act One of a drama I'm staging tonight in Caroline McKelvey's honor. If you'll excuse me, I am going now . . . to powder my nose."

"You are coming back, Anne?"

"Eventually. Just carry on, Alan, until I do."

Peacock Alley was virtually empty, except for the Secret Service.

Anne wanted to observe her prey as closely as possible, but not be observed. She waited beside the glass door, then walked quickly to the turn of the hall and saw Gertrude's black velvet dress just disappearing into one of the elevators.

Anne followed as swiftly as her gold high-heeled evening slippers would take her to the elevator bank and watched the numbers. The elevator was moving up, stopping now on the tenth floor. Using the house telephone, she called the front desk.

Congressman Woodward was registered in Suite 1012. He and Gertrude would have met the President and the First Lady in that suite earlier. The Woodwards would be staying the night as guests of the Northwest America Salmon Industry, which was hosting this celebratory evening.

Anne dialed another number in the hotel and got Simone Gray's husky calm voice.

"We're ready for action." The ABC correspondent's tone was all business. "If this plan of yours works, Detective Fitzhugh, it's going to work . . . big."

If it doesn't, there's egg on my face, thought Anne. Or worse.

"Nicky placed the call to Woodward's office as planned," she told Simone.

" 'Urgent . . . secrets . . . press scandal' are magic words. Janet Sutton showed up at the dinner and whisked Shannon away from the festivities. Oddly enough, Gertrude Woodward went out with him."

"Have they gone over to the Press Club?"

"No, the three of them are upstairs right now in Woodward's suite. I don't know what's happening. We're going to wing it, Simone. I'll stay in touch. By the way, you're not alone, are you?"

"Jesse is here with me. He'll stay out of the way. He insisted on coming."

"I'm glad," said Anne. She returned to the Willard's mezzanine floor. Laughter, piano music and a soft wave of voices floated into the hall from the Crystal Room.

She could not go in . . . not yet.

The Pennsylvania Avenue lobby was quiet. There seemed to be a lull between the constant pulse of those going out for the evening—a few limos were still waiting at the door—and guests coming in. Anne found a secluded place on a leather sofa to the side of the front desk and sat down to wait and watch. She hoped she looked as if she were waiting for someone.

She was . . . but she wasn't certain yet who it would be.

"Hello." Jesse Clore was standing over her. "I couldn't stay in that room with Simone and wait for something to happen. I'm too damn nervous." He sat down on the sofa beside her, picked up a magazine and sheltered his face from the view of those passing by in the lobby. "On the other hand, Simone is cool as a cucumber."

Anne saw Alex Shannon pass through the lobby and go out through the brilliant brass swinging doors. He looked purposeful, intent. He turned left . . . toward Fourteenth Street, the National Press Club.

"The bait's been taken." Anne pressed Jesse's arm.

He looked at her with admiration. There was color in his face. "I can't believe we're doing this . . . that I am doing this. In fact, what *are* we doing?" He cleared his throat nervously. "I am not exactly sure."

"Nicky is at the Press Club. Her job is to get Shannon agitated. She's going to do it as only Nicky Nelson can. She will suggest that she has the incriminating documents about Jim Woodward and his financial ties to Safe Guard America, that indeed she has copies of those papers."

"Shannon's a cool sort of devil. He isn't going to roll on the floor and play dead for Nicky Nelson."

"Of course not. Nicky's ploy is to get him agitated . . . and angry as hell. We want to see what Shannon does when his cover is shaken. It is his play. Then, ours."

"What is . . . ours?"

Should she tell him the whole game plan? She liked this man, liked him a lot. She only smiled in response. "Just wait and see, Jess. This is television. Bright lights and illusion. Simone says 'if it's going to work, it's going to work . . . big.' "

She sent him back upstairs. "Stay with Simone. We'll be up soon enough."

Anne powdered her nose and went back to the party. They were just starting dessert and coffee. The room smelled deliciously of cordials and brandy.

"Really!" said Alan. "You missed the entrée. And almost missed dessert."

He was teasing her, but he was curious, concerned and entirely serious. "Is everything going all right?"

Anne studied the head table. Gertrude Woodward's place was still vacant and that struck her as strange. Wouldn't she have returned to the dinner while Alex went over to the Press Club in answer to Nicky's summons?

Gertrude Woodward knew enough not to be absent too long or people would notice and talk. The President of the United States was her dinner partner. It was imperative that she be here doing what she was supposed to do—gracing the political ship.

"No, everything is not going all right," she whispered back. "I need your help, Alan. Let's get out of here fast."

Without a word, the congressman from Virginia rose. Their good-byes were quick and gracious, with vaguely apologetic smiles to those at their table. "Sometimes the less said, the better," Alan murmured as they headed for the door.

"Maybe they'll think we are having a fight," whispered Anne.

"We are," responded Alan grimly. "You've been mysterious and remote as hell all evening, and now you're dragging me off before I've had my coffee. What the hell is going on?"

Anne opened her purse and took out a scrap of paper. "I need your help, Alan. Please go to the bar upstairs, the one called the Nest, the piano bar that looks down on Fourteenth Street. Ask for a table by the window . . . do you mind? When you see Alex Shannon coming . . . he will most likely be with a fierce young woman with a head of wild dark hair . . . but maybe not, go to a house phone and call this number."

"Whose number is it, and what am I calling for?"

"Simone Gray will answer and you'll say, 'Alex Shannon is on his way.' "

"What about the dark beauty? Shall I say if she is along?"

"I didn't say she was a beauty, Alan. 'Fierce' was the word. Actually it doesn't matter if she's with him, or not. Nicky will have done her part. Alex Shannon is the one we care about."

As for Nicky, Anne admitted to a certain apprehension.

Dakota would see to it that Nicky was safe, Anne told herself as she took the elevator up to the tenth floor. Nothing would happen to Nicky Nelson as long as Dakota was watching over her.

There were two doors to Suite 1012. Both were closed.

It won't do to lurk about, thought Anne. The night maid was coming down the hall. She was a small oriental woman, with a pushcart, towels over her arm, a box of chocolates in her hand. She looked intelligent, capable.

Anne removed her police badge from the beaded gold purse.

"Please," she said, "I'm a police officer and this is very important. I need you to go into 1012 right now. I want you to do just as you normally do, turn down beds or whatever. Then come out of the suite and leave the door unlocked."

The woman studied Anne for a moment with thoughtful eyes. "I do," she said. "I do right now." She gave a small graceful bow.

Anne headed back to the turning of the corridor.

"Oh," she said, bumping squarely into James Woodward.

"Oh, hello." He looked as though he didn't quite recognize her. He was frowning slightly. "Somehow, I've lost my wife." He was making an effort to sound genial. "I came upstairs looking for Gertrude. I just slipped away for a few minutes."

"Marvelous party," Anne called over her shoulder as though she were in a hurry to return to it, "particularly the salmon . . . "

"That's just what the President said." Woodward chuckled, took out his room key and disappeared through one of the double doors to Suite 1012.

Anne took a deep breath and glanced at her watch. It had been six minutes since Shannon left the Willard Hotel. It would take him no more than five minutes to reach the Press Club. Nicky would keep him no more than ten minutes, then five minutes back.

It was all point, counterpoint. It had to work out right.

The maid was coming out of the second door of Suite 1012. When she saw Anne, she bowed and pointed behind her. "Into kitchen area. Is best way, I think."

Anne nodded her thanks and gingerly opened the back door to the Woodwards' suite. She found herself in the suite's kitchen. She could hear a television's low but insistent rumble from the sitting room to her right. She sensed a hallway somewhere to the left, bedrooms . . . probably two of them, each with a bath. She stood quietly in the dark while she got her bearings.

"No, I don't understand!" It was Woodward's voice

from the sitting room, sounding angry and petulant. "My wife and my top aide walk out in the middle of the most important dinner of my career. And now you won't tell me why . . . or where Alex has gone."

"It's nothing for you to worry about." Gertrude's voice soothed. "A minor problem, but we are handling it fine."

"Come on, Jim," Janet Sutton spoke. "I'll go back down with you. The evening is almost over and it has gone so very well. It's terribly important that you are there when the President leaves. Maybe you should even go out to the car with him."

"He came on foot to the Willard . . . didn't you know that?" Woodward sounded testy. "Didn't you realize the President and the First Lady walked over from the White House? There were Secret Service everywhere and press and cameras. It is great PR for the Willard, great PR for me. Where were you, Janet?"

"Sorry, Jim." The young woman sounded contrite, also condescending. "I got sidetracked tonight. Really, I got . . . sidetracked by something important that came up. Now you must go back down to the party. I mean, you *are* the star, you are the whole show! You have got to be there when the President leaves."

"Why the hell aren't you coming too?"

He was, Anne reckoned, talking to his wife.

Gertrude answered but her voice was so low-pitched it could not be heard. In a moment, Anne heard the front door of the suite close decisively. Jim Woodward and his press secretary were returning to the mezzanine and the Crystal Room.

Where was Gertrude Woodward, and what was she doing?

Anne moved quietly to the shadowed darkness by the door to the lighted sitting room. It was a handsome room with a view from its windows of Pershing Square and the Ellipse.

A large scrolled mirror hung on the far wall above the television set. Anne could see Gertrude in her black velvet dress reflected in the mirror. The silver-haired woman was standing in the middle of the room, her face was buried in her hands. Her shoulders shook as if she were crying.

As Anne watched, Gertrude Woodward straightened as if with sudden resolution. Her face was not tearstained but determined. She reached for her purse on the coffee table and took something from it . . . something small and solid that lay on her palm for a moment.

Was it a compact . . . a comb?

No . . . it was a cigar cutter in an antique holder. Anne's heart leaped as she recognized it. She had seen this cigar cutter—or one just like it on Shannon's desk. She had seen it in Alexander Shannon's hand yesterday.

Gertrude removed the small tool from its pearl-encrusted case and turned the small tube upside down, the guillotine end pointing down. At a press of her fingers, a recessed knife shot out from the bottom of the case. It was a short, blunt knife that could be used to open a cigar box.

In the mirror, Anne caught only a glimpse . . . a shard of light, a reflection on the blade of the knife. It was enough for her to form a clear impression. This particular blade was not so blunt. It looked thin and razor-sharp.

28

"That cigar cutter is the weapon that killed Caroline," Anne said when she joined Simone and Jesse Clore in Simone's room on the twelfth floor. "A small tool sharpened. Razor-sharp. It has to be the murder weapon."

Simone's hands clinched . . . her only sign of nerves. "Gertrude Woodward . . . "

The twelfth-floor room was set up for an interview. A table had been moved to the center of the room, two chairs. The camera was waiting, trained on the scene, two spotlights in place. The camera was shrouded. It was a stage set.

"I think we've miscalculated the actors in this drama." Anne looked at Jesse, who was standing by the darkened window. "I could see Gertrude clearly in the mirror. The expression on her face was anger . . . a certain horror. She knows that cigar cutter is the murder weapon."

"I cannot somehow imagine Gertrude Woodward killing anyone." Jess Clore shook his head remorsefully. "I've known her for a long time. I know the road she's walked. In her years as a congressional wife, she's seen her life change and not always for the better. The political wife . . . her role, as it were, lost value and she resented that. She had to become something new . . . the career sort . . . independent although still supportive, *and* chic. 'Wife as asset, wife as trophy' . . . that's how Gertrude put it to me once. It irked her. It took some doing. But I rather thought she'd pulled it off."

Anne was staring into space. "The part that confuses me is . . . if that cigar cutter belongs to Shannon . . . if he used it to kill Caroline, then why did he have it lying on his desk afterward? And, more importantly, why does Gertrude have it now?"

"You're talking about a pearl-handled cutter, about five inches long?" Jess asked.

Anne nodded, seeing the cigar cutter clearly in her mind's eye. She'd noted the pearl-handled cutter on Shannon's desk, had studied it, inspected the wrong end . . . and she'd recognized it immediately in Gertrude's outstretched hand ten minutes ago. How could she have been so stupid!

Jesse rubbed his chin. "There's some story I've heard . . ."

The phone interrupted, a low, piercing buzz on the bedside table.

Simone leaped to answer it. She turned to Anne. "Congressman Foley is calling to say that Alex has returned from the Press Club. He came in the Fourteenth Street entrance and took an elevator up. According to Foley, Shannon looks . . . mad as hell."

It was all going according to plan, but not quite. Anne nodded. They would just have to brazen it out . . . she and Jesse and Simone.

"Foley says Alex is alone." Simone was frowning as she hung up the telephone. "Where the hell is Nicky Nelson?"

Nicky had not accompanied Shannon back to the Willard Hotel. Why not? Anne had been certain the aggressive dark-haired girl would stick like butter until it was all over.

Nicky Nelson's job had been to alert Alex that Simone Gray was closing in, was about to make a public ABC challenge that would knock James Woodward right out of the political water. All Simone Gray needed was documentation of the connection between Secretary-designate Woodward and the phony environmental PAC organization called Safe Guard America—an organization that was, in bitter fact, sabotaging hemispheric environmental efforts.

Nicky had been instructed to tell Shannon that she was

to meet with Simone Gray in a room on the twelfth floor of the Willard in less than an hour and supply a copy of the damning information about Woodward and Safe Guard America. Nicky would claim that she had that copy in her possession and judge Shannon's reaction.

Nicky was then to relay in her own harsh way that she was prepared to two-time Simone and deal directly with Alexander Shannon if he would give her exclusive rights to the story which she would break after the Senate's confirmation. That was the bait. The magic word "after." Damage control would be in place. Denials would be forthcoming. It was believable, and it was to the point. The challenge would force Alex Shannon to take some kind of dramatic action.

Anne had pointed out that this scenario would put Nicky in some danger, which was why the abrasive young woman was to draw Shannon to the Press Club bar—a public place—for their meeting. It was also the reason for Dakota's surveillance.

Nicky Nelson's dark eyes had glittered when she heard the plan. It had been Anne's assumption that Nicky would stay close to Shannon until the drama was over. It was going to be Simone Gray and Nicky Nelson's story for ABC. Where was Nicky now?

There was a firm knock on the door.

Simone Gray gave her characteristic catlike shrug. When she opened the door to the hall, she spoke in a voice only a shade more caustic than usual, "Oh, it's you. What the hell do you want?"

Anne could hear anger in Shannon's voice. "I want to know what kind of crazy trick you're pulling, Simone, and why you are baiting me with that girl?"

"I don't know what you mean?"

As soon as Alex Shannon entered the room, he looked toward Anne and Jesse Clore standing by the darkened window. If he was surprised by their presence, he did not betray that emotion. He gave them a only brief, curt nod. His words were all for Simone. "I didn't believe a word of that story Nicky gave me about two-timing you and going for this story on her own. You put her up to it.''

"What are you talking about, Alex?"

Alex Shannon was taut, cold with control. "You've hated Jim Woodward's guts for years. You've been looking for some way to destroy him. And now, you think you've found it. I am calling your bluff, Simone." Again he looked around the room, took in the darkened camera, the spotlights. "I think this is all a setup. I don't think you know the hell *what* you are talking about!"

"Of course I do. And you know as well. I'm talking about a front PAC organization called Safe Guard America that has pumped thousands of dollars into Jim Woodward's coffers through independent funding and bogus donations. Why? So he would go easy on chemical dumping in certain rivers and along certain coasts. And I am willing to say that he has done just that. I am willing to allege that Jim Woodward had purposefully focused his attention elsewhere and given the chemical industries time to make their profits before they clean up their act."

There was only contempt in Shannon's voice as he responded. "You're going to have a hard time proving those accusations. It has just been a matter of priorities for Woodward, no more than that. We've focused on key hotspots . . . nuclear spillage, air pollution. River and waterways . . . they were coming up next. That's why Caroline McKelvey was on board. It was her research area. Only she got a little hungry for scandal-mongering. She started snooping around in matters that didn't concern her. You put that in her head."

"You are damn right, I did!" Simone said. "And she found what she was looking for. Caroline found . . . what she didn't want to find."

"How do you know that?" His voice tightened just slightly.

"She told me what she had found, Alex."

"She *told* you. But, you never *saw* that alleged evidence, did you, Simone? It was all talk between you and Caroline. Have you ever thought that maybe she was trying to impress you . . . her idol, the great muckraker Simone Gray?''

"That's rubbish." Simone's voice was scornful. She stood with her arms folded. Challenging, belligerent. "Caroline found incriminating evidence and that's why she was killed. In fact, it's all coming together for me now. I am convinced that it was you who killed her!"

Anne was watching Alex's face closely. There was no alarm, only a quiet kind of alertness.

"Caroline adored you," Simone went on in a sharp rush of words. "She talked about you all the time. How bright you were and dedicated . . . and fine. My God, Alex, you can turn the charm on when you want to! Yes, you were just the right kind of romantic hero for an idealistic young woman like Caroline McKelvey. You wooed her, Alex. You made love to her."

It was a challenge, flung out as only Simone Gray could do.

Alex hesitated, weighed his answer. Then he sat down in one of the chairs at the table. Disarming and regretful. He said slowly, "It was a fling, a brief romance. A mistake on my part, Simone, I admit to that. Still, it was nothing."

Simone sat down across from him. She was using her smoothest "Simone digs out the story" voice. "Nothing to you, but important to her. You led Caroline on, Alex. You sweet-talked her. Don't lie, I know you did. And then she discovered the truth about you and your sleazy, lying boss . . . so you killed her."

Alex Shannon's voice was soft. "There's no crime in sweet-talking a beautiful woman. I plead guilty to that. The point is we didn't last. Mutual agreement, actually. Caroline didn't really know what she was getting into. She was a little fool about love . . . about sex, so damn idealistic."

"Yes," Simone admitted begrudgingly, "she was that."

"She came to see the error of her ways with me." Shannon gave an unapologetic laugh. "I'm a total pragmatist at heart. I make no excuses for it. Caroline and I had nothing in common."

"You had good reason to kill her, Shannon. She had the evidence on Jim Woodward. She had tangible proof of his guilt."

"All right, Simone, I was angry as hell that Caroline went snooping around in the office." His voice hardened just slightly. "She took some papers that didn't belong to her. I am not saying what they were. She took them, that's all."

"You see. I told you . . ." Simone sounded triumphant.

Alex Shannon held up his palm to stop her.

Anne felt Jesse's shoulder hard against hers, felt him draw in a ragged breath. She drew in her own breath as well. It was as if they sensed that Woodward's chief AA was about to play his ace . . . to throw a bombshell at Simone.

"I told Caroline I wanted the papers back and . . . she gave them to me."

"She . . . what?" Simone sounded incredulous.

Alex's voice was cream-smooth. "I lied to the police. I did see Caroline after she left work last Thursday. I'm going to tell you the truth now. I'd gone out to the canal to jog and when I came back to my car, Caroline was waiting. She knew where I parked . . . across from Old Angler's Inn. She was standing there beneath the trees, waiting for me."

"Why would Caroline seek you out? You said it was over between the two of you?"

"Of course it was. Caroline said what she wanted to talk about was . . . more important than our recent and painful affair." Alex compressed his lips. "We got in the car . . . we talked. She said she'd thought about it and she'd come to a decision. As she put it, a 'painful decision.' She didn't want Jim Woodward's environmental work to stop . . . she didn't want to put a damper on 'his magnificent influence.' So, she was giving the papers back."

Jesse Clore muttered something harsh under his breath.

Simone retorted. "She wouldn't have!"

"Oh, there was more . . . believe me! Caroline had thought this all through. There were strings attached. She wanted the link with Safe Guard America severed. She wanted a personal donation made by the Woodwards to the Chesapeake Bay cleanup campaign . . . a very large donation, indeed. She had other demands. She . . . "

"Caroline was *blackmailing* Woodward!" Simone's laugh was strong and bitter.

"It wasn't funny. It wasn't then . . . it isn't now." Alex continued soberly, "We parted on that note. I have the incriminating letters. Rather, I should say, I *had* them . . . they've all been destroyed. All those damn letters and the copies. Caroline said she kept nothing and that's one thing I do know—Caroline McKelvey's word could be trusted. There's no hard evidence against Woodward now, Simone. It's all destroyed. There is nothing for you or for Nicky Nelson to use to damage him."

There was a long pause when no one spoke.

Then, Simone asked, "Who destroyed the letters?"

"I don't need to tell you that." Alex Shannon leaned across the table and stared into Simone Gray's dark eyes. He was entirely intent. It was as if he had forgotten Anne's and Jesse's presence. "But, I will say this . . . if you try to build some media bombshell around Woodward and Safe Guard America, you're going to be in big trouble. Jim Woodward is scooping you. He's about to launch a personal investigation into this particular PAC organization with appropriate hoopla. He will offer his apologies to the public for having innocently accepted their donations. Plus, he is introducing new legislation that will call for new and severe penalties for chemical dumping in waterways. He is going to be way ahead of you on this, Simone."

"Your guiding hand, I suspect?"

"In my own way, I do what I can." His voice was amused, ironic.

"You are unscrupulous, Alex. You're cold as a snake. I am not sure I can believe anything that you say. I still believe that you . . ."

"Simone, I hadn't any reason to kill Caroline."

Anne drew in a ragged breath. Alex Shannon was either a marvelous actor or he was telling the truth. She wondered what he would say when she brought up the cigar cutter. She didn't want to rush that. It was close to an accusation. "Miranda" was involved. Alex knew his rights. He was too savvy to rush.

"Well, who was the murderer . . . then, damn it?"

"You are asking me to tell you who killed Caroline McKelvey?"

Alex Shannon smiled for the first time, a flash of white teeth. His voice was sober. "I'm not sure I really know the answer to that, Simone, but I suspect . . . "

A hard rap sounded at the door.

Jesse Clore moved swiftly to answer the knock.

When the door opened, Don Dakota's shoulders filled the doorway. His eyes searched for Anne. He said hoarsely, "I have to talk with you."

"Where's Nicky?" she asked.

There was a film of sweat on on The Cowboy's face. "That's what I want to know! She left the Press Club with Shannon. I waited a few minutes, then took the next elevator down. Thirteen floors, express. When I came out of the Press Building I saw Shannon down at the corner crossing Fourteenth over to the Willard. But no Nicky in sight. I turned back to the Press Building . . . that arcade, all those damn shops! There was no trace of her."

Anne looked at Alex, who stood now beside the table. "Where did you leave Nicky Nelson?"

He shook his head. "Nicky was still claiming that she was going to do a number on Woodward, insisting that she had the evidence. I told her I wouldn't bite. When we came out of the Press Building, she left me abruptly. She didn't say anything, she just took off in the other direction."

"You mean north . . . up toward F Street?"

"She crossed Fourteenth. Yes, toward F Street."

Anne turned to Dakota. "She could have used the F Street entrance. She could be right here in the hotel."

"I can't believe I lost her. I let you down, Fitzhugh."

There was remorse in his voice.

"Nicky Nelson lost you, Dakota. But . . . why?"

"I think I know." Alex Shannon cut in abruptly. He squared his shoulders and said with a certain tone of resignation, "I guess the time's come to tell the whole bloody story."

29

The Woodwards' tenth-floor suite was empty. Alex Shannon opened the door with his key card. The lights were on in the sitting room and the TV was still playing but there was no sign of Jim or Gertrude Woodward nor of any of their party.

Alex turned to face Anne and Dakota. "I guess I was wrong. I thought we would find Gertrude here cornered by Nicky Nelson. We must get to Gertrude, you see. And quickly. Nicky may be stalking her."

"Why?" Anne questioned.

"Because Gertrude is the one who is vulnerable to blackmail."

"The material in Caroline's portfolio incriminates Gertrude Woodward?" Dakota sounded disbelieving.

"I'm afraid it does. Our candidate's wife has gotten herself into one terrible spot. And I'm certain that Nicky is on to it."

"Explain, Alex," ordered Anne. "No more dissembling."

Woodward's chief aide sighed and said, "Sit down, all of you. Please. I said I'd tell you the whole bloody story. And I will." He waited for Simone and Jesse, who had come into the suite after Anne and Dakota to settle themselves in the sitting room.

Alex remained standing. He leaned his arms on the back of a tall leather chair and when he spoke again, his words were directed to Simone Gray. "Yes, Simone, the Woodwards have come into big money in recent years. You're right about that. Dead right. Gertrude's made a killing in D.C. real estate. Jim doesn't have a clue what's going on. He doesn't suspect that all this new wealth is a trade-off The deal is this: Gertrude had only to convince her husband that Safe Guard America is a totally legitimate organization with demands that need his personal attention in exchange for massive independent funding of the Woodward office and . . . some very lucrative real estate deals thrown Gertrude's way for personal profit.''

"Oh my God," groaned Jesse. "Gertrude . . . and political graft. Impossible."

"How would Nicky know any of this?" Simone asked.

"She saw the incriminating papers Caroline took from the office. They were misleading, hard to follow. Nicky didn't put two and two together. But if that girl has half the smarts I think she has, then she's on to the fact that Gertrude Woodward is the one she can use her bluffing act on."

Simone nodded her understanding. "When you didn't fall for her pitch at the Press Club tonight, Nicky decided to go after Gertrude on her own. Is that what you think, Shannon?"

"That's exactly what I think. Some kind of hell will break loose if Nicky pushes too hard. Gertrude is on the edge, believe me."

It struck Anne that Shannon was a master at persuasion, subtle persuasion, who might well have put the impetuous Nicky on to Gertrude's trail. She glanced at Dakota to see if the same thought had occurred to him.

Dakota was rubbing his thumb absentmindedly. He looked exhausted, angry. "Nicky, the damn little fool," he murmured. "Where the hell . . . ?"

The important thing, thought Anne, is to get the characters in focus. Gertrude. Jim. Nicky. A telephone call to the piano lounge brought Alan Foley on the line. Anne spoke quickly. "Alan, important question. Did you see Nicky Nelson follow Shannon down Fourteenth Street from the Press Club and enter the hotel?"

"Can't say. I don't know what she looks like . . . except she's no fierce beauty."

"Well then, did Gertrude Woodward just come downstairs? Did you see her in the lobby in the company of a dark-haired young woman?"

"That I can answer. I was just down in the lobby. Gertrude appeared some minutes ago all by her lonesome, and stood arm in arm with her husband to wave the President and First Lady off. She was all graciousness and vivacity. She pleaded illness at dinner but said she was feeling fine now. She still looked rather pale to my eyes."

"Where are the Woodwards now?"

"They've left the hotel to host a champagne and brandy affair on the Sky Roof of the Hotel Washington next door. It's billed as a 'party after the party' for special friends. We're invited by the way. Everyone's gone over already, so I wandered back here to the Nest to wait for you. Wouldn't you like to join them?"

Anne's gaze met Dakota's. Her gray eyes . . . his watchful blue ones.

She said into the telephone, "I'd like that very much, Alan. Wait for me in the lobby. I'll be right down."

"This case is not working out as I expected, Dakota," Anne whispered. "Alex Shannon is setting up Gertrude Woodward. How could he do that . . . and why? It's hard to believe he would turn on her, whatever the reason. It's wrong, ungrateful . . . it's disloyal."

"Hell, it's life," the big detective said bitterly. "For the most part, Fitzhugh, life's just a kick in the teeth." They were in the kitchen of the Woodwards' suite. Time out. A few minutes alone to discuss the case, he'd said. Imperative, his eyes said.

Anne heard the frustration in Dakota's voice. More than weariness. She knew where he was coming from, felt his despair. It was more than losing Nicky's trail tonight. The suspension from the department was hurting Dakota. Hot shots in the local media were charging police brutality over the killing of the young woman on Drake Place. The charges stung him hard. Demonstrations. A few broken windows. He was ragged and raw from it all. The Cowboy was a man who hurt badly when he hurt. His pain touched her.

"Life's not just a kick in the teeth." Anne reached inside herself for the words. "Sometimes it can go inside out— the good way. I'm thinking of last night, Dakota. I was as low as I can get, and then I found myself on a houseboat with someone I trust. Sleeping safe. I remember some comfort in the night from a friend. Doesn't that count for anything?"

"It counts for more than you know." Dakota touched Anne's face in the half-dark. Fingers across her cheekbones, touching her lips . . . his palm was warm as he cupped her chin.

"You're a wonder, Fitzhugh." He drew in a breath, kissing the curve of her lip. He pulled back just enough to study her upturned face. "Also, a fine partner and a damn good detective. I can feel you're narrowing things down. You're pulling it together, making things happen. You're going to solve this case."

Anne shivered, suddenly apprehensive. "Come over to the Sky Roof, Dakota."

"No way. This is your case, your crowd . . . your party."

"It might be I could use some help."

"I said you're doing fine, Fitzhugh. What's more, you'll have the good Virginia congressman at your side. I'd be extra baggage."

He was riding her . . . maybe even provoking her. His eyes glittered in the half-dark. He had a wry kind of smile on his face.

She pulled away, out of his arms. But there was no anger in her, only strength from their embrace. A certain power, her own power.

It helped that Dakota believed in her. She saw that in his face.

"O.K," Anne said, sighing. "Simone and Jesse will stay here at the Willard. They'll be waiting up on the twelfth floor, in case . . . "

"They don't matter. *He* does." Dakota was looking past her.

She could see Alex Shannon in the sitting room. He was standing very still by the window, his hands thrust deep in his pockets. He appeared to be staring out into the night. "He tells a beguiling story," Anne agreed, "just enough remorse to make him sound innocent as snow. Certainly he wouldn't implicate Gertrude unless . . . I mean, it goes against the grain. She's been like a mother to him."

"I don't trust the man. Watch him."

Anne nodded, but there was misery in her eyes. "I wish you would. . . . "

"Listen." Dakota put his hands on her shoulders. It was an admonition. Also an embrace. "You asked me to tail Nicky Nelson. I agreed, and I blew it. But this night isn't over. I'll find her. That's the best I can do. I'll bring her to Simone Gray's room and I'll wait there until you show up. Then I'm bowing out of this. It's your case, Fitzhugh."

He turned away, all business, vintage Dakota, emotions under control. "If Nicky shows up on the damn Sky Roof, beep me. Otherwise. . . . "

"Otherwise, it's my case . . . my party." Anne could not resist a shake of her dark head. "Yes, I got it, Dakota."

Dakota didn't trust Alexander Shannon. Neither did she. Alex had that kind of insolent charm that carries him above trusting. She was good at nosing out guilt. The odd thing was that there was none in Alex Shannon. His story was so smooth, so anguished. He was almost believable. And she had seen the antique cigar cutter in Gertrude's hands. Yes, it was almost . . . believable.

Follow your instincts, Anne told herself. You build a case stone upon stone. She took a deep breath and reentered the sitting room.

Alex did not turn from the window but he spoke to her. "It seems we're in a hell of a spot, doesn't it? And, as usual, I'm the one who has to clean up the garbage. I like being in control, making things happen. I'm good at that. I don't like cleaning up the garbage."

Was he talking about Gertrude and Safe Guard America?

She could see their reflections in the scrolled mirror. Alexander Shannon in his well-fitting tuxedo and the shimmer of her gold dress, her sleek dark head close to his shoulder. "You're the man who runs Jim Woodward's show, you are the brains behind the brains. That means the whole package, Alex. I guess it also means cleaning up the garbage."

He turned and gave a slight smile with some of the old charm in it. "Poor Jim. He's going to be crushed when he knows the truth. Woodward lives on his own illusions. I knew that from the first. I also knew that my job was to have no illusions. Everyone is greedy and self-serving. I play it that way."

Anne studied his face, wondering if Alex Shannon really meant that cynical statement. "Everyone? Have you forgotten that Caroline returned the incriminating papers to you. That was hardly self-serving."

"Are you saying that Caroline was an exceptional person?"

"I think maybe she was. She didn't need to die, Alex."

They turned out the lights, walked toward the door.

"She was a beautiful creature I'll say that," he said. "She saw what she wanted to see in me, and I'll admit that was heady stuff. For a while I thought I was in love with her. I was as carried away as she was." He closed the suite door behind them. "Only she asked too much of me. The trouble with Caroline was she was unrealistic, a bit of a fool."

"She was an idealist. They're never practical," Anne said. "Idealists believe in possibilities . . . amazing possibilities, honorable solutions."

"Honorable solutions," he echoed as the blue and white carpeted hall led them toward the elevator. "Honorable . . . solutions speak to the good in human nature. How lovely. How false. I would argue that most solutions are reached pragmatically. One seeks and finds the weakness in the other side and takes the advantage of it."

"You are talking like a cynical lawyer, Alex. You've been on the Hill too long."

"And you are wise enough to appreciate the power of persuasion. Persuasion is the very keystone of politics, the pulpit and of the media." He gave Anne a knowing smile. "Jim Woodward has his own way of persuading others to go along with him. His position allows him to lean on certain people. Did you know that Marcus McKelvey was the President's personal choice for the new cabinet position? We have a powerful office, good friends. We called in a few chits. And word got to the President that Woodward was the party's choice. Ah yes, the power of persuasion. Jesse Clore uses his charisma to persuade. And Simone Gray has her own unique way—it's called intimidating to expose."

Anne considered his reasoning. "One finds the weakness . . ."

He chuckled. An unexpected but easy intimacy lay between them. "Are you agreeing with me then . . . that anyone can be bought if the price is right?"

He expected her to say "yes." That was evident in his voice.

"Not at all. My husband couldn't be. I don't believe that Alan Foley can be manipulated. McKelvey may be pompous and made of emotional marble . . . and he wears blinders on certain issues, but no, I don't think he can be bought."

Alex shrugged again, disregarded her words. But he did not argue the point.

They entered the marble-floored elevator in silence.

As they reached lobby level, he turned to her. "Are you going to the Sky Roof to arrest Gertrude? Is that your plan for tonight?"

No sympathy in those eyes, noted Anne. No fear. Only curiosity. A certain carefulness. "No, I'm not interested in Gertrude's manipulation of funds. That's for Simone Gray to expose and a congressional committee to look into. I'm a homicide detective, Alex. I'm looking for Caroline McKelvey's murderer."

"Don't you understand?" He sounded annoyed. "I've been protecting Gertrude. Call it gratitude, affection. Call it loyalty, but it's time for me to let go. I saw her only briefly last Thursday evening. It was about five-thirty when I got to the house in Chevy Chase and she went storming out about six-fifteen. I'm afraid I can't really say where Gertrude Woodward was at the time Caroline was killed.''

What was Shannon's game? Anne was not certain. She was only certain that he was manipulating her. Or attempting to. In his own artful way, he was playing his aces. Puzzled, she stepped out into the milling crowd in the lobby.

The Sky Roof of the old Hotel Washington was one of Anne Fitzhugh's favorite places in town. The long, open porch on the roof of the hotel looked down on the Treasury Building, the Mall and the grounds of the White House. It was a popular spot in which to wind down the day and had about it a European ambiance, small tables, intimacy, fresh air . . . the sounds of the city below.

Anne allowed herself a mixture of sadness and pleasure as she and Alan Foley stepped out upon the roof terrace. Her pleasure lay in the vista of black velvet sky cut with stars and the whisper of a jet making its way down the Potomac toward National Airport. The office buildings of Crystal City in northern Virginia gleamed like a magical Oz on the horizon.

The sadness was a rush of memories.

Anne paused to regain her emotional equilibrium.

''Over there.'' Alan indicated a table near the southwest corner of the porch, a dozen or so people with chairs close together around several tables. Beyond them was silhouetted the Lincoln Memorial, the rooftops of Constitution Hall, the Corcoran Gallery against the dark sky. Voices rose in animated conversation.

Alex Shannon had just joined the party. Anne watched him now place a hand on the shoulder of the host, Jim Woodward. The older man rose to his feet. In a moment, the two had stepped aside to the porch rail. They were speaking in low tones.

Alan followed her line of vision.

"You've got me nervous as a cat. I don't know how to act."

"Act natural, Congressman Foley. We're guests of the Woodwards, nothing more. I don't know what's going to happen, myself."

"Maybe I can move things along." Alan straightened his tuxedo tie. "Should I say, 'Will the real murderer please stand up?' "

He was offering her his support. Alan was safe ground, a man to be counted on. He should be her love, her future . . . he wasn't. He never could be. She put her hand in his, squeezed his fingers. She was thinking of Jesse Clore and Simone Gray waiting next door at the Willard Hotel . . . and Dakota out in the Washington night, looking for Nicky. A web spun thin, waiting for the catch.

"You're shivering," whispered Alan. "Are you cold?"

"No," she whispered in return, "I was just thinking how complex all this is. I am just thinking that Woodward is a good man. He's climbed a long uphill road and now he's probably going to fall off the mountain."

"Politics is made of slippery slopes. The hard climb, the precipice, the fast fall. There's a strange challenge in it."

As they moved among the crowded tables on the canopied porch, Anne was conscious of heads turning. She heard someone murmur, "Congressman Foley of Virginia and Fitzhugh's widow. You remember, Rob Fitzhugh . . . "

Jim Woodward turned from the rail to greet them. The new secretary-designate looked deathly tired, faintly gray around the gills, but he was gracious as always. He kissed Anne on both cheeks. As he and Alan talked about the cabinet appointment and, in particular, the words of support offered tonight by the President, it was obvious to Anne's watchful eyes that Jim Woodward was distracted but covering. An old pro—on stage.

Alex Shannon made a gesture with his head as if to draw Anne aside.

They moved away from the others toward the rail.

Alex's whisper was for her ears only. "I couldn't tell him what was going on. Only that there's trouble brewing—which involves the press, Simone Gray, naturally.''

"Where is Gertrude, Alex?"

"She's right behind you at the table. You'd think to look at her that there's nothing wrong. She is Marie Antoinette . . . about to have her head chopped off and she's drinking champagne and acting the life of the party. The next thing you know she'll be singing a torch song at the bar.''

Anne glimpsed Gertrude Woodward, the twinkle of her bracelet, the artificial brightness of her smile. The congressman's wife was bent toward the wispy little senator who was seated on her right. She was leaning toward him, talking intently as if he were the most important man in the world. Only her cheeks, flaming with color in a white face, disclosed the range of her emotions. She seemed entirely focused upon their conversation.

"I want you to know," continued Alex, "I will suggest to Jim that he not accept the President's appointment to the cabinet. He'll storm a bit but he'll go along with whatever I say. We'll make the announcement tomorrow. We are going to salvage what we can—no matter what kind of damaging confession Nicky gets out of Gertrude tonight.''

Anne could only stare at him. There was a certain quality of dare in Shannon. Agility. Conceit. Pragmatism. She could not sort out the qualities she sensed in him.

"Jim's been having some angina." Alex's tone was persuasive and as reasonable as if he were speaking of canceling a boating trip down the Potomac. "That can be the excuse. The truth is, Anne, he shouldn't be in the executive branch. Jim Woodward's best off just where he is. He does what he does quite well as long as he's managed. Of course, that's all beside the fact," he finished.

"Yes, it's all beside the fact." Anne said.

"I'll handle the problem." Alex didn't finish with, "for all our sakes." It was what he meant. He continued, "We'll distance ourselves from this bit with Gertrude and Safe Guard America. After all, Jim didn't know. Nor did I. Not the extent. Not all the details.''

"You didn't know of Gertrude's involvement, Alex? I hardly believe that.''

"Most of the underpinnings were put in place while I was still in law school. Until Caroline dug up those letters from the files, I didn't sense the extent of the problem. A costly mistake on my part. I underestimated the danger." He grimaced. "If Caroline had let those papers fall into the wrong hands . . . "

"She gave them back to you."

"I know. I accepted Caroline's terms on behalf of the Woodwards. I should have left it there, handled it all myself. I made the mistake of going to Gertrude. I left the canal last Thursday afternoon and went straight to Chevy Chase. I gave Gertrude back the letters in the portfolio and told her everything Caroline said."

"What was Gertrude's response?"

Alex was breathing quickly as if he'd been running. "She exploded. She said some threatening things. That Caroline was asking for trouble, that she ought to be 'dealt with' rather than 'bargained with.' "

"What did she mean?"

"At the time, I thought it was just her anger speaking. Gertrude is very emotional. And she had everything to lose. Everything that mattered to her."

"Including, above all, her husband's respect."

Alex nodded. "The next morning . . . when I heard that Caroline was dead, I knew that Gertrude had gone to The Alhambra and killed her. It was reasonable."

"It was reasonable that Gertrude Woodward was Caroline's killer." Anne repeated his thought as though it were a fact, not as a question.

"Of course. Reasonable people kill out of desperation, as a last resort. You'd have to have a damn good reason . . . "

"Which Gertrude Woodward had," Anne said. "Her husband's reputation and her own. Fear. A certain desperation."

"Right. Political survival is what it is called."

"You had the same reason, Alex."

"I didn't benefit from Safe Guard America. Not directly. My name wasn't on any of those papers. I'll simply claim I didn't know about the depth, the complexity of involvement. I'd say that under oath. There's no way I can be tied to that business.''

''I agree. Not with Caroline McKelvey dead.''

''Look''—Alex Shannon straightened his shoulders—''Caroline was snooping around the office and I was down on her. I've admitted to that. There was some bad blood between us. A love affair that soured. Then Caroline brought me that damnable portfolio of papers. Just changed her mind and brought them back. She surprised the hell out of me. I had no reason to kill her, Anne. None!''

Jim Woodward loomed suddenly between them. ''What the hell are you talking about? I'm damn upset. I don't understand what all this secretiveness is about tonight, Shannon.''

The younger man paused for a moment, then addressed his chief ''You're going to have to talk with your wife about that, Jim.''

''That's just what I mean.'' James Woodward gestured toward the empty chair behind them at the table. ''It's just like at the dinner tonight, without a word to me she's gone. Damn it all, Gertrude has disappeared again, Alex! What the devil is she up to?''

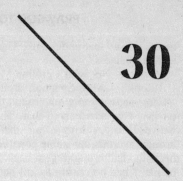

30

Dakota knew that Nicky Nelson was up to no good. He hadn't liked her from the first and watching her tonight hadn't sweetened his impression. From the far side of the bar at the National Press Club, he'd observed her behavior with Alex Shannon. Nicky had leaned toward Shannon in a way that was both pleading and intimidating.

Whatever that female had up her sleeve—and Fitzhugh hadn't gone into any details—it was obvious that the top AA in Woodward's office wasn't interested. Or if he was interested, he was going to play it out his way.

I mean, it was coming across like a soap opera. Dakota reflected on the case as he waited for the elevator in the Willard Hotel. Father Anthony Jesse Clore and Simone Gray turn out to be brother and sister. The congressman's wife—who looks like everybody's idea of a perfect lady—is raking in piles from a PAC organization that's committed to everything her husband is fighting against. And the murder weapon, claims Fitzhugh, is the congressman's antique cigar cutter.

With all that, Alex Shannon is Fitzhugh's main suspect.

For a moment, Dakota reflected on his partner. She's standing there just ten minutes ago in the kitchen of the Woodward suite, telling him all this in a tumble of words. Standing so close to him, smelling like the sweet side of heaven, wearing that damn gold knit dress. And she comes out with all this. How Caroline McKelvey was on to the corruption in Woodward's office because Simone Gray told her what to look for.

And how Caroline was killed because of it.

How Alex Shannon was making it look like Woodward's wife was the murderer. The lady was threatened with exposure. Hence, the murder. A desperate action by a desperate woman. That's how Shannon was making it come together. So the congressman's wife had gone after Caroline McKelvey in a fit of rage . . . using a cigar cutter just like Shannon's, but her own . . . the one she always carried in her purse, the recessed blade sharpened in the kitchen in Chevy Chase before Gertrude Woodward drove the few blocks to The Alhambra.

"Actually"—Fitzhugh had taken a deep breath and finished the story with—"it may have happened just like that, Dakota. Shannon's story is strangely convincing and I saw the weapon in Gertrude's hand an hour ago. I saw the look on her face."

For Dakota's money, it was Alex Shannon all the way.

He'd met guys like this before who gave him the same uneasy feeling. Psychopaths, antisocials, whatever. They are bright as hell and terribly convincing because they haven't any damn scruples. They don't see the difference in right and wrong. If number one gets his rewards, then the hell with everybody else. That was the attitude. All the therapy and all the prison time in the world wouldn't make a dent in their personal belief that they are just a little smarter than everybody else.

Did Shannon kill the beautiful Caroline? Dakota had watched the guy across the Press Club bar. The pieces fit. Shannon was savvy and tough as they come. He had the cool to carry it off.

Still it was Fitzhugh's case. Dakota had confidence in her. He hadn't been putting her on one bit when he said that. Not that he could ever understand her way of handling a murder case.

She didn't do things his way . . . sorting through the evidence, adding it up so that one and one equaled two. No mistakes. No loopholes. That was the right way. It was painstaking but it worked. A killer leaves a trail. A competent investigator sniffs it out, stays on it and "breakthrough time" comes soon enough. I mean, Jesus, he should know . . . he had an impressive stack of solved cases to his credit.

Did Fitzhugh work that way? Not at all.

She had her own method—muddling through, quick-witted and . . . charming. With that odd sort of intuition that damned if he wasn't coming to respect. Now, riding down in the elevator, he got a twist in his chest thinking about her. Such an exasperating love of a woman. And tender. He hadn't known how tender until last night. It was a side of her . . . a side hidden deep beneath the composure and classy ways . . . and it turned him to jelly.

Hell, was he going to let himself fall in love with Anne Fitzhugh?

Maybe it wasn't even a question of . . . letting himself. Maybe it was inevitable, the best things in life usually were. Jesus, it scared him to think about. It excited the hell out of him at the same time.

Dakota shook his head. He had a job to do. He'd promised Anne that he was going to find the nitwit, Nicky Nelson, and he would do that. From a telephone booth on the Willard's mezzanine, he called ABC News. Nicky Nelson had not signed into the building in the last hour. A fumble there. One quarter down.

Dakota dialed The Alhambra. Harold Perry was working the door tonight. "No, sir . . . Lieutenant, Miss Nelson hasn't come home. I been here in the lobby the last hour and I haven't seen nothin' of her. If I hear anythin' of her, I'll call to headquarters and leave a message for you. I sure will."

Maybe he would. Harold was not a man to be counted on.

It was just luck, reflected Dakota when he'd hung up the receiver, that Caroline's murderer had managed to find that unlocked door. Harold steps away for a few minutes . . . yes, just dumb luck, and leaves the door unlocked. In and then out of The Alhambra moves the murderer. Unseen and unnoticed.

People are coming in and going out. Nobody is keeping account. Last Thursday evening, just at dusk, and nobody is thinking of Caroline McKelvey. No one is keeping tabs. Was that true? Dakota had a thought, stroked his mustache. Why hadn't he thought of it earlier? He reached in his pocket for another quarter. He dialed Boccucci at head-quarters.

Anne was exasperated at her own carelessness. . . . While she'd been absorbed in her conversation with Alex, Ger-trude Woodward had managed to leave the Woodwards' table and disappear from the Hotel Washington's Sky Roof.

"I believe there was a telephone call," one of the guests at the table offered. "A waiter brought Gertrude a note. She didn't say anything, just left. I think it was a telephone call . . ."

The waiter shook his head when Anne questioned him. "It wasn't the telephone. A lady asked me to take the note to Mrs. Woodward. Said it was important. Real important."

"A lady?"

"A young lady. Black hair. She stood here . . . looked kind of nervous."

"Did you see them leave together?"

"They took the elevator down. About three minutes ago . . . no more."

Anne went back to the party. "Please stay with your guests," she said to Jim Woodward. "Your wife is under a big strain. You'll understand everything in time, but now it would be best if you just wait it out. Let me find her for you."

She whispered to Alan Foley, "Stay with him, please."

Alex Shannon accompanied her back to the Willard Ho-tel. He asked no questions of her, nor did he hesitate for even a moment. It was close to midnight when they left the Hotel Washington. They did not talk. Their heels sounded sharply on the sidewalks as they rounded the corner of Fif-teenth Street onto Pennsylvania Avenue.

Even at this hour, the Willard's lobby held a surprising bustle. The theater crowd was returning to the hotel. A lady in a dark mink jacket was sitting on the great Victorian pouf that dominated the center of the public area. Lobby vases were overflowing with handsome arrangements. All was rich, subdued color. Polished brass and dark wood gleamed above the rose-flowered carpet.

"Anne." The strong voice reached her through the hum of voices. Dakota was coming down the steps from Peacock Alley. He said, "Nicky is here in the hotel. She came in a few moments ago with the congressman's wife and took the elevator to the twelfth floor. I assume they're headed for Simone's room."

Anne's eyes were intent upon Dakota's face. So why the guarded look?

"If ABC is going to get a story tonight, it will be Gertrude's . . . an exclusive," said Anne as they moved through the mulling crowd to the elevators. "Nicky must have convinced Gertrude that she can possibly save her husband's career by giving her own account of the story to the public before it's leaked out as a media bombshell. Gertrude is just loyal enough . . . "

"She'll incriminate herself right into prison if she talks." Dakota jabbed the elevator button. "She must know that she's heading into trouble, big time."

No argument with that, Dakota, thought Anne. Only Gertrude is already in trouble, big time. How deep . . . as deep as murder? She turned to Alex, who had said nothing since they left the Hotel Washington. He looked pale and wary now. His eyes were anxious. Was there a weakness here? The thought gave Anne a grim sort of pleasure. Instincts, my girl, she told herself.

She began to test him slowly. "Political graft is one thing, murder is another. All I care about is the murder, Caroline's murder. Until tonight, Alex, you've claimed that you and Gertrude were together at the time Caroline McKelvey was killed. You stated that you were together until nine-thirty or ten last Thursday evening. Are you saying that it wasn't true?"

"It wasn't true, but we'd agreed to say that, Gertrude and I."

Anne raised an eyebrow. "How convenient. You gave each other an alibi."

"It was actually my idea to tell it that way. Gertrude was obsessed with the fact that Caroline had taken those incriminating papers. It haunted her. She'd been threatening Caroline in a subtle way for weeks."

"What do you mean?"

"Gertrude would come into the office and watch Caroline. She shadowed her in the car, called the apartment and then hung up when Nicky or Caroline answered. I thought she'd be relieved as hell that the papers were returned."

"And she wasn't?"

"Maybe, at first. She destroyed the portfolio, right there in her kitchen. Sharpened some scissors and cut the papers up and then burned them in the sink . . . all the ashes went down the disposal. She had a drink, then another. She said she couldn't believe it was going to be that simple, she said maybe there were copies of the documents. No, I said, I don't think so. Caroline McKelvey has power over us, Gertrude kept insisting, 'She has power over us and always will.' The story would eventually come out, Gertrude was certain of it."

"She didn't believe Caroline would live up to her word?"

"Gertrude knew how much was at stake politically. Suddenly she grabbed her car keys and went storming out of the house. I couldn't stop her. She said something about 'getting things straightened out for once and all.' I took it she was going to the club to tell Jim everything."

"Come clean, as it were?"

"Right. I figured they'd return home soon and we'd talk the problem out . . . I knew that I could convince Jim to go along with Caroline's terms. We had to do that. Or Jim . . . all of us would be ruined. So I hung around and waited."

"What did you do?"

"I fixed some cheese and crackers. The news was on. I was too tense to pay much attention. In about an hour and a half, Gertrude returned alone. She looked exhausted. All she said was that she lost her nerve. She couldn't bring herself to face her husband with the truth. She told me that she drove out Connecticut Avenue ... past the club, out toward Rockville, and then turned the car around and came back home.''

"Did you believe her?''

"Of course I believed her.'' Alex seemed entirely intent upon his own story as they rode the elevator up to the twelfth floor. "Gertrude seemed calm ... strangely calm. I was reassured. I told her again that, in my opinion, we had to meet Caroline's demands. Call it ... damage control. There was still a chance that Jim would never have to be told anything. I told her to get some sleep. And I left. I went straight home.''

"Jim Woodward still hadn't returned home?''

"No. I left Gertrude alone. She was making herself a drink.''

For the first time, Dakota looked directly at Alex Shannon. "It's still your claim that you did not enter The Alhambra on that Thursday evening between 6 and 9 P.M.?''

Alex answered with obvious impatience. "I was not at The Alhambra that evening, Lieutenant. Gertrude Woodward was the one on a tear and unaccounted for, not I.''

Dakota shrugged his broad shoulders and looked away.

Anne knew her partner. She knew how Dakota's mind worked. This was her case. He was going to let her handle it. But there was something else happening here ... something he was on to. He had a piece of the puzzle. In his own time he would give it to her.

Jesse Clore was just coming out of Simone Gray's room. He had a pole lamp under one arm, a rope of electrical cord in the other hand. He said to Anne with relief, "You're right on the money. I was getting worried.''

"Gertrude ... and Nicky. Dakota says they've shown up?''

"A few minutes ago. Gertrude says she is willing, even anxious to talk. God knows why! She's going to tell her story on the air in ten minutes. Nicky is taping.''

"Where are they now?''

"Gertrude wanted to do the interview in her own suite. They've gone down to ten. Nicky has the camera and most of the gear, and this is the rest. I'm on my way down there now.''

"Damn Nicky Nelson,'' Dakota muttered under his breath.

Anne glanced at Alex Shannon, who was standing behind them. The burnish was definitely off, a white line of anxiety showed around his compressed lips. But he seemed entirely in control.

More in control perhaps than anyone else. But then Alex Shannon knew the truth and she and Dakota were only close to it. "I want you''—she was looking directly at Shannon—"to stay where I can see you.''

Illuminated by floodlights in the living room of the Woodward suite on the tenth floor, Gertrude Woodward sat on the sofa with her hands folded in her lap. She looks like any seasoned politician's wife on the podium waiting for one of her husband's speeches to begin, thought Anne.

For the second time this evening, the maid had allowed them into the suite through the rear door. Alex Shannon stood beside Anne in the familiar dark of the kitchen as Jesse Clore adjusted the brilliant spots to highlight both Gertrude Woodward and Simone Gray, who was moving a chair close to the sofa.

Anne could see the older woman clearly in the scroll mirror on the far wall. Gertrude's face made her think of a scene in Shakespeare's *Macbeth* . . . of Lady Macbeth. There was a similarity. Something theatrical . . . something desperate. A great sense of tragedy.

"I find it terribly warm in here,'' said Gertrude. She put her hand to her neck as if she felt a flush. "Can you raise a window?''

Jess moved to do so, pushing back the heavy drapes.

It did not seem warm to Anne. Her own hands were icy and she wished she had the Glock. She had never been on duty without a gun within reach until tonight.

She would have to depend on her wits. She was alone in this. Dakota had abruptly disappeared. A touch of his hand to his forehead at the door to the Woodward suite and he was gone. He'd found Nicky Nelson and that was the bargain. He'd made a gesture toward Shannon that said "watch him," and then he'd taken off. There was something on The Cowboy's mind. Just what it was, he hadn't said.

For the moment, Anne concentrated her attention on Nicky Nelson, who was setting up her camera. The girl moved efficiently. Give the devil some credit. She'd come up with this new scenario. And she and Simone Gray were carrying it off.

The camera came on, a red light at Nicky's shoulder.

Simone leaned forward, one high-heeled boot crossed over the other ankle. Filling up the screen with her energy, thought Anne . . . dark triangular brows, that special smile with just a touch of lioness in it. The hard-hitting correspondent that all America knew . . . or thought they knew.

"Ladies and gentlemen, this is Simone Gray with an ABC exclusive . . . "

Simone was into it now, the marvel of her quick, smooth words making the intricate background easy to follow. Congressman Jim Woodward and his wife Gertrude . . . from a factory town in New Jersey. Small-town kids without money or influence. Their young marriage, the long climb up the political ladder . . . the hard times and the good. There had been no children to bless this marriage. Only an adopted son who'd come to them in his teens.

But Jim's career *was* their child—to be sacrificed for, and worked for and delighted in. The commitment to America and her principles and Jim's growing involvement in environmental issues. The great successes. And finally, Jim Woodward's appointment to the President's cabinet.

A newly created position, one of great power and influence—Secretary for Hemisphere Protection. It might be the road to the White House. It sounded like a fairy tale.

Now Simone turned the story. Here was the pivot, the hook.

This program . . . *this* television exclusive . . . would not be about Jim Woodward and his success. No, Simone paused for emphasis. It was going to be about Gertrude Woodward. It was going to be a confession.

Anne's nerves were stretched. . . . She knew how much depended on the next few minutes. She was aware of Alex Shannon standing tautly at her other side.

Illuminated to almost beauty by the spotlight, Gertrude Woodward had begun to speak. At first she responded softly to Simone's questions. The early years . . . yes, they had been hard. But also full of dreams. Academia, then politics. She had been her husband's office manager, always his unpaid adviser, his campaign manager. Better than the pros was Simone's guess.

Gertrude smiled at that. Yes, she listened . . . she read everything.

No, it wasn't easy being a political wife. Everyone expected something . . . something different from you. No one really understood what your life was like. The long hours spent alone and the hard hours spent "out there" . . . where you sometimes didn't want to be . . . with people you usually didn't want to be with. And the press criticizing how you looked and what you said or didn't say.

And then . . . there were victories. It got better.

"Better?" Simone questioned.

"On the surface better," admitted Gertrude. More power for Jim and a bigger staff, more committees. More clout within the party.

And for her . . . for Gertrude? What about for her?

Actually, that had been the hardest time for her. Gertrude seemed to be oblivious to the camera. She clasped her hands in her lap. She was talking directly to Simone, pain in her voice. "Times changed, you see. The helpmate wife was out of fashion. I wasn't beautiful enough . . . or clever enough. I hadn't a career, not anything that was mine. Just mine to point to. And there were all these women out there making a fuss over Jim."

She smiled with a certain irony. "Not that he took advantage of it. My husband is too . . . honorable for that. But he noticed. He appreciated the strident young beauties. I was middle-aged, the worn-out horse he didn't *need* to ride anymore. But, of course, he did stay loyal. Jim believes in loyalty."

"I think you are being hard on yourself," said Simone Gray.

"I had to change." Gertrude leaned forward earnestly. "I decided to make him proud of me. I always managed the finances in our marriage and in the office. I had friends who were making money in Washington real estate . . . so I got my license. And it was a windfall! We'd never had much extra money . . . hadn't thought it important. But Jim liked having some cash for a change. He was proud of me . . . he bragged about me."

"Then you moved to the house in Chevy Chase, joined the country club?"

"Not right away. I didn't strike it big until . . . "

"Until Safe Guard America came into the picture."

"Right." Gertrude visibly paled. "It was about eight years ago. I was still managing Jim's office then and I thought this was just another environmental lobbyist group. They came around often . . . really nice people. One of them wanted to buy a house in Washington. I helped him find one in Georgetown. There were a few things like that. They always spoke so highly of Jim. I mean, I was totally taken in."

"When did things begin to go wrong?"

"About six years ago. Safe Guard America was already doing some independent funding in Jim's office. Anonymously. I knew that, of course. I'm not dumb. I was grateful. And they asked me to find a house in northwest Washington for one of their research people. And then a house for one of their executives. Pretty soon, I found I was getting a generous check from them every month. 'A retainer' they called it. For something I'd done, maybe just a few phone calls I'd made on their behalf. They said they owed me . . . that I was like a consultant to them. I thought . . . "

"You thought this was a worthwhile organization?"

"Yes, that is the point! I thought they were totally behind Jim. I thought they were our allies. Of course they sometimes disagreed with his interpretation of a bill before the House. They would explain their side of the story to me and usually I could see where they were coming from. I . . ."

"You influenced your husband?"

Gertrude put her hand to her neck in a defensive gesture. "Jim hasn't time to read much. He has always depended on me to keep up with things and, well, yes, once or twice he listened to me and changed his vote. I thought I had done a good thing. You see, I believed everything Safe Guard America told me."

"And the money kept coming in. You made investments, good ones. And the money kept coming in." Simone was leading Gertrude Woodward with all the finesse and fine-tuning that was her style.

"Jim was so very proud of me. It all went hand in hand, his success, our success. People looked at us differently. Money does that, you know. Somehow I couldn't turn it off . . . even when I began to see that I was being bought."

"Is that how you'd put it . . . you were bought?"

"Of course I was. And even when I knew it, I went on with the charade. I'm talking to you"—Gertrude took a long steadying breath—"to set the record straight. My husband doesn't know that I am giving this interview tonight. Jim is a wonderful man. He's just what the President called him at dinner tonight . . . 'an honorable man.' "

Simone's tone was skeptical. "An honorable man . . . who didn't know his own affluence came from those who pollute . . . for profit?"

"He doesn't know . . . he won't know until he sees this broadcast. Jim shouldn't be blamed politically for what I have done. That's why I am talking to you so publicly. Understand please, everyone . . . that I alone am the guilty one!"

The pain and defiance in Gertrude Woodward's voice rang true. Anne sensed the congressman's wife had carried the moment and she felt a surge of admiration for the courage it had taken. It might just work, it might disarm . . . it would certainly take the ammunition out of the hands of Jim Woodward's enemies. Still, the humiliation of the moment was searing.

She stared at Gertrude, who sat with bowed head, her hands folded again on the lap of her black dress. "How extraordinary this is," Anne murmured under her breath. "Gertrude will go to any lengths . . . "

"To any lengths," Alex murmured at her elbow. "She is strong. And determined. We understand each other, Gertrude and I. . . . "

Simone Gray was rising to her feet. She unfastened the mike from her lapel, motioned to Nicky with an authoritative gesture. "Cut the camera. I'll do the windup later."

"Really, Simone, a few minutes more." Nicky was unwilling to lose control.

Simone blocked the camera. She put her hand on Gertrude's shoulder. "Thank you. I'm sure this was a difficult interview. But you said what you had to say."

It was a gesture of compassion. Honest. Like Simone.

A gesture like the one Jesse Clore now made. He had been standing in the far shadows of the room. Now he moved forward, held out his arms to Gertrude Woodward. A friend, a man of God . . . no judgment made. He moved out of the way of the camera. He was standing by the window.

Gertrude Woodward rose from the sofa and took a few steps toward him. She moved as if in a dream . . . moved as if she were sleepwalking. She spoke in a quiet resigned voice as if offering an explanation to Jesse Clore alone. "You get into things without knowing the price you'll have to pay. That girl, Jess, she didn't have to be murdered. Such a lovely girl . . . to be so stubborn. To want things her way."

Jesse shook his head, bewildered. "Do you mean Caroline?"

"Of course I mean Caroline." Her tone was hazy and distant.

"Do you know who killed her, Gertrude?"

"Last Thursday night, the cigar cutter . . . so nicely

sharpened. In my purse, so nicely sharpened. I couldn't believe it. And then I realized . . . it had to be like this. There was no other way." She was close to Jess Clore and even closer to the open window. She took out the cigar cutter from her purse, held it up for him to see. "Murder, you see. So very simple and easy to do. It's just as well she's dead. There wasn't much hope for her, was there?"

"Caroline McKelvey had *everything* to live for."

"No, she'd gotten herself into a dead-end. She asked for too much, expected too much. She had to die, Jess. Like I do . . . I have to die now."

For a moment, no one caught her meaning.

Then it came to Jess Clore. "Gertrude . . . don't!" He reached out both hands.

It was an instant too late. Determined upon her course, Gertrude Woodward had reached the window. The black skirt flared as she turned for a brief moment. "I shall look for forgiveness in heaven. Pray for me, Jess."

She was gone. A hoarse cry in the night. Then all was quiet. The faint steady noise of traffic. There were only the stars, the lit buildings across Pershing Square . . . the illusion of constancy.

There was a rush for the windows. Anne kicked off her shoes. Alex Shannon pushed her aside and thrust his head and shoulders out of the window through which Gertrude had jumped. "I can see her body below," he cried hoarsely. "There's a sort of roof or ledge. Beyond into the courtyard. I believe she's landed there."

Simone was crying in harsh ragged sobs. Jess Clore put his arm around his sister. He was murmuring something under his breath. It sounded like a prayer.

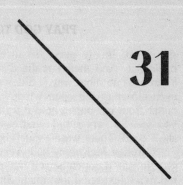

31

"I can't believe she really jumped." Nicky Nelson's eyes were huge in her pale face. "It's not my fault. I mean, she didn't act despondent or anything when I told her about the exposé. She said she wanted to be interviewed. Really, it isn't my fault!"

"No one is blaming you, Nicky," said Anne.

Nicky spoke heatedly, as if feeling the need to vindicate herself. "It's true that I came to her suite tonight to pressure her. I lied. I said I had copies of the papers Caroline took from the office. I knew she feared just that. Now I understand everything. Gertrude was the one who'd been stalking Caroline . . . the one who had me scared shitless since Caroline was murdered. It all fits together in my head."

"How did Gertrude react when you confronted her?"

"I told her I knew she'd been following me. She didn't deny it. And then the phone rang and her husband said she'd better come down because the President and the First Lady were leaving, and she went . . . she just looked at me over her shoulder and went out the door."

Nicky was rubbing her hands together nervously. "There was an important story coming together here. I knew if I pressed the woman hard enough, it would happen. So I followed the Woodwards and the rest of their party to the Hotel Washington. They were all out there on the Sky Roof talking and laughing. Gertrude looked like she hadn't a care in the world. But I had a scoop and I knew it, so I sent her a note, and she came out to talk to me and I told her that

ABC was going to break the story about Safe Guard America funding Woodward on the eleven o'clock news. I mean I was bluffing, but I saw that she was wavering. So I called Simone at the Willard and . . . ''

Simone was white with shock. "I never dreamed she was the murderer, Anne. I never suspected that Gertrude Woodward was the one who killed Caroline."

It seemed to Anne that something had gone off track. She looked around the room at the earnest, pained faces. "Is that what you think? Simone . . . Jesse? Does everyone think that Gertrude Woodward killed Caroline McKelvey?"

There was silence in the room, a confirming silence.

"Yes," said Jesse Clore slowly. "It is pretty obvious, isn't it?"

Nicky Nelson nodded. "My God, she killed herself!"

"I am afraid it makes sense," agreed Simone slowly. "You heard Gertrude's words, 'Caroline asked for too much, she had to die.' ''

Anne looked directly at Alex Shannon. "What about you? What do you think?"

He was standing by the window. "I suspected as much. I'm afraid it adds up."

Had he pulled it off then? Anne was more certain than ever that Alex was the killer. In her bones she knew that it was he and not Gertrude who had used the cigar cutter to cut the young woman's throat. He stood there looking back at her with that watchful, cool manner that was so characteristic of him. There was no pain in Alex Shannon's face.

"What about Woodward?" She changed the subject abruptly, her eyes still on his face. "We must tell the congressman before he hears the sirens, before the press . . . ''

Alex spoke with his usual, quick competence. "I'll go to him. Jim needs to be handled carefully through this. He needs . . . ''

"No." Anne thrust a wing of dark hair behind her ear and turned to Jess Clore. "I'd like you to do this. Go as quickly as you can to the Sky Roof . . . right now, before anyone else gets to him. Find Jim Woodward, take him to a private place and tell him that his wife is dead. Tell him . . . a fall from the hotel window.''

"Only that?"

"Only that, Jess. And bring him here to the suite. We'll take it from there."

The report came over the squad-car radio. It was directed to all patrol units in the area: "Accident. Female. A fall from the tenth floor of the Willard Hotel. Happened three to five minutes ago, just called in. A paramedic team is on its way."

"Oh, God, it might be Anne." said Dakota. His heart lurched in his chest.

"A fall . . . maybe pushed." Boccucci came down hard on the Ford's accelerator.

They were rounding Scott Circle, moving west toward Pennsylvania Avenue. Dakota was seeing it happen in his mind's eye . . . Anne tumbling from the window, smeared in blood, broken on the pavement.

The squad car slowed in a snarl of traffic in front of the Treasury Building.

"I'm out of here." Dakota swung out on the passenger side. "I'll see you both at the Willard," he said to Boccucci and the passenger in the back. "Step on it."

The Cowboy could still move when he needed to. Despite a few extra pounds and a bad knee, it was still in him. He kept his head down, traveling the sidewalk past Old Ebbitt Grille. His legs stretched out. It helped to run . . . eased the pounding in his heart. He crossed F Street, downhill all the way now, rounding the corner by the Occidental Restaurant without even slowing the pace. A siren sounded far off. No crowd gathering.

The Woodward suite on the tenth floor faced west . . . toward Pershing Square, the gleaming Ellipse. Its windows had looked down on the inner courtyard.

Dakota sprinted up the white steps that led past the elegant Willard shops. A plaza, plants, two fountains, shop doors. One was Chanel's. There was no one in the darkened court. Except Anne . . . and Alex Shannon.

Dakota caught sight of them in the half-light of windows. He broke his run, took a deep breath and fell back into the dark. They were at the far side of the court, standing beside a body. A woman with silver hair. Yes, of course. He recognized her from the press conference earlier this week. He knew at once that the dead woman was Gertrude Woodward.

The big detective stepped deeper into the shadows. He was flooded with relief that the body wasn't Anne's. He pressed against a shop window where he could see what was happening but not be seen. He was a private citizen tonight. He had no weapon, no clout. Still he had to be there for her.

Anne sensed his presence. It was only a change in shadows . . . a slight crunch in the gravel. She knew it was Dakota. She was glad he was there and relieved that he was staying back. She had come this far. She knew what she had to do. They had brought a sheet down from the hotel room. She watched Alex Shannon spread it over Gertrude's body.

"Shall I ride in the ambulance . . . with Gertrude?" Alex asked her soberly.

"She's dead. That won't be necessary."

A nice gesture. And like him . . . cleaning up the garbage, he'd said. She weighed the power and control Shannon had now regained. She noted that he had recovered his usual assurance. All the circumstantial evidence pointed now to Gertrude Woodward. He had the power to persuade. Even Gertrude's own damning final words would be interpreted as a confession to murder.

She had only her last cards to play. She asked, "What did Gertrude mean . . . about Caroline getting herself into a dead-end?"

He considered the question, standing beside Anne in the cold darkness. "I can't say."

"Caroline was holding some rather considerable political power." Anne paused. "Emotionally, well . . . that's another story. Maybe *that* was the dead-end."

"I don't know what you mean." His tone was noncommittal.

"I am talking about the pregnancy. She was pregnant with your child. It must have been a painful dilemma for her . . . and for you."

Shannon folded his arms across his chest. "If Caroline McKelvey was pregnant, what would make you believe that I am . . . was involved?"

Anne said, "Caroline told Father Clore."

It was partially true. Caroline had told Jess Clore that she was pregnant. Unexpectedly . . . and without defenses. Jess had finally shared this confidential information with Anne earlier tonight in Simone's apartment. It wasn't easy for him to talk about. Caroline told him that she'd believed herself in love when the child was conceived. She refused to say who the father was. Only that the father was unworthy, and that she didn't trust him. She refused to marry him. It would be a travesty. And she couldn't see abortion. Or giving the baby up. She had the means to support her child. That meant raising it on her own.

"You have to tell the father," Jess had counseled her, "no matter the problems between you. It is only fair, Caroline."

Jess said she'd fought him on that. "Caroline could be stubborn." He couldn't see how the pregnancy was relevant to her death. "It was Caroline's secret. That is just the way she was."

Forthright . . . idealistic. A shining soul, Caroline McKelvey.

Anne was beginning to see clearly, beginning to understand. She was banking on the likelihood that Caroline had changed her mind, that she'd decided to tell Alex that she was carrying his child . . . that she had told him on Thursday afternoon on the banks of the canal. That she had brought him that bombshell of information . . . along with everything else.

"Caroline said that no one knew about the pregnancy. She hadn't even seen a doctor yet." Alex said.

It was an admission, a slip on his part. Had she found the weakness?

Anne said, "She'd only talked with Father Clore, who was her spiritual adviser."

A hard sigh of exasperation from Alex. "It wasn't a spiritual matter."

"Oh, in a way it was," Anne responded. "She fell in love with you . . . a knight in white armor. She adored you, Alex. Maybe too much in the beginning, maybe that was the problem."

"I told her I'd pay for an abortion. 'Let's get this over with.' 'No way,' she said. Then I told her I'd marry her. She laughed at that. Can you believe it? Holding something like that over my head. No marriage . . . a child out of wedlock. Can you see what this would do to any political career that I might . . . ' "

"Caroline was a liability to you and to the Woodwards."

There was silence. When he spoke, Alex Shannon's voice was soft and persuasive. "Yes, a liability. That's what Gertrude kept saying. That's why Gertrude killed Caroline. On Friday morning when Nicky called to tell me that her roommate was dead, when I realized . . . you can understand I felt relief. Some regret but also, relief! Awful to admit . . . but it's true."

Anne heard a siren wailing to a stop in front of the Willard. "But you already knew she was dead, Alex. You knew because you were the one who killed her. You'd gone to The Alhambra that night, found the door unlocked. Pure Shannon luck. You killed her. Not Gertrude Woodward."

He stared at her hard, then laughed. "Consider Gertrude's last words, Anne. It was a confession, plain and simple."

"A confession to mistakes. Errors in judgment. Not a confession to murder."

He was annoyed now, short with her.

"You can't prove any of that, Detective Fitzhugh. You've nothing to offer. Any case you might bring against me would be conjecture on your part. Motive? Yes, perhaps I had motive . . . but so did Gertrude."

"And the means. Caroline was killed with a cigar cutter. Sharpened. I believe it was the cigar cutter that I saw on your desk, Alex . . . "

"My cigar cutter is still on my desk at the office. And

the recessed blade is dull, unsharpened. Would I be so blatant as to leave it out if I was a murderer? Would I have left it there?''

Anne understood immediately. "You were very smart. You were protecting yourself. You were setting up Gertrude. The murder weapon was *her* cigar cutter, the one she always kept in her purse."

"Yes, they were alike, gifts from one of Jim's admirers. We kept them handy so Jim wouldn't be testy. Caroline was indeed killed with Gertrude's cigar cutter. As you say, the one from *her* purse."

"On Thursday night, you had access to the murder weapon, Alex. When Gertrude left the house, she took her car keys. That's what you said, 'she grabbed up her keys.' We might assume then she left behind her purse. You were in a turmoil. Gertrude was going to find her husband and confess all, which wasn't going to help matters. Jim is so inept at this kind of thing. It was all up to you, as usual. The only way out . . . was to get rid of Caroline. But how?''

"How?" He stepped closer to Anne in the darkness.

"You took the cigar cutter from Gertrude's purse, sharpened it on the knife sharpener in the Woodward's kitchen and went to The Alhambra . . . ''

"Do you mean this cigar cutter?" He pulled it from his pocket.

She remembered. He had picked it up when Gertrude had dropped it on the carpet upstairs. She stared at the small tool in his hand, sensed a threat in the way he was holding it out toward her. "Yes, *that* cigar cutter. When you returned to the house after killing Caroline, you returned it to her purse. Gertrude had no reason to look at it, no reason to think that it might be a murder weapon and you . . . a murderer."

As she watched, he flipped the cutter upside down and pressed the handle. The blade sprang up. A short blade, razor-sharp. She could see the set expression on Alex Shannon's face. Dakota said one doesn't argue with psychopaths for they have no conscience. But they can be bluffed.

She did not step back. "Poor Gertrude. She got in deeper

and deeper. Caroline McKelvey has the incriminating papers. Then someone murders her. Abruptly murders her. How sad, thinks Gertrude, and how fortuitous. Especially since her husband is about to have the cabinet post. But Nicky Nelson and Simone Gray are on to something . . . searching out the truth. What if they find out about Safe Guard America? She is terrified. How difficult, how painful this becomes, how threatening for Gertrude . . . ''

Alex was fastened on Anne's hypnotic face, listening to her words.

"Her worst nightmare is coming true," Anne continued. "She hasn't anyone to lean on but you, her ally, her adopted son . . . she thinks you two are in this together. Anything to save the political ship, anything to save Jim. Then Gertrude finds the cigar cutter in her purse has been sharpened, and she knows. She knows you have set her up. She's going to be the guilty one. She . . . and she alone."

"You have an ingenious mind, Detective Fitzhugh."

"Poor Gertrude was the one dead-ended. Her name is all over those incriminating papers, the murder weapon is in her purse. The confession. She gave you that. And you . . . you will walk away, an innocent man, Alex."

"An innocent man. That's the way it is." He snap-shut the blade and put the cigar cutter back in his pocket. "I'm sorry about Gertrude. She was valuable, important to Jim. All this is going to hurt our image, you know, muddy the waters. But then there is the sympathy angle . . . if I can play it right."

"And Caroline. Are you sorry about Caroline?"

He admitted nothing. Only his taut shoulders said that he realized that Anne knew the truth. The night air was bitter, hard on their faces. They turned toward the sound of voices, the rush of footsteps as the paramedics entered the courtyard.

"You killed her, Shannon. And I'll prove it. I'll find some way to put you at the scene of the crime."

"Dead angels don't talk." Alex was victorious, even amused.

Then Anne saw Dakota coming out of the shadows. He

was looking down the steps toward Pennsylvania Avenue. Boccucci was entering the courtyard behind the rush of paramedics. Emile Farrare was with him.

She saw the young man step away from the rest and look calmly around as if searching someone out. Why was Farrare here . . . and looking for whom?

Anne narrowed her eyes against the beam of flashlights, the spotlights' glare. Emile Farrare, who had loved Caroline and waited for her in the green Cathedral close. When she didn't come, he had gone down to the park across from The Alhambra. In the softness of an October twilight, he'd been waiting for Caroline . . . waiting and watching.

He was watching now. Anne observed how slowly and carefully the stone cutter was scanning the quickly gathering crowd in the courtyard. When the dark thoughtful eyes reached Alex Shannon, they lingered. There was a flicker of recognition.

Then Emile made a fist and pointed at Shannon.

Dakota had come from the darkness. He gave Anne a "thumbs up" sign with both of his hands. A triumphant grin. For a moment she could not take it in. She was diverted by the bustle of the paramedics and police officers around her.

Then the resolution of it all hit Anne Fitzhugh with full impact.

The stone cutter had been waiting and watching. Of course he would have seen Shannon enter The Alhambra last Thursday night. He'd recognized him. Alex Shannon was not someone you forgot. It would be Emile Farrare who would place Alex Shannon at the scene of the crime. A crucial piece of the puzzle had just fallen into place.

"Don't go," Anne said to Alex, who was about to leave the courtyard. "I want you downtown. I'm going to read you your rights loud and clear. And then, I intend to book you for the murder of Caroline McKelvey."

Shannon's face wore a look of shock. "You're bluffing. You don't have any evidence, any witnesses. I don't understand . . . "

Anne looked up at the shimmering arc of lights above them. "Take it on faith, Alex." She could see Dakota pushing through the crowd toward them. "You don't have to understand. Yet. Just say, an angel was watching . . ."

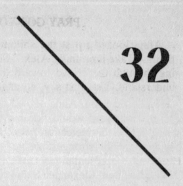

32

The bells of Washington's National Cathedral do not generally peal on weekdays. Unless it is a holy day or there's a wedding or a funeral in progress. One golden morning in late October, the bells of the Cathedral pealed for Gertrude Woodward.

A great many autumn flowers filled the Bethlehem Chapel on the lower level of the Cathedral. This was a private funeral, a small but impressive crowd in attendance. Mourners and friends . . . political friends and sympathizers.

Anne Fitzhugh sat alone on one of the back pews.

The ABC special had aired on Saturday night at seven. Gertrude's suicide had changed its tone. The television news special took not the expected muckraking approach, but a subdued and philosophical one. Its focus was on the pressures in Washington politics and the unique stress inherent in the position of "political spouse." Simone Gray handled the commentary well . . . no holds barred, but without judgments. The special was a *coup* for her. It was also a *coup* for young Nicky Nelson, the show's director.

Actually the show hadn't hurt Jim Woodward either.

He was sitting on the front row in the Bethlehem Chapel now, pale with grief, but supported by close friends and staff. A story was going around town that he would decline the President's nomination for the cabinet post. His health and this personal tragedy would be the reasons given. The truth was, as Alan had speculated, Jim Woodward could afford no political risks now. He would stay in the House of Representatives where his support was solid and his influence strong.

A wise decision, Alan noted, the only possible one.

A wise decision, Anne agreed, for many reasons.

Jim Woodward would ride out the Safe Guard America storm before the reelection race came around. And he was psychologically strongest on the familiar ground of the House of Representatives . . . especially without Gertrude Woodward and Alexander Shannon to look after his interests.

Rumor also had it the President would offer the cabinet position to Marcus McKelvey. An excellent choice, everyone agreed. It was a turn of events that would have pleased his daughter, thought Anne with a certain irony.

She left the chapel before the last hymn and went up the great stone stairs to the main level. In the wide hall called the Westminister porch of the Cathedral's north entrance, she waited for Alan Foley, who was sitting with the congressional delegation.

The mid-morning sun laid patterns of gold in the pale marble floor of the hall. Anne watched, appreciated the beauty of the moment. But she was spent. Without emotion.

In a few moments, mourners began to appear at the top of the stairs and stream past her through the bronzed doors out to their limos waiting in the circular drive. There was a somber mood. Not many of the mourners stopped to talk. Most looked preoccupied; some few smiled to be out again in the sunlight. One or two glanced at their watches.

So, Washington goes on. So indeed, life goes on, thought Anne.

Jesse Clore was suddenly beside her, distinguished in his purple and white vestments. He took both Anne's hands in his. At the service he had spoken briefly and eloquently, about forgiveness. Now, his expressive face was drawn. There was guilt in his eyes. "Somehow I can't believe all this really happened, Anne. It's still too much . . . too real to take in. If I had known how much of Caroline's secrets to reveal . . . ''

"I've been struggling with it too," Anne admitted uneasily. "I keep thinking about Gertrude's fall, her sudden leap from that window to death. I keep thinking if I hadn't allowed the interview, if I hadn't . . . ''

"No regrets on your part, please. You found Caroline's murderer. You and Dakota did that for us. You proved to us all that it wasn't Gertrude who was the murderer. . . . You did *that* for her. Don't be hard on yourself. Listen, we aren't infallible." He grinned then. Wickedly. The old Jess. "Well, maybe a few of our politicians are!"

His dark eyes held hers intently. Jesse Clore continued in a softer voice, "I'd like to see you again. I feel I've come to know you, Anne. Maybe to understand . . . ''

"To understand?" Anne laughed gently. A certain irony in that. "Do you remember your question to me that night at the party in Woodward's office, 'What's a nice girl like you . . . '?''

"I remember what I was thinking anyway. 'What's a beautiful and classy female like you doing in the messy business of homicide'?'' The dark eyes were warm, expressive. "I don't know that I have the full answer yet. But I understand more and more who you are—a seeker, a yearner . . . a cheerleader."

"A tiger. A she-tiger."

Now he laughed, really laughed. For the first time in a long time. "No doubt about that, Anne. Listen, can we have lunch soon? I don't want you out of my life."

Yes, she'd like that. Maybe they'd have lunch next week or maybe the next. Jesse Clore was the kind of friend that she needed. Anne returned the squeeze of his hands and went out into the sunlight. At the bottom of the steps she turned to smile a farewell to him.

Above the North facade she caught sight of the graceful stone carving of *The Creation*—a young man rising from the stone, all his tender vulnerability caught. And the soft faces of young women. Anne let her eyes glide over the lights and depths of the carving and thought again of Caroline McKelvey.

So much loss. Always in the living of life, there was so much loss.

There were no real answers to life's tragedy. No excuses for loss and pain. She was finally coming to see that. You never really found the answers. You just kept trying.

Alan Foley's footsteps crunched behind her in the driveway. "There you are. And looking thoughtful. You need some lunch, I think. Let's find someplace quiet."

She shook her dark head. "No time today, Alan. I've got court in an hour. We're arraigning Alex Shannon today for the Caroline McKelvey murder."

"It still amazes me that you got a confession out of him. Clever, ambitious Alex Shannon. I wouldn't have thought he'd break and admit his guilt."

"He lost control. Of everything, himself included. Shannon's a man who has always lived on his cunning, his bravado and his persuasive skills. He thought he handled the garbage, that he'd won—that he was out of danger. And then out of nowhere appeared the mysterious E. Ironically enough, it had been Alex who alerted me to his existence. Emile Farrare, this 'out of the blue witness' that Alex had never seen before and certainly never expected would be a major witness against him."

"But Farrare had seen Shannon?"

"Exactly. He'd seen Alex Shannon enter The Alhambra on the night of the murder. At 6:35 P.M. Emile was certain of that, decisive. He even knew what Shannon was wearing . . . white running shoes. White with yellow ties. No coaxing by Dakota or Boccucci, Alan. Everything finally closed in on Shannon. His alibi was shot and he hadn't any defenses left. I can't say he's repentant. He's not, at all. He'll plead temporary insanity. But I expect the prosecution will ask for a life sentence. Caroline's murderer deserves that."

"You solved the case. You're a damn good detective, Annie."

"I had some fine help." She was thinking of Dakota.

She was thinking that Alan was right, she just might be a damn good detective.

It seemed to Anne Fitzhugh as she said good-bye to Alan Foley that the air was unusually luminous, everything around her seemed full of both sunshine and shadow. There was no glare at all. This day was going to be the rare golden kind that held the best of Washington's autumn. She'd be off at three this afternoon. It might be the thing to do some shopping, maybe buy a new dress. She might even call a friend.

Call a friend . . . now, there was a thought.

There'd be a full moon tonight, and she had an invitation to spend the night on a boat in the Potomac.

Anne walked to her Porsche parked along the North Drive and slid into the driver's seat. She had to think about this particular invitation, test it out in her head . . . consider its implication in her heart. An evening on *The Reliable Source* meant bluefish on the grill, cold beer to wash it down and some low, sweet jazz to soothe the spirits.

That's all the man said he had to offer. That is what he said.

This strange difficult loving man who was down on his luck. Down, but not too down. Dakota would make it through. He had that kind of grit.

Anne looked at herself in the rearview mirror. The gray contemplative eyes looked back. She was considering . . .

A moonlit night . . . a red dawn above the Potomac.

With a man who would hold her close to his heart, a man whose touch was fine and gentle. A man she trusted. One who could make her laugh and make her cry. Could she risk it?

A man with the devil's own blue eyes. Dakota.

Anne smiled at herself in the mirror. She was thinking she might just be ready to risk loving again . . . for a man like that.